GOAT'S HEAD

GOAT'S HEAD

BRIAN LUPO

www.pulpvein.com

Cover by David Richardson

Copyright © 2018 Brian Lupo

All rights reserved. In accordance with the U.S. Copyright Act of 1976, the scanning, uploading, and electronic sharing of any part of this book without the permission of the publisher or author constitute unlawful piracy and theft of the author's intellectual property, except by a reviewer who may quote brief passages in a review to be printed in a newspaper, magazine, or journal. Thank you for your support of the author's rights.

All characters in this book are fictitious. Any resemblance to real persons, living or dead, is coincidental and not intended by the author.

ISBN: 978-1729619841

Printed in the United States of America

For Riana

PROLOGUE

Shivering beneath the twinkling heavens, restless under a full moon's gaze, the miniature city of Yucaipa was hankering to put to bed the formidable veil of phantoms and nightmarish devils on another Halloween. Eager to ignore, desperate to sleep but too terrified to dream, the children waited, expectant, eyes edgy and bellies sickened from candy. They watched for lingering demons blowing outside their windows, casting ghostly hues as they tap a last to be let in. These unfortunates, unable to shake a dreadful intuition that somehow, something out there had already snuck in and was waiting...

The befouled idea warped formative minds with creepy images of nameless horrors which might pounce on the mattress from the darkest recesses of the room and snatch them out of bed. The wise among them left the lights on, sleeping together to keep at bay the disfigured shadows that climbed the walls. The others...what others? It's one o'clock. A new day, supposedly banishing the witching hour and the power to cast a spell over the people of this haunted community. Though, if they dared listen to the early morning wind, a relic cry would be heard. Unanswered in the shadows. In the darkness of shadows, screaming since unknown time.

CHAPTER 1
Sneaking Out
1993

1

Tossing and turning, I tucked myself up to my nose in my sleeping bag, cradling my flashlight. My ears filled with the wind's push and pull of the night. The fluorescent lantern gave me the nerve to close my eyes. *What-if the batteries fail?* My eyes opened, again. The Ones Who Dwell in the Dark held sway over my mind. A faint scent of firewood reached my nose. *Who else is up?* Lying there with my friends, I was jealous. *How could they sleep, knowing what was coming?* My thumb rubbed the knobs of the flashlight handle. *How?*

2

Jarrod's Swiss army watch sounded, slipping us out of our bags to mobilize. He placed his authentic M1 helmet on, turning the angular light under his face to highlight a Sharpie beard. "Ready, men?"

"Let's go kick some Nazi ass," I said.

"Oorah," Ethan replied.

Jarrod drew back on his knees, pinching the bridge of his nose. "That's Marines, Ethan, you freakin' *Mee-yamee* face."

"How would I know that?" He squirmed.

"You're American; that's how." Jarrod grimaced, slipping on his tan field-pack, equipped with visible shovel and canteen. He strapped it tight around his Parson's jacket, retrieving his flashlight as he waited for a rough gust to pass before unzipping the entrance flap. "Let's move out."

Ethan turned off the lantern, and we clicked our flashlight beams to life. My exposed skin froze to the touch of the air outside the encampment. A wind surge whisked autumn debris into our faces, leaving me blinking at the stripping trees.

The deep freeze was quick to sink into the hide of my leather jacket and pants, making my Mad Max costume an unfortunate pick. At least my feet were warm, having boots and calf-high socks. Poor Ethan though. Dracula was a terrible pick. I knew he had to be suffering something awful.

Jarrod, our leader, set off at a rapid clip despite his crouched gait, waving for us to keep our flashlight beams low as we approached the first checkpoint, Becca's Room. He pointed a warning at Becca's window before signaling us to move. Pressed against the wall of the house, he dipped below the sill to pass under. One false step could end any one of us; Becca would plunge a bayonet right down into our chest. We safely passed under the window and made it to the other side.

Ethan and I hung back, waiting for our signal to move to the front of the house. Three flashlight clicks signaled us onward to checkpoint two, The Iron Gate. Our leader opened the six-foot barrier, careful to manage the whining metal. He raised a clenched fist, and we held position. Pulling binoculars from his pack, he scanned the potentially hostile terrain of the front yard. He waved me forward. I took charge of the gate. As briefed, I held it for the men and closed the noisy hinges during a concealing wind gust.

When I caught up, I fell to a belly crawl in line with my team. We scurried under Terri's Bedroom Window, checkpoint three. Swastika flags flapped above us. My hands grew numb to the touch from the freshly cut grass jabbing my palms. In the thick of it now, our position optimal for snipers, we broke into a cautious running formation. We rounded anti-tank Czech hedgehogs placed along the perimeter to reach checkpoint four, The Driveway. The front lawn was bordered by a lengthy moat that stretched the width of the perimeter. It had been embedded with metal and wooden spikes angled too high to attempt a jump. The saying *'sitting duck'* came to mind. Crouching behind German tanks, we avoided the searchlight above the garage. Timing its passing, we individually hightailed it toward freedom. We reached our final checkpoint, The Street. Our risky mission to cross enemy territory unobserved was achieved with our escape.

3

Free of enemy territory, thus no longer preoccupied by capture or death at the hands of Jarrod's Nazi sisters, I thought about what was approaching. *We're not going. They won't go through with it, no way.*

"Sir, we can't go on. Look at Ethan," I said, grateful to see Ethan shaking uncontrollably in his Dracula costume.

"I'll be-he, be, fin-ine, guys-s-s."

"Wait here, men. I'll sneak a jacket from camp. Hang in there, soldier; you're gonna make it. Private Vince, if I'm not back in five minutes, take command of the mission. Failure is not an option, soldier." Jarrod stealthily ran back towards camp, risking being grounded for life.

"Sorry-y about this-s."

"Ethan, man, don't sweat it. I can't imagine how cold you must be. I'm freezing, and I have on way thicker stuff. It's not the right night for this."

"You're-re sc-scared?"

"No, it's just not the right night." I took a good look at Ethan, unable to stop myself from bursting out laughing.

"Prick-k-k."

"I know; I'm sorry. You have—" I couldn't stop laughing as Dracula wiggled like a hula dancer in the full moon.

Jarrod returned with his blue naval peacoat. The coat draped Ethan, turning his hands into sleeves. "Vince doesn't want to go."

"I didn't say that; I said it's not the right night for us to go." *Snitch.*

"How so? It's Halloween, private. What's a better night?" Jarrod asked.

"The weather sucks tonight."

Jarrod broke character. "I can get you a coat?"

"Nah, it's cool, I'm game. Ethan is mad because I laughed at him for shakin' that ass in the moonlight." Jarrod snickered.

"That's what you told me. You said—"

"Whatever, *Mee-yamee* face."

Back in command, Jarrod ordered, "Stop bickering, men. We have a skull to claim."

"That's what you said," Ethan murmured, loud enough for me to hear.

We moved up Ivy Avenue to Jefferson Street, hanging a right to overlook the dirt road that would lead us to the tree line. There it swayed in the distance: a string of ridged contours set against rolling hills. It was the gateway to Goat's Head. We followed a rusty barbed-wire fence aslant on decaying farmland. The arrest stories told by Jarrod's dad began to replay in my head: blood rituals, flayed bodies, human sacrifices, animal mutilations and butchery. The ghost of Blackie Wilson, the evil force who was said to haunt the grounds and his followers, the Watchers, materialized at the forefront. I sensed them watching us now, out there somewhere in the neglected field.

Appearing fearless, we dug our heels into the dirt road, flashlight beams out thrown. Abnormal silence settled among us. Harmless things took on creepy guises. Nature made noises not fair for human nerves. I swung my light left to the sound of coyotes howling and was startled by the vampire at my elbow. The darkened fabric of Jarrod's coat enhanced the contrast of Ethan's white head and blood-red lips.

A screech erupted somewhere out in the unseen, catching our attention. Agonizing screams of a small animal slowly being picked apart had us quicken our pace. We could hear its terrible cries with each of the pack's snapping, snarling attacks. The poor animal's final feeble cry was the worst. It sounded like a voice being torn in half. We shared a wide-eyed look at each other and no one said a thing.

Sneaking Out

4

We passed Carter Street, the midway point of our mission. The trail of trees formed a hand, welcoming its guests in a 'come hither' gesture. *It's the wind.* My heart's irregular beats became apparent. An itchy compulsion to run in the opposite direction yanked at me, yet the wind swept my feet forward. I fought the command, wiping my sweaty palms against my leather pants.

I labored against my cowardice to Goat's Head, where it redoubled its efforts. Our lights twisted open the tree-lined path. We shone the beams over the ushering pines, facing my seizing fear straight on. I watched the towering evergreens sway in the wind, urging us to enter. I looked back the way we came. *Run.* The vacant dirt road looked no less terrifying to venture through alone in the dark. *Run for it!* I coughed, choking on a dry throat.

"To the victor goes the spoils, men." Jarrod made a running start around the wide, deep trench at the foot of the hill, sticking his combat boots into the steep-graded dirt as he climbed to the top. Reluctant but afraid to be last, I used his packed footprints to climb up. Jarrod and I helped Ethan after he about ate shit on his second attempt.

My heart was pounding. *It's because you ran up the hill.*
Is it?

5

The three of us slowed atop the elevated path. Our weak beams did nothing to penetrate the tunnel of deep-seated darkness. *Tell them to turn back, that we'll come back tomorrow during the day.*

I can't! They won't let me live it down. Jitters took ahold of me to where I thought I might beg to leave, not caring any more about my potentially ill-fated reputation.

"Move out." Jarrod's tone was mild. We ventured inward, me in the middle, Ethan to my left, and Jarrod at my right. Our lights were made up of yellow misty dirt swept up from the wind. The trees tightened around us. Their rustling canopies blocked the skylight. *What are you doing? Run!* As the wind died down, our breaths and crackling steps became increasingly apparent. We drew close and touched shoulders. *Run, stupid, RUN!*

"Combine the lights." Jarrod ordered with a hint of quiver in his voice. A single, brighter beam formed. The beam brought to light previously unseen green, spindly limbs reaching for us. The sound of my breath amplified in my ears, bringing my attention to my breathing and a sensation of gradually being smothered. The dirt steadily snuck into my lungs as I tried to catch my breath. An unrelenting sensation of suffocation emerged with a chalky taste in my mouth. In, out, in, out, in, out. *RUN FOR IT!* The narrow entrance of dark blue sky was snuffed out of existence by colliding trees.

I stopped, frozen, nerveless with a hideous thought. *What if I can't get out? You need to leave!* I was unable to take a decent breath, unable to move, unable to think clearly. I couldn't deal with losing that small piece of the outside world. "Jarrod, Ethan! Let's go! I don't want to do this any more!" A prickling about my scalp trickled down my body. "I'm done!" IN, OUT, IN, OUT, IN, OUT!

They failed to respond. My heart sunk at the absence of their shoulders' weight against mine. The beam from my flashlight was again weak and alone and, as it appeared, so was I. All alone. Alone in clouds of strangling dirt. Alone on a path lined with extensive reaching limbs. Alone among rustling whispers and unnatural darkness that offered no release. *Trapped!*

IN, OUT, IN, OUT, IN, OUT! "Jarrod, Ethan, where are you?" I swung my light around in every conceivable direction, finding nothing but a billowing yellow dust cloud built around my frantic legs. No sign of them or their lights. In my disoriented state, I had lost the exit. INOUTINOUTINOUT!

"Vince!" I heard the voice of Jarrod, pulling me forward a step in no known direction.

"Jarrod, Ethan, I'm here! Follow my light!" I yelled so hard that I burnt my tonsils to an instant headache. I waved my beam, gasping as hot sweat dripped in my eyes. *I CAN'T FIND THE EXIT!*

My heart beat at the speed of my chaotic eyes. "Jarrod! Ethan! Look for my light!" INOUTINOUT— my airwaves cut off, my heart sky-rocketed. The harder I tried to breathe, the worse I made an awful gagging sound. My stomach compressed into a tight knot. "Jarrod! Ethan! ETHAN! JARROD! I CAN'T BREATHE!" My heart was going to puncture my chest. After barreling into branches and trunks I managed to find the night sky hiding in a small corner of the dark. My legs flew in the direction of that wonderful blue light. I was dying, having a heart attack from fright. I couldn't die in this wicked place. I knew, no matter what, I had to make it out.

My body shook relentlessly as I fled. All joints and limbs had turned to jelly. A new darkness enveloped my vision, tunneling in all around my insignificant light. An oppressive, swirling blackout cloaked the already blackened wall of trees.

A solid snag at my shoulder pulled me backward midstride. My legs ended up out in front of me with a firm crack on my back. My heart knocked against my ribs and I could have sworn my brains dashed out. The flashlight dropped and spun out of reach. The fall stopped my screaming long enough to hear the comforting voice. "Relax, private!" It was Jarrod. I tried to catch my breath, hacking from burning lungs.

6

My face rolled on the crunchy ground towards my fallen light. The black tunnel circling its weak beam was receding and it disturbed me to discover that I alone had caused the swirling darkness. I tried to speak but my throat was dried shut and caked with powdered dirt. I had difficulty creating enough saliva to swallow. When I did, it stung my throat like a hornet. Jarrod helped me to a sitting position.

The sound of running footsteps came up behind me. *Ethan*. A firm embarrassment was settling in. My heart slowed and I tried standing. "Guys…ah…hand." The two lifted me to my feet. My hands released from their grips to fall on wobbly knees. I looked in the direction of that far-flung pocket of blue sky that marked our way out, determined to get out of this black box. Light-headed, I nearly fell over. "Give me…a…sec…"

I attempted to stagger in concert with the Earth's noticeable rotation. "…a…second…wow…holy shit." I swayed like a drunk to pick up my flashlight, lifting in a straightening breath to test my balance. A surge of heat waved up and down my body. I slapped my pants clear of debris, keeping the light pointed in the direction of the exit.

I tightened my face to swallow so I could talk, turning back to Jarrod and Ethan to tell them we were leaving. "Guys, wher– why'd you turn off your lights?" I couldn't tell which of my friends whispered back.

"We don't wish to be seen." The comment gave me goosebumps. I could hear debris crack underfoot as my friends came closer.

"Hey, come on, turn on your lights."

"We don't wish to be seen," the same voice whispered.

Throw your light on them.

I can't, I'll lose the exit! "Real funny, guys. Turn on your lights." The feet moved closer to me. "You're not scaring me."

"Aren't we?" The whisper blew on my face.

"I swear I'll sock you. I'm not kidding!" I made a fist.

I perceived a faint movement coming towards me in the darkness and I threw a sloppy punch at it. "You missed," the whisper taunted. Sloppy or not, I couldn't have missed. I found myself strong-armed by steely fingers clamping down on my forearm.

"What the fuck? Get off me!" I fought by kicking but my legs flew through open air. The clamping hand tightened to where I thought I would drop my flashlight from the crushing pressure. I could feel every wrinkle my skin made underneath my jacket, burning the muscle with crippling pain until I thought the insides of my arm might split. "Stop, fuckers!" I screamed out against the sound of twisting leather. I turned my light on Jarrod and Ethan's face to blind them. The sight of nothing there was worse than the pain. All that stood around me were clouds of yellow dirt and the pit of darkness receding behind it. The grips disappeared, replaced by a continuous flow of throbbing throughout my spasmodic arm.

The speed at which I ran shook my brain harder than my beam. IN-OUTINOUTINOUT! My heart was ready to burst. Over my screams, I couldn't tell if those things were chasing me. My light strobed, swinging out of control. Bristly limbs slapped me, attempting to tie me up. The night sky began to spread the trees apart. I may have heard my name called. IN-OUTINOUTINNN! The swirling blackout spun me around.

MAKE THE EXIT! I gagged. My eyesight was hijacked by the swirling black hole carouseling the trees and the sky. My face cracked in my ears. I had the sensation of being thrown head-first into a brick wall and everything went blank.

CHAPTER 2
First Session
1996

Friday, 3:30pm

1

The doctor's full head of winter-white hair blended seamlessly with his connected beard. His trained grey eyes were centered on me. He reclined back in his leather chair with squeaky springs, his hands threaded over his protruding sweater vest. "Lie on back, Vince. You want a drink? Water, tea?"

"No, thank you." My hair gel crunched against the headrest.

"Better?"

"Yes." The white ceiling tiles displaced in my vision. *Sit up*. My focus fled to the wall of diplomas.

"What are you, six-one, six-two?"

"Six-two." *What-if I can't make it to the car?*

"Tall for your age." My arm jerked, and I accidently bumped my elbow on the recliner. "You lift weights?"

"Yes."

"How did you get involved in weight training?"

"Doctor Morgan suggested it." I took a shallow breath. *You can make it if you leave now.*

"Doctor Morgan's your primary, correct?"

First Session

"Yes."

The doctor squeaked his chair forward to skim some sheets of paper on his desk. "Where do you work out?"

"At home."

"And has it helped you?"

"I'm definitely stronger."

"How about with your anxiety?"

Breathing in, I made an unintentional wheezing sound from my nose. "Maybe."

The doctor leaned into his desk, writing on a stationery pad. "Speaking of working out, I should get myself to the gym. I have a membership to the club, and I hardly take advantage of it. I am paying for it after all."

The ceiling steadily lowered down on me. At the far end of the desk was a black-and-white photo of a football player taking a knee by his ball.

"Is that you in the photo?"

The doctor withdrew from his writing.

"Are you feeling anxious?"

Heat from inside my face pushed my skin outward.

"No, I was just curious if that's you?" I rubbed my palms against my jeans. *He can see, he knows.*

With his pencil at attention, he observed me.

"It's okay to be anxious, Vince. There is nothing wrong with it."

A vibration built in my neck.

"I was, I was just curious about the photo?" *He knows.*

"When I was younger, I played football for a brief stint with the Giants." The New York Giants memorabilia around the room now made sense.

"Wow, that's cool. Why'd you stop?"

He reached over his desk to move the photo closer to him. "I was injured."

"That sucks. What'd you injure?"

He did not take his gaze off the athletic, dark-haired younger version of himself. "...What is it you asked?"

"What'd you injure?"

"Oh, my ACL..." He pushed the picture back. "but that's ancient history, this is your time... Vince, are your hands sweating?" The heat of my face returned. "Is that why you keep rubbing them on your pants?"

I stopped, unaware I was even doing it. I let out a loud exhale of air. "Sorry."

"Don't be, there is nothing to be sorry about."

I placed my hands on my chest but the sound of my heart and the pressure of my hands was too restrictive. I moved them to my stomach, but then I couldn't breathe with them there, so I placed them at my sides against my pants to soak up the sweat, cautious not to rub. *What-if you panic? Won't you look stupid.*

I can run to the car.

You won't make it.

Yes I can. Yes I will.

"Do you wash your hands frequently?"

"...Yes."

The doctor leaned over to jot on his pad. A new layer of sweat formed on my palms. "Do you experience alterations to your perception?"

"I don't know what that is."

"Well, it's when your perception becomes disconnected from reality. What's perceived around you can seem unreal."

"I think so. Sometimes my vision feels like a movie screen of everything."

"That's it." The doctor gestured with his pen.

"What causes that?" *How'd he know?*

"Anxiety. It's termed derealization. It's a harmless symptom of it. How about sensations of floating outside your body?"

"Sometimes I can feel like I'm floating out of my head. I know, it sounds stupid."

"No it doesn't. It's a common symptom."

A strange tingle went off in my gut. "How do you know all this stuff?"

"I've been in practice a while. Plenty of patients with anxiety have come through the same door you have. What you're experiencing will appear unique

First Session

to you, although anxiety is common. A lot of people have it, especially females after pregnancy."

"Really?"

"Certainly. I've had to cope with anxiety problems in my own family with my wife after our son was born."

You're not alone. Contemplating what was said, I ran my thumbnail under my opposite hand's fingernails to the sound of his pencil and a fountain's trickle. The doctor squeaked back in a restful post where he examined my hands that came apart. I felt like a rat on display in a lab.

"Vince, do you know what hypnotherapy is?"

"Not really."

"Hypnotherapy is guided relaxation techniques, used to transform the conscious and subconscious mind. Over the next few months I will show you how to better manage and eventually alleviate your panic attacks." I sat up on my forearms, having difficulty swallowing. "You alright?"

"Yes. I was uncomfortable." My chest grew tight as he stared at me. I went to grind my twisted tooth, but stopped myself. *You can make it to the car if you leave now.*

"What I was saying is that, with a few simple techniques we'll do together in the office and you take home and practice, you'll be able to eventually manage your attacks on your own."

"That'd be great."

"It's important to understand what a panic attack is." My eyes went from wall to wall to stop the spin from gaining momentum. "Let's get a few things straight, right out of the park. First, you are not going to die. Nobody dies from a panic attack. It's a survival trait to help you survive attacks, not die. The worst that can happen is you'll pass out, the body regulates, and you wake back up." The doctor shrugged. "Like falling asleep. Don't misunderstand me, I am not understating the unpleasantness of an attack. I'm saying one will not kill you."

The room is tightening.

"Second, you will not have a heart attack, especially at your age. The heart races to pump extra blood for you to fight or flight. Third, you are not crazy. It will not drive you crazy. What makes these attacks scary, Vince, is that they seem to come out of nowhere— Are you grinding your teeth?"

"No."

"…What makes these attacks scary to the individual is that they seem to come out of nowhere, for no reason."

I laid down to hide the shakes building in my arms. *You won't make it. I told you, get out.*

"I realize it's uncomfortable for you talk about at present. It's important, though, to understand your body and its physiology to cope with what occurs during an attack. The more you understand what's happening, the better you can deal with it."

An urge to cry came upon me. *Get to the car. The walls. You won't make it.* "You mentioned you could alleviate the attacks?"

"Certainly can."

"How long will it take?"

"That depends on you. Make your appointments. Practice the breathing exercises I will show you, which will retrain your breathing pattern, and you'll see a drastic improvement in as little as three months."

"I can be completely rid of my attacks?" My breath went short.

"Primarily, it's up to you. Have you ever taken a martial arts class?"

"No." *Breathe.*

"Well, are you familiar with the purpose of the belt system?"

"Yes."

"It's to show how skilled you are in a particular style, right?"

"Yes." I lifted back up on my forearms. *Breathe, stupid.*

"Right."

Be cool. Run.

"You are the equivalent of a white belt. Your goal is to be a black belt in anxiety control. Learn the skills and techniques to progress and you will. Your treatment progression depends on you. For example, a sensei does not punch or kick for the student. He merely provides the right technique and support. The rest is up to you. Right?"

First Session

"Yes." My airways opened. The dizzy spells eased. Instantly my chest was lighter, my palms drying. The news sent tingles throughout my body. Excited, I wanted to walk to Plarek.

"Let's talk about fight or flight. We all get it at some time or another. A fight or flight reaction is a normal response to any real or perceived harmful event threatening our safety. When you get in a fight, your heart races due to adrenaline. This is that reaction at work. In your case, your brain is perceiving threats from otherwise normal circumstances. Thus, in accordance, you panic and since there's nothing to fight, you inevitably flight. It's caused by a chemical imbalance."

"What causes that?" The room shifted again.

"Well, that's essentially what these sessions are for. To find out what happened to have triggered your anxiety. Those answers will come eventually."

I took an extended breath. *Breathe.*

"Having spoken with your mom, it's my opinion that you have what is called separation anxiety. Meaning, you worry about being alone or separated from your familiars. We will work to retrain your brain to understand nothing is wrong with being alone. Once you train your brain to understand the truth, the attacks will begin subsiding and stop holding you back from living a normal, healthy life."

What-if Mom has to use the restroom? "Does it go away permanently, or does the anxiety come back?"

"Everyone has anxiety, I have it. You're not human if you don't. It's a natural response of the body. I cannot cure you of your body's natural response, nor would you want me to. That's like asking me to cure you of laughing. What will go away permanently are your panic attacks."

"Really?"

"You sound uncertain."

Come on, breathe. I took a deep breath. "It's just, I've seen a bunch of doctors and they didn't help me. You don't prescribe pills, do you?"

"No. What medication did they put you on?"

"Xanax and Paxil first, then Ativan and…Diazepam."

The doctor's fluffy eyebrows went high. "They gave those to you?"

"Yes." *Breathe, please.*

"How did you do on the meds?"

I let out an involuntary sharp breath. "Terrible, I heard voices telling me to kill myself. I had a crying fit I couldn't control in front of my neighbor. One slowed my reactions to where I felt like a zombie. Another made it look like it was raining when it wasn't, it sucked. And when I complained about the side effects, they blamed my anxiety." I could feel a pressure of tears curl around the back of my eyes.

"I can relate. I too, am pill sensitive. Vince, pills…" The doctor shook his head at the ceiling. "…are not the end all cure for anxiety. It's important for you to be treated by a specialist who deals with your specific type of condition."

"Then why didn't they send me to you?" The backs of my eyes pressed.

"Well, not everyone is pill sensitive. Pills work for some people, others not. That's the specialist's job to determine if medication is necessary. In your case, it's my opinion it wasn't. Doctors are people, they make mistakes. Your doctors might not agree with me. They thought they were doing what was best for you. What did you say the name of the pills were?" The doctor readied his pen.

"Xanax and Paxil, they put me on those together. Ativan then Diazepam, I took individually."

"And which gave you which side effect?"

"I don't remember." The tears pressed to get through.

"Also, I want to tell you everything that we discuss in my office is one hundred percent confidential. If you want to share what we discuss with your parents, that's your prerogative. I will not, unless you tell me otherwise. I may ask for permission, but I won't share anything unless you allow it. There are two exceptions to this rule: if you tell me you are going to hurt yourself or hurt someone else. I have to say something."

The image of the gun sparked in my head, its metallic taste momentarily replaced the sweet taste of blood.

"Do you ever feel suicidal, other than when you were on the meds?"

"No."

First Session

The doctor tapped the pencil on his pad. "It's important to be honest. I will not judge you, Vince. Keep in mind too, if it's in the past, I will not report the incident, it's in the past."

"Only on the meds." *He knows, breathe.*

The doctor looked briefly away through the open blinds at a patch of grass where three small trees were spaced evenly apart. "Depression is not uncommon in conjunction with anxiety, so let me know if you do get depressed. It's treatable. Don't be afraid to tell me."

"I won't be."

He clasped his hands together to put them behind his head, squeaking back in his chair.

"Go ahead and lie back down for me."

You're dizzy. What-if you can't get back up? What-if your mom left?

Shut up!

"Comfortable?"

"Yes." *Get up.*

"Whenever you feel anxious, I want you to perform this breathing exercise. No matter where you are or what you are doing. Drop everything and practice it."

I inched my neck to look at the door. *You won't make it.*

"I want you to close your eyes and listen to my voice."

The falling ceiling was closed off. My thoughts grew louder. The twitches of my body increased.

"I will count to six, at which time I want you to take a deep breath in through the nose."

What-if you can't open your eyes?

"Let's begin. A deep breath in through the nose. One, two, three, four, five, six."

My nose felt blocked and my chest quivered. *You can't breathe.*

"And exhale, slow and easy, through your mouth. Visualize your worries being blown away."

If you don't breathe right, you'll panic. Breathe!

"Again for a count of six, in through the nose." I wanted to yell at the doctor to give me a second to catch my breath. "Breathing in positive energy. One, two, three, four, five, six."

You can't—

"Exhale out the mouth, your worries blowing away." My nose opened and my chest eased. "In through the nose, clean air fills your lungs. One, two, three, four, five, six."

You— The twitches lessened.

"Out the mouth. Feel the stress empty out, the unwanted anxiety leaving you to a calm and restful state."

Warm breath streamed out of me. I could feel the stress leaving. Fleeting tingles of excitement raced around my insides. *I can breathe.*

"One, two, three, four, five, six." I counted along, taking in a strong breath. My body was warm, relaxed. Not a twitch was felt. My chest lifted high and dipped low. "And out, relaxed, free of worry, free from unnecessary anxieties. Free."

At last. The doctor's voice disappeared behind the black curtains of my eyelids, to hear my own count. My open hands restful, my legs unresponsive. I gradually stumbled into rest, never more at peace with it.

2

"Vince." The afternoon light coming in from the venetian blinds stung my eyes. My head slumped to the side, bringing an involuntary yawn. Below, my neck remained unmoved. The doctor's white socks under his desk were comforting. The trickle of the fountain weighed heavy on my eyes.

"How do you feel?" The sound of the doctor's voice stirred me renewed.

"Amazing." The rest of my body was waking up. I stretched out and felt perfect.

"Any time you have anxiety, you can always rely on this breathing exercise to relax; it will not fail you. You are always in control."

"Good stuff."

First Session

"Vince, I want you to tell me about your first attack." My body tightened. My heart skipped a beat and my breath lost a cycle, crumpling my legs inward.

"The question bothers you?" I hated my transparency.

Why'd he have to...? "A little." I tried to disguise my discomfort in a stretch, to look at the door.

"No reason to be bothered. We can always repeat your breathing exercise. Tell me what you recall?"

"My friends and I snuck out to a place called Goat's Head."

"What's Goat's Head?"

He knows. "My parents didn't tell you?"

"Some, but I would prefer to hear it from you. As I am confidential with you, I'm confidential with your parents, unless otherwise instructed."

Digging my thumbnail under my other nails, I searched for an answer.

"Listen, communication is the key if we are to build a rapport of trust and get to the bottom of what's bothering you. It will not work otherwise, it's that simple. You want to overcome these panic attacks, don't you?"

You won't make it! "Yes."

"Then let me help you."

"Okay!" The doctor was momentarily taken back. "I'm sorry," I said, now unable to look at him.

"Not a problem. What is it you're nervous to tell me?" he asked in a soft, caring voice.

He'll think you are a freak.

You are a freak! "I don't want to sound crazy."

"Vince, you're not crazy. People who are crazy don't usually reflect on being mentally ill because they are unaware of their mental illness. There are always exceptions to the rule. You are not the exception. By the way, I broached the subject by using an incorrect term to indicate a point to which you could better relate. You are not mentally ill. It's important to note, mental illness cannot be dismissed as someone being crazy. The affected people are at the mercy of their condition. Treatable by a specialist in most cases, usually with medication."

"My point is, you are not mentally ill. You have a disorder caused by a chemical imbalance, not a mental illness. Mental illness is a disease, yours is not. You have a disorder, a meaningful difference. I apologize for using an inappropriate term, I shouldn't have. Not to go off on a tangent either. If you would, tell me what occurred at Goat's Head. By the way, why is it called Goat's Head?"

Don't tell him. You won't make it. Run. "It's why we went. We wanted to impress everyone at school by getting the skull of a goat that everyone says is there. That's why it's called Goat's Head."

"I see, and did you get it?"

"No…I had the attack." *You're so stupid, he's laughing at you.*

"How did it occur, what were the circumstances?"

Don't do it…don't you do it. I'm telling you, you'll regret it.

I have to be honest or I'm not going to get any better!

The room displaced in my vision. I closed my eyes, reflective of the calm state I was in. "The Ones Who Dwell in the Dark were there. They pretended to be my friends and attacked me." *You idiot, you stupid idiot.* The tear pressure loaded on the back of my eyes and I lost my train of thought.

"Who are the Ones Who Dwell in the Dark?" I could hear the pencil lead move.

"They're dark—" *Don't do it. Run!* "Dark-like shadow people, who live in the dark. I know it sounds stupid but I swear they're real."

"Doesn't sound stupid, I've seen them."

I braved a glance at the doctor to see if he was humoring me and laughing privately. He wasn't, he was writing.

"The Dark Ones, they caused your attack?"

"Yes, no, well kinda, yes. Yes, I lost my friends in the dark. I had two attacks. One when I lost my friends and one when the Dark Ones pretended to be them, when they attacked me. I can't remember what happened after that." My voice died out. *Come on, breathe, please breathe right.*

"Was this the first time you saw the Ones Who Dwell in the Dark?"

I couldn't help blowing out a big breath.

First Session

"No, I see them anytime the lights are out. I first saw them when I was younger; my dad turned off the light in my room and one came out of the darkness at me."

"Can you describe it?"

It's enormity resurfaced in my mind. My eyes pulled themselves open, my head shook, out of control.

Run! I jumped out of the chair, my heart leaping out of my chest. "Doctor! I'm having an attack!" The room went blurry. I struggled to get a paper bag out of my pocket, fumbling with shaky hands. The doctor said things to me, lost in translation. The answering weight of his hands gripped me from running for the door. Every part of me shook in his restraining grip. "I CAN'T BREATHE, I CAN'T BREATHE!" I pleaded in his stolid face. He forced me back down on the seat.

"Focus on your breathing."

"I CAN'T BREATHE! THE TUNNEL'S COMING!"

The secretary ran into the room. The doctor waved her off, irritated. She rushed out.

"NOOO!" I yelled, gasping. "I'M GOING OUT! DON'T LET ME!"

"Vince, breathe with me."

The tunnel closed in. I gasped like someone going under water.

"Do you have a girlfriend?"

"What?"

"Do you have a girlfriend?"

I did hear him correctly.

"Let me...my bag."

The doctor's restraint lessened on me.

"Do you?"

Stop asking me! I thought about what he was asking. I shook the bag open and smashed it over my mouth. My head tucked between my legs to breathe. The doctor released my shoulders. *I didn't pass out. I'm breathing.* My fingernails were pink. The tunnel vision had left without my knowledge. *Do you have a girlfriend?*

I laughed into the crumpling bag. The doctor slumped back down in his chair as if nothing ever happened.

"You haven't answered me." I laughed in the bag at the absurdity of it.

"No," I said, embarrassed beyond belief.

"Why not?"

I couldn't look at him. "I only know one girl."

"And?" A pressure to laugh came over me as it sunk in what the doctor had done.

"She's my friend…my only friend…left. I wouldn't jeopardize what…we have," I said in breaths.

"What is the young lady's name, if you don't mind me asking?"

"I don't mind. Melissa, she's my neighbor across the street."

"She's your age?"

"A year younger, fifteen." I tried to look at the doctor.

"We will get you back to school, don't you worry. By the end of these sessions, you will have no trouble finding friends. Not to mention a girlfriend."

"You think so?"

"Absolutely."

"Can't wait. Hey, I know what you did by the way. I was like, is he really asking me if I have a girlfriend?"

"Simple distraction. Where your head is at matters. You can't concentrate on panicking with your mind somewhere else."

"Like a *what-if*?"

"What's a *what-if*?"

"I get these *what-if* thoughts. My dad says my problem is that I'm too self-absorbed."

"Give me an example of a *what-if* thought."

"Okay, take our session for instance. My mind said, *what-if* my mom has to use the restroom, I have a panic attack in here and I run out to the car and she's not there." The doctor put down his pencil and folded his hands on the desk.

"Well, I would answer: you don't need your mom. You had an attack. You mom wasn't here, you beat it."

First Session

"With your help."

"Vince, I asked if you had a girlfriend. That's it, you did the rest by yourself. The power is in you. If it was that simple, I could send you away today and say if you ever have any troubles, have someone or yourself ask you if you have a girlfriend. Do you think that would work?"

"No."

"No, it wouldn't because you did it yourself. You're giving my distracting comment credit, not yourself. You've had one session and have already beaten an attack. That's immense progress. How do you feel?"

Despite the chest pain, after shakes, headache, cold hands and feet, I answered, "Pretty good." No bad thoughts, no breathing problems. *He's right, I did it.* "Good, I feel good." The pressure behind my eyes returned.

"It's harmful to rely on people for control. Their instincts are to coddle you and treat you like a victim. It worsens the attacks. If they treat you as a victim, you will react like a victim. You are not a victim, you are in charge of your mind and body. You and you only."

I'm done being a victim.

The doctor glanced at his large silver watch. "Vince, I think that's enough for today."

"Can I ask one more quick question?"

"Certainly," he said, standing.

"So…you see them too? The Dwellers in the Dark."

"I almost forgot. I'm glad you brought that up." The doctor slipped his shoes on, walking to the front of his desk to lean against it. "Imagine a world before recorded history, where our ancestors were hunter-gatherers living in small travel bands across the undeveloped world. Living in caves, possibly without even the knowledge of how to harness fire. It would have been a dark, harsh and scary existence, wouldn't you agree?"

"Yes."

"There would be no telling what predator might come out of the dark and attack you. You might have a spear or rock to throw at it. Against what? A saber-toothed tiger? My bet is on the tiger. Our survival was dependent on being overly cautious in the dark over millions of years. This is why we see things in the dark that are not actually there. It is an evolutionary advantage that has carried over, though unnecessary today."

"That makes sense, but what about when they attack you? Why would you feel it?"

The doctor walked over and planted his hand on my shoulder. "Paramnesia. Next week we will discuss it in detail. I hate to do it, but I am running late for my next patient."

"No problem. Thank you, doctor."

"Call me Bruce, Vince. My, you are tall. Between you and my son, I must be shrinking." Bruce walked me out. "When's your next appointment?"

"I haven't made one. Can it be Monday?"

"Certainly. Make it with Susan."

"Can I...make it with you? I'm a little embar—"

"Yes, same time?"

"That'll work."

"In the meantime, dedicate yourself to the breathing exercises we practiced today. Six counts in, exhale air out. I would also recommend looking into getting a mouth guard to keep you from grinding your teeth."

"I...I will, thank you, Bruce. I'm excited about these sessions."

"As am I."

CHAPTER 3
It Had No Face

Friday, 5:41pm

1

Bruce placed his briefcase down and locked up. Mentally drained, he was eager to get home. The phone rang. He peeked at his watch. Resolute to leave, he zipped up his Giants football jacket, reclaimed his briefcase and left the caller to voicemail. As he walked down the hall, he waved goodbye to the open windows of neighboring physicians, technicians and secretaries having to work late. Encapsulated at the gate's archway was a tequila sunset. It was exactly the catharsis he sought to clear his head. He had left New York's unpredictable weather to experience this type of usual pleasantry in California, so he told himself regularly.

Bruce slumped into a 7 Series Beamer framed in his ex-team's royal blue and turned the station to his classic preset. Private roads were both dark and bright in the hands of Beethoven's "Moonlight Sonata". Beneath the street lamps the pavement unwound, rounding the narrow curves of affluent houses in upper south Redlands. With their manicured yards, the properties were elevated on hilltops to overlook the city lights and mountain range to the north; magnificent views no one seemed to take advantage of outside their windows.

Bruce looked around at the lonely street. His thoughts always led to the same end: *we should move.*

He was on his block when he saw his neighbors gathered outside. He knew something bad had occurred because his neighbors were outside. His throat locked. The people were congregating close to his house. Red and blue flashing lights painted the spectators. As he drove closer, he remained incredulous to the fact it was his house they gawked at.

2

Bruce unfurled from his seat belt and fled the car mid road, forgetting to close the door. The sound of the office phone rang in his head, associated with feelings of regret. He ignored the nameless faces that corralled him for insight, wedging between the onlookers. He could see his seemingly uninjured family atop the driveway; a sight of unbelievable relief. A flat palm went into his chest.

"Sir, please stay back."

"But, officer, I live here."

"Name?"

"Bruce McGrail."

The officer turned his head to the top of the driveway. "Sarge!"

"That's my wife and son." Bruce could see his wife Elaine, son Michael, Michael's girlfriend Debbie and his neighbor Doug talking to the sergeant. The sergeant waved him up. The officer's arm dropped. "Go ahead."

Bruce rushed up the horseshoe driveway to the waiting assemblage. The sergeant was a bald, rangy man whose nickel-sized eyes were reflective mirrors to the glare of the disturbed craftsman. "How do you do, Mr. McGrail? I'm Sergeant Wilkins of the Redlands police department." The officer spoke in a commanding southern accent. He extended his hand in a firm shake. Bruce scanned everyone for injury. Michael and his girlfriend's composure was relaxed. Elaine and Doug is where he sensed a controlled perturbation.

"What's happened?"

"Your house was broken into. Accordin' to your wife and son, nothin' appears to have been taken. My men are workin' a perimeter search. We have K-9 out combing the area. The suspect, we believe, is a male who has absconded, accordin' to Doug's testimony. He may or may not have had an accomplice. We're investigatin' the possibility—"

"Where's Darla?" Bruce twisted at the sudden realization.

"Excuse me, I—"

"In my room, she's fine," Michael answered.

"Darla's the retriever?" The sergeant verified.

Bruce sighed. "Yes."

"I have a bulldog. I get it, they're family. Nobody was hurt. What we have thus far is, Doug observed a male suspect from his kitchen window, possibly wearing an ape costume, climbin' into your bedroom window—"

"My bedroom, an ape?" Bruce stroked his beard.

"That's correct. The suspect came in through your bedroom window. My belief is said suspect made contact with the retriever, was frightened and cornered in the hallway and jumped out the window at the end of the hall. I'll show you; the backside top window is shattered. We found foot impressions in the ground below."

"Sergeant!" a female detective called from the break-in side of the house.

"Be back with y'all in a minute."

"Take your time. Thank you for everything." Everyone piggy-backed on Bruce's appreciation.

Bruce pulled Elaine close. She clung to her husband, placing her cheek on his jacket. He rubbed her silk-robed shoulders. "My bear," she said in a hushed tone. "Honey, it was simply awful."

"Tell me what happened."

Elaine pulled her head back, swiping shiny black bangs from her aged cerulean eyes.

"I was in the shower. I heard Darla barking, how she does on occasion, and I thought nothing of it. It wasn't until Mikey came and told me to get out of the shower that I thought something was wrong. He was in the room with me—" Elaine couldn't continue.

"Yeah, Pop, Mom had no clue," Michael said, wrapped securely around his cheerleader girlfriend Debbie Janson. "When we pulled into the driveway is when Doug came and told us someone was in the house."

"Mike had it totally taken care of, Bruce." Doug made an uh-hum cough. "I was thinking, if you know what's good for you, dude, you'd better not let Mike catch you." Debbie's light-blue animated eyes widened. Michael adjusted the brown knot on his gi and clutched her curvaceous body tighter; an air of agreeable conceit on his smooth, angular face.

Bruce turned from the mental heavyweight to endure Doug's details. "What did you see?" Doug patted an iron golf club off his pink polo. He could have doubled for Donnie Osmond. Around the same age, the two men shared similar features; a trimmed – once black, now graying – white man's afro and a wide forehead dipping into a pointed jaw.

"From the beginning?" Doug asked.

"Obviously, yes." Bruce didn't mean to come off so curt.

"I had finished playing eighteen holes with Doctor Fisher at the club. You've met Doctor Fisher?"

"Uh, sure."

"He's from Barton Medical Center, next to my office in Redlands. He and his wife are the ones that make the brick oven pizza we adore. The couple Veronica and I went to Europe with a couple years back—"

"I've met him."

"Of course you have. Anyways, I came home from the club with a thing in my stomach and I was looking for the Pepto-Bismol."

Bruce wanted to strangle Doug for his ostentatious, gasbag nature. "Doug, start from where you saw the intruder."

Doug adjusted his white Pro-line pants, insulted. "Bruce, I'm getting to it, let me tell you. I thought you wanted to hear it from the beginning?"

Bruce composed himself with a sigh. "I do. I'm tired, Doug. Please continue."

"I find the Pepto-Bismol and while I put back the cap, I spot out my kitchen window a—" Bruce noticed there entered a slight higher inflection in

Doug's voice. "*Person* climbing the side of your house, wearing a gorilla suit. I thought it was you, Bruce." Bruce ignored the remark. Elaine, Michael and Debbie had taken to talking amongst themselves, tired of hearing Doug prattle. "To be positive, I went to my room to get my glasses. I can't see a thing without my glasses, far away anyway, and when I returned I witnessed it wasn't you. Whoever *it*—" There went that higher inflection.

"Was, slipped into your bedroom window. Of course I immediately called your house, figuring Elaine's Mercedes is in the driveway, she might be home, to warn her and she didn't answer because she was in the shower like she said. That's when I called the police and right about then Mike and Deb arrived. Of course I came right over to warn them. I intended to come for Elaine too. I was not about to let anyone hurt your family. I grabbed my trusted Big Bertha—" Doug flashed the golf club's signature. "And came immediately over."

Bruce felt bad for having ill-feelings towards him. "Well, thank you, I appreciate it."

"Hey, we're neighbors, neighbor. It's what we do. We look out for one another. It's what we do." Doug's neighborly comment came off gaudy, but Bruce knew it was somehow genuine. Doug couldn't help being Doug.

Bruce turned away. "Mike, did you see this ape man?" Michael had inherited his mother's eyes, amongst the majority of her facial features and her hair on a larger canvas. Doug raised a tentative finger to Michael to say something additional.

"No, I didn't."

"Doug is trying to tell you something, Bruce," Debbie said, clueless as always. She pointed at him with a chewed wingtip of blonde hair. Bruce, however, did not want to continue the tiresome discussion from Doug's perspective.

"Doug can tell you what happened better than I can, Dad, he witnessed the whole thing."

"Well, Doug, tell me—" Bruce acknowledged his neighbor. "What happened?"

"Can we talk?" Doug signaled to the side of Bruce's house.

"Certainly." Bruce unzipped his jacket, placing it around Elaine. "I'll be back."

The open house was lit from top to bottom. The bottom story was accessible for anyone wanting to have a look-see indoors. Bruce hated the exposure. He wanted to close the front curtains. He walked beside Doug, taking in the circus of officers and neighborhood gawkers. Doug's uneasy stare bristled his neck as they rounded the house. Two detectives were examining the siding beneath, taking photos. Sergeant Wilkins was among them, examining what appeared to be gashes in the siding. Doug led Bruce to the edge of his lawn where he stopped. He tapped Big Bertha against his shoulder.

"What is it?"

"I don't want to scare you. I thought you should know..."

Doug gave a cautious look around for eavesdroppers. "I didn't mention *it* to the police, your family or mine. Nobody knows except you and me."

"What didn't you mention?"

"It wasn't a gorilla suit."

Bruce's eyebrows drew closer. "What was it?"

"Not easy to say what you don't believe."

"You can tell me."

Doug took in a rush of air.

"When I got my glasses on, I watched *it* climb up your wall with no support. *It* was climbing using its bare hands and feet."

"You're suggesting it was an actual ape?" He felt ridiculous asking.

"Worse." Bruce stepped to steady himself. "*It* was two of you. Taller than Michael. Three hundred plus pounds of solid muscle. *It* had the head and body of a silverback gorilla. *It*s extremities were elongated and massive. Picture it...what would you call *it*?" Bruce stroked his beard.

"I would have no idea. Why haven't you told the police?"

"I did, it's what I can't."

"What can't you?"

"*It* had no face." Bruce's eyelids lowered.

"So it was an outfit, he was wearing a blank mask."

"No, it wasn't an outfit, that is what I'm trying to say." Doug's eyes hooked squarely on the window, its yellow, rectangular light sitting in his pupils. "*It* had no face. I saw *it*…" Doug, nonplussed, struggled to find the words. "Become a contorted shadow…*it* molded its body to fit into the window frame."

Vince Marino crossed Bruce's mind with the word "Shadow". His brain filled in "People". "So you're mistaken; biological and neurological effects can take place on what we think we see—"

"You're wrong!" Doug looked around, lowering his voice. "I know how eyes function. Don't treat me like one of your patients." Bruce straightened with a sigh, resigning himself from an argument. "Besides, you're preaching to the choir. I don't believe it either. I did, however, see *it*. How else do you explain something *it*'s size fitting through your window?"

"Well…perhaps you misjudged its size. I'm not saying you did. I'm saying it's not impossible you didn't."

"Why would a burglar pick the topmost window to break in? Why not the larger, double-hung window below? Do you even lock your doors? Cause when I was with Michael, we walked right in, he didn't use a key."

"I thought about that, doesn't make a whole lot of sense, does it?" Bruce stole a glance at his 22 by 33-inch window, his eyes resting on the three still inspecting the siding. "I saw marks on the house, maybe it was an ape. Maybe someone was keeping one in their house and it got out."

"No, I saw *it*. *It* wasn't an ape. I don't know what *it* was. I haven't told you yet how I know *it* didn't have a face."

"How?"

"When your visitor entered your house, *it* leaned into the window seal so *it* could stare at me make the calls. *It* didn't have eyes, but *it's* head was facing directly at me for a while, a looong while. Long enough to call your house and the police. *It* had a solid black cone-shaped head, with no face on *it*."

Bruce paused. "You don't think you could have perceived it wrong?"

"On my wife and kid, no. While *it* stared at me…" Doug shook his head. "I don't even want to tell you, you're not going to believe it."

"Doug, don't play games. Who cares what I believe."

"*It* had claws and *it* threatened me. The threat was made loud and clear, neighbor. *It* threatened to slit my throat."

A horripilation ran down Bruce's neck. "What do you mean, claws? Like a bear?"

"Large claws, like a bear, yes. *It* ran one large curved blade across *its* neck. This was no bear though."

"Well, let the cops do their job. Find out whoever it is, or whatever it is. Let them handle it, it's what they're paid for. There's nothing we can do about it."

"We're leaving tomorrow morning for the desert. Told the fam we'll stay there a week till things mellow. I suggest you lay low for a while, take everybody on a trip. You can come with us?"

"Tempting." Bruce made it sound sincere.

"You should see the resort were staying at, it's a beautiful five-star luxury for half the price. Veronica's girlfriend at the hospital got us a great deal. We're talking golf, a hot springs spa—"

"That's great…I want to hear about it, I do, but later. When I can think straight. I'm tired."

Doug's voice became serious. "Okay, but there is one more thing I ought to tell you, the police are wrong about. There is no way in hell your geriatric dog scared the thing I saw out the window. No, no, no way. *It* would have—" Doug shook his head. "I'm not buying it. In fact, when Mike and I went inside your house, Darla was at the foot of the stairs, cowering."

"Honey!" Elaine took Bruce out of his head. She waved the two to come back over. Sergeant Wilkins was with her.

"Coming!"

"Was the window broken when you went upstairs?"

"Mike went upstairs, you'll have to ask him."

"I want to thank you for having the courage and presence of mind to help my family."

"Of course, we're neighbors." Doug slapped his back. "I'd lock up extra tight tonight. Let's keep an eye on our houses."

"Believe you me, I will. Would you tell them I'll be right there?" Bruce asked with a nod of his head in his wife's direction.

"What are you doing?"

"Just want to ask the detectives a question. I'll be right there."

Bruce approached the house. "Excuse me." A female detective exchanged private words with her partner, pulling away from the wall to head him off.

"Sir, this is an active crime scene."

"I'm the owner of the house. I just wanted to see what damages were done."

"You have some scratches you might have to fill in and repaint."

"You know what caused it?"

"It's under investigation." The detective created an awkward silence for Bruce to leave. Her stern countenance was ungiving. Bruce looked over her shoulder at what he could see of the severe gashes. Her male counterpart stood in the way. "Sir, is there anything else I can do for you?" She sought to bring his eyes back to hers by stepping her head into his view.

"No, thank you." Bruce stroked his beard, walking away, her eyes following him off.

CHAPTER 4
Walks to Plarek

Friday, 4:33pm

1

As I left my session with Bruce, I felt alive for the first time in a long time. I wanted to live. This feeling left me overstimulated and starving for more treatment. I was desperate for a walk to Plarek. I ran out to the car. *See, I told you she was there.*

"Vin, I can't see!" Mom had the blind look, an unblinking stare of brown eyes on white saucers. *Clean your room.* I grabbed her purse and felt around until I cornered her seizure medication and shook a pill into her hand. *How long has she been sitting here alone in the dark?* I shook free from the thought.

"You want me to call Dad?"

"No, stay with me." She squeezed my hand. "The pill will work soon."

What-if you panic?

Shut up.

What-if?

Shut up.

What-if you panic?

I will carry her to Bruce.

What-if she forgets who you are?

I will get Bruce, shut up.

"Talk to me." I explained and demonstrated my breathing exercise to calm us both down.

Fifteen *what-if* free minutes later, the lively brown of my mom's eyes blinked. "I can see."

"Enough to drive?"

Mom looked around, blinking. "Yes." She patted my hand to take hers back and start the car.

"It's weird," I said.

"What? Don't drop my pills."

"I won't. We were just talking about pills in the session. How some people need pills and some people don't. Bruce says I don't."

"I never thought you did. Those doctors didn't know what they were doing."

I shook the tube to reassure her the bottle was sealed. "I'll place 'em in your zipper section."

"Thank you." She gave the look, brow up, creased corner lip.

"Four Colors?" I asked in anticipation.

"Four Colors."

"Are we talking two comics?"

"We'll see," she teased. She knew my weakness, it wasn't fair. She knows the comic store is my sanctuary, a place of great reverence for me and hankering for an overdue walk to Plarek as I was... what a day, what a wonderful day.

2

Dad was home from work, his Grand Prix hogging the curb. He hated to park in the driveway, a habit he'd picked up to avoid the trash cans on trash day. I raced out of the car, over the monster crack in the walkway to the front door. A feat, considering I held my comics the way a butler carries drinks at a cocktail party. I was eager to show my dad these Bronze Age beauties but I couldn't get the stinkin' screen open to foot-kick the door. "Come on, Mom." She was slumped over in her seat. "…Mom?" I hesitated to walk over. "Mom?... Mom?" Her head lifted and the window rolled down. I took in an absent breath.

"I'll be in in a minute."

I walked over to the car. "What's wrong?"

"The Dilantin is bothering my stomach." My mom circled her hand over her abdominal area. "I'll be in in a minute. If he asks, tell your father I'm listening to the rest of my program. You know how he gets." She switched on talk radio at a low volume.

"Are your pills still working?" *Clean your room.*

"Yes. Go take your comics in and show your father what you got. Show him your breathing exercise, he'll want to see it."

"I'll wait for you."

"I don't want your father to come out, Vin."

"Mom, he's in his undies, he ain't goin' no place." Nauseous, she relented easier than usual, placing her fist to her white-streaked temple and rolling up the window. She knew I was right, I was not going to leave her alone. I placed my beauties delicately in the backseat. Our camphor tree's branches were calling my name.

3

Dad was in the living room watching the news, reclined upon his upholstered throne. He wore a butt-hugger and white sock combo. The man had no shame in his kingdom. "Hey, how was it?" he asked, holding the lazy man's snack, a peanut butter sandwich and glass of milk.

"Good. Vin had an attack during the session and he was able to pull himself out of it. The doctor gave him a breathing exercise to practice over the weekend." If Mom was still sick, she didn't show it.

"Comics?" Dad said.

"He earned it."

"Let me see what you have."

"I will, let me wash my hands." There was no unclean touching of my beauties.

"What have I been telling you? It's all in your head."

"I know!" I shouted from the adjoining kitchen.

"When does he go back?"

"Monday at three-thirty."

"Can you take him?"

"I'll work it out."

"…because I can't."

"I can."

"Are you ready for Ghosts number nine and Unexpected number one-forty-one?" I hastened into the living room. My dad's attention was split between me and the TV. "Don't you dare touch my babies with your peanut butter fingers."

"Take it easy. You would think he was holding an original *Orlando Innamorato*."

My mom laughed from the kitchen.

"He doesn't know who that is."

"Matteo Maria Boiardo's epic poem—"

"Cool, I don't know what that is."

"Would it kill you to be cultured, Son?"

"It might."

"Very funny, Murruda. I ought to comb your head." My dad mimed a prepared smack of half-eaten sandwich.

I painstakingly removed one exquisite beauty from the paper bag, holding it from underneath before him, in all its glory. My timing couldn't have been better, it was a commercial break. "Ghosts number nine, artwork by Nick Cardy." Dad's brown raccoon eyes rolled down the cover and shot back up at the TV, then me.

"What's it about?"

I spoke from memory. "The captainless crew of an adrift cargo ship are caught amid a raging sea. Two deck hands hurry to the ship's wheel to see why the ship has lost control. What do they find on deck? Mysterious footprints of sea water coming straight out of the ocean. Something has broken a giant hole in the side of the ship and has made its way to the wheel. A shipmate yells out in horror to his mate. The captain's skeleton is manning the ship. Or is it their captain?"

Dad peeked at the TV. "Let me see the other. Actually, let me see it later. Can I see it later? After dinner I'll check 'em out with ya."

"Yeah." I knew he wouldn't. His attention went straight to the TV.

I headed to my bedroom, leaving the door ajar so I could spy on some honest conversation. "His problem is that horror and sci-fi junk, I'm telling you. Sixteen and he has to sleep with a night light. Give me a break, Paula. You're not doing him any favors buying him that shit either."

"You're right, it's just… I wanted to give him incentive. Melissa was right; therapy was a smart move. He was able to steady his hands for me."

"I hope you're right, for our sake. You can't keep taking him to work. At this rate he'll be living with us forever. It's not healthy. We should drop him off in the desert and have him find his way back—"

"Stop it."

"That would cure this psychosomatic bullshit. We can't even take a vacation—"

"Enough. I don't feel like having this conversation, I just got in the door. I would like to take a shower, change and get dinner started." Mom's footsteps sounded to their room. All the energy was drained from my body. *How come they don't see them? Dad's right, you are a worthless dead weight on your family.*

Turning on the light, I shut the door, quietly locking it. I took a look at Claude Rains as *The Invisible Man* watching from the poster above my bed. His spectacles beamed green rays at me. I slumped down on the side of my mattress, placing the comic beauties out of harm's way. *You're not junk.* Gritting my teeth, I socked myself in the jaw, a solid blow. The second sock was a tad harder, searing through both layers of teeth, causing an uncontrollable chatter. My knuckles cracked an egg on my jaw for the third serving. I grinded my twisted tooth to ignore the searing pain until I was released from the worst of it.

A dull ache circumvented my head. *Give yourself another, you deserve it.* The heightened sock landed too perfect, triggering a swishing of sweet blood, compliments of the twisted tooth's receding gum. I fell back on my bedspread, numb, having gotten over-zealous. My eyes were blurry. My tongue touched the smooth roof of my mouth and I was made to lie that way for a minute. I drank the sweet secreting blood, lifting to a wobble. I held the mattress for balance, continuing to grind my tooth. The blood oozed out. I stopped knocking myself around. I wouldn't want to leave a mark, after all. I've annoyed everyone enough already.

My beauties were given refuge in my closet's comic collection, where I gently pulled out the acid-free cardboard storage box labeled DC horror. I bagged and boarded the comics with a watchful eye. I gave a closing look at Ghosts #9 and Unexpected #141 in their new sealed homes. The artwork's characters had a cheerfully spooky effect on me, I was able to trade in my fears for theirs. Securing the closet door, my eyes connected with my sketch desk. The picture I drew of Plarek reminded me and invigorated me. I went over to the stereo and pressed the power button. The low hiss charged up the silver box, set for tape. I clicked Play to release Metallica's "Ride the Lightning," yanked my blinds shut, removed my comforter and climbed aboard my bed ship, ready to begin my journey.

4

I walked around the sink hole in my bed, bowing from innumerable adventures. Metallica had played me into Plarek. Without warning, I was brought back, plucked straight out of bliss by a knocking at the door. "To go order!" Mom yelled.

"Coming!"

"Can you turn the music down? We can hear it clear in the living room."

I leapt the incurving base, dialing down the tape. *Your face?* "Mom, I'm not dressed. Can you leave the plate in the hallway?"

"Watch it, it's hot." I awaited her departure and forcefully twisted the knob while pressing my thumb against the lock, a method I used to silence the loud clicking sound it made. I swiped a steaming bowl of fettuccini and broccoli. Mmm, did it smell good. I was famished. After scarfing dinner down, I dialed the music up and was back to Plarek, walking out what remained of the evening while the tape flip-flopped the playback.

5

My alarm sounded. I went to the bathroom to review my face in the mirror. Not a trace of bruising was evident, only a slight swelling near the right side of my mouth. A cold shower cured it. I changed into pajamas, fixed my bed and retrieved my trusty flashlight out of the top drawer of my night stand, placing it face down by the alarm clock. Going between the TV antenna and metal supply cabinet that held the stereo, I lifted the heavy aluminum blinds into an elevated locked position by way of a worn nylon pull cord, careful not to bang them against the window. I gently rolled the squealing window open and pressed out the screen to land silently on the grass. I turned on my TV and muted the volume before the sound could escape the speakers. Fetching a shabby blanket from the metal cabinet, I headed for the door and opened it with my method to quiet the lock. "Good night!"

"Good night!" Only Dad answered, which meant Mom was likely asleep. Closing the door, I gingerly pressed the lock button with my thumb to a flat subtle click. Locked in, I secured the blanket along the seam at the bottom of the door and turned off the bedroom light.

While getting into bed, I was struck by a lack of breath. My throat compressed. The walls and ceiling closed in on me. I threw myself out of bed, heading for the door. *Get out! Get out!*

I can't! I couldn't get a gulp of air to save my life. I managed to drum up a single breath, wrenching at my neck. It wasn't enough, I was trapped! The room grew tighter, tighter, tighter. Screams hung on the roof of my mouth.

GET OUT! My hands and toes curled as the room fell in. My heart pounded in my ears. I went for the knob with slippery hands. *GET OUT!* A scream for my parents was ready to spill. *DON'T! YOU CAN'T! NO!* The lock clicked and I yanked at the door, it didn't open. I had forgotten in my panic about the blanket wedged underneath. It wouldn't budge. *GET OUT!* The swirling black hole traced the corners of my vision. I was too scared to bend over, too dizzy.

GET OUT, YOU HAVE TO GET OUT NOW! My body convulsed and it was then that I knew I would not make it to my parents. *YOU'RE LOCKED IN!* My legs threatened to give out. I tried a breath in through the nose. *One, two—*

The first count clipped off, forcing a short exhale. *STOP! BREATHE RIGHT!* My lungs were exhausted. I spun into a wall from dizziness. *The Invisible Man* whirled by me. *One, two, three. One, two, three, four.* The ceiling was floating upward and away. It was working. *One, two, three, four, five.* The dark swirl receded back behind my eyes. Tingles went off in my gut. My face lifted from the wall. *One…two…three…four…five…six.* I exhaled a full breath.

My mind switched gears. Panic and I had parted ways. I relocked the door, confident I could without further trouble. My claustrophobic hell re-opened. It was over. My breath exercise continued unabated, bringing back my bedroom's normality and my stability. *You did it!*

I DID IT! I DID ITTTT!

A sticky, drained wreckage, I climbed into bed and settled myself down before I caused myself another attack. I continued my breathing exercise until I heard the backyard gate latch lift. Airy steps patted over the pavement to the ladder, switching to a rustle on the grass. A swinging beam shone into my window. Melissa's backpack made a cushioned thud on the carpet, joined by the extinguished flashlight. "You got it?" I whispered.

"Yep." Melissa's small hand anchored itself on my bedroom wall. Her jungle of swinging honey-blonde curls were bleached by the TV's white noise. Melissa eased herself in, carefully managing the window and blinds closed. She was wearing her pink iron-on sleepover shirt of the punk band Snail Bones. The long-sleeved shirt captured her butt nicely in the TV radiance. I tried not to look, but I did. It was hard to ignore. She plopped down onto her side of the bed and removed her glasses. I rolled to my side facing the door, groping my pillow underneath my head. Bad thoughts rolled around in there.

I heard her set the alarm. She glided into bed, slipping into the center depression as her voluminous hair gathered against my back. "How was your appointment?"

"Great, we are definitely onto something. I just had a panic attack before you came over and was able to bring myself out of it. Third today. Bruce, my therapist, gave me a breathing exercise and it works miracles."

"Sweet."

"We'll see what happens. I'm optimistic. I think the solution is to distract yourself. You have to find something that distracts during your attack, some outside influence and you'll forget you're even having it."

"Interesting."

"I am worried about my mom, though."

"Why, what happened?"

"She lost her eyesight again while I was in my appointment. I'm afraid her pills are starting to not work."

"What does that mean? I mean, there has to be other seizure medications she can take?"

"I suppose. It's the transition period I'm worried about." *Clean your room.*

"Tell your mom to see her doctor and see what options are available. Sooner the better."

"I will…I'm hitting the hay. I'm exhausted."

"I bet. Congratulations on your progress today."

"Thanks."

"Thank you for letting me stay over." She said the same thing every night. I smiled, still a little high from beating the panic attack and it felt good to be of value to her in my own pathetic way.

"Anytime."

CHAPTER 5
A Familiar Visitor

Friday, 10:11pm

1

The neighborhood had gone home. Bruce drank another sip of tranquilizing Cognac. Michael and Debbie had gone to bed upstairs with Darla. Elaine came in the sliding-glass door, talking security systems with Sergeant Wilkins. They convened at the butcher-block island where Bruce rested his glass.

"We'll be havin' uh couple of units patrollin' the neighborhood tonight. If you folks do see somethin' out of the ordinary, which I don't anticipate, just call us. We'll be right over."

"We will," Bruce said.

"You bet we will," Elaine added.

"I gave your wife my card. Rest assured, I don't expect the suspects or suspect is dumb enough come back tonight, or any night for that matter." The sergeant's micro expression betrayed him to Bruce. "In any case, I would recommend installin' a security system and fixin' the window when you have the opportunity. Merely a preventative measure."

"Sergeant, did you find out what caused the scratches on the side of the house?" Bruce asked.

"It was probably somethin' they climbed up with, a ladder I suspect." Bruce discerned the same micro expression. He would review the markings in the daylight and see for himself. The image of Doug's faceless ape with claws haunted him. "I'd check your homeowner's insurance, the damage ought to be covered."

"I'm going to," Bruce said.

"Unless there's anything else I can do for you folks, I'll be on my way."

"No, thank you. We appreciate it. Can I get you anything? A water? Tea for the road?" Bruce asked.

"No, thank you kindly. Be sure and lock up and get yourselves some sleep, you hear?" Bruce gave a pathetic smile. Elaine, being the ever-bred hostess, walked the officer to the door, expressing the depth of her undeniable gratitude.

Bruce stroked his beard, draining the Cognac in an ample pour. He revolved around to the liquor cabinet, turned the skeleton key and retrieved a bottle of Kelt X.O. from the top shelf, swilling from the bottle. When Elaine returned, the cabinet key was restored, Bruce was securing the sliding-glass door and the drink was doing its job.

"Bruce, honey, let's go to bed."

Bruce's beet-red cheeks faced her slender glass reflection. "Let me-es secure the locks."

Elaine didn't acknowledge his sloppy speech as she headed out of the room. "Don't be long."

"No." Bruce hiccupped, turning off the backyard light. What limited sight he had vanished into the dark. A sensation of vulnerability came over him, for he was backlit to the outside hills.

Bruce checked the windows and doors downstairs. As he turned off the lights, he remained a step ahead of the dark. He stopped in the entrance hall, one hand on the newel post leading upstairs. His father, Ronald McGrail, and his childhood voice played over a symphony of fearful thoughts.

You want my strap, boy? Well, do you?

No, Daddy, I don't. Please don't hit me any more, I'll pray.

The almighty is the answer. God will cast those demons out of you yet. You bring the Devil into my house, poison your mother and me. We're susceptible to demonic possession because of you. Pray, boy. Pray or I shall see you punished in the name of the Lord.

Don't hit me, please. I'm not possessed. I don't see demons any more.

The Devil has left a rotten print on you. Pray to Jesus with me, lest you be reinfected by sin. Lord Jesus!

Lord Jesus.

Remove from me these bonds of demonic oppression.

Remove from me these bonds of demonic oppression.

Allow not Satan to possess my soul—

Don't let him, Daddy! Don't let him get me!

God is punishing you for being a sinner. Join his army and take your righteous punishment to prove your penitence and self-worth unto the most high.

Do I have to?

Yes you must! The Lord demands it of you, to be clean.

The sound of the body being flogged rung out. *Your savior is a redeemer; salvation shall be yours!*

Bruce hiccupped, his wet eyes probing the dark rooms while he maneuvered back through them. He would not let this uncommon hold on his sensibilities take charge of him. He ended up at the back window, his eyes adjusting to the night. The yard's verdure leaned back and forth with small currents of quiescent wind. He stood there a minute skimming the black hills, reflecting on how silly he was being. "Ridiculous." With a painful hiccup, he headed back to the stairs.

Taking a full hand of banister to balance, he proceeded up the curved steps. Parted by a professional family photo, a pair of shaman masks set back in wall niches faced down upon him. The art pieces were gifts from his anthropologist friend Dr. Anthony Pritchard. They gave the impression of watching him. Bruce regretted the supposed loosening drinks he'd overindulged in, debating going back to the kitchen for a glass of water and a bite to eat. He reasoned to head straight to bed instead and sleep off his weary nerves. A suspicious thought questioned the reason behind his hasty resolve. *I'm exhausted.*

With hand steadfast on the railing, he ascended the steps hard-footed, verging on the lower mask. It hailed from Central Plains, China, was said to be a warrior's headgear. The red-painted wooden mask had bulging eyes with black pupils, red irises and white sclera. The brow extended in the shape of a black bat whose wings outstretched the length of the domed forehead to touch the wearer's ears. The center teeth were human in design. Two white outward-curved tusks bisected the edges in a horrifying grin on the top row. Rotund cheeks gave the fullness of the cleft chin a hilly roundness to the bottom section. Bruce watched the unbroken impression in passing, causing himself to stumble. He hiccupped a nervous laugh, shying away from the warrior.

The deer mask at the top of the stairs was less sinister, but it too watched him pass. Its origin was a mystery. It was said to have come down from many fathers, over many moons. Anthony had acquired it from Mongolian traders in Ulaanbaatar. He said it was likely used in ritual dancing for speed, strength, versatility and night vision to conquer supernatural forces. Carved out of wood and painted overall in brown and white, it had a remarkable life-like quality. It's authentic, wide antlers had been designed to fit in the niche. The nose and inner ears were black with daubs of white paint. The eyes carried the spirit of the animal with wide, smoky brown and black marble-colored authenticity.

Bruce reached the top of the steps in a liquor sweat, having to center his breath. His legs had gone part numb from drink. He flicked off the stairwell light, doing so without looking back. The hallway corridor clung moth shadows to the Purcell friezes wallpaper coming from three overhead slipper shade chandeliers. At its end was the window taped over with black plastic. Somehow permissible despite rational effort, an incurable sensation came of a presence waiting on the other side of the covered glass. *You're being childishh*, he told himself in a mental slur. He strode forward towards his bedroom. A slap of the plastic had him jump out of his skin. *Air from outside pressed the plastic.* Still, he surveyed. Catching his breath, he condemned his blasted disconcerted behavior.

Bruce was inelegant in getting to his room and undressing for bed. He left his robe on the nightstand and retrieved a loaded revolver from the closet. He climbed into bed next to Elaine, who was fast asleep, and observed the light

A Familiar Visitor

he'd left on in the hallway from the crack in the door. *Satan is coming for your soul, boy, repent while you can.* Bruce had the absurd notion to pray.

2

Darla whooped a series of whines, her legs twitching in a dream chase. The cat was almost caught when she sprung from sleep. Her brownish-blonde ears went alert, drooping hazel eyes attentive. Michael was asleep on the bed, huddled over Debbie. The room was peaceful. Darla's head spun to the hallway where a receptive warning issued. She struggled to stand, her hip joints cracking. She went as far as the door frame.

The hall appeared empty and was deathly quiet. Breaking this uneasy quiet was the smallest crinkle of plastic from the window, claiming Darla's interest enough to have her dark chocolate nose sniff the scent. Satisfied the latent warning came from elsewhere, she prowled cat-like down the hall. Her head bowed at the lightless foot of the stairs, searching that which cannot be seen by people. She advanced, pausing on one leg to peer in her master's doorway to see Bruce sleeping. Darla swung her head to the stairs, letting her leg down. An unmistakable presence was perceived. After a few tiny whimpers escaped her maw, the quiet reclaimed the house.

In a spinning turn, Darla faced the concealed window. Her back became rigid, her hackles raised, hazel eyes fixed keen and wild. A slight pressure on the plastic covering pinched her nose. Darla's attack posture took to the front legs, her muzzle fraying white, bristled hair around bared teeth. A guttural growl seeped out from behind her fangs. It was a slap of plastic that sent her off barking in the direction of the unwelcomed visitor, emboldened by her owner's pack.

Michael came ready for a fight in his boxers, a bat in hand. He was carved from stone with not an ounce on fat on him. Debbie sat up in bed, the covers bunched under her chin. "What is it?" she asked.

Observing Darla, Michael targeted the window. "Deb, out of the room." She scrambled out of bed, bouncing in Michael's red-sleeved baseball t-shirt and threw on a pair of his boxers. Running into the hall, she clung to Michael's hips.

"What is it?"

"Don't know, back up. I don't want to accidently hit you." Debbie backed away, crossing her tense arms over her chest. She watched Michael head to the window to have a look behind the plastic.

"Michael, don't!" Bruce said, tightening the robe around his waist, his revolver in hand. Elaine was stuck at his heels. Darla drew close to the window frame, barking. The whites of her eyes were tracking Michael's attitude to determine just how bold she would remain.

Bruce did a sudden turn towards Elaine. "Keep an eye on the bedroom window."

"Debbie, come with me."

"For sure." Debbie grasped Elaine's outreached hand.

Bruce ran up to his son. "What's the matter?"

"Not positive, if anything. I woke up and Darla was barking at the window. I was gonna take the plastic down and see what it was."

The ape creature jumped through the window in Bruce's mind. "No don't, you'll cut yourself. Do you have the cordless in your room?"

"Yeah."

"Get it." Bruce's headache began to give over to the barking. "Darla, quiet!" The plastic slapped Bruce's heart down with a whap. Darla erupted in disobedient barks as Bruce raised the revolver in a stumble backward.

"Here." Michael handed his dad the phone and Bruce dropped his aim.

"I'm going downstairs to turn on the backyard lights, see if Doug can see anything. If he can, I'm calling the police."

"Yeah. What do you want me to do?"

"Give me the bat." Bruce exchanged the bat for the revolver. "Safety's off. Something comes through the window, unload on it. Stay here and watch over your mom and Deb."

"Yeah. What about you?"

"Don't worry, you'll hear me. If you do, come running."

"Yeah." Bruce headed down the hallway, dialing Doug. Elaine ran to the doorway to meet him in passing, seizing the door frame. Debbie stood at the window observing and listening.

"See something?" Bruce asked.

"No, are you calling the police?"

"No, Doug."

Elaine's face went crooked. "Doug? Call the police, Bruce!"

"Elaine, let me handle it. Might not be anyone out there. Keep an eye on the window."

"Come back here. Where are you going?" Bruce steadfast, flicked on the light to the stairs, descending with the phone to his ear.

"Mom, we have it handled."

Elaine, sick with worry, placed her forehead against the door frame, twisting back towards Debbie.

"Mrs. McGrail, Mike will protect us."

Bruce ignored the shaman masks, navigating his descent. He waited at the foot of the steps for Doug to answer, his sobering headache pounding to each ring. "*It's* back, isn't it?" Doug answered, excited.

"We're not positive." Bruce wiped the cold liquor sweat from his brow. "Listen to me—"

"I am listening—"

"Listen. I'm going to turn on the back lights. Tell me if you see someone."

"Where is…?" Doug murmured.

"I am going to turn on the back—"

"I heard you, Veronica is…hang on." Doug covered the receiver.

"Oh." Bruce's eyes ran around the foyer, searching high and low in the partial light. He investigated the wingback chairs, Chesterfield sofa, end tables, fireplace, book cabinets and grandfather clock down to their finest articles.

"Alright, I'm heading to the kitchen," Doug whispered.

"Me too. Veronica okay?"

"I told her you can't sleep."

"Smart."

"Alright, I'm in the kitchen," Doug said.

"Okay, I'm almost to my kitchen. You have your glasses?"

"Yes, of course. Uh oh."

"What, you see someone?"

"Impossible, there's a fog bank outside." Bruce sighed. He maneuvered furnishings using the bat while his eyes adjusted to the dropping light. The glowing white fog was visible in the kitchen windows. Darla's non-stop barking mingled with the creaking floorboards above and below. The unsettling noises prompted Bruce to vacillate in the company of deceitful shadows which tried his reason. *Shadow people. Get it together.*

"Are you there?" Doug's voice startled Bruce.

"Almost, I'm flying blind here."

Bruce stepped under the archway of the living room, gaining improved sight. Outside, the sliding-glass door cooked a rolling fog belt, a glowing brew of brume. The dark prowler skulked about within its incandescence. The shock stanched Bruce's blood flow. "I see him, call the police!"

"Calling." Doug hung up. Bruce dipped down beside the bar island table, peering askance at its side. The prowler's lanky stature stalked toward the glass. It was not near the size Doug had embellished, except for its height.

Bruce dropped the bat and phone to the floor, attempting to run in what felt like slow-motion. He overheard the police officer's radio call just before he witnessed his figure being struck by Michael's bullet. The lead sent the officer sailing into the swathing clouds. Fog vapor swallowed him and spun the bullet hole in the glass to elucidate the reality of what was an inconceivable nightmare.

"Michael!" Elaine cried out when she retained her voice. Bruce rammed the wall with his shoulder, flicking the living room light on. His son hardly had support of the rattling revolver. Michael stared at his father for guidance. Not since he was eleven, when a bully gave him a black eye, had he asked for anything. Bruce wanted to hug him and tell him he would make it better. Elaine and Debbie's mouths hung open, their eyes stricken with horror. They, too, stared at Bruce for an answer. Darla hid somewhere from the sound of the shot, her whining distinct.

"Put the gun down, Mike. Put it down." Bruce beckoned. Michael's arms fell, useless.

"He has a vest!" Bruce answered, wishfully thinking. Acting on impulse, Bruce blew out into the murky fog and retrieved the radio the officer dropped, finding it covered in a crimson consistency which adhered to the skin. The substance was sticky like blood. The evidence increased his greatest fear; that it was too late. He espied a head poking out of the vapor. A coned head lifting under the weight of a lanky body, indicative of the officer's height. "Are you hurt? It was an accident!" Overtaken by emotions he could say no more. Not receiving a response was unbearable. *Don't be hurt.*

The figure's torso swung wide and it occurred to Bruce the figure had stood up sideways. Only its side profile was beguiling the width of a slender man. An impression set in of ants crawling over every inch of his body, the sensation intercepting his steps. The figure was on the move, rising and expanding the closer it approached. Bruce made steps backwards, tightening his robe. The muscles on his face twitched. *Can't be IT.*

The gorilla charged on tree trunk legs. It's bulldozer chest tore away the curtains of fog, thrusting black anaconda-sized arms like pistons in motion, linked at the ends of bowling ball fists. Turning tail, Bruce ran back in the direction of where he believed his house to be, having caught himself in a labyrinth of foggy web. At any second the simian would tackle him and pick him apart. The fog grew denser. "Dad!" Michael's voice drifted across the yard. Bruce went in the direction of his voice. "Dad, where are you?"

"Bruce!"

"Mr. McGrail!" Michael, Elaine and Debbie called out. Bruce panted fire, desperate to answer. He perceived the vibrations from behind getting stronger. It would soon have him. His were the eyes of a hunted animal, whose speed was no match.

"Dad!"

"Bruce!"

"Mr. McGrail!" As it rose its arms, Bruce could feel the swift generated power swing upward at his back. He caught sight of his family's cloudy contours. A tremendous pressure laid down on him. The touchdown of claws was resisted. His foot went wrong into a concavity, hurling him earthward. He closed his eyes when his arm buckled under him as he hit the ground. In a constriction, he braced for the attack. Having knocked the wind out of himself, he hadn't the voice to scream.

"You alright? I found him! Why were you running?" Bruce's eyes cracked open. He could do nothing but pilfer for breath, watching an earthworm writhe in the blades of grass. Someone was saying something, though he couldn't make out who. His world was a painful, dizzy place. The officer rolled Bruce over and he winced in incredible pain, his convulsing hand seized his heart.

"I need medical—"

3

Doug took the call in his bedroom. "*It's* back, isn't it?"

"Listen to me."

"I am listening—"

"Listen. I'm going to turn on the back lights. Tell me if you see someone." Thinking of his wife, Veronica, it dawned on him to see if he'd awoken her. She was not in bed.

He found her standing in her white nightgown, facing out the bedroom window.

"I am going to turn on the back—"

"I heard you. Veronica is…hang on." Doug covered the receiver. "Veronica, what are you doing?" The tint of night traced her shoulder-length hair in silver.

"I wanted to see the fog. Why, is anything wrong?" she asked mechanically, not bothering to turn.

"Bruce can't sleep, I'll talk to him in the kitchen." Doug snatched his glasses off the hutch and closed the door behind him. "Alright, I'm heading to the kitchen," he whispered.

"Me too. Veronica okay?"

"I told her you can't sleep."

"Smart." In the dim lighting, Doug thought he saw his son, Vaughn, near the entrance to the kitchen. Doug squinted, putting on his glasses. As he drew closer, the semblance appeared to merge with the wall. He brushed it off as the dark playing tricks on his eyesight.

"Alright, I'm in the kitchen," Doug said.

"Okay, I'm almost to my kitchen. You have your glasses?"

"Yes, of course. Uh oh."

"What, you see someone?"

Doug gazed out his panoramic window. "Impossible, there's a fog bank outside." Doug studied the thickness of brume which surrounded the McGrail's property and strangely not his. The sight was something out of "Creature Feature." "Are you there?"

"Almost, I'm flying blind here." Doug thought he saw something when Bruce startled him. "I see him, call the police!"

"Calling." Doug hung up. Feet stamping on the marble floor behind him caused Doug's fingers to misdial from a shudder. "Veronica?" Disconcerted, he could see the vague outline of a person standing in the room with him. "Vaughn?"

"Yes, we're here." The darkness of the room amassed a drove of lurid outlines from the walls, floor, and ceiling. Before Doug could reach the light switch, unspeakable inhuman things ascended upon him, rendering his faculties worthless. His mouth was yanked open by the many and he was force-fed a squirming thing of the night. Doug was then taken into the house's inner darkness.

CHAPTER 6
Safety Zones

Saturday, 4:38am

1

I awoke charged. Beating three panic attacks produced a high probability I could be cured. From my optimism came a formulated, ballsy plan. I practiced my breathing exercise until Melissa awoke.

2

I told Melissa my plan. I would use neighbors as safety zones while I walked around the block. If I had an attack, I would stop and ask that neighbor for assistance. I would practice my breathing exercise with him or her and keep going. Worst-case scenario, I could call my parents to pick me up. It was brilliant. Melissa told me good luck, gathered her things and snuck out. I worked out, showered, got dressed, stuffed my pockets with bags and ate my breakfast while watching my favorite movie, *The Invisible Man*.

3

I heard a lawn mower start outside, now was opportune. I ran from my bedroom to the backyard where my parents were sitting under the umbrella patio table. It was a perfect clear blue sky. "And where do you think you're off to?" Dad hawk-eyed me.

"A walk around the block."

"I don't think so. You got chores to do. Supposed to rain tomorrow, I want to get some work done today."

"Why can't I take a walk?"

"Because your mom and I are trying to enjoy our morning coffee, that's why."

"No, I meant I'd be going alone." The response caught him off-guard.

"That's what I like to hear."

"I'm not making any promises. I'll see if I make it." I caught myself wiping hand sweat on my jeans.

"Always think positive. Remember, stay away from *what-if's*," Mom said.

"You just have to stop thinking about yourself. Tell yourself, 'it's all in my head' and be a man." Dad added.

"I will. If I'm not back in say, ten minutes, come look for me. I will be face down on the concrete."

"Will you listen to yourself? You're dramatic like a woman."

"I wasn't being serious."

"If you're not back in ten minutes, I will come get you. Make it around and I'll let you out of your chores today. How's that for incentive?" Dad shared a look with my mom. "You can dance to your terrible music to your heart's desire." Dad motioned me off with his mug; Mom with an encouraging smile. I walked over to the fence, lifting the latch. *No turning back.*

"Positive thoughts," Mom said.

I walked along the side of my house listening to the lawn mower. I couldn't contain the excitement clenching my entire body. Melissa was across the street, mowing in her yellow summer dress, pretending not to see me. She's amazing. All my other friends have gone, dwindled away. But not her for some reason. Maybe it's just because we're neighbors. Didn't matter. What mattered is that I had to make it around the block now, if not for me and my parents, definitely for her.

A mile. You can do it. I stepped off the curb of Oak Street, becoming hyper-aware of my legs and their ability to support me. Each step was surreal. I became amazed at how the brain could steady me and make my legs move. *What-if your legs give out?* It was strange how they functioned. My brain began disorienting their stride, like I was walking on stilts and the ground seemed to wobble beneath them the further I went.

My confidence hedged each step. I reached Erdmore Street, which connected the circular block to the main thoroughfare of California Street. I could no longer hear Melissa mowing. I glanced down to see if I could spot anyone. No one was out. *What-if your legs give? You won't be able to make it back. If you head back now, you can make it, just run.*

I can do it.

No you can't, you will panic.

No, I can.

No, you can't. What-if your legs give? I tried my breathing exercise but I couldn't concentrate. My focus went to my hampered breath. *You won't make it, run. What-if you pass out? The darkness will come. What-if you can't swallow?* My focus went to my difficulty in swallowing. *What-if you choke to death?*

What-if, what-if, what-if…I can't swallow! I can't breathe!

I felt the dreaded tremble take hold, stuck in a conflicted imbecility. I touched the bag in my pocket. It wasn't enough, my heart began to pound. *RUN!* I sprinted back towards my house, legs in full operation. *'You won't make it!'* I fought the inclined street of Erdmore. *YOU WON'T MAKE IT!* I hadn't yet reached Oak Street when, frightened out of my wits, the sum of my muscles convulsed, threatening to drop me. My heart rammed my chest, head and ears. That's when I heard the miracle. The sound of a house door closing, back down Erdmore. Spinning around faster than I could think, I spotted the blonde-haired lady heading to her car. *GET HER!* The dark trim of the tunnel was forming. If I didn't get to her soon I was going out. As luck would have it, she held a coffee which slowed her pace.

She was near her car. *MOVE IT, MOVE IT!* I pounded the pavement, my chest rattling, my legs on fire. I had to reach her before I collapsed. *SHOUT AT HER! SHE'S GETTING IN HER CAR!*

I CAN'T! I was too embarrassed to shout. The car started up, the parking brake released and the vehicle started to pull out of the driveway.

YOU WON'T MAKE IT! The swirling tunnel framed my vision. I made it to the driveway, the bumper coming at me. *WAVE YOUR HANDS.* The lady's garage door lifted and the sound of a radio playing inside ran me to the opposite side of the street. The white Honda backed out and drove off, unaware.

I had switched to a casual walk, where I took my pulse like I was exercising and had to stop to catch my breath. My pulse was knocking impatiently at my wrist. I don't know how convincing I was to the two guys circling a classic car in the garage, with me wearing jeans and puffy-tongued footwear. At least my heaving breaths proved I'd been running. They looked at me suspect, I assume because I was looking back at them. I waved. The dark-haired one gave a simple wave back. The fair-haired one didn't bother. I turned the corner at the bottom half of Oak Street, taking heaving breaths. I anchored quivering hands on my cramping sides, practicing my breathing. I had my first safety zone, Guys in Garage.

It occurred to me in seeing Fred gardening down the street that my brain's distortion of the ground, my ability to swallow and the stability of my legs was, at that moment, no longer a problem. I cleared my head of the morbid ideas of what else a brain might be capable of doing to a person by focusing on my number two safety zone, Fred. I admired the landscaping that Melissa's mom, Jacklyn, did in each achieving step of freedom. *You've won!*

Don't jinx it.

Fred was placing fertilizer spikes in the ground for his impressive rose collection, humming an unfamiliar hymn. "Hi, Fred." He pushed up on his hands, his eye creases making wrinkles at me.

"Hello there, Vince." He looked back for my parents.

"I'm alone."

He took off a glove to scratch his grizzled hair. "So you are. Beautiful morning we're having."

"I know, it's awesome."

"Soak it in. Supposed to come down tomorrow."

"That's what my dad was saying. Jacklyn did an incredible job on your yard."

"Didn't she?" Fred admired the florid variety of roses edging his property. "I told her, Melissa and her ought to start a nursery."

"Definitely. I didn't mean to take you away from what you were doing. I'll see you. I'll be walking around the block."

"Tell your parents 'hi' for me."

"I will."

The last street was a breeze. My house was right around the corner and the safety zones were in abundance. *You did it.*

"Look at you, stud." Melissa surprised me from behind my dad's car. She was outstretched on the curb, leaning against the mailbox. "How was it?"

"Beginning was rough, I won't lie."

"How are you not freaking out? You-u-u walked around the block." She scissored her legs. Her emerald eyes paraded question marks behind thin black frames. I didn't want to celebrate, I wanted bigger challenges. The rush she and I expected was left somewhere back there on the road.

"I want to go around again. When it gets easy, then I'll get excited." I left Melissa with her mouth open and went to the driveway to tell my parents I was back. I could only see my dad's black hair from where I was. "I went around!" My dad's head lifted and craned over the fence. "No chores, ha!"

"See, what'd I tell you?" My dad said something to my mom and she wandered into view.

"We knew you could do it!"

"I'll be going around again!"

"That's it, keep at it," Dad said.

"I will!"

Melissa pushed her fairy-tale hair to the back of her ears, pushing them outward like an elf. She held that question mark look. "What?" I asked to get the question out in the open.

"I'm impressed."

Safety Zones

"Don't be, it was a couple of blocks." Her knees touched, tenting her yellow dress between her short, lean legs.

"Small steps lead to big ones, you watch."

"I don't want to get too far ahead of myself. For now, I just want to focus on a flawless walk. I had trouble on Erdmore and it's messin' with me a little. If I can get the block to be routine, maybe I can try some driving with the same safety zone plan. Then I could use shops, stores and gas stations."

Melissa's face lit up. "Oooh, will you take me for a ride?"

"How would I be facing my anxiety with you in the car?"

"I don't know, pretend I'm not."

"Oh, okay," I said in a goofy voice.

"You suck." Melissa crossed her arms, play-pouting her lips.

"Can we please not get ahead of ourselves? Let me see if I can lick the block first."

"Don't be silly. You will. When you do, will you take me for a ride?"

"Melissa, your mother wants you in back!" Dick yelled from across the street. Melissa gave me an annoyed look. "Hey, Vince."

I partially turned. "Hi, Dick."

"Out by yourself?" He smirked.

"Appears that way."

"Be careful you don't get shaky." Dick mimed a shaking fit.

"I'm sorry," I heard Melissa say.

"Just having fun with you, don't panic over it."

"That's cool. Maybe when I'm old enough to drink my problems away like other people, I won't get the shakes." Melissa brought her lips in to avoid laughing. I could hear the beer can being crushed in Dick's hand.

"Did you hear what I said, Melissa?"

"Coming! So when should I come over for my ride?" she asked, walking backward.

"What?"

Melissa dragged her feet.

"Hurry up, Melissa! I'm missing the race!" Dick yelled.

"Six-thirty."

"See you at six-thirty." She did a twirl and her dress and golden locks danced.

Crafty little devil. I walked away, ignoring Dick's glassy stare. I wanted him to see the future Vince Marino. *Could I ever use a walk to Plarek.*

4

Dick walked in front of Melissa who lingered behind. He owned the face of an asshole. His tank top read in yellow letters, "I flexed and my sleeves ran away." He wore American flag harem pants and sandals with bottle openers sewn in. "You're letting the flies in." Dick held the screen door open.

"I'll use the front."

"It's locked." She preferred not to hear him. Dick muttered. Melissa rushed to the front door and knocked to no answer. She peered in the window under the shade of her hand, looking for her mom.

Dick reveled in the notion of a defeated Melissa, who would have to come crawling back and obey him. He knew Jacklyn was in the back-yard gardening. Standing by, he anticipated his dominance, playing out the scenario. After ample minutes passed, he grew frustrated and impatient. He walked around to the front of the house to find no Melissa. "Jacklyn, you bitch." Dick lumbered back to the side door, slamming the screen.

He wedged back into his fart-stained recliner with a fresh cold beer glued to his hand and went back to Nascar. "Whew, I'll teach you order yet, you bitch." He leaned forward to be heard in the backyard. "Tell her the news!" Dick settled back into the race with an irresistible urge to smile. "Cunt," he said under his breath.

Moments later, a vicious argument could be heard building from Melissa's room. He listened to the drama, slurping down beers in a buzzed ecstasy. It was a fitting revenge, exceeding expectation. When the argument was abrupt to stop and Melissa's door slammed, Dick lowered the TV volume. To his delight, he was rewarded with Melissa's hysterical sobs. "See what you did? You made the cunt cry. Boo-hoo, boo-hoo." He laughed, adjusting his member. He settled deeper in his chair, satisfied. Minutes later, the crying stopped and Melissa's room door opened. Dick muted the tube. *Would she attempt to start some shit?* Feet moved along the carpet in his direction. He placed his beer in the recliner's cup holder, pushing his seat back into an upright position. An unease pressed him to investigate. He began leaning forward to stand when he found himself face to face with Melissa.

Dick's liquid courage welcomed any verbal assault or physical attack Melissa could muster; he prepared his fists to beat her down. "Do something." He smiled, wry. She uttered not a word, locked in a stare down of vengeance. "Jackie, come get your daughter!" Melissa's hair fell over puffy eyes of interminable hate and rage. Every fiber of her being trembled. Her finger nails oscillated at her sides, having trouble deciding in what order to start scratching. "You want a piece of me bitch, come get it. I'm your daddy."

"Ahhh!" Melissa yelled. With hopping speed she drew to a dangerously close range. Dick threw a packed punch but miscalculated and missed. Melissa spit, hitting him in the right eye.

"You fluckin' bitch!" Dick's eyes clamped shut as he scrambled to pull the bottom of his tank top up to clean his eye.

"What happened?" Jacklyn asked the fleeting figure of Melissa, nearly sideswiping her.

"Stop her!" Melissa ran out the front door, slamming it behind her. A framed picture of girls standing at a western bar, ass out in bottomless chaps, fell to the floor.

"Why, what did she do?" Jacklyn asked, buying her daughter time. Dick tried to roll up on his feet and Jacklyn grabbed his right arm to aid him. Dick gained his legs, pulling his arm away.

"What does it look like she did, retard? Your whore daughter spit in my eye."

"No...she didn't."

"That's it, Jackie. That's fucking it, I'm finished. I want her out of my house."

"I'll talk to her. Let me talk to her? She will apologize for her actions, I promise. This is unacceptable. Let me just talk to her. She will apologize." Dick grabbed her brown curls, yanking her head down in a yelp. "You're hurting me." Jacklyn blocked her face.

"You want forgiveness for your brat, then you will take her punishment."

5

I parked my mom's Monte Carlo at the gas station, overlooking Interstate 10. I sat there, idling the engine. *How far can I push it?* The day was already an unbelievable success. I had traveled nineteen streets and conquered the block. Why'd I have to pile so much into one day? An inexorable high had me hooked on freedom, locked into a dangerous curiosity of just how far I could push my limits. My hands left perspiration marks on the steering wheel as I flirted with the idea of joining traffic on the 10.

Are you crazy? What's wrong with you?

The fear of wrecking my parent's car with no license was not to be taken lightly. They had allowed me to take a few close side streets under the strict condition that if I was pulled over, I was to tell the officer "I took the car without asking." I would have to suffer the implied consequences of the D.M.V. and the ramifications of my parents. *So why am I in line waiting to enter the freeway?* These impulsive acts were getting out of control. Redlands will be where I put my foot down and call it quits.

The plan was to stamp the gas to Ford Street to the next safety zone, Gas Station, a three-mile stretch. If the traffic was to jam, I would drive in the emergency lane. The signal light changed green. *What am I doing? Too late.* I glanced down at my pile of brown paper bags stuffed in the driver side console. Holding the wheel with ten fingers, I stamped on the gas. It turned business real quick as my foot challenged the motor. I was in the slow lane going anything but, unable to stop holding my breath. The highway consumed me. To my left, cars rocketed behind me like meteors of metal. Vehicles weaved out of my lane, left in the Monte Carlo's six-cylinder dust.

You're not breathing.

I'll make it. The hand tremors came despite my stranglehold on the wheel. My heartbeats pumped in my ears, the shakes gaining momentum.

You have to breathe!

I will!

What-if you crash and kill someone?

Little late! I can make it! The thought of killing someone did a good number on me. I tilted, feeling like I was going out. I shook off the terrible feeling. My body convulsed, urging me out of my skin. I wanted to pull the safety belt off my restricted chest. I wove around those too stupid to get out of my way, coming darn close to colliding with those who honked in response.

Your mouth is dry! What-if you can't swallow? What-if you choke?

I CAN'T SWALLOW! A scream welled in my throat. I tried frantically to swallow. It was a race against the clock through the tunnel of swirling darkness. The exit sign for Ford Street flew over the windshield like a green and white bird. I could swallow again. My speed dropped and I felt myself starting to breathe.

The come-down felt like running superfast on a treadmill and jumping off without a cool down. I continued to drop the speed as I exited, slowing around the curve to a stop at the light. "Yes! Yes! You are the man! You are the fuckin' man!" I hopped in my seat, pounding the steering wheel, snapping the right blinker on. My safety zone was across the street. "I can't believe I did it." The rush was intense.

I stopped at the gas station for a bottled water in case I was to have another dry choking spell. I knew Mom and Dad must be flipping out from concern. I took a swig of water and was back on the freeway heading towards Yucaipa. It was an easier drive. My lead foot was a feather. My breathing maintained an orderly rhythm. Scrambling through cars was replaced by a blinker. I thought about those I had seen speeding on the freeway with my parents in the past, thinking they were just jerks in a rush. Those jerks could have been people like me.

The freeway run was a breeze. I decided I would drive past the Yucaipa Boulevard exit and take the shortcut at Live Oak Canyon. A quarter of a mile stretch further with a quarter of the safety zones. The nearest was a pumpkin patch farm. I passed the Yucaipa Blvd on-ramp and, without warning, I panicked. I punched myself in the face for being so stupid.

YOU ARE GOING TO PASS OUT! A fellow driver honked at me. *WATCH OUT!* the voice screamed in my head. I veered back in my own lane. My seatbelt locked down like a strait jacket.

I CAN'T BREATHE! UHT, UHT, UHT! I tried to take a breath but couldn't get one. UHT, UHT, UHT! *STOP IT! YOU'RE MAKING IT WORSE!*

The freeway wobbled in my vision. My shaking hands gripped the sweaty wheel, haphazardly in control. I was incapable of operating the barreling machine. The pedal was to the metal and I was out of my mind.

My speed became irrational. A terrific heat secreted from my pores. I raced through tunnel vision to the freeway exit; the pumpkin patch my destination. The darkness pressed in with haste around my sight. By luck I could not conceive, I managed to screech off the freeway. The car careened off the exit, close to rear-ending a red car stuck at the red light. I screeched the brakes to a halt, causing the vehicle ahead to inch forward to avoid a hit. Tattooed arms lifted at me in the red car. I was caught in an unreasonable terror and could not have cared less. The pumpkin patch banner was in view, carrying on about leftovers for Thanksgiving. It taunted me just off the on-ramp. Traffic was obstructed in both lanes with no shoulder, blocked by a cement traffic barrier.

I'M GOING OUT! HIT THE RED CAR! THE DRIVER WILL HAVE TO STOP! My head bobbled. *THEY WILL HAVE TO STOP AND HELP YOU.* My breath was freed. I began my breathing exercise, achieving deep breaths. *You're not alone. You never were. Drivers can be your safety zones.* I unbuckled my seat belt and whirled around to see all the vehicles and the people in them I could use. I could hit anyone of them. The realization drove me home with not a single *what-if*, or concern for the next stationary safety zone. There was always a car around. I was, for the first time in three years, free.

6

My dad's Grand Prix was gone. *They went looking for you!* I pulled into the driveway to formulate a plan, using the visible neighbors three houses down to hold my cool. My dad wasn't gone, he was out back, lugging a ladder. "What the hell?" My dad acknowledged my return with a thumbs up. I grabbed my water and crammed a paper bag into my pocket. He had some explaining to do.

"Is Mom out looking for me?" I asked with some justifiable attitude.

"No, she went to see the doctor, she's been having stomach problems. She might be pregnant." The answer suspended my reply.

"Are you serious?"

"Yes."

"Is it healthy to have a baby at her age?" My dad's expressive brown eyes held back distress.

"I don't know. We're not positive that she is, so let's just wait and see. Talk to me, I want to hear about your drive." Dad shouldered open the sticking garage door, walking the ladder across the room to place it against the wall by my weight room. He retrieved a can of black paint from the middle shelf and placed it on the splotched sawing table. "Drive went smooth?"

"Yeah it did, better than expected."

Dad popped the lid off the paint. "Good, and we have Friday's appointment to thank for your improvement?"

"No doubt about it. Bruce is a miracle man. He gave me this breathing exercise that has completely changed the game."

"Your mother and I discussed it and we want you to attend therapy twice a week. What do you think?"

"I'd love to. Can we afford it?"

"We can afford it." Dad confronted me with a look that said "don't ask again". A stern look which thinned his already angular features. "I want you to do me a favor."

"What?"

Dad stopped stirring, reaching in his tattered jean pocket. He pulled out a wad of twenties. "Here's two hundred dollars. You can take the car tonight. I want you to take Melissa somewhere special."

"But, Dad—"

"Take it."

"It's not like that, we're friends." He took my hand, pushing the bills into my palm.

"So what do I care, go as friends. Your mother and I want you to take her." His hairy, dirty hand held onto mine. "Just don't damage the car. You haven't damaged my car, have you?"

"No."

He released me and began stirring.

"Melissa came over here crying to your mother, asking us to hide her from Dick and her mom. Apparently, Jacklyn's pregnant."

"No…"

"Yeah… something must be in the water. They got into a massive fight over it, I guess. I didn't ask questions. Always advisable to stay out of other people's family affairs."

"Is she here?"

"No, she left."

"To where?"

"Said a friend's house."

"Whose?"

"What am I, Colombo? That's none of my business. She was excited about your six-thirty ride. I told her you were taking her out to dinner."

"What! Why would you do that?"

"To make her stop crying."

I couldn't argue with that logic. "What's the big deal anyway? Melissa's a sweetheart."

"She's awesome. I'm not saying she's not. We're friends. It'll be awkward."

"How are you my son?" My dad gave me a look of bewilderment.

"What do you mean?"

"You have a lot to learn about women. She's nuts about you. Take her out tonight. I have a suit you can wear and woo her with the Marino charm."

"A suit? I will be way overdressed, no."

"Vince, Vince, Vince." Dad shook his head. "Make no mistake, you have a suit and tie date in a couple of hours. You can thank me later when you don't look like a mameluke and she comes over dressed to kill."

"How do you know she's dressing up?"

"She will."

"What about Mom?"

"I will take care of your mother. You take care of Melissa. Be supportive but stay out of her family affairs. Let her tell you when she is comfortable, don't press. Unless you want to become the enemy. Be a gentleman and respect her space." Dad's eyes lifted. "Capisce?"

"I will. Thanks for the money."

"I'm proud of you." I fought the water welling behind my eyes. He tapped me on the cheek with a release. "Scat. Go listen to your terrible music."

CHAPTER 7
The Hospital

Saturday, 9:36am

1

"I don't know how, Pop, and I don't care." Michael propped two pillows behind Bruce's back. He was hooked to a heart monitor. His casted left arm fixed across the outskirt of his belly to fit under the breakfast tray carrying cold oatmeal, a crusty English muffin, one hard-boiled egg and a bitter cup of lukewarm coffee.

"Sergeant Wilkins told you?" Bruce asked in a groggy voice.

"Yes, honey. Let it be," Elaine said, her eyelids ready to fold. The column-framed window shone a golden-wheat sunrise over the guest chairs that Elaine and Michael occupied.

"How could we have mistaken it? How?" Bruce asked.

"Let it be. Eat your breakfast." Elaine placed a spoon in his weak grip.

"Get your vitamins in," Michael encouraged.

"They didn't find anybody?"

"No, honey. Don't let it bother you. It's insoluble. Wilkins told us no officer was shot."

"What about the man who chased me?"

"It was foggy…"

"Well I didn't do this to myself, Elaine!"

"Don't get excited. No one is saying you did, Pop. We'll figure it out."

"I'm not excited, I'm exhausted. I want to go home, rest in my own bed." Bruce fed himself a spoonful of oatmeal, squishing his face in a groan.

"My poor bear." Elaine stroked his covered leg.

"I don't want you two returning to the house unless I'm with you."

"Honey, where are we supposed to stay?"

"Carol's watching Darla?"

"Yes, bu—"

"Then ask her."

"Honey, uh…" Bruce winced, struggling to reposition himself.

"No worries. We'll stay at Aunt Carol's," Michael said. Elaine considered her son in disapproval. Michael's response read: 'Agree on behalf of his condition.'

"We'll stay with Carol," Elaine said.

"You hungry?" Bruce offered his food.

"I'm not." Elaine waved it away.

"Mike?"

Michael gestured being arrested. "No thank you. I'd rather eat raw sewage."

"It is awful."

A courtesy knock was heard at the door. "Hello, doctor," Elaine said. The room quieted.

"Don't stop on my account. The food is not appetizing. Though, I have to say, I wouldn't prefer raw sewage," Dr. Eloa Angeles remarked. Michael flaunted a specious smile at her. The doctor walked into the room towards the right side of the bed and stood opposite Elaine. She darted judgmental brownish-green eyes from the food to her clipboard. Michael observed how well-proportioned she was in her lab coat.

"Hello, Mr. McGrail, I'm Doctor Angeles. How are you feeling?"

"Tired, otherwise fine."

"Excellent." The doctor leafed through her paperwork. "You didn't have a heart attack. Your EKG was normal. Your blood pressure mimicked one. When you were brought in, your blood pressure was two hundred thirty over one hundred fifteen—"

"Bruce!" Elaine blurted.

"Yes. He has since come down. Last check was…one hundred twenty-two over eighty. Your earlier reading carried a high probability for stroke. You have to take it easy for a while. No stresses, no alcohol." The doctor eyed him.

"Yes, Doctor."

"We gave you some medication which will maintain your blood pressure. The compression socks will aid this in conjunction. We would like to keep you overnight for observation. I know…" The doctor read Bruce's face.

"Okay." He sighed.

"Do you have any questions?"

"No."

"Then I will be back. You hang in there with the food." The three thanked the doctor. She made her way out the room, passing Michael whose eyes and smile flirted with her openly. Her head dipped a smile and she could sense him watch her out of the room.

Michael's stride slid him out of his seat and over to the bed. "Dang, Pop, you hit the jackpot. You should tell her your penis is broken and let me switch places with you.

"Michael!"

"What? It's funny. I'm trying to make him laugh." Bruce had a huge smile, so Elaine eased off.

"Mikey, be an angel and get me a glass of water, would you?" Elaine asked, searching her Prada bag.

"No worries, be right back. Maybe the doctor can tell me where I can find some cold water."

Elaine gave a parental glance of disapproval and pulled out her old anxiety medication. "Poor Debbie."

"You're having trouble?" Bruce asked.

The Hospital

"Since everything, eh." Elaine rocked a pill in her hand.

"Attacks?"

"Nothing of the kind. Stop stressing. Eat some food."

Bruce leaned back. "My gruel." He scooped more oatmeal in his mouth, pushing it down with coffee. Michael returned, handing his mother a Styrofoam cup.

"Thank you, Mikey."

"She's married. Should have caught the ring finger." Michael flopped down in the chair.

"You asked out the doctor?" Bruce asked, impressed. Michael surveyed the entryway.

"You bet I did. I thought I had a shot too."

"How would Debbie feel about you asking out other girls?" Elaine glared at him.

"I'm young. I'm not getting married to Deb." Michael looked pained at the thought.

"Shame on you. I raised you better than that."

"The doctor is educated. No offense, Mike."

"None taken."

"You two are terrible. Debbie deserves better."

"What are talking about, Mom? You are always complaining to me that she's hanging her breasts out for everyone to see."

"Well, she does."

"She's bound to end up on a pole."

"Pop gets it."

"You're the one dating her, what does that say about you?"

"That these boots were made for walking."

Bruce nearly choked on his food. Elaine rolled her eyes. "I bet she's cheated on me and I don't care."

"I can't do it." Bruce pushed the breakfast tray away.

"Poor bear. You want us to pick you up something to eat?"

"No, I'd like to get some sleep. Mike, I want you to stay with your mom."

"I can't, I got that thing." Mike pointed at a watch he didn't have. "Don't be ridiculous…yes, I'll be with Mom."

"Smartass. Too bad it takes me being in the hospital for you to spend any time with us."

"What? That's not true. Let the man sleep, he's delusional."

"I'm delusional?"

"I don't have to take this abuse from an invalid."

"I'll show you an invalid." Bruce shook a low fist. Elaine dipped over Bruce, pushing his hairline back to kiss his age spotted forehead.

"Call Carol's if you need us. I'll check on you later. Love you." The two stared into each other's eyes.

"Love you too. Will you call Susan, let her know what happened? Tell her I'm not coming in next week and to cancel my appointments."

"Yes."

Michael gave his dad a lopsided hug. "Later, Pops. You want the curtain closed?"

"If you wouldn't mind." Michael closed the curtain and the two loving smiles were covered. The death monitor's low-toned buzz filled the room.

2

Bruce was shaken to arousal. A blurry needle was in his muddled sights. In a raise of his head, an Asian nurse came into focus. Her brown eyes and upturned nose lifted at him.

"Sorry to wake you, I have to take blood. On the bright side, you have a visitor, yaaay. Be tough for me, 'kay?" Her miniature pony tail swept into view as she turned to his abused vein. Bruce avoided watching the needle. He concentrated on his friend, Anthony Pritchard, sitting in a guest chair. Bruce's eyebrows waved to him. He signed back. The prick made his eyelids blink.

"All done."

"You're insidious," Bruce said. The nurse bandaged the purple blot, smiling white teeth and healthy pink gums.

She packaged the sample. "Be back."

"Don't rush on my account."

"You're so funny."

Bruce waited for the nurse to leave. "She's a menace to society."

Anthony laughed. "How are you, my friend?"

"I'm dealing."

"Broke your arm?"

"Yeah."

Anthony combed his hand through thinning salt and pepper hair.

"What happened to you?" Bruce referred to a square bandage on his friend's forearm.

"I contracted leish in Columbia from sand flies."

"Are you okay?"

"Oh yes. I cover it because it's not very attractive. Has the appearance of leprosy."

"Jeez. What were you doing in Columbia?"

"Fieldwork for the museum, with the Jaguar Shamans. I'm interested in their ancestral systems. I'll be doing a lecture about my findings next month. You and Elaine should come."

"We'll come, sounds fascinating."

Anthony leaned forward and made a pyramid with rocky palms. "I spoke with Elaine, she let me know what happened."

"Yeah."

"Wanna tell me about it?"

"I can…what time is it?"

Anthony checked his cracked watch. "Five twenty-seven."

Bruce echoed the bizarre details, holding nothing back.

"What do you make of it?" Anthony's muddy-brown eyes were wrapped in thought.

"A considerable amount. Did they say when you are to be released?"

"They want to keep me overnight, keep an eye on the old ticker. Barring no unseen complication, I'll be out tomorrow."

"Would you mind if I accompany you home with a friend of mine?"

"Course not. Why, though?"

"I believe she can assist."

"How?"

"She's a medium."

"Tony, you can't be serious?"

"I am. I realize your stance on psychic phenomena."

"Mediumship is nonsense. You're an educated man." Anthony's lean face became rigid.

"I would say the events you've experienced would at the least warrant an investigation. You have an unbidden ape thing that morphs into your window. Your neighbor swears it climbed the wall. You, yourself have found markings on the siding. Police look for it, can't find it. It returns.

"Michael shoots what is perceived to be the ape in front of three reliable witnesses, but then an officer's radio call is heard. You run out into a convenient fog bank to look for the supposed downed officer, find a bloody radio and are then chased by what you admit was what your neighbor says he saw. You come to find out that no officer was ever shot and no bloody radio was ever recovered. A patrolling officer responds to the gun shot he heard and finds you running scared in the fog from that thing, which he claims not to have seen. Sounds preternatural to me."

"Maybe I had an incident of paramnesia. I have no idea, I was exhausted." Vince Marino crossed Bruce's mind and he laughed.

"What's funny?"

"Oh, I just saw a patient and I said the same to him."

The anthropologist arched a frayed eyebrow. "Regarding what?"

"Panic attacks. The young man thinks shadow figures took the form of his friends and attacked him while he was panicking. I told him it was paramnesia."

"When did your patient tell you this?" Bruce paused with a stare at the ceiling.

"Don't suggest a connection, Tony, please don't."

Anthony eased his features. "I'm not saying anything. I was just curious when you heard this story."

"Why?"

"Could be responsible for what you might have mistook?"

"That's certainly possible. It was Friday."

"Yesterday?"

"Yeah."

"I don't know what to make of it. Would you mind telling me more about what your patient told you?"

"I don't see the point."

"Humor me." He went on to tell Anthony what Vince and his mother Paula had told him.

The moment Bruce finished, Anthony stood. "I hate to do it, but I have to be on my way. I have errands to run."

"So I will see you and your friend tomorrow, then?"

Anthony looked at him squarely. "Yes, you will."

Bruce sighed. "There was no excuse for my behavior earlier, I was rude. Can you forgive your friend's slip of character?"

"On one condition."

Bruce was a tad surprised. "Name it."

"You humor your bizarre friend."

"Absolutely, how?" Anthony removed a blue sack tied with black yarn from his cargo pants pocket. He poured the contents into his rough hands and blew the dusty powder to the four corners of the room.

"Tony, I assume you're paying my cleaning bill?"

"There will be no trace." Bruce checked. Anthony was right.

"Close your eyes."

'Whaa!' Bruce felt whatever it was blown onto him. "Thank you for that. I said I was sorry."

"It will protect you." Anthony walked over to a bouquet of blue hydrangeas placed beside the door, pouring the majority of the bag's contents into the soil basin.

"What is that?"

"A little of this and a little of that. Can I get you anything before I leave?"

"No."

"Then I will see you tomorrow."

"Thank you for blowing powder in my face."

"You're welcome." Anthony left. Bruce inspected his gown, pinching the fabric and rubbing his fingers together. Nothing tangible was there. He licked his lips. No taste either. Even his face felt clean.

3

The dirt path channeled through the deserted landscape. Its outlying edges spanned into obscurity. *I'm lost. Have to find shelter.* Run-down residences came to be, their frames dislocating in creaks. *Where am I headed?* Two rows of trees were gathered at the path's horizon. Rain was strained in drops of black onyx. *I hear the screams of many, the shrieks of children.* The ground was deluged in black fluid. *Where are my legs?* Bruce persisted, waist-deep in the fluid, towards the trees. *Pristine black. Where are my hands? My heart hurts.*

"You are safe if you stick to the path," a mysterious voice said.

"Who's speaking?" Bruce asked.

"I am."

My heart hurts.

"You are safe if you stick to the path."

"Elaine?"

"Yes. You see the wayfarer at the trees?"

"Yes."

"Hearth will guide you."

Something's wrong. "You're not Elaine."

A second voice chimed in, "Ignore the siren, Bruce."

"Hearth calls. You are safe if you stick to the path," the first voice said.

Something's wrong.

"Get off the path," said the second voice.

"Pleasant bliss, my love," the first voice said.

"Get off the path, Bruce. That's not Elaine."

The Hospital

Bruce's house sprung up from beneath the rising black sludge. His motion off path was imperceptible. If not for the house coming closer, he would have thought himself stagnant.

It's not water! Bruce fought a sea of black bodies with a lack of configuration. They lunged at his missing limbs, screaming for help with arms outstretched. Innumerable numbers rained down from oblivion above. "Get off of me!" The oozing carpet of tarred bodies converged on him relentlessly. "These are your children, stop!" The children were trampled to the depths by the adults. The house was close but too far to reach. *I can't take it!* The screaming holes were runny veils of black gunk. Screaming bodies pleaded and thrashed. *I'm dreaming. Wake up, wake up, WAKE UP!!!* The door to his house opened.

Bruce leapt awake in a night sweat, wide-eyed, shaken and addled on his living room couch. The nightmare freed from his mind with some jerky head movements around the still room. A few breaths later, his head rested back down on the damp cushion. A white glow from the back-sliding glass window traveled over the couch. Bruce hoisted his neck to eye the glowing fog belt rolling outside.

A couple of black-figured angels holding hands flew into the fog, coming into color as they drew closer. "Mom, Ronald?" Ester and Ronald swooped to the center of the glass. Their white feathered wings sprawled lengthwise across, ratcheting up and down in the angelic light. They wore respectable dress, fluttering back and forth at the window. Ester was in her green skirt suit and Ronald in his wool brown Sunday suit.

"My boy. Glory be! How we've missed you. Thankfully the Lord has allowed us to be reunited. Praise the almighty. Halleluiah!" Ronald said.

"Halleluiah," Ester repeated.

"Come open the door and receive the holy spirit." An intuitive forewarning made Bruce stay put.

"Come outside, join us in God's loving arms. You have a place set between your mother and I in the kingdom of Heaven." His intuition won out and Bruce stayed put.

"Brucie, we love you, don't you love us?" Ester asked. Bruce felt hot water run down his face. "We miss you, haven't you missed us?" Truth be told, he did love and miss his mother. Bruce tried to close his eyes. *I have no eyelids?*

"We have prayed for your return. The Lord has answered our prayers. We are proud of you. We hear of your accomplishments in Heaven and how hard you've worked to get where you are. The other angels can't wait to meet you. We talk about you often. They say your presence is felt already," Ester said. Bruce could hear himself blubber.

"You have made me proud. I knew if I was tough on you and the Lord thy God saw favor in you, you could end the cycle of poverty. No demon hath touched you. Halleluiah!" Ronald said.

"Halleluiah," Ester repeated.

"You've done it and we couldn't be prouder. Come outside and join us. Meet your maker," Ronald said.

"*No!*" A voice in Bruce's head spoke aloud.

No? Bruce asked himself.

"We love you, come to us." Ester said.

"No!" The disembodied voice protested louder. Bruce sat up. The beckoning call of his mother was brutal not to obey.

"That's it. Come, my child," she said.

Take a closer look! The words rang out through the vestibule of Bruce's thoughts. He peered at his parents, resulting in a gasp. The angelic glow ebbed. The wings fell off and floated downward into the unknown. Their eyes were torn holes, their feet torn off. Their yellow skin undulated from black tentacles shoved up the ankle openings to animate the puppets.

Ronald's animator thudded him against the glass, a thud that should have shattered the window into a million pieces. The mouth slit of Ronald spoke with an unfamiliar, penetrating deep voice of the ventriloquist. It was a voice of hunger and thirst. "Enough, let's be honest. I grow tired of false persuasion. Be dignified and give yourself over to Argauthartera. God can give you what you seek. You're obese and old, Bruce. Frail like a twig. Your son doesn't respect you. He is embarrassed of you. Your failures sour him. He finds in you a quitter."

"Your wife doesn't want you. She rejects your nudity. She finds your skin wrappings unflattering. You could have been their hero, a football star, but alas you are not. You are the snake oil for the ruined, a hypnotherapist. You were swindled, Bruce, your existence amounts to failure. You live vicariously through your son's achievements. You secretively desire what he has, his Debbie; how you pretend you don't see, how you pretend you don't hear. He's embarrassed that the potbellied pig at his judo tournaments is his seeder. Why else would he not introduce you? To him you are defunct."

"Your wife can't bring herself to be honest and admit her disappointments in you. Other suitors cross her mind steadily, who she could have known. She could have loved, she could have truly loved. If she had it to do over, the story would be different. She's stays with you because she is old. She loves your money. It is what pleases her. That and her son is only why she stays. You will die unfulfilled, tacked forever in misery. Incrementally compounding your woes. Sharing false devotion…unless that is, you decide to come outside. Argauthartera can make you who you desire to be, who your wife and your son desire you to be. Your wife will love you, Bruce, truly love you. Your son will idolize you. You could be his hero. You will be superior to anything on Earth and a god to your family. If you only come to me."

Bruce was compelled to the window, he stood dejected at the thing which read his mind.

"*No!*" the internal voice spoke.

"I didn't say that," Bruce said.

"Then come quickly, open the door," said the summoning voice.

"I can't move."

"Don't you want it, the fulfillment of your desires?"

"Yes, it's not my fault. I can't move!"

"Bah! Show us you can be the champion you formerly were! Come outside!"

Bruce was stuck in place. "I can't!" The manipulated puppets manically hit the window to get inside. The tentacle feelers concealed within them were thrashing around to get out of their disguises, contorting the sallow faces into hideous extensions. Bruce's parents were torn to shreds, releasing a mass of flapping black tentacles slapping against the glass.

"Come outside!" it roared.

4

Bruce's stomach constricted as he leapt awake in a night sweat, wide-eyed, shaken and addled on the hospital bed. It was a look at his cast that brought him back fully. *It was a dream.* He went to stroke his beard and winced. A sharp bitter taste was in his mouth. Sips of water couldn't remove it and he was too tired to brush his teeth. He lay back down on damp sheets. There was a burning pain circulating his right arm. In his peripheral vision he was startled by a faint movement behind the curtain. The obscured figure's shadow moved in the strip of hallway light.

"Hello?" Bruce lifted with great effort to a position comfortable for his aching buttocks. His pulse throbbed. "Hellloo?"

"Mr. McGrail?"

"Yes?" Bruce recognized the voice.

"It's Sergeant Wilkins."

"Everything okay?"

"Your wife and son didn't come home."

"You can come in. They're fine, they're not at the house."

"Where are they?"

"You can come in, I'm decent."

"It's not visiting hours, I can't."

"My lips are sealed. Come on in."

There was no response. Bruce pushed the nurse's call button, sensing something was not right. "They went to Arizona with my neighbor." The room ushered in an uneasy silence.

Bruce remained quiet, watching the shadow's silhouette on the floor. Flashes of the ape hassled him. The shadow strode from sight. Steps stamped down the hall in a scuttle. "Hey, stop!" A tall male nurse with curly blonde wicker hair rushed into Bruce's room, pulling the curtain aside. "Who was that?"

"Said he was Sergeant Wilkins of the Redlands police department." The young man's face drew back, taking after the stranger. Several other staff and security personnel soon followed. Bruce's leg reminded him that he wasn't dreaming when he pinched it.

CHAPTER 8
The Non-date Date

Saturday, 6:04pm

1

Jacklyn sat on the couch, not watching nor listening to the fishing program. She held a cold pack against her polished shiner, teetering on a breakdown. Standing, she was no longer capable of being in the same room as Dick. She blocked the television as she tried to slip by. "Get me a beer." Dick ordered.

Jacklyn turned a murky green eye on him. She wanted to say, *Can I get you a knife and slit your throat?* "I will, I have to pee."

Heading to the bathroom, she came across whispering in Melissa's room. She didn't realize Melissa had come home. She was aware of her occasional window retreats to Vince's and figured that's how she snuck back in, considering the doors were locked by Dick. She knew she was helpless to stop her from sneaking out, and understood Vince was important to her so she was thrilled Melissa had him. Other than gardening, the subject of Vince was how they connected. But, most of all, she had him to thank for Melissa no longer cutting herself.

Jacklyn lowered the ice bag, tiptoeing to the door and placing her ear against it. She couldn't make out what was being said. She didn't want to spy on her daughter, but she had to be sure it was Vince with her, as Melissa was sometimes known to talk to herself. Jacklyn did not want Vince to get caught by Dick, so she knocked lightly on the door to quiet them down, the secret knock that mom and daughter shared. It signaled Dick was soused or on the warpath, typically a mixture of both.

Melissa's room hushed. Jacklyn left and went into the master bathroom and locked the door. She dropped the cold pack on the sink. The mirror threw back the train wreck that was her aged face. Her hair was frazzled and matted, her eyes lined, her face sun spotted, wrinkled and emaciated. She did have a thin figure with ample breasts, though, without a bra, they were stretch marked and loose. In her mind, these were still her most valuable assets to attract a new filler companion. It stunned her how haggard she'd become with Dick over a few years. She took a considerable assessment, in disbelief at the damage done. *I can't leave him and have an abortion. Who would want me? With what money? How would I take care of Melissa?*

She rubbed her veiny hands, taking a seat on the toilet, thinking of her late husband Edgart. The memories flowed in. How awkward he was about asking her out. How shy he was to kiss her. How nervous she was to kiss him. The songs they dedicated to each other, the love letters they wrote. The places they traveled, the stars they gazed. The restaurants they dined in. The gentle sweetness of his eyes. The sensitive caress of his touch. The feel of him within her. She recalled Melissa in his arms and the sheer joy he had of holding her. Their first car, their first house. The nursery they owned. How happy they were as a complete family…how in love.

The thoughts brought her hands to her mouth, she would have cried aloud if she hadn't. Jacklyn pulled a towel off the rack to muffle a scream. She recalled the final hours; his withered body, his positivity in dying. His loss of appetite and taste, the struggle to breathe. The prayers to live. He just wanted to be with his girls, it wasn't fair. Edgart loved Melissa beyond comprehension; losing her broke him. She recalled the accursed rocking chair, his inability to sleep in the bed. Those final moments she held him while he wheezed. How Melissa struggled to be close and admit he was dying. They watched him off, to suffer no longer. His gentle eyes closed for a last. *That was the night I died.*

Jacklyn reached under the sink, placing drain declogger and industrial cleaner on the counter. She watched herself in the mirror. A self-loathing wretch peered back. "Jackie, where's my beer!"

"Coming! She reached for Dick's shaving cream, writing on the mirror "FUCK YOU! FUCK YOUR BABY!" She took the cleaner, placing her mouth around the container, patting a decent portion into her mouth. The stuff released an acidic chalk taste clinging to her saliva, coating the inside of her mouth in froth. Burning her throat, she washed it down with the drain declogger. The taste was abhorrent, bubbling and sizzling in a miasmic gas which sent forth a cocaine burn throughout the canals of her throat. The combined flavors of old batteries, cod liver oil, congealed milk and sour candies entangled the taste buds to produce a stench of rancid durian fruit in the nasal cavity. She slavered to hold it down, thudding the table with her palm to keep it from spilling out in a ball of foamy puke.

She stumbled backwards onto the bed. The drooling mess foamed and spurted out of her lips and onto the floor. "Bye, baby." The thought of Melissa brought about regret for the impulsive act of selfish insanity. She staggered back into the bathroom and jammed a finger down her throat to puke.

"Hurry up!" Dick howled. Jacklyn fainted, her head hitting the sink as she fell to a sprawl on the floor with a fizzing tongue sticking out of her frothy blue and grey face.

2

I heard a knock at the front door as my barber's comb perfected the part. Taking a step back from the mirror, I rolled up the sleeves on my dad's white dress shirt, admiring the blue pinstripe waistcoat, pants and tie combo. For a vintage suit, it looked impressive. I was the likeness of an Italian gangster from the Prohibition era. "Vince, Melissa's here!" Mom said.

My heart was tumbling. *If she's not dressed up, man alive.* I grinded my tooth and toweled the sweat off my hands.

"Vince, Melissa is here! Answer the door!" Dad shouted.

"Why don't, uhhh—" My heart palpitated, a rushing nervousness of excitement pumped through me, different from the norm of anxiety in that I wasn't fearful of it. I just wanted to be able to contain it. "Why couldn't you guys get the door?"

Dad confronted me with a "you should answer it" look. "Sorry, Melissa, hold on!"

I practiced my breathing to the door, taking a deep breath before opening it. I wasn't ready. The stunning beauty that was Melissa snatched my senses, she was breathtaking. She had styled her hair in a pompadour fishtail that braided down the side of her slim neck. It twisted down a white mini dress to the middle of her trim waist. Her long lashes fluttered over green emeralds that shone vivid without the overshadow of glasses. She wore a balmy red lipstick which heightened her femininity. Her little ears, cute button nose and dimpled smile took on new notice. Around her neck lay a fancy sparkling diamond necklace, spread out over her breastbones. "Can I come in?" she said in a shy eagerness.

"Yes, sorry," I said with serious effort to stop staring.

"Melissa, you're gorgeous!" Mom gasped.

"Thank you." She blushed. Mom was beside herself, not that I could blame her.

"Greg, will you take a look at Melissa?" My dad had to fully turn from the TV, which he did with resistance.

"My, my, Melissa Saunders. All grown up. Your ravishing sweetheart. *Sei bellissima.*" My dad strummed his heart.

Melissa's rosy cheeks darkened. "Thank you."

"You tell me if he is anything less than a gentleman tonight."

She laughed. "I will."

"I have to get a picture." Mom went to get her camera.

"You do look great," I said.

"You too, you look hot. Where'd you get the suit?"

"I've had it." I could feel my dad look at me.

"I like it, you're handsome." Our eyes met and I found myself tongue tied. I turned aside thinking of what to say next, pretending I was checking the clock above the sink.

"Where are your glasses?"

Her eyes had not moved. "I'm wearing my new contacts."

"Are they comfortable?"

"They weren't to get in. They say it gets easier."

"You look great." *You already said that, stupid.* I couldn't help myself. She was striking. My mind was abandoning me.

"Vince, you make a funny face in my picture and I will kill you." Mom rushed to get in front of us. "Close in."

I cradled Melissa in my arm, pulling her close. The warmth of her body aroused me. *Don't you dare get hard, you stupid bastard. I should have masturbated.* Melissa snuggled into my ribs. She smelled of watermelon candy perfume. *Mom and Dad having sex.* My chub died down.

"Smile," Mom said.

I thought the pictures would never stop, if not for Dad. "Paula, enough."

"Alright."

"Vince." I stopped at Dad's command. "You get pulled over tonight…"

"I took the car without asking and kidnapped Melissa." I expanded on the conditioned response.

"Not funny. Drive safe."

"No speeding," Mom added.

"I won't."

Melissa grabbed her flashlight that she left on a wicker chair on my front porch. I could hear Dick yelling from his bedroom across the street. Melissa pretended she couldn't hear it. She rushed us to the car the best she could in high heels. I rolled my window down to air out my collar once we were out of range of Dick's voice. He had killed the mood.

"Don't let Dickhead bother you."

She summoned a weak smile. "I—" She was interrupted by the siren of an ambulance bearing up Erdmore as we were turning onto California Street. "It's not him, it's my mom. She wants to marry him for security." She looked out her window.

Don't press. "Sucks, I'm sorry." Her red lips slightly parted to say more, I assumed about her mom's pregnancy.

"Not your fault."

"Sucks all the same."

She turned straight and her chin touched her chest. "Can we talk about something else?"

If she wasn't going to talk about her mom's pregnancy, neither was I going to talk about my mom's.

"You want to eat somewhere on Hospitality Lane?"

"Are you comfortable driving that far?"

"With you I am." The emeralds of her eyes brightened with a smile.

"Are you hungry?" she asked in a soft voice.

"I could eat. Are you not?"

"Hospitality it is," she said, turning forward.

"What, no. Why'd you ask?"

"No reason...I'm just not that hungry."

I should have assumed she wouldn't be. "Then...where did you want me to take you?"

"Wherever you'd like. I'm happy to tag along for the ride. If you're hungry, let's eat."

I wasn't. "Alright, we can drive around."

She didn't answer right away. "I...have an idea..."

"What?"

"If you're not okay with it, no pressure."

"Tell me."

Melissa bit her bottom lip. "If you're not okay with it, don't say you are." Her hand landed on my thigh.

"I won't." *Parents having sex, parents having sex, parents having sex.*

"I've always wanted to see Goat's Head."

The suggestion stunned me. "To what, drive by it?"

"Yeah." *She won't get out of the car wearing what she's wearing.*

"I'll drive by it." I disguised my uneasiness.

"Really? If you have problems, we'll leave."

"We're just driving by?" I confirmed.

"Just driving by. Your anxiety has really improved, I'm impressed."

"I know, it's bizarre. I don't believe it myself."

"I knew you could beat it."

"Thanks, by the way, for suggesting Bruce."

"You're welcome. Therapy helped me and I figured it'd help you."

3

"This is the road."

Melissa straightened in her seat. "It's spooky." The ranch house near the entrance of Cherry Croft Drive was to be my only safety zone within close proximity. Some of its windows shined awake with light. The house had one street lamp above it. Beyond it, the veil of night crouched in the dark. We were heading in. I rolled up my window and locked the doors. We left my safety zone behind. The street lamp became a shrinking orb in the mirrors. Melissa pressed against her seat, giving a nervous laugh as she scissored her legs.

"You want to head back?"

"No." Melissa took my arm, causing an erection to build an outline in my pants. I couldn't stop it. It was the pants' fault, they were too tight around the crotch. I had to just let it be and hope she didn't notice.

The sound of gravel being pressed under the tires filled our ears. We stared into the interminable darkness of the unpredictable roadway, split in two by inadequate headlights. "We do need to be careful of The Watchers. Lots of druggies and squatters come here at night also."

Melissa squeezed my arm, moving in closer. Something about her fear lessened mine. I could smell the sweet watermelon scent coming off her, it was intoxicating. The road curved off to the right, slicing through mounds of dirt, then left. The mound on our right leveled off to decaying farmland blocked off by the indelible barbed-wire fencing. It brought back unpleasant memories. The car began to jostle with the straightening of the road. "The trees will be coming up soon on your right. In the daytime, you can see the tree line from the curve."

Melissa gripped my arm harder. My erection pulsed and I started sweating in my suit. I wanted to roll the window down, but was hesitant. I found that if I focused my thoughts on my sexual fantasies about her, I wouldn't think about my fear as much. I thought about riding her doggy-style, her sexual moans of ecstasy crying out of control from my thrusts, like the elastic girls in my dad's secret VHS tapes.

The car took a sudden drop, along with my fantasy. The depression scraped the undercarriage. *Dad's going to kill me.* The road was getting bad. *Fuck me!*

"I'm sorry," Melissa said.

"You didn't know." I avoided what I could. The road had worsened from what I remembered. I went slow, but not too slow to avoid getting caught. The depressions tossed us around, scraping the car. I had to keep free of the road's edge or we'd get stuck in the soft dirt. I grew nervous realizing we couldn't turn around. It was Carter Street or nothing. The tires caught and released, creating a ball in my throat.

What-if you get stuck? You'll have a panic attack in front of Melissa. My chest fluttered. *No! You're stuck!*

"You alright?" Melissa asked.

"Yes." I could feel my breath abbreviate. *Not now, No, NO, NO!* My heart pounded, I couldn't control it. *DO YOUR BREATHING! I CAN'T! YOU'RE STUCK!* My hands trembled on the wheel.

"Slow down, you're going wreck your dad's car." The car banged the dirt.

I CAN'T BREATHE! "I'm having an attack." She was aware. My sweat pores opened from one end to the other around my forehead and neck. *YOU STUPID ASSHOLE, YOU EMBARRASING FUCK!*

Melissa reached down and put her hand on my erection, stroking it. My thoughts did a 360 and panic declined into surges of pleasure.

"Watch the road," Melissa said.

I did my best to drive. By the time the road smoothed out, the pressure to release myself was intense. I stopped the car at an angle on a flat slab of land, removing Melissa's hand.

"We're good," I assured her. I did not want to finish in my dad's pants.

"Thought I'd distract you," Melissa said with a devilish smile.

Down, fella. "It worked, you distracted me. Too well is the problem."

Melissa giggled. "Penny for your thoughts."

There was no way I was telling her what I was thinking. "We're here, Goat's Head," I said in a deep, unsatisfied breath. Melissa looked out at the brooding tree's darkened contours. Her gaze was full of the mystery that is Goat's Head. I was more interested in reaching between her alluring legs. My dick was pulsing for me to finish. *Parents having sex.*

I looked at the entrance caught in the car's headlights. The trench, the steep graded hill, the straggly branches of evergreen, all just as I remembered. It dawned on me to turn on the high beams so we could see deeper into the trees. The place was dead silent. It wasn't as frightening as I remembered. If anything, it was sad and pathetic, like it wanted to die but couldn't.

"It's creepy. Blackie Wilson's house is down there?"

"It was, the city may have torn it down. From what I heard last, it was on the verge of collapse." Melissa took back my arm. *You have a girlfriend.*

"Thank you for taking me." She squeezed my arm, placing her head on my shoulder.

"I wonder if they got the skull out?" I asked.

"Who, your friends?"

"Yeah."

Melissa smiled at me. "Someday you'll find out."

Here was a chance to reclaim a fraction of my manhood. "You want to take a closer peek?"

Melissa gave me a look of utter disbelief. "Are you serious?" Her fingers tightened around my arm.

"Are you scared? Ooooh." I wiggled my fingers at her.

The Non-date Date

"From the stories you've told me. Yes, yes I am. I don't want to end up a lamp shade."

"Just to the entrance. See if we see anything inside."

"What about the Dwellers?" Melissa asked.

"We have light, I brought plenty."

"How'd you know...?"

"I'm always prepared."

Melissa made a nervous laugh. "I don't know..."

"Come on, I'm with you." I cringed at the stupid comment. "We can leave the headlights on."

"You'll stay with me?"

"Cross my heart. Any sign of trouble, we're blazing a trail. If you draw your attention to the front of the car, you will see I have already strategically placed the wheels for a clean getaway."

She looked out at the trees. "Let's do it."

"Shit, I forgot about your heels, nevermind."

"I'll leave 'em." Melissa began slipping them off.

"I have to grab the lights out of the trunk. Can I borrow your flashlight?" Melissa handed it to me. I left my door open with the keys in the ignition. She trailed my every move. I shone the flashlight on anything I found suspicious, making several scanning circles. What I found was what I counted on; bushes, dirt, posts of barbed wire and the trees. With a wary eye, I lifted the trunk and retrieved two camping lanterns.

It was then that I heard steps coming out of the dark. My light beam drew to my right. I saw a dark figure come running at me from around the car. I stood paralyzed. Melissa wrapped around me.

"Couldn't wait?"

"Nope."

I tried to create distance by handing her a lantern so she couldn't feel my heart pounding. The night brightened in a white florescent glow. I touched the bag in my pocket, closing the trunk. I took her hand and tossed her flashlight in the car as we made cautious, measured steps toward the entrance. I had left the car open and glaring headlights on. "Watch the trench." I shone my light on it. I didn't recall it as deep as it was. "I'll climb up, then help you," I said.

"Okay."

I scaled the steep incline to the top, doing my best not to scuff my dad's dress shoes. I grounded myself, swaying my light over the depth of the entrance. My gaze sunk into its deep-rooted reaches.

The terrifying memories of these baleful trees summoning me to their death call was appearing to have been over-exaggerated head fantasies. The place was eerie, no doubt. The shadows made a thousand misconstrued fancies and, given its history, it was not a place to be toyed with. I just couldn't ignore the pleasant scent of woody resin, the calm droopiness of the trees, and a path littered with Mother Nature and transient trash. The tranquil path did not resemble the narrow, suffocating, yellow swirling horror I had memorized. It was wider, brighter and sparser than recollected with no clouds of dirt. I had a private laugh at my expense. *Could it be that I imagined the Dwellers? What about the power outage, was that in your head? What was it Bruce said I had, peramizia?*

Turn off your light and find out.

Are you crazy, no way.

He's wrong and you want to believe he's right.

I went to assist Melissa. "Melissa?" She was gone. I looked over at the car, she wasn't in it. My heart dropped in a whirl of the light. "Melissa!"

"Over here." I caught her white dress through straggly limbs, bounding down the path between two trees. "You won't believe what I found, come here."

"How did you get up?"

"The same way you did, silly. Come check this out."

Keep your voice down. I couldn't have missed her, could I? I went after her full-tilt, intending on leaving.

What are you scared of?

Quiet! "Whatever it is, it can wait for daylight. We should leave. The keys are in the car unattended. We can come back tomorrow."

The Non-date Date

She slipped from between the trees, beckoning me to silence. Her gentle hands glided around me. I took a wary look around. The place was restful but eerily shadowed. "Let's take it to the car," I said.

Her body crawled on me, the smell of watermelon was strong. Her sweet red lips pressed to mine. I placed the lantern down and our tongues coiled, tasting one another's sweet flavors. She guided my hand down the curves of her dress, over her breast and I grazed her erect nipple. My hand went down over her tensing stomach to the smoothness of her legs. She fastened my index finger to my middle finger, lifting them through the narrow passage between her legs. I felt the tender wetness of her vagina. She slipped the fingers inside her with care, moaning in pleasure as her warm lubricant coated them. She then guided me up the slit of her pussy to its peak, making circular motions on the fold.

"I want you to fuck me."

"Let's take it back to the car."

"No, take me here."

A brightness penetrated my eyelids and my arms fell. My eyes opened to the impacting glare of florescent lighting. My hand raised to deflect what it could. "Why are you ditching me?" The watermelon smell was replaced by a smell of rotten apples. I started spitting, finding my mouth full of dirt. "Melissa?" I said, when I could speak.

She emerged, trembling from behind the light. "You said you would stay with me." She was hugging herself, fresh with tears.

"What are you talking about? You just – what was I – wasn't I just holding you?"

"What do you mean?" The tears took a break, sensing something more serious at play.

"Answer me. Was I just holding you a second ago?"

"No, you called me and I couldn't find you."

I recoiled in horror, my eyes darting around for who or what I held. My brain searched for a suitable explanation. I knew it wouldn't find one. The trees darkened, looming over us. Their spiky branches seemed to reach down, invigorated. I snatched my lantern and stole Melissa by the arm.

"That wasn't me."

My heart stampeded. *What-if you're holding another fake Melissa?* The emeralds of her eyes caught my fearful glance and it occurred to me that I hadn't seen the other Melissa's eyes because they were disguised by the dark. *It's her.* A loud twig snapped underfoot. I thought it was my spine. I was not about to look back. We trained our sights on the exit, running as one body.

Goat's Head summoned me. I could feel its call. My ears sharpened to where I could have heard ants. The Dwellers were moving towards us, their rustling on nature's floor was many. "Move," I said, pulling Melissa's shorter legs.

"I am."

"Stop soldier! No man left behind!"

"Wait for us guys!" The disembodied voices belonged to Jarrod and Ethan. My brain conjured disturbing images of what followed. We reached the ledge of the crest.

Inasmuch power as I could muster in a decision of terror driven desperation, I scooped Melissa in my arms and leapt across the trench. We barely crossed the opening in a rib smash landing where I took a digger. Melissa fell from my arms, as did my lantern. She was quick to get back to her feet, but I could not match her pace or catch my breath. She assisted me to the car, tossing her lantern in the backseat. "I'm good, get in," I said.

"Freakin' Mee-yamee face!" Jarrod's voice yelled. I watched her get in before closing my door, afraid to look directly into the treeline. "Mee-yamee face!" Jarrod's voice etched in my mind. I locked the doors. Melissa was pale and visibly shaken. She held herself in a bear hug, her dress torn and covered in debris. I was on the gas when my head rang from her scream. An old man was at Melissa's window rapping the door handle. The window thudded from his head banging it, caught in the pull of the car. The man in the red robe was joined by a crowd of ugly people leaping onto the hood, all wearing red robes. Men and

The Non-date Date

women, twisted and staring sickly at us, painting a deadly earnest picture of their intentions. I smacked the shit out of the undercarriage to shake them off.

What-if you get stuck?

Fuck off!

"Leave us alone!" Melissa yelled.

We could hear hoots, wicked laughs, and hollers from all around the car. *Get to Carter.* The Grand Prix's suspension reared the brutality of the road. The Watcher's voices faded.

Even though the experience was terrifying, I was exhilarated from it. The feeling of being alive coursed my veins and with Melissa by my side, a slight invincibility became present. She had pulled something bloodthirsty out of me. Her panic empowered my courage. I was redeemed. Melissa looked out the back window. "You think we lost 'em?" she said, steadying herself.

"Yes," I said, looking out of the rear window at blackness. *What-if they have a truck?*

I'll dust their truck! I took a sharp left at Carter, watching my rear.

The alignment was damaged, the car now pulled to the right. My dad was going to kill me, but I was too high to care. We took side streets home, losing all headlights that came into view. Melissa apologized profusely for asking me to Goat's Head, and I said again and again that it would be okay. We pulled up to my house.

"I have to shower," I said.

"Tell me about it, I feel disgusting. Sorry I ruined tonight."

"You didn't, stop it. It was cool." Her eyes dipped from mine in a moment of guilty silence.

"What do you think they would have done to us?" she asked.

My high died down to the reality of what could have happened. "I don't want to know, honestly."

Her eyes stayed down. "Yeah. Too bad we can't call the police."

"I'm not worried about it."

"I had a nice time with you, despite—" She shrugged.

"Regardless of my punishment, it was worth it, to be with you." Her eyes lifted at mine, red lips inviting. She moved towards me, her kiss soft and sweet to the taste. Unfortunately, the kiss was similar to the one earlier. "I have to shower, I feel gross," I said, pulling away.

"Me too."

"You're more than welcome to take a shower here?" Her eyes turned to Dick's dark house.

"I wanna change."

"I could do for a walk to Plarek."

"When should I come back over?"

"Let's say an hour and a half, cool?"

"Yeah. I'll tell Greg you were a perfect gentleman," she said, bright-faced.

"I'll watch you to the house."

"Okay." She grabbed her flashlight and heels and climbed out of the car. Her body was poised in a purposeful, sexy walk. Dirt stains, tears and all, she looked incredible.

4

Melissa removed the loose screen from her ajar window, sliding it open. She tossed her heels on her bed but they didn't land easy, like she intended. She stuck the flashlight in her mouth, stepping on the side of a potted plant. Placing her palms on the seal, she lifted herself in butt first, managing a turn a leg at a time. She jumped in and fell forward onto an unstable surface, causing her to spit out the light. She planted her hands on an ungiving, wooden material. Shaking her head, she winced to push herself up. In the scant lighting of her flashlight she discovered that she was on the back of her overturned dresser.

The light to the bedroom turned on. Dick was at the doorway, shirtless. He held a brown belt that dangled from a firm, clenched hand. His cold-blooded eyes mercilessly glared. In a terrifying, confused snapshot, Melissa's eyes spun around the room. A hurricane couldn't have done this damage. The blood abandoned her face. "Mom!" Melissa screamed, heading for the window.

"No you don't." Dick leapt.

The Non-date Date

Melissa felt a staggering slap of leather penetrate her hair down to her neck. Her necklace broke and she involuntarily curled up, falling backwards onto the dresser. Lashes beat down on her defending forearms. Dick's tremendous weight was on top of her, pinning her with his knees. "Mom! Dad!" she wheezed, emptying her lungs. Her battered arms fell, depleted of strength.

Dick eased the pressure off her stomach, releasing gulps of air into her tingling body. The strap waved from his taut grip. "You want more, you keep fighting, missy. Behave and there's no reason why we can't be friends." Melissa's eyes rolled to the ceiling, her body a statue. Dick sat back in a profuse alcohol sweat. The sound of his zipper was loud. "That's a girl, I'll be gentle. Looks to me, you and Vince have done some rough housing of your own." Sweat dripped down onto her dress. His chest and belly hair was a wet, blackened mat. Dick wrangled his pants down. "That's my girl." Melissa's teeth pressed together. She felt her dress lift, the air circulating her panties. Dick made noises of someone dying of thirst who had finally found drinkable water. He pulled his underwear down.

She took his bare hand. "What are you—" Dick snapped.

"Give me your hand." Her voice was kind.

"Don't be dumb, girly."

"Secretly, I've wanted this." She slid his fat open fingers around her red lips. Dick was steeped in drunk fascination. Melissa let the fingers dip inside her mouth, where she sucked on them, moaning.

"Dick!" Dick's head swung back toward the unknown voice. The crunches that followed pulled his jaw down in a such a way that it threatened to tear the seams of his elongated mouth. Melissa had chewed straight through four fingers, leaving the thumb. Dick held the erupting nub in front of his face, screaming at it.

Melissa burst up and dug finger nails deep into his scrotum and tore the sac from the root, spitting his fingers at him. "Fuck you! Die!" she shouted with a mouth full of gore. She had torn with every ounce of strength, dropping a chunk of unraveling tubules onto the dresser. Dick plummeted into a convulsing heap. Melissa pulled her tilted legs out from underneath him. Dick rolled off the dresser onto the floor.

"Kill him, baby!" The voice cheered.

Melissa put on a single high heel, stomping Dick in the head hard enough to break the heel off. She put on the other one with the same result. Dick's gurgles indicated a dying man; his blood was pouring out of him by the gallon. Dick made a huff and ceased moving.

Melissa spurned Dick's corpse, spitting out the gooey, rancid taste of him. "Good riddance," she said with the bloody webs between her teeth. Her body trembled while her sanity and breath caught up.

"My baby girl..." The wall spoke with Edgart's emotional voice.

"I'm alright," Melissa said. A bloody smile vertically slashed her jerking face.

"Are you?"

"I am...fantastic," she said, admiring her handiwork. "I'm glad he's dead. My regret is that I couldn't extend his suffering."

"I hate to see you like this."

Melissa's head lifted to the coffee-brown wall. "I got him to Goat's Head."

There was hesitation in Edgart's answer from the awkward switch of subjects. "It's that dress, it's magic on you."

"Was..." Melissa peered down at her torn and blood-dipped dress. "I imagine the contacts didn't hurt. I can't wait to get them out. I have dirt caught in my eye."

"We've got him! Did Vince say anything?"

"No, not yet. He might have if we weren't interrupted by the fucking Watchers. If not for that, I would have made more of it. It was perfect, too. When I left him alone, the Dwellers attacked him. I thought it might jog his memory."

"And no?"

"No, because of the Watchers. But, the night is young. I'll see what I can do."

The wall gave a discontented breath. "Do what it takes, I give you my permission. Whatever it takes." A quiet was shared, an uneasy one that kept her eyes allergic to the wall.

"I have to get a painkiller," Melissa said. The bruises on her body were ripening.

Melissa was on her way out of the deranged room when a sudden concern entered her. She had forgotten. "Where's Mom?"

"Jackie's in the hospital."

"What do you mean?" She recalled the ambulance she and Vince passed earlier.

"She tried to kill herself." Melissa stared fixed at the wall. "My baby, be strong. It will be over soon, I promise. No, don't cry…"

5

Melissa spotted Vince walking circles on his bed, wearing headphones. His intense greenish-brown eyes were far off in a distant world. She found a discarded stick that had fallen from the Japanese plum tree beside his window. She slid the window open and poked him back to Earth. She had worn her long-sleeved "Snail Bones" shirt and hair down to disguise the majority of the marks on her body. The rest were concealed with cover-up. Vince gave her a hand with her backpack and flashlight, then her.

"Easy on my arms," Melissa said.

"Sore from the fall?" Vince gave her an un-thought-of excuse for the bruising.

"Yeah, it did a number on me."

"Sorry."

"Don't be, it was my bright idea to go." Vince eased her inside with the aid of the step ladder.

"My dad has Ibuprofen."

"I'm alright," she said, keeping her bruises and puffy eyes out of direct sight. Melissa sat on the side of the bed, suppressing her concerns about her mother.

She slipped under the covers. The room was lit by the TV. Vince climbed into bed, slipping into the depression against her back. Melissa cradled his arm over her to spoon, placing his hand on top of her breast. Accelerated heartbeats united. "Tell me about Plarek."

"It's basically what I want it to be. There's no anxiety. My friends stay friends and there's no Dickhead."

"No, there's not," she muttered.

"What?" Vince lifted to better hear what she said.

"Nevermind."

"It's what this world could be, if it were bent to my whim."

"Am I there?"

"No. I can't imagine you surpassing the person you already are." She pulled his hand from her breast and kissed it.

"How come you never asked me out?" Melissa asked.

"Truth?"

"Yeah."

The words were carefully decided. "I felt I wasn't good enough." The sound of crickets outside filled the absent conversation. Melissa twisted to say something, but stopped herself, waiting for him to continue. "I never told you…but before you suggested going to see a hypnotherapist, I did think about killing myself." Melissa released a jarred breath. "I came close, I had my dad's gun loaded and put it in my mouth."

"What stopped you?"

"Truth?"

"Yeah."

"You."

Melissa tugged on his arm. "You get tired of waking up in fear every morning. Tired of feeling worthless to others, always in the way. My parents are miserable."

"No, they're not."

"Yes, they are. I just overheard my dad complaining that they can't take a vacation because of me. My so-called best friends ditched me. If it wasn't for you..." Tears pressed his eyes.

"I'm sure your friends had their reasons."

"Yeah, I bet. You know how many times I've tried to get ahold of them?"

"They'll come around, be patient."

"What? When I'm better, fuck them. It's been years. I just want to know what I did wrong. It's the mystery that screws with me."

"You didn't do anything wrong. A number of things could have happened. I wouldn't hold a grudge over what you don't know yet. When you're better, which it looks to me you are, visit and ask. If it turns out they ditched you, screw 'em. But I would find out first."

"You're all I have left beside my parents and now that I'm getting better, I will make it up to you for sticking it out with me. You will be my forever, if you'll have me."

"I will." She squeezed his hand to her breast, her heart pounding through it. "I never had to stick it out, I wanted to."

"I love you, Melissa."

She rolled over facing Vince, holding back her tears. "I love you too. Since we're being truthful, I never told you. I've had a crush on you since we met. I was in a pretty dark place when I left Arizona after my dad died. When you introduced yourself and we began to hang out, the pain eased. You made living tolerable." Vince had seen the scars on her. The rows of white lines on her wrists, forearms and ankles. He knew it wasn't the cat she used to own, like she blamed. He also knew not to bring up her father, it would put her in a funk. "You are not worthless. You are my everything," Melissa said.

"And you're mine." Vince kissed her. Tears of happiness welled over her lips.

"I didn't think you found me attractive," Melissa said.

"Are you nuts? You're beauty at its finest."

"Lie back," Melissa whispered. She slipped under the covers, twisting around. Her body pitched a tent covering Vince's pelvis. Vince felt his pajama bottoms and underwear being tugged. He helped slip the pair off his legs. In the hush of loud breaths, she eased him inside her.

CHAPTER 9
It's Not a Dream

Sunday, 1:10am

Pray for Jesus. Lucifer's demons have come for you! Bruce willed the voice of his father from his thoughts. A chest pain came on, leaning him back against damp sheets, his mind reeling. For a time, the floor was quiet, until two sets of steps carried on down the hall. Patients called the nurses with no audible response. The two staff members gathered at the threshold of Bruce's room. The strip of hallway light bounded the two in a blue filled outline. They disclosed a whispered interest in Bruce's bouquet of blue hydrangeas. "Excuse me?" Bruce asked. The two heads turned in his direction. They were wearing white surgical masks. The shorter one closed the door, leaving the room dim. A repugnant stench drifted in with his visitors. "Why did you close the door?" Bruce demanded in a false tone of authority.

"You're in danger, Bruce. You and your family." Bruce's skin crawled at the taller one's low, graveled voice.

"Who, who wants to hurt us? Why?"

"We Harbingers have come to warn you," the shorter man rasped. The curtain swooshed open. Bruce rapped the nurse's call button. The foul odor permeated the room with a slaughterhouse scent.

"Of what?" The smell crept into the openings of his face.

"Argauthartera." Bruce pinched his leg skin, twisting it. *It's not a dream.* His finger went back to rapping the call button.

The tall one spoke loud, his tone discordant and cracked. "The hour has arrived. A fate worse than everlasting death draws near. Argauthartera, God of Consumption, will harvest all life into its belly where it will wallow in suffering for eternity if not repelled. You will see to Argauthartera's failure."

"How can I...?" Bruce managed.

"Listen closely and adhere to every word. It's vital." Bruce gathered what he could of himself. "You are to keep your appointment with Vince Marino on Monday. Is that understood?" Bruce found he couldn't speak. "Do you understand?"

"Yes!" Fear pushed the word out.

"I cannot understate the importance of keeping it. Hearth is who stalks you. The malevolent spirit will stop at nothing to possess you to get to Vince's forgotten memories. You are a vessel to extract where he hid Iosk, the Goat's Head skull. Hearth is not without company. Legions serve the spirit who serves under Blackie Wilson, an antediluvian sorcerer who sought Argauthartera for your world's destruction. Our position is dire. It is not our intention to scare you. We want to protect you, do you understand?"

"Yes."

"Your family's survival will depend on you. Can we count on you?"

"...Yes."

"Your family must band together. You will need each other to fight the forces of darkness. Attaching spirits like Hearth are less likely to bind to a host within a spiritual war party. Your spirits will organize and can overwhelm a formidable opponent in battle when unified. This is necessary when you find yourself surrounded. In such a case, evasion is the course of action to take. You cannot, at any cost, become attached to Hearth or any other spirit possessor or you will die, along with everyone else, including us. Whenever necessary, run. Do not confront Hearth. You will lose. Do you understand?"

"Yes. How...do... I... I— My family, how do I protect my family?"

"Who cleansed your room?"

"Anthony...tossed a powder," Bruce blurted.

"Stick with Anthony. Your friend is wise. He saved your life from Hearth tonight. Tell him what we've told you and do not miss Vince's appointment Monday. Do not tell Vince any of what we have told you. The bonded spirit in him will kill him. Do you understand?"

"...Yes."

"Failure is not an option. We have to leave you, but before we do, I have to show you something we deem crucial. Its purpose is not to scare you. It is for you not to question what we say."

Where's the nurse? Bruce swallowed past the thick blockage in his throat.

A swooshing of scrubs brought the taller one forward. "Do not be afraid, I will not hurt you."

Bruce braced himself. The bed lamp turned on and he gasped in terror. No amount of preparation could have prepared him for the horrific aberration. Maggots disgorged out of the caved-in eye sockets, tumbling on Bruce's legs. The meat of the lips ebbed back to chipped or missing teeth. Tufts of brown hair sprang here and there. The head was strung over an incomplete neck, splintered with perceivable bone. The sight was more than Bruce could bear; he clenched his eyes shut. "I'm dreaming! Wake me!" He shook his head.

Bile gathered in his throat. The involuntary pressure opened his eyes to an empty, lamp-lit room. Bruce bent over the safety rail and vomited. He then slumped backward while reclaiming his breath. His body was weak and his chest hurt. He moaned, lifting again to see his legs. The maggots were nowhere to be found. They were gone and yet the rotten smell lingered. *Did I imagine it?* Just as the thought occurred, a maggot appeared from under his leg. He managed to muster the strength to reach over and pinch it up, bringing it close enough to see its dotted brown eyes.

The blonde curly-haired nurse returned. "What's that smell?" The nurse recoiled.

"I threw up." Crusted vomit had hardened on Bruce's lips.

"We'll get it cleaned right away."

"I found a maggot."

"Where?" The nurse moved to inspect what Bruce was holding.

"On the bed." The nurse pulled gloves out of a back pocket and proffered the waste basket.

"Any more?"

Bruce examined the bed. "I don't think so. Did you catch the man that came to my room?"

"Yes, we apologize for the disturbance."

"What did he want?"

"It was a confused patient. He's been taken care of. Hold tight." The nurse hurried out.

It wasn't a dream.

CHAPTER 10
That's My Girl

Sunday, 5:49am

1

The TV's white noise gave over to an unfolding, clouded grey dawn which petered out the shadows of the bedroom. Melissa slipped from the clingy sheets. Tears began streaming down her cheeks. Her muscles aching, she returned home, making a surreptitious dash for her bathroom. There, she hustled into the shower, breathing a sigh of relief at the feel of the water washing the evidence of sex off of her. She did not want to have that conversation with her father.

Her muscles eased. She pulled herself out of the water's renewing embrace, gathering a clump of honey-blonde hair into her hands, fanning it out. She saw her razor on the window sill; its alluring silver blade glistening. She bit her lip at the memory of skin separating, the terrific sting that radiated throughout her, followed by the warm sensation of trailing blood. Ambivalent, Melissa opened the window and flung the blade outside. She pulled her attention away from the white scars over her veins, her breath lessening from more than the steam. A dollop of conditioner brought her out a new person.

2

The answering machine picked up the call. "Hi, this is Doctor Patrad at Redlands Community Hospital. Could you please give me a call back regarding Jacklyn Saunders—"

Melissa rushed to pick up the receiver. "Yes, hello? I'm Melissa Saunders, Jacklyn's daughter."

"Hi Melissa, my name is Doctor Patrad. I'm the physician overseeing your mother's treatment."

"Yes."

"Your mother is in our intensive care ward. She is stable."

"Okay."

"Her length of stay at present is undetermined due to the significant damage done to her throat tissue."

"Can she talk?"

"Afraid not. You can talk to her, she just won't be able to respond. She is mentally sound however, there was no brain damage."

"Okay." Melissa whimpered.

"I do regret to inform you, the baby was lost."

"Was it?"

"I am sorry. You're free to visit her when you can."

"I will be by soon, thank you."

"Very well. See you then. Goodbye."

"Bye." Melissa slid the phone from her ear, placing it on the cradle.

"How is she?" Edgart asked from the cream-colored wall behind Melissa.

"She can't talk, her throat is damaged but she's stable. I'll head over and see her."

"She'll be alright. Don't say anything."

"Like I would."

"How will you get there?"

"I'll take Dick's car."

"You're positive Vince has Iosk?"

"Yes, stop worrying." Melissa hoisted her backpack with an aching arm.

"You're cutting it close."

"Oh, by the way, I won't be back. I'm meeting some friends I wanna see before I leave. I'll be at Vince's afterward. I want to continue what we've set in motion. Might be able to get it out of him early. If I can, I'll see you tonight. Either way, I will see you tomorrow."

"I can't wait. Did he agree to take you to his appointment?"

"He'll do whatever I tell him to."

"That's my girl."

"See you tomorrow." She went to the wall and pecked it. "What kind of a kiss was that?" She went back, tonguing the cream paint. A wet substance, not her own, slavered down the outer coat, interloping with her taste buds.

"Bye, Daddy. Love you." She wiped her mouth on her jacket's sleeve.

"Bye, love you."

3

The recovery center was flat white, like Jacklyn's complexion. Her section was curtained off, as were the other patients. Melissa sat back in the visitor's chair and folded her tender arms, disguised within a green jacket and long-sleeved shirt. Even though she tried not to show her emotions, her expression was of a hollow sadness that her mother could determine.

Jacklyn reached her frail hand out in an apology, a PICC line attached at her right bicep. Melissa took her hand in hers and summoned a weak, accepting smile that went along her face. Their green eyes met, but Melissa's did not stay. The brittle smile diminished. She laid her mom's hand back down with a circular massage of the thumb and forefinger. Jacklyn made a weak, pleading noise. The sadness in her mother's eyes was too hard to bear. "I forgive you," Melissa said, hugging her.

CHAPTER 11
Discharged

Sunday, 9:00am

1

Bruce was wheeled out to the patient loading zone where he was introduced to Rosalyn. She was a tall, lissome woman in her mid-twenties, clad in gypsy garb. She climbed in the backseat of Anthony's olive-green, hardtop Jeep while Bruce was carted to the passenger side door. Anthony locked his wheels and offered an unnecessary hand to Bruce. "I got it, thanks." He managed to climb aboard the Jeep single-handed.

"Taurus." Bruce crossed eyes with Rosalyn's in the rearview mirror.

"Huh?"

"You're a Taurus." Her voice was youthful and charming, having a seductive sway like her turquoise eyes.

"I wouldn't have the faintest idea."

"Mike convinced Elaine to stay with Carol. Darla is with her," Anthony said.

"What he'd tell her?" Bruce asked with a sigh.

"You'll have to ask Mike."

"Where is Mike?"

Discharged

"We're waiting for him. He and Debbie went to get the car. Get some rest, we'll talk later."

2

Debbie ran a hand through her straight bleached-blonde hair. The wind from the drive was tossing it in her face. "You should be nicer to your dad, Michael. Bruce is not fat." Michael gave her a delusional expression. "You're wrong, he's not. He's pleasantly plump. Makes me wonder what you say about my body when I'm not around." Debbie studied him for an answer, expecting the right response. Michael averted his eyes.

"Don't try it."

"What?"

"You're compliment searching and you know it."

"Plenty of men would love to be with me, Michael, if you're not satisfied."

"Be with them then, I'm not stopping you." Debbie gave off the impression she didn't care, even though it affected her deeply. She loved Michael. "Besides, what are you talking about being nice? You call your mom by her first name. How disrespectful is that?"

"Whatever, she's my stepmom. There's a total difference. Bruce is so nice, you're lucky to have him and your mom in your life."

"All I was saying, was that this could have been avoided if my dad was in shape. He needs to stop drinking and get himself on a treadmill."

"I agree with you about the drinking." The death of Debbie's' dad caused by a drunk driver crossed Michael's mind.

"Not the weight loss?"

"Talk to him, if it bothers you."

"What would I say? Hey, Dad, you're fat. Lay off the drinking, you closet alcoholic. I realize you hate your life because your dreams of being on the Giant's team were never fully realized and you tried to cover up an abusive childhood so you got a job you didn't want, married my mom and had me just to give your life purpose. But that's okay, just don't think about it. Hey, think on the bright side, you make great money. No thank you. I would hate my life too, if I was him."

"Can I see you tonight?" Debbie asked.

"Yeah, why? Aren't you staying?"

"I can't. Have to get the car back to Brenda. Her and her boy toy want the convertible."

"Remember the stains?" Michael's lips peeled back to expose perfect teeth at the thought.

"What the fuck, why would you say that? Jerk." Michael laughed at getting slapped. "God, you're gross."

"I didn't do it! Although I would be willing to stain the backseat." He smirked.

"Grow up, Michael."

3

Rosalyn could feel the area's nonexistent energy. The opulent houses were like flowers on a grave. The Jeep curved up the driveway, parking behind Bruce's BMW. Debbie's red Cadillac wasn't too far behind. Anthony kept his focus keen and nose to the ground while he helped Bruce's sagging body out of the vehicle. Rosalyn's long legs and tall frame stepped out, her senses hyperactive. Anthony and Rosalyn heard the Cadillac drive off, sharing a sidelong glance. Rosalyn hastened for the back of the Jeep. Michael was ascending the driveway. "Where's Debbie?" Rosalyn asked, not letting on her concern.

"She went home."

"Debbie went home." Rosalyn told Anthony who walked beside Bruce. Anthony and Rosalyn did not openly exchange their elevated concern.

Rosalyn waited for Michael, immune to his pompous bearing. Naturally, he took the opportunity to get an eyeful; he dug her exotic appeal. She wore a colorfully ornate velvet jacket over a white peasant tunic. Her assuit messenger bag and tall brown boots accentuated her brown sugar skin. A chain of dangling silver coins draped downward at an angle around her waist.

Rosalyn watched in the direction that Debbie drove off. Michael led with his trademark specious smile. "We never did get a chance to formally meet. I'm Michael." He held his hand out. She didn't bother to notice it left hanging, strolling toward the side of the house. "Pleased to meet you, rude ass," Michael murmured.

Rosalyn eyed every little thing near and far, touching the house as she went along. She fingered the deep inlaid scratches on the siding, receiving past happenings. Doug's kitchen window and the lawn area underneath the broken hallway window received extra scrutiny. She touched the grass below the broken window, searching for more of the story. Hearth's presence of fear was of particular interest. The narrative brought her to the slope at the edge of the lawn in the backyard where there was an incredible view of the Highland mountain ranges. The vast range rolled under the ceiling of an approaching storm, the bolts of which zapped electrical veins down the jet-black clouds and into the peaks.

She searched the hillside's vacillating wild brush. She then headed to the bullet hole in the sliding-glass door, ignoring Michael's unwelcomed leers coming from the other side. Her finger rounded the bullet hole, turning her to face the wind-leaning vegetation.

She rounded the house, her talents bringing her to the bottom of the driveway. Her search ended across the street, looking up a long, curved date palm tree that extended high above the city of Redlands. "Found you." Screened within the wind-swept fronds was Hearth.

The mighty spirit's claws crushed fronds in a warning to stay back. Rosalyn crossed the street to the slope that dipped towards downtown and was brought to a standstill near the palm. A vociferous uprising came from a swarm of spirits prowling the darkened regions of the slope. Cryptic languages exclaimed threats. She gathered it was an assembled ambush waiting for the intermittent sunlight to dissipate, seeing how none of them would breach their darkened confines. It was impossible to conceive the latent coverage and just how far they extended in either direction.

Rosalyn lifted her head back to look at Hearth who was thrashing at the tree top. The leader dropped from the great height to the base of the palm in a sizable thud. Hearth did not share the light boundaries. The spirit's black frame was banded with sunlight escaping the clouds and palms. The aggressor charged with drawn-out razor-sharp claws typical of a bear. Rosalyn reached into her bag with jittery hands. Hearth would be on her in seconds. She pulled forth an unordinary human skull. Carved in the bone were mystic symbols derived from the Masters of the Ancient Wisdom.

Hearth rushed back up the tree. Pandemonium ensued across the slope and a new set of cryptic sounds gripped the air. Rosalyn headed back towards the house, chasing the front door. She barged in and set her back against it. She placed the skull back in her handbag, catching her breath. She could hear Anthony and Michael talking in another room through the kitchen archway. She went to inform them when she was distracted by a spate of messages coming from the shaman masks that were propped in the stairwell wall niches.

4

Anthony and Michael stood to the alarming way Rosalyn came into the living room. Anthony was in the process of delicately explaining to Michael the details his father had relayed to him. "Where's Bruce?" Rosalyn asked.

"Upstairs, asleep," Anthony said.

"I had a run in with Hearth."

"The ape?" Michael asked Anthony.

He nodded once. "Where?"

Rosalyn paced. "Across the street. The house is surrounded. When that storm blocks out the sun, we're done for." The trio faced the storm spilling over the sky outside the sliding-glass door. "Wake Bruce, Michael, we have to head to Yucca's immediately. I will explain on the drive over." In a trail of confused thoughts, Michael dashed from the room.

He swung around the newel post in the foyer, his eyes drawn to the masks, which appeared to be staring at him. He bounded up the stairs where the Chinese warrior mask had fallen out of its niche and landed impossibly upright, given the jaw's curvature. The mask faced him like a balanced dreidel. Michael's hairs rose in a hesitation. He was under the influence of Anthony's tale. He contemplated logically that, in his heavy-footed steps, he had pitched the mask over just right. Its tumid eyes bore intense black pupils into him, giving an impression between menace and urgency.

He retrieved the mask, placing it back in its spot. A feeling came over him to take it, but he ignored it, continuing on. He heard a noise behind him and spun around. He would have fallen if not for the banister. The Chinese mask defied logic. It held the identical position on the edge of the step. His ego kept him from calling Anthony.

A shadow swept over the house's windows. It was the impetus which charged him to take the mask with him. Michael hastened down the hallway and opened his parents' door without knocking.

"Couldn't sleep, Pop?" Michael said, low enough not to startle his dad. Bruce did not answer. He sat dressed in work clothes at the foot of the bed in front of the window. Michael walked towards him. "We're leaving. Tony and Rosalyn say we have to leave."

Bruce gave a sigh. "When you were a boy, your mother and I discussed whether or not to tell you about Santa Claus. I thought we should. My thinking was to protect you from becoming an outsider among your peers. It was the first day of first grade. You came home crying because a boy told you Santa was your parents—"

"We don't have time for this." Michael vaguely recalled the day.

"You asked if we were putting presents under the tree. Well, we denied it. I explained some kids are naughty and their houses are skipped—"

"Seriously, we don't have time." The sky was tipping the room from yellow to grey.

"You haven't had time for me in a while. Always busy…" Bruce broke off, never shifting his attention from the window.

"Is that what this is about? We can do whatever you want, after you rest. Right now, we're leaving."

Bruce didn't budge. "I certainly wouldn't have let you down on purpose."

Michael kneeled, his eyes on his father. Bruce's eyes would not leave the window. "Dad, you need sleep."

"A year later, you caught me putting gifts under the tree. I let you down. You trusted me."

"You didn't let me down. I don't care about any of this."

"I care. I betrayed you. Your impressionable world was shattered. It's my fault. You cried hysterically. I haven't forgotten, you blamed me—"

"We're leaving." Michael placed the mask on the bed and took his dad's right arm, urging him to rise.

"I realize I haven't been the father you want—"

"That's not true. You're tired." Michael tugged with no real force.

"I can't leave. I now know how I can make it up to you. You and your mother. I was given a revelation—"

"Dad, move it." Bruce pulled his arm free. Michael let it out, not wanting to hurt him.

Bruce tapped his temple with a well-padded finger. His grey eyes fastened tighter to the reaches out the window. "All my life, I've been absolutely wrong. Instructing you poorly. I told you there was no God. There's a god, innumerable gods and demons. My father was right. Argauth—"

"Dad, don't make me get rough."

"Watch your grandfather's blood. It runs in your genes." Michael was shocked by the comment. The man was a religious extremist and he hated him. "Leave, I will stay. Hearth promises me they will not hurt you, as long as I stay. You, Tony and Rosalyn are free to leave." Michael twisted with indecision. He almost called Anthony but was afraid how his dad might react.

"Dad, if you love me, you'll come with me."

Bruce broke his stare off the window to look at his son. "Mike, don't you understand? That's why I have to stay, because I love you and your mother so much. I will not let you two down anymore."

Michael went for his arm again, putting power behind his pull. "Michael, stop it. Leave me be. You don't know what you're doing. We can't win against Argauthartera. Michael, stop! You're hurting me." Bruce was losing the struggle.

His right hand clutched his son's thick wrist, relaxing his grip. "God is coming to clean the mess we've created. We are parasites. We deserve permanent quarantine. I have the ability to save us from it. Mike, I want you, your mother and Darla at the side of God, protected. I can atone for us. I can be the father I should have been from the beginning. It is my obligation to our family. We can't fight Argauthartera. We are due for consumption, I have foreseen it. We deserve it. Hearth let me see what will happen if we are not stopped. It's terrible what we are capable of."

Michael's flesh crawled. Bruce's attention was summoned to the window. Michael wanted to know what it was he was drawn to. The grey outside had deepened and in its shelter roamed a myriad of black figures. Michael watched in shock as the house was strategically surrounded, just as Rosalyn had said. A forgotten memory surfaced from when he was a child, seeing similar hideous creatures that would lurk in the dark. His father would reassure him that they didn't exist, that they were figments of imagination. But there was no logical reasoning that could explain what was happening.

"Hearth is not our enemy, we are. Leave, I will stay."

"Tony, Rosalyn!" Bruce launched off the bed, making for the door. Michael, confused by what he was doing, didn't respond. Bruce locked the door. He then shielded his face with his cast in a blitz for the window. "What are you doing?" Michael caught his dad and judo threw him onto the cushion of the bed. Bruce cried out as he flew back.

"We're going to die! I can't leave!" Bruce lashed out.

Michael was caught in an unpredictable struggle for restraint; his father was trying to bite him, scrabble, pull hair and hit him in the groin. The locked door pounded with yells. Bruce fought with unreal strength to no avail against Michael's grappling. "Dad, stop it!"

"I have to! I have to stay! We will die otherwise! Don't you get it?" Bruce raved in his son's face.

"Dad, stop fighting!" The inarticulate sounds that expelled from Bruce began to sound more primordial beast than man. Michael was concerned his father was going to have a heart attack. Bruce was cherry red. The veins of his neck managed to root into his corrugated forehead. Michael caught a slipped knee in the groin. He repositioned to take control when something caught the corner of his eye. The mask was moving on its own.

The door caved in and in rushed Anthony and Rosalyn. Anthony and Michael were able to contain Bruce. Michael leveraged a free hand to retrieve the mask. The instant he did, his hand automatically brought it down on Bruce's protesting face and his body went limp.

Michael's head swung back and forth at Anthony and Rosalyn. "He went berserk on me."

Rosalyn spoke, holding the deer mask in her hand. "The warrior spirit has intervened on your father's behalf. You can get off him. He will remain reposed while the mask quells Hearth's possession of his faculties." Anthony freed Bruce.

Michael leaned back, uncertain. "They're everywhere outside, like you said. Dad wanted to stay. Said Hearth told him they wouldn't hurt us if he stayed." Rosalyn went to answer when a brilliant-white flash painted the interior. The heavens opened a torrent of pelting rain on the house, followed by a crack of roaring thunder.

"Let's get your dad out," Anthony said, glancing out the window at a storm crowded in evil. Michael sprang off the bed.

"He mustn't be separated from the mask," Rosalyn said. Anthony went to assist Michael but, before he could, Michael scooped up his father with minimal effort.

"You got him?" Anthony asked.

"Yeah, he's light." Michael tossed his father up an inch or two. Anthony hurried to beat him to the broken door so he could hold it open.

"Watch the stairs," Anthony said.

"No worries." Anthony and Rosalyn shared eye contact at the young man's strength.

Michael, aware of impressing Rosalyn, was motivated further by ego. He descended the stairs at a rate in which they had to hustle to keep step.

"Easy, Mike," Anthony said.

"No sweat, I got this." Michael laid his dad beside the front door. A burst of thunder boomed behind it, lighting the windows in vivid flashes. "We're not all going to fit in the Jeep. I can take my car if you want?"

Anthony took a break to think. "Yes, get your keys. Rosalyn can ride with you. I'll take your dad and the deer mask. Do you know where your dad keeps his office keys?"

"Yes, should be in the kitchen near mine."

"Grab them."

"They're waiting for us," Rosalyn said to Anthony.

Michael riffled through the clutter in the kitchen drawers. He had found his keys. Not a moment later, the office keys were spotted.

"Michael?" His attention shot around the room for the lost voice.

"Deb?" He placed the keys in his jeans.

"Michael?" Debbie's tone was filtered by a speaker. A roll of thunder played over the house. "Michael, can you hear me?" Debbie's voice came from the kitchen phone which had been left off the hook, hidden behind the dining table. Michael fished the cord and placed the receiver to his ear.

"Deb?"

"Mike! You have to—" The phone went dead with a snap. Rosalyn held the pulled phone cord.

"That wasn't Debbie. Did you get the keys?"

"Yes."

"They will operate through those closest to you. Do not be fooled." Rosalyn headed for the foyer, waving for him to follow. Michael placed the phone down, uncertain.

5

Braulio and Candela were driving to service, already late. They detested being late; how the congregation would judge their tardiness. It was tough being punctual with a toddler. The strident double doors of the church would announce their overdue arrival. Candela would rock fourteen-month-old Sofia while Braulio searched out two seats in the rearmost pews. The coughs, whispers and stares would be equal to that of the sequestered single mothers.

The aggravating anticipation subsided at the scene of an accident. "Have mercy!" Candela exclaimed. Braulio pulled off the road, turning on the hazard lights. Sofia became upset in her rear-facing car seat.

"Stay in the car." He stepped from the vehicle, assessing the tipped Cadillac. The broken glass cracked under Braulio's tentative steps. The rear tire was still in a spin. According to the conspicuous skid tracks, the convertible had come from the opposite side of the road. Braulio did not see any ejected bodies. "If it be your will." He prepared himself for a confrontation with death, stepping around the trunk. "No one's in the car!" Candela heard him but was busy tending to Sofia's worsening mood.

Another car stopped.

"Hey!" A teenage boy poked his head out the window. "We'll call an ambulance."

"No one's in the car. They might have been thrown." The teenager receded, talking to the driver and the car drove off.

The windshield had fresh blood smeared across it and there was a crack where the driver must have smacked her head. Braulio inferred the injured person was a female from the strands of long blonde hair knotted in the cracked glass. The black leather seats glistened with her blood. Braulio ran to his car and ripped off his blazer. He reached to throw it in and noticed Candela was not in the car. Braulio swung around. "Candela!" His voice faded in the overgrown thicket of weeds. Dropping his black coat on the passenger seat, he leaned in to check on Sofia, who was also missing. "Candela!" he shouted into an all-too-quiet setting.

Braulio could see far down the street in both directions and across where there was a wall of lifted earth. He detected movement amongst the overgrowth coming in and out of sight and he moved toward it. "Candel—!" He rolled his ankle on a pump. It was Candela's. The bushes were slightly out of shape from where the pump lay, travelling to where the movement was stirring. "Candela!" There was no reply from out of the insect-infested undergrowth.

Discharged

The corpulent Braulio walked inward, nervous and worried. He remained cautious of the holes in the ground, unsure of rattlesnake season. The movement ceased in the bushes ahead. "Candela!" Stickers, bur and foxtails slivered inside his church slacks. "Candela!" He was answered by a baby's cries.

"Sofia!" Braulio bounded over the bushes, scraping up his legs. Dust billowed over him, making dirt patches of the sweat stains on his dress shirt. He could make out split and torn flesh stooped between the foliage. Overblown breaths brought him closer to the bruises, taunt contusions and lacerations on what he discerned as a ribbed spine that jerked upward from a crouched position. His feet lost themselves as the blonde teenager sprang from Sofia and onto him, her bloody mouth tearing through the cords of his neck. Braulio was no match, he fell awkward on what remained of Candela. Layers of blood drew over his eyes with every spurting crunch until his head detached.

The sound of truck breaks played over the weeds. A city electrical worker had stopped to see if he could assist. The man faltered when he saw the nude teenager crawling on all fours. She came towards him carrying a screaming Sofia in her mouth, like a wolf cub. The shock chased the man to his truck. She stalked him with lurid black pools for eyes, her face a river of dripping blood.

A faint ambulance siren sounded. The teenager shook the screaming bag of bones quiet and dropped the half-dead baby to the asphalt. She uttered a brisk clanging noise while performing a slanted, front-sided pushup over the body. The creature went on to place her lacerated left hand on one of Sofia's fragile legs, crushing it into bone meal. The baby screamed in a bid for survival; her three tiny, pudgy limbs flapping.

The monster's mouth opened, displaying pleasure in what life was left in the child. Human teeth began falling out of her mouth, one by one, sprinkling Sofia. They were replaced by developing sharp teeth, similar to a dragonfish, with rows that left no space in the mouth. The unrecognizable, subhuman head flew down on the child, striking like a Cobra. Instead of toddler flesh, the monster was met by a blowing impact from a wrench against its now indented, blonde and pink-covered scalp.

Two scowling eyes of the darkest sea bottom rose up. The city worker postured for a fight, clutching the giant wrench. The mouth full of jutted dragonfish teeth clanged. "Shoo! Shoo! Get out of here!" the worker said, unaware of what it was he was speaking to. When his shouts didn't work, he thrust another blow down on the elongated head. His tool was caught and wrenched away from him by the creature's mutated mouth. The heavy-duty steel whined to the pressure that seized it. The worker wavered and ran. The wrench was bent into a sinuous rod and hurled back at him.

Guttural clanging raised the creature's ravaged nudity into the air without the use of the legs which dangled beneath the body, crippled. The middle of her stomach started to split from the navel button, tearing the firm stomach in a complete ring. It snapped apart, falling into two separate halves connected by mere bones. The top half of the body hovered with a demented cheery aspect. The worker passed out at the grotesque sight as the creature's deformed head twisted downward, it's loads of curved teeth hooks spread open. The cheery quality fizzled.

Sofia was dead, the baby's life essence puddled around her. A clamor of clanks burst forth out of the mouth of the creature, venting at the passed-out man. When the ambulance arrived, there were four mutilated victims, a sideways Cadillac and an electrical work truck. Braulio's car was not among the remains.

6

Braulio's car drove deep into a large driveway, parking alongside a Hummer. The creature crawled on its hands out of the vehicle, separating from its bottom half and leaving it in the driver's seat. Lacerated palms paced across the asphalt towards the backyard. Like a grasshopper, the oozing disfigurement sprang over an eight-foot security fence, landing on green fescue. Male moans penetrated a downstairs window. The black pools peeped on what was behind the glass. A woman in her thirties was performing fellatio on a man, bobbing up and down between hairy legs. The window smashed apart, spraying glass. The woman did not recognize the monstrosity that was her stepdaughter.

When the screaming stopped, the creature moved onto the bed and over to the phone, its torn hands dialing. The phone lifted under blood-matted hair, the voiceless mouth busy as the phone rang. "Filthy spirit, what have you done?" Rosalyn asked.

The butcher's mouth hesitated, not expecting a confrontation.

"She's in the darkness with us." A light blue flickered and withdrew back into the black pools of the creature's eyes. The voice was a perfect imitation of Debbie's.

"Then we have no business to discuss," Rosalyn said, dropping the phone down. Debbie's possessor glowered, the black pools darkening a shade.

"Argauthertera will seal you, bottom feeder!" the spirit clanged. Rosalyn had abandoned the conversation. The possessor sat on the phone as instructed by the internal messages received from Hearth.

7

"Office keys." Michael handed them to Anthony, who slipped them into his cargo pocket.

"Mike, get your dad into the back of the Jeep, we'll do a switch of masks there. I want you to take his mask for protection," Anthony said.

"Do I have to wear it?"

Rosalyn jumped in to explain. "No, you just have to have it with you. The masks are what fought off Hearth during the break-in. They contain warrior spirits. When united with our spirits on the spirit plane in the realm of light beyond form, we become stronger."

"Gotcha." Michael nodded, not getting it.

"Rosalyn will be riding with you in case we get split up. Do not wait for me. We will run into problems with Hearth. Be prepared for it."

"You don't have to tell me," Michael replied.

"You ready?" Anthony asked.

Michael lifted his father. "When you are." Rosalyn traded looks with Anthony to signal that she was ready. The three heartbeats thumped between their teeth as Anthony turned the knob. In that plunge through the thrown open door, their hearts sank in a burst of feet.

The front yard was deceivingly vacant. They loaded Bruce into the Jeep and switched masks. The downpour soaked all it could touch. Michael made for his blue and white striped Mustang, leaving Rosalyn. He did not question her delay. Constant splashing in the face made it hard to judge distance. Hearth and his band were nowhere to be found. Still, Michael couldn't outrun the premonition of something wicked on his heels. He reached the car, keying it in his haste to get in.

The raindrops beating down echoed in the car's interior. Michael checked on the whereabouts of Rosalyn, but was unable to see out the fogged windows. He started the car, turning on the windshield wipers and heat to blast the defrost. The engine coughed, warming up. "Where is she...?" The red mask sat in his lap. He avoided any sight of its menacing stare. The squeak of the wipers dueled the considerable vats of rain and the window's fog began clearing. The Jeep came hazily into sight, but no Rosalyn. Michael's head jerked to look out the windshield, pulled by an intuition of baleful influence. He was stuck in absolute fear.

A dense horde of faceless black fiends blocked the driveway. They were crowded together in considerable number, each varying in alien aspect to create a cluster of one horrible contorted formation. The body of the outrage flailed weird disjointed appendages around. From out of the front and center of this bizarre mass, a gorilla impression separated from the others.

A darkening exterior swung over the car, where the ever-encroaching numbers strobed in a flash of lightning. All manner of creepy things fringed on the car's outskirts. Michael faced the firing squad, his body pulling backward. A thunderclap sent him into the roof. The busied black beings bent out of shape and twisted in their grim, disfigured shells. The mask in Michael's lap began to shake. From the thick of the massive hoard behind Hearth arose a tower of mangled beings high in the sky, gathering in a tsunami-sized tidal wave. Michael's eyes glided up what they could. The fear welled from his stomach into his throat. The things upshot out of sight into the dark, grey sky, blanketing the vehicle in a darkness that blocked out the rain.

Michael fumbled to turn on the interior lights, followed by the brights, which amounted to the combined power of a few miniature candles. His hands went to the wheel, his foot hovering on the gas pedal. "Rosalyn!" he yelled into the alive, abysmal darkness. The warrior mask in his lap fluttered violently. The windshield wipers became loud without rain. Michael felt claustrophobic, on the verge of losing control. Unadulterated fear had taken him hostage. He didn't want to abandon Rosalyn. In desperation, he revved the engine. The close-quartered darkness stayed put. He revved his engine harder with a fierce yell of frustration. The grey of the sky made a brief return. The swarm was in a frenzied composition.

With cannon ball fists, Hearth hammered Michael's headlights into pieces. The car waved to the blows until only a candlelight flicker kept the Mustang's interior visible. Michael froze. A powerful variety of cryptic hollers emanated from the surroundings, followed by the ground being struck by an intense force. He could feel the car draw underneath him to the great rumblings. He stamped on the breaks to keep the car from sliding. The darkness peered in around him.

The disturbing vibrations shook Michael's intestines and sent his head, teeth and shoulders rattling. The car slid to a lean, despite the applied brakes. The grey of the sky opened, wider and wider. The black mass was hysterical, scattering about in a perceived panic. The wave that took the sky came crashing down, along with the rain. A drenched Rosalyn came into Michael's view from the passenger-side window. From his confines, he could see she was holding a skull outstretched in her hands. She moved without falter as the black aversions retreated. Hearth and the minions equaled a mega quake. Their cryptic chorus raised to a piercing choir.

Michael tried to push open the passenger-side door for Rosalyn but at the angle to which the car leaned, gravity wouldn't allow it. He rolled the window down, letting the rain in. His ears wanted to bleed from the increased sound. "Rosalyn!" His vocal cords could not compete against the fury of noise. The car slid down the lawn sideways, pulled in a deluge of giving ground and a chaos that chainsawed into the Earth itself. Michael rolled up the window, regretting ever putting it down. The dispersing amalgamation released a deafening cry. Michael clutched his ears and closed his eyes. For the first time in his life, he found himself praying to any god of virtue listening. The mask's fluttering eased in his lap. Michael could feel the energy of the formidable mass lessen and he wondered, with peeking eyes, if his prayers had been answered.

Like roaches discovered by light, Hearth and the spirit's minions had fled to parts unknown. The dark grey sky was back to flush the car. The mask was steady. Michael wasn't, however. He turned to search for Rosalyn but found her getting into the car. Michael's ego mitigated his state instantly. She plopped down in the tilted passenger seat. She was a water fountain of glistening beauty. Strands of sable hair plastered to her youthfulness. "Catch, Anthony," she said, arranging her handbag on her knees.

Michael hit the gas, going nowhere fast. He could hear the dirt being kicked beneath the wheels. "Try it in reverse," Rosalyn said. Michael tried, switching back and forth, rocking the steering wheel. Anthony honked from the street.

"I can get it." Michael gained and lost turf. The car interior darkened. The warrior mask fluctuated.

"Mike…" He didn't bother to look at the returning horde. His undivided attention was on the sound of his wheels.

"Grip, you mother—!" Michael's fist struck the steering wheel. The car plunged into complete darkness. Rosalyn retrieved the skull from her bag, pressing it to the windshield. The mask shook. "Yes!" Michael yelled as the car flew forward. He slugged the gas pedal. The engine let loose drumfire, spitting land.

Michael steered on instinct through the augmented horde. The Mustang's fender bisected the black mass with no headlights to guide and speed to kill. He felt the touchdown of pavement, veering to the left. The spirits let out fierce sounds of dissonant blusters. The warrior mask jostled out of Michael's lap. He perceived the contact of his tire's tread from the driveway to the road, swinging another left. The blockade of evil was smashed open at full throttle and the sports car blasted through the gap.

Doug, Veronica and Vaughn ran into the road, flagging the car down. Michael slowed down. "Don't! They're not your neighbors!"

"Are you sure?"

"Yes!" Michael watched their faces sadden as he sped by. Doug Fenton's family was an exact replica.

"You're positive?"

"Yes, I can tell the difference." In repeated rearview glances, Michael watched the despondent family assimilate into the horde.

"So, my neighbors are clones or what?"

Rosalyn shivered. Her brown sugar skin was dappled and her hair dripping. "Here." Michael fixed the heater vents on her, his eyes crossing paths with the skull. *What the hell is that?*

"Thank you," Rosalyn said, as she placed the skull and warrior mask into her bag. "Yes, they're clones." Rosalyn adjusted a vent from underneath to blow on her face. "It's my mother's."

Michael took his attention from the road. "What?"

"You were asking about the skull. It's my mother's."

Michael's mouth fell open. "I..."

"You don't have to, I'm telepathic." Michael's mind went in several directions at once, wondering mainly what lewd thoughts she heard and it occurred to him to stop thinking about it. "It's not my choosing. It's a gift and a curse, depending on the circumstance. I don't want you to take it personally. It's not my intention to intrude on your privacy or I wouldn't have told you. I can't turn it off. I would if I could, but I can't. I, myself, made peace with my abilities only recently. It wasn't easy, I assure you." Michael remained quiet, afraid to think. He focused on the road. "I'm thick-skinned. I've heard everything there is to hear under the sun. From strangers to lovers to family alike. I'm numb to it. You needn't be concerned about offending me, or embarrassed."

The car illuminated with a flash and thunder soon followed, rolling to a break. "Beautiful. I just love storms. You?" The interruption served her. She tilted her head to gaze at the heavens when Michael didn't answer. The buckets of water on the windshield didn't share much of a view. "You like storms?"

"What? Um, yeah." Michael concentrated on what to think and say. He became hot and found the heater an irritant.

"You can turn it off," Rosalyn said. Michael turned on her twice in both amazement and fear, cautious not to lose sight of the road. Rosalyn laughed. The mirth struck a negative chord with his ego. "You're afraid to speak with me now, are you?"

"No." Michael made a dumb jock face. He was bothered that he couldn't blank out his compunction.

Michael went to apologize. "I hear you've heard of Goat's Head?" Rosalyn said first.

He seized the opportunity. "Yeah, yeah. I've not been personally, but I know where it is. I told Tony we are going to drive by it…or rather, the road that leads to the trees. It's on the way to Oak Glen. We're heading up to Oak Glen, right?"

"Yes, Yucca's."

"Then yeah, we're going to be driving right by it."

"Interesting."

"Is this your house, we're headed?"

"No, I live abroad."

"Who's this Yucca then, if you don't mind me asking?" Michael asked with keen curiosity.

"Yucca is an elder. He's one of the 'People of the Pines', the Yuhaviatam tribe. He is a great many things, including a healer. He can heal your father's madness."

"Can he help us with our situation?"

"Yes, as long as we are unwavering in our commitment to succeed, notwithstanding the sacrifices required, we can prevail."

"What kind of sacrifices?"

"Whatever may come. The alternative is terminal. Our cause must prevail, whatever the cost."

Michael sighed. "What's your mom's name?" he asked, to break the generating vibes of discouragement.

Rosalyn peered at him with interest. "Lavinia." She ran a gentle hand over her mom's lump in her bag.

"May I ask...?"

"Her spirit leads me on my journey while I reach for ascension, a form of elevated perception." Michael went along with the New Age jargon.

"What's with the writing on her face?"

"It's script from the Masters of the Ancient Wisdom."

"Is that something like Masters of the Universe?" Michael laughed flat.

"What is that?"

"A failed attempt at humor, it seems. You don't know *He-Man*?" Michael thought of the cartoon.

Rosalyn's eyes rolled. "Very funny." She made a teensy smile and the car's atmosphere lightened.

"I hate that you can read my mind."

Rosalyn gave a theatrical gasp. "I beg your pardon? It's worse to have the ability. You try dealing with the world's dirty secrets on your own. What people truly think, especially when it pertains to you. Gross is an understatement. Thankfully it's not how they act, for the most part. Men in particular." Rosalyn's head waved side to side. "Although I must admit, women can be just as disgusting and cruel."

Michael withdrew before he replied, "Dang, how do you trust people?"

"Umm...usually when people find out I can read thoughts, they either force maturity or lie continuously. I'm not popular, if that's any indication of people's quality of character. It's difficult, but when you do meet someone genuine, they can bring you a rare joy."

"Sorry." Michael was not referring to her plight. He was apologizing for his earlier thoughts and conduct.

"I accept, if you mean it." Michael didn't answer right away. Instead, he gazed out the windshield.

"I regret it."

"I appreciate that. Will you learn from it, is my question?"

"All I can say is, I can try."

"A positive start."

"I'm a decent ear, if you ever want to talk to somebody."

"I appreciate it."

"You didn't finish telling me, what's the Masters of the Ancient Wisdom?"

"They were spiritually enlightened beings. My mother was a ninth initiate. She was a 'Lord of the World', which translates to having a life wave capable of spiritual office and union with the gods."

Michael nodded. "I have no idea what you're talking about."

Rosalyn sat with a gracious smile. "It's because you're a Scorpio."

"How'd you figure that out? I wasn't thinking it," Michael said, intrigued.

"You wear it on your sleeve."

CHAPTER 12
The Clean your Room Incident

1

Northwest Smith was folded in the tentacles of *Shambleau*. Pulsing wet worms slid and writhed all over him. The door knocked, bringing Vince from Mars back down to Earth. "What's up, Mom?"

"I want you to clean your room." Vince glanced around. His room wasn't dirty.

"Can I do it in five minutes, I just have a few pages—"

"Clean your room!" The scream swung Vince out of bed.

"Mom?" He stood petrified, eyeing the door. The *Weird Tales* pulp fell from his hands. The scream was blood-chilling; Vince had never heard anything like it. His mom's footsteps moved away from the door. He stayed put for a period, not certain what to do. It was his anxiety which eventually shoved him out of his room. "Mom?" he called around the quiet house. Anxiety turned Vince's search into utter desperation to not flee out the front door, shouting for someone, anyone.

He barged into his mom's bedroom. "Mom, what's the matter?" She sat on the bed, facing the wall. "I'll clean my room right now, I swear I will." Vince made his way around the queen bed. A blank stare was on Paula's face. "Mom, why aren't you answering me?" Her brown eyes were open, each vacant.

"Who are you?" Paula asked. Vince was stirred to panic. His shakes pervaded him.

"I'm your son." He convulsed. She remained expressionless. He pulled the bag out of his pocket. The shakes rattled him out of the room to the kitchen on the verge of an attack. Jerky fingers dialed with adversity. "Don't do this to me." Just the delay of pushing numbers on the phone panicked him. The swirling darkness appeared in the rims of his sight. "Nooo!"

"Yucaipa Physical Therapy."

"Kim, it's Vince! It's an emergency! Get my dad!"

"Yeah!" Kim's phone struck the table. Seconds later, Greg was on the phone.

"What's the matter?"

Vince couldn't breathe. "I don't know! Mom doesn't know who I am!"

"I'm on my way home!"

Vince gasped for breath. The only person he could think to turn to was Bill next door. He ran out the front door and pounded on Bill's door. He had to take a seat on the iron porch bench to avoid passing out. He was hyperventilating, the tunnel was closing in on his sight. He put the bag around his mouth, blowing into it. Bill answered. "Bill, I—"

Vince's eyes opened from the miserable dream. The storm outside ran a waterfall off the shingles. He realized that Melissa wasn't beside him and assumed she had gone home. The room smelled of petrichor. The dream had been vivid, the ruthless images lingering. Vince reflected on how that incident played out.

Bill sat with him and his mom. She had forgotten who she was and where she was. Bill tried to explain, but she was brain-dead. The circuits had gone haywire. When Greg arrived, Paula gave him the mindless gaze of a total stranger. His dad explained that Paula was weaning herself off Dilantin to see if she could stop taking it. With one pill, she was back to being his mother within twenty minutes.

Lying on his bed, Vince tried to rest. He thought about Melissa to distract himself. She was too good to be true. He had thought it many times before. The

The Clean your Room Incident

fear of losing her had worsened, even at this peak of having her. His grey-curtained house was brighter than it'd ever had been and, for some reason, he couldn't enjoy it. He kept thinking that, one day, she would leave him, alone. Restless, he went to get a glass of water. The house's abnormal quiet tugged at him. Curiosity and a pinch of anxiety had him investigate his parents' whereabouts. "Mom? Dad?"

"What, Vince? Your mom is sleeping." The answer came in the form of a hushed whisper from his parents' bedroom.

"Just wondering where you were." Vince headed to the bathroom to get ready for the day.

2

Melissa parked Dick's car behind a Bronco beside a weed-infested field, overcrowded in bare paper birch trees. Concealed behind the field was a drab white-walled house with dark windows. Melissa gave a cautious inspection of her lonely surroundings and proceeded out of the car carrying a bag labeled "Fun Corner, Costumes and Makeup". After a second inspection, she pulled her jacket's hood over her head and hurried through the rain toward the secluded house.

CHAPTER 13
Yucca's Place

Sunday, 11:57am

1

"Slow down," Rosalyn said. Rain blotted Cherry Croft Drive. Her gaze roved the muddy, puddled road that led to Goat's Head. Michael sat back so she could better probe the impalpable world unseen by most. A renovated, late nineteenth century green and white farmhouse edged on the left with an overgrown field on the right. The dirt road itself waved and coursed into what would have been mountainous arches, had not the storm stonewalled the upper background. Rosalyn didn't take long to find what it was she was searching for. She sat back and listened to Michael's thoughts. "We'll come back." Michael drove off, getting the gist.

2

Oak Glen's main artery wound the Mustang and Jeep up a bosky mountainside community built by the fall apple season. The orchards were ripe, dangling their subdued colorful fruit under the accumulated weight of the weather. The stores, restaurants and petting zoo were open for an unusual crowd of no one.

The cars split from the loop into the recesses of the mature forest. After this way and that, the obscured streets concluded the group at a dead end where the trees obstructed the clouds and met the mountains. A quaint log cabin was carved and nestled in from those trees, bellowing smoke out of the chimney.

3

Yucca sat in a wooden chair on the porch. His cracked clay skin and long white hair rocked under a worn, raven feathered hat. The once-white brim dipped just below the stem of a broad nose. He took the rocking chair arms in hand to stand. His umber eyes lifted from beneath the brim. They were bold and tough-set. His orange ocher jacket spoke of a high-ranking tribesman. Rare shells and beads of a motley assortment circled his hardy neck. He was tall, statuesque and noble in appearance. The marks of Kruktat were upon him.

Yucca waited under the shelter of the porch for his company. Rosalyn switched Bruce's mask, taking the deer mask in her hand. Michael retrieved his father from the Jeep's backseat. The elder took a step forward. He spun a lengthy arm around the porch's wooden pillar and scrutinized Bruce's inert body. Out of the splashing drops, the group ascended the porch steps, Anthony at the rear. "His mind has been corrupted by Hearth," Rosalyn said, leading the group.

"I am aware of the spirit of whom you speak," Yucca said, solemn with the visage of a sea turtle. "What's your name?" he asked Michael in a brusque tone.

"Michael," he answered, feeling assaulted.

"Rose, show Michael the guest room. Place him on the bottom bunk." Rosalyn opened the creaking front door.

"Mom's home!"

"Hi, angel. Watch out." Rosalyn tenderly pushed her daughter back. "Let us get settled, okay?"

"Okay." The little girl walked backwards into a stack of old books. One of many stacks under the vaulted ceiling. Michael didn't think twice about his surprise of Rosalyn being a mother. The little girl's unflinching, mellow turquoise eyes fell on him.

"Hi there." Michael's voice wrapped her fidgety hands behind her back. She was the spitting image of Rosalyn, only with baby fat. She was no older than five.

"Hi." The reply came in her size.

Michael went from the shy sable-haired little girl to the wall-to-wall library. "Unreal," he mouthed under his breath. He was mesmerized by the impressive collection of antiquated books flickering in the light of the flames. The musty smell of Old World literature competed with wood, smoke, oil and wax. He wandered the walls made of built-in shelves. The custom job bordered the three bedrooms and fireplace. An expansive cherrywood desk, characteristic of a king's scribe, centerpieced the room, complete with a red-cushioned dais. The desk's balustrade legs were enveloped by organized volumes of animal-skin bindings. Piled on top the desk was a continuation of these ancient works. In the middle of the desk was a magnifying glass inside an open book which was showcased with tulip oil lamps.

Michael followed Rosalyn into a cramped guest room. She turned on a lamp in the shape of a gnarled bough. The bulb expelled the gloom of grey adhesion coming from the curtain-tethered window where the storm poured over the forest. The room held minimal amenities: a bunkbed, lamp, table, writing pad and pen, chair and three modern books.

Michael laid his father down on the bottom bunk. Rosalyn fixed a pillow under his head and realigned his cast across his belly. Bruce's unconscious body weighed poignant on his son. It was too representative of death. He hadn't time to dwell on it, however, because no sooner than Michael had set his father down, Yucca spoke up. "Michael, why don't you warm yourself by the fire while we adults put your father right."

"Can't I help?"

"You will be, when you leave." Michael's eyes turned to ice on Yucca. He met his, unintimidated.

"Permit us privacy, please, Mike. We'll take care of him," Anthony said, patting his back in a friendly ushering out. As close as Michael and Anthony were, he still felt an urge to swing at him for protecting the jerk.

"It's for your dad's sake," Rosalyn said. Michael slackened his stare from Yucca and sidled past him and Anthony. The urge to shoulder the elder in passing was strong but he controlled himself.

"Close the door," Yucca said in his stern, dismissive manner. Michael did not turn. He instead slammed the door in response, stirring the cabin's curtains.

"Oooh, I'm gonna beat that motherfucker. Bitch-ass motherfucker, talk to me that way." Michael grumbled to the fireplace, clenching his fists red. He fought not to be *that guy*. People turn into the bad guy when they throw the first punch. He seemed to always end up being the shit starter. *It wasn't his fault*, he thought, *it was assholes like him who provoked him*. Michael spread his hands across the screen of the fire. The warmth created a soothing shiver within him.

He shook his head over his right shoulder, having the feeling of being watched. His irritation subsided at the sight of spying turquoise eyes over a fort made of books. He became conscious of his filthy mouth and considered with regret whether or not the little girl had heard him. "What's your name?" he asked in a soft tone.

The eyes dropped out of sight. Michael's face went wry at the thought that he scared her. A sound of a rattle and chants came from the guest room. It captivated Michael for a bit. His attention was then drawn to the mysterious volume on the desk. He walked over to it, sidestepping book pillars.

Michael leaned on the dais and examined the spread animal skin against the tulip lights. Its crinkled pages were bound with shaved bone. They contained an unfamiliar, gilded handwritten writing system, similar to the cave art of stick figure trees that he'd seen in history books. Each individual tree had a varied set of branches with a number below, written in a red, classic font. The compressed golden script captioned a monochrome square illustration at the center of the right page. Michael moved the magnifying glass over it.

At once, a sinister feeling enveloped him. The deeper he inspected the black and white atrocity, the starker the feeling grew. The five monks were divested of their robes and undergarments. They were placed just off the tips of an enlarged five-branch tree symbol. The brothers' semblances displayed remonstration for their sinful acts, performing devilry for the fulfillment of the malignant spirit, which had enclosed a smoke ring around them. The face of a Punch doll demon displayed blasphemous mirth at the torment. Its body was that of a genie with a fit male torso and an attenuated lower half of smoke, blending into the ring. The demon hands were strangling each other from pleasure, held outward before its sunken stomach.

The monk just off the highest branch that went skyward had a tilted head and was performing anal copulation on himself with a cross. Moving counter-clockwise, where the branches stretched the longest, the second monk was made to eat gold coins. His covetous stomach was ready to burst. The third, bottom-left monk used overgrown fingernails to pare the skin off his body with his flayed chest skin yanked outward in his unholy hands. The fourth, bottom-right, pleasured himself to the damnation of his brethren. Then came the fifth. Michael found the fifth the innermost bothersome. It was of a monk praying on his knees. On his forehead in bold print were the letters "**Abra**". The demon loomed above the five. It's dark, smoke-filled eyes looked down upon the fifth man, the man on the shortest branch.

In the background, upper-right corner, was a subverted monastery, fallen to ruin. The venerated walls were askew and overgrown by the land, sprouting black grass from its eroding stone. To the lower-left of the monks was a dingy forest of thorn trees, realistically drawn. Its gnarled, jagged branches twisted towards them. Michael wrenched his eyes from the piece in a sudden intake of breath. He stumbled backward from the dais, caught by the bookshelf wall. His arms gave way to instinct and protected his ribs with an inward agony. He could have sworn he saw the monks turn on him in despair.

"You're not allowed on Yucca's desk." The voice was subdued.

Michael sought the little girl. "Why not?" he said in no one direction. Her tippy toes lifted her sable hair over the front of the desk.

"It's dangerous," she whispered, being spotted. The guest room was quiet. The crackling wood of the fireplace and the pelting drops on the ceiling held sway over the house. Michael moved away from the wall. His eyes averted from the terrible page, putting on an unbothered front.

He went around the desk and kneeled to lessen his height. The two were separated between a row of clasped books. "My name is Michael. What's yours?" Marissa played with the buttons on her overalls.

"Marissa." She looked up towards him and he noticed her eyes would move slightly side to side.

"That's a pretty name." She did a mini twist from the hips, dipping her eyes back down on her busy hands.

"I got new shoes. Wanna see?"

"Yeah." She lifted a pink and white sneaker outward.

"Neato. Did your mom and dad get you those?" Her foot dropped.

"My mom did. My dad doesn't visit me." She gave him a timid glance.

Michael considered his response. "They're stylish. Say, Marissa…do you know, does Yucca have a phone?" Michael wanted to call Debbie.

"Uh-huh." She nodded with her eyes on her silver buttons.

"Where is it?"

"Umm…" Marissa did a slow 360-degree pan around the room, exchanging a hand on the books for balance while turning. Michael realized the girl might be blind. "I think it's in Yucca's room. I can ask my mom for you."

"That's alright, I'll ask her."

"You wanna play with me?" She bounced on her tippy toes, setting both hands on the books for support. Her face brimmed a hopeful smile.

"Yeah. What did you want to play?" Marissa's face lengthened in surprise. Her tiny fingers felt along the pathway of leather books to reach him. It was then that it occurred to Michael, the books were organized so Marissa could use them to navigate the room.

"We can play dolls in Yucca's room. You can be the boy doll and I'll be the girl."

"No, Marissa." Marissa stopped. Her head upswung in disappointment at her mother. Anthony and Yucca entered the room behind her. Yucca went on to the kitchen. Michael stood, eyeing the elder like a predator. "Mike and I have to have an adults only talk. Why don't you play dolls with Grandma?" Rosalyn retrieved the skull from her bag.

"Michael, you wanna play after you're done talking?"

"Angel, he's busy. Grandma wants to play with you. Play with Grandma." Marissa executed the piles in her path with precision, taking the skull in hand to Yucca's bedroom. The sight of the child playing with a skull sent a chill down Michael's spine. Her reticent walk carried a doleful bearing.

"We can play later, Marissa," Michael assured.

"Uh-huh," she said over her shoulder.

Yucca's door closed before Michael spoke. "How's my dad?"

"Better," Rosalyn said.

"He's asleep," Anthony said.

"Where is Yucca's phone?"

"You can't," Rosalyn blurted.

"Why not?"

"Who do you want to call?" Anthony asked.

"He wants to call Debbie."

"Mike, you can't," Anthony said.

"Awe shit! Why?"

"Mike, my daughter."

Michael gritted his teeth. He threw his hand in the air, gesturing "who gives a damn", even though he did.

"Calm down." Rosalyn was clearly nervous of his uncontrolled behavior. Her reaction only stirred his emotions. "They'll influence her to get to you." Michael combed his hands over his hair.

"Take it easy, will—" Anthony was cut off.

"Hey, macho Mike. Would you like some tea?" Michael's inner impulse was to fight.

"Depends, you putting poison in my drink?" Anthony and Rosalyn stood in ineffectual alarm.

"Depends, are you man enough to stop me?"

Michael ignited. His intension transmitted to Rosalyn. "That's it!" Michael's thoughts became pure violent impulse. Anthony and Rosalyn caught up with him in the kitchen. Michael loomed over Yucca in a bully's posture. "Say it to my face, bitch!" The elder sat placid on a wooden stool, sipping tea. Michael's eyes bore into his tilted downward brim, his features full of detestation. Michael slapped the cup and saucer plate out of his large hands, causing it to shatter on the floor. The impassive elder rested his hands in his lap.

"Mike, stop!" Rosalyn cried. Anthony stopped her from intervening.

"Talk your shit, old man!"

"You appear angry," Yucca stated with a calm demeanor. Michael flicked Yucca's hat from his head where it glided to the ground.

"Do I, asshole? Talk your shit!" The elder's wrinkled eyelids were closed. Michael regarded this as a sign of weakness.

"What would you do now, demon?"

"Demon?" Michael took a step back. There was a parting of provocation in his voice. Yucca's eyes opened onto Michaels. The umber pair were more compassionate.

"Yes, I see you, demon. I will drive you out." Yucca spoke in his native tongue.

Michael drew back from Yucca's voice, his breath unsteady. His eyes flicked on Anthony and Rosalyn who were glommed onto each other, engrossed at his intervention. Michael eased down into a seat at the kitchen table. His features contorted at the realization. "I belied to you, Michael. I wanted to agitate the demon. I saw the evil spirit in you when you arrived. You are our greatest physical strength, yet because of your sickness it is my belief you would have easily enough turned our foe."

"The demon who possesses you is a selfish, angry spirit, driven by fear. Your true divine spirit has been at war with the dark seed for many winters. Your impurity did not come from Hearth or Blackie, but from your past. I tested the demon's weakness for anger and, with light effort, you see it failed." Michael stared at the plaid red and white tablecloth. He listened to two sets of dialog, Yucca's external and his incriminating internal.

"The china you broke was handed down to me by my parents. They had passed it down to me so I could take pride in my upbringing. When my parents fought to protect our village from the white settlers, they acquired the tea set from battle. My tribe was displaced from Chimney Rock. The tea set gave my parents pride to know we hadn't lost everything." Contrition overwhelmed Michael. His tongue pushed the soft palate of his mouth to avoid falling apart. "I say it not to shame you. The tea set represents a wise teacher whose lesson is that rash decisions carry unperceived consequences. Take the lesson with you into battle and, remember, think before you act. The triad is heart, mind and spirit, united you will choose wisely."

Michael observed the floor of blue and silver shattered pieces. "I can glue it," Michael said. Yucca cracked a carefree smile.

"Let it remain a sacrifice for the benefit of a lesson learned and a spirit cleansed. I've prepared tea for you, have some. It will give you the strength you will require." Michael turned in the signaled direction. There, on the counter beside the stove, were four steaming tea cups. Michael's head went back to the elder who nodded a proud recognition of his sincere regret. Michael got up and did not take a cup. He instead walked past Yucca's stool and retrieved his hat. After a brief glance for dirt or damage, he handed it back to him.

"I'm sorry." Anthony and Rosalyn drank to the heartwarming sight. Yucca grasped the hat and Michael's forearm in a callused grip. He slid the raven-feathered hat over his head of white hair. Michael waited for the message from under the brim that tilted toward him.

"The tea tastes better hot." Michael made sufficient haste in gathering two cups, bringing one to Yucca. The elder toasted him. "To victory, my friend."

"To victory," Michael repeated.

Anthony and Rosalyn saluted the union. "To victory." The four raised their cups and drank.

Something inside Michael awoke after he took a seat back at the table. He drank another sip of the sweet tea. "I have a confession to make to you all. A few..." His focus was on the steaming, ornate tea cup. "I have been confronted with certain peremptory traits of mine lately that I'm not proud of. My dad told me that I ignore him, that I'm ashamed of him." Michael bit his inner cheeks as he spoke. "Was it Hearth talking through him? I don't know, but that's not the point. What bothers me is that he wasn't wrong. I don't want to blame being possessed. I've had choices but I've made foolish decisions. A lot of…realizations of late." He slouched forward with stooped shoulders and watched the hypnotic serpentine steam flow upward.

"I've treated my girlfriend, Deb, unfairly. I justified my behavior because I think she has wandering eyes. Meanwhile, I'm the one cheating. My mom was right, she was right. I don't deserve her." Michael's fingers tapped his cup. "My dad's hurting, I've hurt him. My girlfriend deserves better. The end of the world could be approaching and what do I do?" The words clumped in his throat. "I think lewd things about Rosalyn. I flirt with her, my eyes wander on her. Why? Because of a demon? I don't believe that's entirely accurate. I love Deb, but I'm not in love with her. I dated her because she was the hottest cheerleader. How shallow is that? That was the choice I made. I chose looks over brains. I had options for the smart girl, incredibly smart girls. Not that she's…not smart. She has unique qualities, all her own." Michael circled his neck.

"When Rosalyn told me in her kind way that she knew what I was thinking about her, I felt…just disgusted with myself, and rather than face it because I knew she would hear me, I bottled it. It's interesting. She mentioned once people know her ability to read thoughts, they change. Once you are held accountable. It took that accountability for me to realize what I was doing was wrong."

Michael's focus zeroed in on the cup. "I don't like who I've become. I want to do the right thing because it's me, not some pressured circumstance. I have to think about it, have ta…find out where it all went wrong." Michael's eye line raised to Yucca's. He was locked on Michael's feet. "I'm a spoiled brat, it's as simple as that. Everything's has been handed to me. I think that's why I love judo. Nothing comes free in judo. It doesn't care where you live or what you drive. How you look, who your friends are. If you're dating someone hot. It doesn't care. It's real. Michael went around the room. "I apologize, Yucca, Rosalyn, Tony, for my behavior. I'm ready to change for the better, on my own."

Rosalyn and Anthony, like Yucca, were locked in a gaze at Michael's feet. He eyed the wood floor beneath him and saw something move under the table. "What is that?" Michael's chair screeched as he jumped up, startled. No one else appeared alarmed. In fact, they didn't give Michael's reaction any attention. They were too fixated on the sight underneath the table. Michael lifted the tablecloth with an outstretched hand, ducking under. His features altered in amazement. The roots of his hair tingled. The shadow figure huddled under the table's shelter, curled up in a cowering position. The demon's hand covered its eye. The exorcised spirit was an eleven-year-old Michael, nursing a bully's black eye.

"Be at peace, dejected spirit," Yucca said, carrying on in his native tongue. The eleven-year-old reached out a hand to Michael.

"I..." Michael shook his head with the utmost sympathy. The boy disappeared in front of his eyes.

"Come, we are without time," Yucca said.

CHAPTER 14
Jarrod's House

Sunday, 1:24pm

1

Inspired by Melissa's comment, Vince got it in his head to attempt a visit to his friend Jarrod's house. He contemplated a possible reunion if the opportunity presented itself. He still hadn't made a concrete decision one way or another when he went to ask permission to use the car. Vince didn't want to disturb his mom but the cold light of outside made his anxiety itchy, as it always did in gloomy weather, and he felt he had to get out. Part of the reason for going was to prove the weather didn't bother him. He took a deep breath, tapping at his parent's door.

"What?" his dad answered. Vince heard whispering feet on the floor from what sounded like more than two people.

"Sorry, can I take the car on a drive?"

"In the rain?"

"I'll drive safe."

"Alright." There was a lot of hushed moving around heard from the other side. It sounded like a room full of people.

"Is there anyone here?" The sounds of movement quieted.

"No. Your mother is trying to sleep. Will you let her get some sleep? Take the car." The atypical quiet of the house seemed to worsen in that instant. Vince didn't know what to say. *Mom must be sick. What-if she's having a miscarriage?* He ground his tooth.

2

A hooded Vince ran through the yard to his dad's Grand Prix. Thunder rolled overhead. In starting the car, he noticed his nervous hands. *It's the weather.* He glanced over and saw that Dick's car was gone. *Let's invite Melissa.*

Later. What bothered him about overcast days, and especially rainy days, was the weather was reminiscent of tunnel vision; the way the cold, dark light closed you in. Vince rounded the street, the car's alignment pulling left. He stuck to the main streets for safety zone protection. The anticipation of what might take place between him and his ex-friend grew along the way.

It was in passing Oak Glen Road that he had noticed the now-absent traffic. He gave an affected throaty cough, looking at his water in the cup holder. There would be no more businesses on the way, the last being well behind him. What few houses there were directly on Bryant Street were not easily accessed. Vince wiped his sweaty hands on his pants. *What-if Jarrod's not home?*

I'll get out of there. The rain persisted to taunt him with its suffocating nature. He pulled his upper seatbelt strap behind his elbow to keep the restrictive pressure off his chest.

Ivy Avenue came into sight. He curved up the street and pulled to the curb, feeling like he should turn around. He had forgotten how long a street it was. He cast his eyes down at the car's floor. *You can do this.* Vince white-knuckled the steering wheel, driving on. *You can always turn around.* He focused his concentration on his breathing exercise and a calmness followed.

Vince saw a man in his yard walking out of his barn. The man glanced at him and then continued into his house. He had his safety zone. The street didn't feel as long after that. He arrived at Jarrod's house and turned the car around for a quick getaway. He gave the direction towards Goat's Head a look, even though the weather would not permit a clear view. It felt closer then he recalled.

He parked along Jarrod's curb. There were no cars in the driveway and the yard was unattended and half dead. The brick and white stucco ranch-style

Jarrod's House

house was as he remembered it. It was the front window that caught his eye, Terri's bedroom. There were no curtains up and, from what he could tell, the walls looked bare. *Take a look.* Vince stepped out of the car, opening his umbrella. He glanced towards Goat's Head again.

What-if Jarrod comes out?

I'll have another safety zone, won't I? He walked up the driveway to the front door, peering into Terri's room. The room was unoccupied with not a thing in it. *Maybe they moved? That's why their line was disconnected. Why wouldn't he tell me he was moving?* The door to the house was ajar. Vince knocked and the door creaked loose, back and forth. "Hello?" No answer. He pushed the door open. The guts of the house had been removed; it was just fading walls, dirty tile and stained carpet.

Vince stood at the doorframe. "Hello?" He took a look behind him and walked inside the lonely house. There was a musty smell accompanied by urine. *Don't go too far from the car.*

I won't. He walked down the entrance hallway which branched off in three directions. To the left was another hallway of four rooms, which included Terri, Jarrod and Becca's bedroom and their bathroom. To the right was the kitchen were cockroaches could be seen scurrying on the floor. Straight ahead was the living room that led to another back room and the staircase that would take you to Jarrod's parents' bedroom. Vince headed for Jarrod's room, peering into Terri's to check on his car, but more so to check on what lie beyond it. The rain patter on the roof added a negative effect on his nerves that left him always checking behind him.

Jarrod's room brought back memories. Vince reconstructed the furniture, the posters, the toys, the models, the games; the way it was in his mind, reminiscing playing with *Star Wars* action figures, reading comics, trading cards, playing Atari and Nintendo, strategizing their war games and talking girls. He could hear his friends' voices in his head, like they were in the room with him. But these voices were dashed by another. An uncanny voice, terrifying in its delivery, which had no explanation.

Vince was paused, motionless with fear. He was brought momentarily to a place where thought didn't exist. Every hair on his body was lifted, every nerve tingling. His olive complexion blanched. The gurgling wail had come from somewhere inside the house. Maybe from behind him. Whirling around, Vince ran for the front door as fast as humanly possible. The apprehension of whoever it was waiting to jump out at him from behind the wall as he passed was unbelievably cruel.

Whatever it was, he didn't want to see it. The sound shrieked at him. As he rounded the small hallway leading to the entrance, he found the front door closed. He went to open it, but the door wouldn't open. He yanked on the door handle that came off in his hand. The thing was getting closer. *Jump out the window.* He had no choice. He turned, his heart pounding to get out of his chest. Vince threw the knob in the disturbing voice's direction. The unprecedented sight was a shock to the nervous system. The brain delayed in retrieving what it saw in those few seconds of running by.

The woman avoided the knob and extended out an arm, making that horrible noise repeatedly. Her gaunt face was bent out of shape and had the appearance of melting. Her hair was thin and balding, her teeth mangled and broken. Her eyes were cavernous, colder than the outside light. She was startlingly white, her body emaciated and nude. Between her legs she was smeared with a dark fluid of some kind. Her breasts hung like sacks of meat while the rest of her skin sagged on her middle-aged body.

Vince ran into Terri's room intending on jumping through the window but, instead, rational thought grasped him at the last second. He threw it open and leapt out, pulling it closed in case whoever it was followed. Jetting through the yard, he jumped over what was once a garden at the foot of the property to access his car and proceeded to burn rubber. The swirling black tunnel around the rim of his eyes lightened with the crossing of his safety zone. Soon after which, he claimed back his breath with a return to a safe surrounding.

3

Dick's car was not back yet when Vince arrived home. He went over to tell Melissa what happened to him but no one answered the door. There was a spoiled odor in the air. He couldn't figure out if it was coming from inside or out. "Where is she?" He gave her house one last look before returning home.

4

A gleam of firelight extinguished within the drab white-walled house, giving the windows back their dark emptiness. For a while, the rainy atmosphere was undisturbed and then Melissa appeared, running amid the birch trees. She ran over to Dick's car for a moment of privacy, practically falling in from sobbing. She laid across the seats, rolling in pain and despair. "I'm sorry, I'm sorry..." she said to her stomach. She cried with a quiet, seemingly ceaseless desperation.

CHAPTER 15
ABRA

Sunday, 1:51pm

1

Four hands were outstretched before the stoked fire. "What are we summoning?" Michael asked.

Anthony's brown eyes thickened around traced flames. "A demon."

"Why are we doing that?" Michael whispered.

"To perhaps reach a deal for Argauthartera's cessation. It's our understanding there's only one who has the authority to summon Argauthartera and the dominion to repel the deity, and that's Abra." Michael's bottom lip went limp at the designation. The bone-bound book's illustration rebounded in his mind. "We assume Blackie has made a deal with Abra to summon Argauthartera, unless the sorcerer is dealing in a magic unknown to us, which is a possibility. Either way, Abra would be a useful mediator."

"Will a new deal nullify an old one?"

"Yes."

"Wait, say it did. What's to stop Blackie from doing the same thing to us?"

"We think his deal is not yet complete. Why else would the Harbingers be here? Why would Hearth be coming after your dad? The answer lies with the appointment with your dad's patient, Vince. We're counting on Abra to fill in some of the blanks. The difficulty is that we cannot ask outright."

"Why not?"

Anthony shrugged. "We're not allowed to. We do not want to anger the demon or else we will be at the mercy of the Harbingers."

"Can we trust the Harbingers?"

"We think so. They broke the seal I set to protect your dad at the hospital, a sign they're not malevolent. The imperative question for the time being is what Abra will require for a new deal." Anthony's worry sent Michael's attention to the flames. They danced in the pupils of his eyes, while he made the shapes of his thoughts out of fire. "You holding up?" Anthony asked in a low tone.

Michael's head craned towards him. "What choice do I have?"

Anthony threw an arm around him and pulled him close, touching temples. "We have to be tough. We're in this together." Anthony shook Michael's rounded shoulder. "You get my back, I have yours."

"Always."

Rosalyn came out of Yucca's room. "I'll be back soon. You and Grandma have fun." She closed the door behind her, holding onto the handle. Every fiber of her being dithered. She heard the door lock from inside, then tried to open it. Satisfied it was secure, she went along and blew out the tulip lamps. The fireplace struggled against the prevailing dark. A vague profile of Yucca shook shells and beads through the lambent atmosphere. Michael and Anthony turned on the benighted room. The flames swam the walls in ripples of dark red, orange and yellow. The covered windows whispered wind to the sound of wood and rain colliding. Anthony and Michael thought of separate threatening matters, heightened by the room's surly influence. The mood was deathly somber.

Yucca came toward Michael. His face was cut deep with shadow, his umber bold eyes ablaze. In his large hand was the raven feather from his hat he'd put away. "Mike, take the feather for the evocation. It will bring you unending courage. Do not drop it..." The elder's long finger raised in caution. "Or there will be great consequences." Michael clasped the quill. Upon contact, he knew no fear.

"Rose, let's begin," Yucca said.

On a loose part of the wooden floor in the center of the room was imprinted a golden tree symbol with four branches like the ones Michael had seen in the Abra book. He was directed to the largest branch. Unlike the monks in the book, Michael was instructed to stand on the tip of the tree branch, not slightly off. Rosalyn said, "To move will be your last mistake. Stay put on the vein." She buried her eclipsed eyes in Michael's darkened skies.

"No worries," he said, fearless. Rosalyn instructed Anthony to the second largest branch below Michael. After which, she took her own place on the shortest branch, the single branch on the right side.

"Anyone one moves from the vein will become a prisoner of Abra. You've seen what can result, Mike," Rosalyn said. Michael looked unperturbed at her concern.

Anthony and Rosalyn anchored in place, fighting the portent shakes traveling up and down their spines. The three participants faced the flare of a struck match from behind the desk. Twelve black candles were lit across two golden candelabras. Gradually, the combined yellow wicks presented a beaded Yucca from the brooding waves of the fireplace. The elder was attired from head to toe in an undergarment of buckskin, on top of which multicolored beads rested in uniform stripes. Abra's book was at the elder's service. Caution stirred in the human spirit.

Yucca produced a veiny wrist to the clack of beads. His cut-out eye holes bent over the calfskin pages of symbols of cant. The elder began clinching an upside-down fist in an orderly sequence. It occurred to Michael what Rosalyn meant when she said, "Stay put on the vein." The symbols are human veins, not branches. Yucca went from book to wrist. He discerned the elder was clinching his wrist per the number code beneath the vein symbols.

The fireplace extinguished, seizing the room's occupants. Michael stood still with mere curiosity and amusement. They were interposed by illimitable darkness outside the candle's reach and an afterglow of the golden vein in which they stood steady. The sound of rain dispelled. No corners of the room could be visualized. The pit of Rosalyn and Anthony's spirit wavered. "Do not move!" Rosalyn said. Anthony felt himself wave against his will. Yucca continued the evocation. The candle flames throbbed. Then, one by one, the sound of sizzling wax extinguished the wicks until total darkness engulfed the golden vein on the missing floor. Yucca's beaded legs and moccasins appeared from out of nowhere at the vein's apex, just before the last flame flickered out.

The feeling everyone but Michael had was a tilting that promised you would fall off a tight rope into endless dark if you did not remain absolutely still. The key was to be calm. Michael was this in spades. He had no comprehension of the miasma, only of his orders given. The surroundings gave forth a scent of burning sulfur accompanied by a calescent atmosphere. No participant could be seen above the knees by the others. The flowing heat upshot as the darkness seemed to judder. The candelabras relit, one by one. Their flames sputtered as they swayed afloat in midair with the book hovering between. The desk was gone, along with everything else the original room housed.

A diaphanous smoke ring formed above the book. Anthony and Rosalyn's hearts collectively sputtered like the candelabra's flames. The amorphous forms the dark spirit created defied what was possible. Its morphing stages gave seconds of identification for the human mind that in no way could be comprehended. The whole process of illumination was a visual volley. The illustrated demon was molded. A genie, the Punch doll presence, resurrected. The wicked spirit's smoke-pitted eyes bandied the summoners. A toothless grin stretched its elongated half-moon head, pierced in the middle by a hook nose. Vaporous pointy hands came together in a blast of smoke, strangling with intent.

"For what purpose have you summoned me?" The demon's voice was subterraneous, belonging to the core of damnation. A voice deceitful, mocking, malefic and imperial in tone. The top-heavy demon floated forward on a string of smoke like a big grey balloon, bringing an aggressive grin down on Rosalyn, the group's speaker. The head's openings became black passages over the candlesticks. The smoke of the body was a solid mass. Abra left the light and went against an invisible wall, stopping short of Rosalyn. There the demon taunted, a nocturnal nightmare. Rosalyn fought the urge to crumble and conjured the strength to speak.

"We have come humbly to ask for a deal." The demon's pointy hands clasped each other.

"Whet my appetite and we shall see. What is it you seek?" The demon held a hideous smile.

"We appeal to you, o'mighty Abra, to stop Argauthartera from coming." The awful face didn't move, held in a minute of reserved thought.

"I have a conflict of interest, per your request, unless…" The demon's eyes poured greed, falling in a slant. "…what you offer is more pleasing?" Abra flickered like a flame bounding from wind. The demon appeared above the candles.

Rosalyn chose her words wisely. "What would please your excellency?" The pointy hands became antsy.

"Regale Abra with your willingness to please."

Rosalyn humbled her sight, aiming it down at the bottomless ground. "If I could know what deal you have, I could offer a deal that would please you absolute, according to your tastes."

Abra's eyes widened into two full pits. The demon's head floated back over a muscular torso. "Appetize Abra, appetize!" The demon's hands strangled from the outpouring of unbound fantasies. "What would you offer me? A child perhaps?" The inflection of cheer in the demon's voice shook Rosalyn's foundation. "I have a proclivity for the wee people—"

"Any child?" Rosalyn struggled out.

Abra scowled. "Strike your tongue, underling, I'm not done!" The roar gave weakness to her knees. "Interrupt me again, I dare you." The disquiet of quiet deafened. It remained this way for a while. "A child, the love of a mother, the love of a lover is what I am after." Abra challenged her to speak with a significant pause. Rosalyn could scarcely have spoken, even if she had fallen for the trap. Her face reflected the insurmountable pain she was in.

"Additionally, I shall require Iosk. You, the simple, designate as the Goat's Head skull. I am firm. No negations. Deal?" The demon relished in her countenance. "You may speak."

"I—"

"Louder! Abra can't hear you."

"Deal." Rosalyn forced out the syllables; they came out like a dry heave.

"Deal!" Abra mocked her agreeable tone and spun around, kneading hands in enjoyment of what possibilities lie ahead.

"Bring your offerings to the place you call Goat's Head. You will find the charnel house onsite. Proceed into the basement of the mansion, where I will be waiting for the first arrival. You have until tomorrow night, at midnight, where the deal expires and, for the defeated, so will they." The demon drew back and faded unceremoniously. The scent of sulfur dissolved, taking with it the calescent atmosphere. A cold entered the participants' bones. The library's musty smell and the storm outside came forth. The candelabras and Abra's book were back on their resting places atop the desk. Yucca had just doffed his beaded outfit when he saw Rosalyn tumble down on her knees, grasping them. He, Anthony and Michael ran to her aid and helped her into the kitchen as Yucca directed.

2

When the feather was taken back from Michael by Yucca, the Abra experience seemed unreal, yet he knew it was real. Rosalyn paced in the corner, listening in on the conversation. Yucca and Anthony were elaborating the details of the deal to Michael and his potential role in it. It was emphasized to him that Iosk was the Goat's Head skull. It was a crucial part of the mystery solved of why Hearth wanted his dad and why the Harbingers needed Vince to attend his appointment. Vince must know where Iosk is.

Michael didn't fully grasp the details, those would have to wait for the road. Michael's thoughts overwhelmed Rosalyn. She watched him from behind with bleary eyes. He was considering being her lover in the deal; the trait of a Scorpio. His bravery intrigued her. Their signs were a love match. Virgo and Scorpio, written in the skies. She chased possibility. In the end, there were no options for any of them and it was made abundantly clear their blood would not be the only spilt. Yucca and Anthony were making it appear that Michael had free will, when he didn't. Although Michael didn't appear ambivalent, Yucca told him a handed-down story.

"Our people, the Yuhaviatam tribe, encountered the sorcerer Blackie Wilson when my ancestors retreated to these mountains, Yuhaviat. We knew him as Taamit Takwish, or Sun Eater. Our history says the attack was sudden, striking with the white people's fury. The baskets had no acorns. Game was infected with disease. Clean water was poisoned. The offspring were being spirited away by the evil lurking in the pines. The infected region was cursed. Gratefully, our leaders employed powerful shamans to bewitch the sorcerer. Taamit Takwish's grasp was wide and they fought many painstaking battles, forming alliances with neighboring tribes to defeat a common enemy.

As one, they prevailed in lifting the curse, but this did not destroy the root of the problem. Taamit Takwish had no heart. The dark spirit did not come from people as we know people. His false flesh was given to the coyotes and the land burnt for purification. The land was abundant in giving thanks. Successful trade commenced between nations. The sorcerer became a bad memory. His return was imagined. That's why the sorcerer's story is handed down. I have the responsibility of my ancestors to sleep in a dark place and you, for future generations, to put an end to the people's wicked subjection."

Yucca stared at Michael with the solemn visage of a sea turtle. Anthony, with the visage of a supportive friend. "We can destroy the root. Finish what my ancestor's blood started. Fear not death, but laugh in its face, a warrior. When I said I saw in your face a demon, what I didn't mention was that I also saw the warrior, the one that would not let the demon take over. The time for renewal is at hand. Will you take your destiny?" Michael's eyes probed the plaid tablecloth.

"What happens when we die?" Michael asked.

"You will receive a pain-free exit and will journey onward into the spirit world where you will find a new beginning, Rosalyn and Marissa as your companions." Rosalyn shivered at her daughter's mention.

"Death is inevitable, Mike," Anthony said, his forehead drawing extra wrinkles.

"I know. I'm not saying no. I'm just asking." Michael came off a tad defensive.

"Okay, okay. There is a chance, however small, that the Harbingers could present a deal benefitting us, but we can't rely on that." Rosalyn's bright eyes shrilled at the possibility of an alternative deal.

Yucca went on to say, "You will die a privileged death, with great esteem. Your placement in the next life will soar and you will be rewarded for your courage." Yucca omitted that he might lose his memory in death.

"You'll save your parents' life, all those you care for, Mike," Anthony said, with a weak smile. A smile that read that he understood what they were asking of him.

"Your reach will stretch far, felt by the world. What greater responsibility could one have?" Yucca said.

Rosalyn's breath was snatched by the question Michael was about to ask. "Now, I'm just asking hypothetically here. Say Argauthartera succeeded. What would happen?" The hairs on the back of Michael's neck rose from the table's reaction. Anthony expressed a look of being on the edge of a precipice, about to be shoved off. Yucca drew back, his hands falling off the kitchen table onto his lap. The elder displayed uncharacteristic signs of discomfort in the cracks of his face. His bold, umber eyes drew up at Michael's wavering blue eyes to speak of the unthinkable.

"Our spirits would be consumed to the god's belly, where no light will ever exist for us again. We will live in a prison of sheer darkness and absolute despair for eternity. We will reside in the crushing crowds of screams, pleading for release, as we scream for ourselves. Your spirit will never die, only suffer mercilessly under these conditions as you perpetually search for an exit which doesn't exist." Michael jerked around to Rosalyn, stopping her in her tracks.

"Can you learn to love me in a day?"

Her shoulders dipped. "Can you?" she asked, just as concerned. He spoke from his mind to hers and hers to his from their eyes.

Michael surrendered his true feelings and her bright, penetrating turquoise eyes exercised their seductive sway. *All I ask from you is loyalty and affection. The rest will take care of itself. I am attracted to you, are you attracted to me?*

"Yes, you'll have it," Rosalyn said, taken by passion.

You'll have mine. Marissa's a darling. You are smart and beautiful. I want you, Rosalyn. We can find love, I know we can. We could kill it together, the three of us. I will not disappoint. Rosalyn lost her passion for a second with the mention of her daughter. Michael's rapid non-verbal sentiment kept her from being able to dwell on it. *Let our love be. What do you say? We're all that stands in our way.* Michael's eyes studied her impassioned expression veering down on him. He needn't be psychic to know her answer was an overwhelming *yes!*

3

Anthony managed the flooded mountain roads with expert skill. He'd been through multitudes of impetuous storms before. This was nothing new, but it was a time hindrance. Yucca followed behind the Jeep in a white Silverado. The elder and Marissa were headed off to the Morongo reservation where they would rally support from the tribal leaders for an inevitable showdown. Bruce was left in bed, back at the cabin. He would remain under a sound sleep by way of a potion Yucca concocted and protected by the warrior masks left to guard him.

Yucca recommended Big John's Guns in town for the closest supplies Anthony required. The Jeep's occupants were off to check out Goat's Head to find the exact location of the charnel house and get a general readout of the area. There could be no mistakes tomorrow. They knew they would come up against possible opposition at Goat's Head, but options were none and spiritual power was in numbers.

Rosalyn laid her head on Michael's shoulder, somber and reticent in the backseat. Her mother, Lavinia, rested in her handbag that wrapped around her fine V-shaped neck. She stared at her daughter through the backseat window. Marissa's undistinguished aspect seemed to be looking back at her from over the dashboard. How much Rosalyn wanted to be with her tore her insides out.

She told herself the Harbingers would act on their behalf. She had to tell herself something favorable. She had to.

On the ride down, Michael was asked what he knew of Goat's Head. He spoke in an uninspired tone. "Goat's Head is Yucaipa's definitive haunt, like Redlands has 'The Gates of Hell.' The property is said to be the headquarters of the Watchers. From what I've heard, the Watchers are a cult group Blackie Wilson started back when. I hadn't heard Blackie was as old as Yucca said. Let me see, what else…" Michael was having issues concentrating. His thoughts would not let up on his family and his friends he'd soon be losing. Would he be able to say goodbye? The oppressive cause was all happening so fast. Michael circled his muscular neck. His shoulder was pressed by Rosalyn's forehead. Her restrained tears came tumbling down. He clutched her back, touching his head to hers. The tears he fought streamed into her soft hair.

Holding Rosalyn, Michael saw Anthony's surreptitious breakdown in the rearview mirror. A revelation dawned on him and he realized Rosalyn's plight. She was taking in all their sorrow, all this time, on top of hers. A remorse overcame him. He wanted to be witty, but he couldn't think of anything proper to say. His humor defense didn't so much allude him as it wasn't appropriate. He had plenty of material from making his buddies laugh on their cross-country judo tournaments, all of which, though, was inappropriate. A mental picture of his buddies came and went. Michael watered Rosalyn's hair. In thinking about judo, a solution sparked. He knew Rosalyn would be aware of what he was doing, but he did it anyway. Michael cleared his mind of concerns, snapping into a tournament mode of thinking. A mode of thinking where a fighter's focus honed in on the task and lived in the present moment and feared not so he could perform under extreme stress.

"So, what I was saying is—" Michael spoke over the tears. Rosalyn's cries lowered as a result. "And try and stick with me here. There are several different accounts. I'll cover what I can think of off the top of my head. It's been a while for some of it." Michael took in an affected breath. "Blackie is said to roam the grounds of Goat's Head at night wearing a red robe. Some say it's a black robe and some say a gold robe and he leads his followers, the Watchers, in ceremonies of black magic." Michael's mind geared toward the tales of sacrificial rites and he rushed away the inopportune thoughts. Rosalyn plucked herself from Michael's shoulder. Her face mirrored the streaming windows. Michael gave her sadness no perceivable attention. "People claim they've seen Blackie fly. Some say he has red eyes and some say he has black. The Watchers themselves are townspeople. Now, some have also said they're the resurrected dead. Take what you will." Anthony was wiping tears out of his eyes.

"Before you go on…" Anthony said.

"Yeah?"

"Do you know why they call themselves the Watchers?"

Michael took another affected breath. "So, when you visit Goat's Head, especially the trees where the formal entrance is located, they're said to be watching you. Thus the name, the Watchers. I don't know their real name, unless it's the Watchers which I—"

Rosalyn's gratitude displayed in her facial movements, stealing Michael's focus. He rubbed her back under her jacket. Her drying face smiled and he placed her in a hug. She dug in around him, resting her head back on his shoulder. Anthony glanced at what caused the interruption. A crooked smile appeared on him. He missed them already. Rosalyn saw Yucca and Marissa take to a separate road and crushed the remaining tears from her eyes. Michael could feel her pent-up pain. He knew he had to start talking fast or he would lose it.

"I'm trying to think if there is anything else I know about Blackie and the Watchers. Oh, the Watchers wear red robes. Remember, none of what I tell you is fact, either. Don't believe me, take what you will with a grain of salt."

"We're aware, we are," Anthony said in the rearview.

"Now, as far as the layout is concerned. The property is old farmland, boarded by fences. It's extensive land." Anthony gave out a huff. Michael almost paused. "The main entrance is a set of trees aligning a path that leads back some ways to Blackie's mansion. That's where I think Abra mentioned the charnel house would be, there in the basement."

"Just so you know too, the mansion is supposed to be on the verge of collapse and that was years ago when I heard that. When you pass the mansion, there's supposed to be a barn. Now the barn is where the Goat's Head skull is, well, Iosk…I guess is hanging, not hanging. Let me start over, that didn't make sense… So, the barn was where Iosk was hung. The place got its name from what people perceived was a Goat's skull, hanging up on the barn. Blackie was said to use it in his ceremonies with the Watchers. I've never heard anyone mention Iosk before. Well, if you continue past the mansion, there's said to be an altar…" The mention of the altar received special attention from Anthony. "With a screaming face. That's about everything I can think of."

"Interesting, Yucca—" Anthony began.

"Wait, wait, wait. Sorry… to interrupt you." Michael broke in.

"No, tell us, please," Anthony said.

"I forgot, something I didn't mention that we might want to be prepared for. I've heard there are shadow people like Hearth who live in the trees, at the entrance. People have claimed to see them and hear them whispering. Just thought I should mention it, before I forget."

"No, Mike, that's crucial information. You tell us when it comes to you," Anthony said.

"It is," Rosalyn agreed.

"So, what were you saying?" Michael asked.

"In order to summon a deity, a considerable sacrifice should be mandatory. We have to see this altar, let Rosalyn get a readout of it. It is possible that the sacrifices haven't been completed yet. It's a slight chance, I'll admit, but worth looking into. Stopping the sacrifices could null the deal."

Michael confronted Rosalyn's eyes straight on. She was already fixed on his, the turquoise glaring with possibility. His smile was warm and unsuperficial. It carried a new anti-specious meaning; a smile of warmth, care and compassion for her. His high cheekbones lifted and having met no reluctance, he pulled her to him where their lips parted and tongues met. Their kiss was a dining out on fatalism.

"Hate to break you love birds apart, but we have to hustle." Michael and Rosalyn's lips separated. They were at Big John's Guns. The group piled out of the Jeep. Anthony bought what would provide maximum coverage from the elements: thermals, flannels, slickers, insulated gloves, camo pants and rubber boots. Additionally, three heavy-duty flashlights and batteries. While Rosalyn and Michael changed at Big John's, Anthony went across the way to Jack in the Box. They had given him their small orders out of custom, not hunger. Anthony insisted they eat something. While in the drive-through, he retrieved a holstered Beretta pistol from his glove compartment and concealed it under his slicker.

4

Coming back from Jack in the Box, Anthony's head tilted sideways from seeing Michael on the complex's payphone. Rosalyn was beside him, pacing with her hooded head down and arms crossed. Michael glanced at Anthony, worried. "What now?" Anthony said. His stomach churned. The smell of fast food settling on the interior made his twisting guts worse. Rosalyn caught Anthony's thoughts. She left the shelter of the overhang and jumped in the Jeep, fixing her handbag under the slicker into her lap. She slammed the door.

"We've got a problem. Michael's mom told Bruce's secretary to cancel Bruce's appointments for next week."

"Call her." Anthony barked.

"He did. The problem is, when Elaine called Susan, she said Vince Marino had not been scheduled for Monday."

"What?" Anthony's neck beaded sweat. His wrinkled features tensed. "Don't tell me this..."

"Michael's figuring it out." Anthony scratched the sandpaper stubble on his sharp-cornered cheek, leaving red trails. Both were staring out the windshield. "He's telling his mom to have Susan set up Vince's appointment for Monday…she keeps pestering him why. He told her he'll explain later and to just do it…he's telling her he'll call her back tonight, that he has no time to talk…she's asking him what's wrong…he'll explain later." Michael banged the payphone head. "He hung up on her."

Michael splashed over to the Jeep. Rosalyn let him into the backseat solo. "My mom—"

"Rosalyn filled me in."

"I have to call Vince. We cannot leave it up to Susan. She might say she tried to call and didn't. My dad will have his number and address on the computer at work. We can get it and I'll call and schedule it myself. If he doesn't answer, I'll make a house call."

"After Goat's Head we will," Anthony said.

"It's my fault. My dad said to cancel his appointments. I forgot."

"It's not your fault. Susan said he wasn't even on the calendar," Rosalyn defended.

"Still…"

"It's no one's fault. Here, eat something. We'll get it figured out afterward," Anthony said, handing Michael his food.

Michael picked at his double cheeseburger, listening to Anthony fill him in on the details. "Iosk is paramount in the deal, we know that much because of Abra. It must be a valuable tool for those in its possession. We're almost positive Vince knows where Iosk is. Your father's patient was attacked three years ago at Goat's Head when he and his friends were attempting to take Iosk. Vince lost his friends and had a panic attack because he was attacked by the Ones Who Dwell in the Dark, as he calls them. Obviously, he ran into mischievous spirits and the spirits pretended to be his friends and scared him senseless. He claims to never have gotten Iosk, at least that's what he told your dad. Vince has suppressed memories from that night following the attack."

"Somewhere along the line, Vince became bonded to. The spirit that bonded to Vince has been attempting to find the whereabouts of Iosk, but with Vince unable to remember the incident, the bonded spirit cannot use him. In comes your father's role as an unaware participant to retrieve Vince's memories of that night and find Iosk. We suppose Blackie summoned Argauthartera prior to that night and needs Iosk for the god's arrival."

"It would explain why Hearth wanted to bond with your dad, and why the Harbingers placed such an imperative importance on keeping Vince's appointment. Both parties must be aware of the time scale they are dealing with. Tomorrow night, at midnight. No Iosk, no deal. The race for humanity is the race to find Iosk."

"So, let me get this straight, Rosalyn and I have two chances for survival in this game. Stop the sacrifices from being completed or get Iosk and hope the Harbingers have included humanity in their deal?"

"You'll survive with your deal too," Anthony said, making a point to look back in the rearview.

"Right, right, just not in this life."

Anthony exhaled. "That's correct."

"What about these friends of Vince's? Why don't we talk to them? Maybe they know something?"

"No time. Besides, it's obvious Vince is the prime interest."

"Yeah, you're right." Michael put a piece of beef in his mouth, mulling over the information. He locked resolute eyes with Rosalyn in the side mirror.

5

The wipers could not match the torrent's intensity as they approached Cherry Croft Drive. The green sign displaying the street's appellation soaked through the streaks on the windshield with soggy letters. Making the left, Anthony switched to four-wheel drive. The sodden roadbed was plagued with depressions of young floods. Michael looked at the farmhouse on his left. Beyond the rain splatter, he could just make out a side window framed in green form a strange, bloodless face of unknown gender. He went to say something, finding Rosalyn looking at the ghostly image with him. "They know we're here," Rosalyn said, steeped in telepathic concentration.

"The Watchers?" Michael asked. Anthony, absorbed by the road, gave a worthless glance.

"Think so." Rosalyn watched the disfigured face diminish into the rain.

"Are they coming for us?" Anthony asked. Rosalyn didn't move. Her flat expression and reticence geared up a nervous energy in the Jeep.

"I can't discern the voices. They're excited…too many talking at once."

Michael followed Rosalyn's probing examination out the back window. "Someone's coming." Rosalyn swung at Anthony, the pulse in her neck visible. A red truck shining low beams came charging out of the rain behind them. Anthony snuck a look back in a halfway turn. His narrow lips drew inward as he shifted for speed.

The truck drew closer in the mirrors. "It's gaining...," Michael said. The three watched the space between the vehicles dwindle. Anthony was at the curve about to turn.

"False alarm," Rosalyn said. Anthony caught the truck turning as he turned. The mirror revealed an open white gate far flung from the farmhouse in which the truck entered.

"Anyone following?" Anthony asked, his eyes busy. Rosalyn swayed around the Jeep's interior.

"Don't sense anyone..."

"I don't see anyone following," Michael said, gazing out the back window. Rosalyn draped her arm across the back of Anthony's seat, looking back and forth.

"Keep an eye out, Mike." Anthony said in the rearview.

"I am." The Jeep had to decelerate between the winding bend of earthen acclivities leading into a byway of increased flooding. Eyes were on everything. In a lively manner, the Jeep trundled along the inundated road, tracked by a barbed-wire fence.

"The trees," Anthony said to their mutual fixation. Despite Anthony's apprehension, there was adventure in his tone. The contiguous evergreens germinated from the grey clouded surroundings. Rosalyn trembled inside. Michael broke the spell of his captivation, looking out the back window. Although the coast was clear, the anticipation he put on that blurring curve would not let him turn back around.

Anthony anchored the Jeep atop an angled surface area. It was the closest, safest, spot he could manage to the tree's pathway, which was raging water from its entrance. Anthony turned sideways. "Mike." Michael faced him, alert. "Stick together and we're in and out."

"Sure thing."

"Getting anything?" Anthony asked Rosalyn. The medium's eyes closed for a deep reading.

Rosalyn's eyes reopened. "Dead air."

The three were pelted as they alighted the Jeep, but despite the rain, they could not take their assailed focus off the miasmic trees. They peered at the flooded threshold through their hoods. A malodorous odor of a skunk permeated their noses. Anthony contemplated the pressing obstacle ahead. In doing so, he waded sinking steps to Michael and Rosalyn. "Mike, you think you could climb up those branches and then assist us up?" Anthony signaled toward low-hanging branches at the right edge of the entrance flood. Beneath which, was a melting acclivity of mud that offered their best opportunity for scale.

"Yeah, I can." Michael handed Anthony his flashlight.

"I'll throw it to you. Watch yourself and don't fall!" Anthony warned deaf ears.

Michael dashed like a man on fire. He faced the wind and rain, ducking his head from the inclement weather to keep his hood on. His resolved eyes were trained on the ledge. Rosalyn and Anthony watched with bated breath. Boot strikes left the ground in a leap to the top where Michael caught the branches in a solid grip. A couple of strong pulls had him fight the downpour. His slip-resistant soles did the rest against the avalanche under his feet, where he mounted the rolling hill with minimal effort.

Michael's gloves released the crippled branches once he erected himself. His eyes strained into the tainted canopy of dripping needles, pine cones and wood that stretched inward to a reservoir of forbidding darkness. His body's integument crawled from what lay within. "Mike!" His name came to him over the loud rush of water channeling the pathway. He was given three feet of muddy ground to execute a turn. "Mike!"

"Mike!" He met Anthony and Rosalyn's determined voices. They called from right beside him but it wasn't his friend and lover he found calling. The sight brought shockwaves from every nerve ending. A distorted head molded of black incongruous outline filled the opening of his hood. "Mike!" The thing yelled in his face using Anthony's voice.

"Ahh, shit!" Michael shouted. The two traded blows. The ground beneath Michael fell away. He was precipitated and his sight inversed, caught in a headwind. He was in a roll, a familiar feeling for him. He was trained on how to move with it, just not when you land in paralyzing cold water.

The splash submerged him in rocky filth. He could hear shouts of warped words that reverberated. Kicked gravel bits bumped him from all ends. A show of hands appeared in brown waves of panic. Michael snagged the bemired lifelines just before a black covering took his sight from him. The pressure of the dark antagonist closed the hood against his face, covering his mouth.

Michael paddled his head back and forth, not releasing his would-be rescuers. He felt himself whisked and pulled, whisked and pulled, whisked and pulled, this way and that, all the while trying to shake the tenacious thing off. Michael was burst from the water in a heave, arms stretched to the limit. The stench around him was awful. He coughed up water as the flaps of his hood were relieved. He pushed his legs against the road, aiding his haulers. Strange bristling shapes admitted him light. "Get it off me!" Michael gurgled. His sight peeled open. A viscid skunk's gnarled body hung a brief moment by a chewed leg where it fell with a smack onto the soaked ground. "*Uuhh!*" Michael recoiled. He pulled his hands free to stand, wiping the gloves on his glossy slicker in repulsion.

"Are you alright, Mike?" Anthony asked.

"Yeah!" Michael sounded irritated. He looked for the shadow person who'd attacked him. Anthony was already on the hunt for the same menace. The anthropologist was studying the inlet with a keen observer's eye. The shadow figure was gone. Rosalyn held both sides of Michael's head in her gloved hands, bringing his face to hers. Her flashlight rattled in his right ear. The medium signaled discomfort in every smooth line.

"Are you hurt?" Her eyes shone concern under long black lashes.

"No, I'm not." Michael's voice was hoarse. "Thanks for getting me out." He brought down her right hand so he could cough and give the spilling entrance another look. After which, he busied himself with an overall look around. "Did you see it?" Michael asked, facing her.

"Yes." Rosalyn drew closer. "I didn't perceive the spirit, I'm sorry. My talents are failing me. It's this place. I can't read properly."

"It's not your fault, Deb. Do you know where it is now?" The effusion of hurt in Rosalyn's face as she withdrew from him was unmistakable. "What?"

"You called me Deb." Michael's eyes lifted in confusion.

"I did?" He subdued a shiver from the water setting into his underlayers.

"Yes." Rosalyn gave him a double-take of hurt, walking away toward Anthony at the base of the hill.

"It was an accident!" Michael sighed hard, taking after her. "Rosalyn!"

"You don't owe me an explanation." She waved him away.

"Listen…Rosalyn!" She drew away from him, her tear-seeded eyes hidden behind the hood. Michael was apologizing in his mind.

"Something the matter?" Anthony asked, noticing Rosalyn's demeanor.

"No!" Rosalyn said. Michael and Anthony exchanged a quick look. Michael had an apology written on his face.

"Mike, I'm going to have you lift me up," Anthony said, getting on with it.

"What about that thing up there?" Michael's gaze never fully left the top of the hill he'd fallen from.

Anthony switched his flashlight on. "They hate light. I should've never let you go up without your flashlight. I should have known better." Anthony waited for a boost under the crippled branches. "Rosalyn!" Anthony held out Michael's flashlight for her to take. Rosalyn snagged it, sharing her hood's opening with no one. "Toss me a light when I tell you." Rosalyn nodded. Michael made a stirrup with his hands. A thought crossed his mind, bringing a quick smile to his face.

"Watch it up there!" Michael said, blinking from the eye poking rain. Anthony answered with a mouthful of flashlight handle. He stepped in Michael's hands, balancing on his shoulders. Without warning, Michael did most of the work, thrusting him on top of the slippery ledge. Anthony scrabbled to his feet with the aid of the crippled branches. The beam shot out at his left. He righted himself, light in hand and scanned the entrance.

"Toss it!" Anthony yelled. Rosalyn handed the flashlight to Michael. She knew his aim would be precise and there could be no more mishaps. Michael wasted no time. His aim *was* precise. The light was tossed into Anthony's glove. Rosalyn held out her light for Michael to take. He shoved the handle into his armpit.

"Why are you smiling at me?" Rosalyn asked, perturbed.

"You don't know?" The comment angered her and Michael realized she didn't.

"You must really like me to get so mad." Her face indicated there was truth to what he said. Michael's smile deepened as he bent over and made a stirrup for her. Rosalyn's eyes followed him down, her face in an internal struggle. "I'm sorry, it was a slip."

The light pressure of her foot mounted on his hands and then her gloved fingers on his shoulders. Like a feather she was raised. She bound her gloves around the haggard branches and her long legs surmounted the hill with ease. She made a cautious turn and watched Michael jogging backward and then bustle forward. She wanted to give him a hand, a hand he didn't require and she knew she couldn't offer. Michael saw her watching him mid sprint and he aimed to impress her. His intense feelings for her culminated in a high jump where his gloves landed on the top soil. He swung his legs into the trunk of the tree whose lower branches were bent beyond repair. Springing to his feet, in a second he was at her side, ready. Rosalyn produced Lavinia's skull from her handbag. The three gave the drenched outside world a brief glance and headed in.

6

The smell of wet sap filled their cold noses and the language of water filled their swooshing ears. The path's blacker than black innards brightened with a three-way formation of lighting, front, side and back in the order of Rosalyn, Michael, then Anthony. Lavinia's skull led the tight-knit group. Her spiritual protection combined with the lights commanded the tree's inhabitants back.

Their thin line of defense was confined close to the right side of the trees, skirting their way on precarious mud between rushing water and rasping limbs.

Rosalyn maintained the power to perceive the cloaked tree spirits and, despite their combined efforts of protection, the spirits persisted in testing their boundaries. Michael and Anthony watched these boundaries being pushed in a continual repeat of human-molded anatomy playing chicken with the streams of light. They would appear and repel, again and again. By the looks of it, there were many.

A gust of whispers whirled through the passage. "Hold on to your lights!" Rosalyn yelled back. The whispers wrung the tree canopy overhead in a weighty spill of collected rainfall. The group's shoulders lifted in a tucked response, hands steel on their illuminated safeguards.

The trek went on and on like this, tree after tree, whisper after whisper, dunk after dunk of water over their slickers. There was no end in sight. Lavinia cautioned Rosalyn of the numbers gathering but Rosalyn was already well aware. They would have to find an exit soon or be pressed through the trees and out into the bushes. No sooner did this thought occur did Rosalyn spot a missing tree from the order on the adjacent row.

An overcast nightfall shed in from the gap. The group braced for another whispered spill from the treetops. The water walloped them in a splash. The polluted atmosphere was overrun. "Michael, Anthony!" Rosalyn called them to her immediate back. "We have to get across there!" Their eyes met on the exit.

"Let's see how far across it is," Michael said, trekking onward behind her and Anthony behind him, with their eyes in the back of their heads. They aligned themselves with the trail's split opening. Michael considered the seven feet of crashing water reflecting the sky beyond. The group clustered.

"We can jump it! I'll go first, that way I can help you across," Michael sniffed.

"Can't, the numbers are too great. They'll snatch us, one by one!" Rosalyn said.

"We can hold hands and jump." Anthony suggested. Anthony and Michael turned to Rosalyn.

"Don't miss!" Her short answer was chilling. Michael was convinced he could pull their weight in the event of a misstep. The three hooked arms, aligned side by side.

"When I say jump, we jump!" Michael said.

"I'm ready!" Anthony said.

"Rosalyn, you ready?" Michael asked.

"Move your lights around when you jump and, yes, I'm ready!"

Michael clamped down on their arms. His strength startled Rosalyn. She knew he was strong but this was abnormal.

"Hurry, Mike, they're everywhere!" Rosalyn said. Michael's left boot drew outward.

"Jump!" The bodies went airborne, being grabbed at by black-strobed anatomy from all around. The combined body weight pulled them free from several tugging close calls. They plopped down in a hunched chain, each releasing a pent-up breath. Michael rebounded in a sprint for the exit, pulling the others like they were made of Styrofoam.

They emerged from the partitioned trees, wading through a split-off waterlogged trail amid knee-high growth. The unrestricted rain came down on them. The Victorian house swung by Michael's eyes. His arms were yanked backward in both directions simultaneously. A searing pain tore at his sternum down both shoulders where he thought his arms would be pulled off. He lost Rosalyn's arm first from the splitting pressure, then Anthony's and his flashlight.

Numerous elongated black appendages clung to Rosalyn and pulled her screaming body backwards toward the trees. The tree spirits had stretched long and out of shape to reach her, gaining their advantage by way of the back of her slicker. Multitudes of black extended arms joined in and clenched down on her. Anthony hung onto Rosalyn's extended hands, being dragged through the soft mud. She strained against the black extensions that multiplied on her body by the second.

Anthony was losing his grip. Rosalyn was steps away from being sucked back inside the wall of trees. The terror in her eyes poured out of the black wrappings, her pleas releasing a beast in Michael, the warrior Yucca spoke of.

Michael came running at full speed. He snatched up Lavinia and the flashlight Rosalyn dropped and pointed them at her captors. He parried the black swinging arms that flung at him from out of the trees, leaping over one that got too close, just to duck another. The whispers voiced their discontent, high over the rain. "Tony, catch!" Michael tossed the skull and flashlight at Anthony, shooting for Rosalyn's waist while avoiding an attempted ankle grab and neck crank. Anthony had to let go of Rosalyn to catch the pass.

Roslyn's hooks burst from Anthony's hands to Michael's slicker. The hit he gave her rattled her insides, knocking the moment's scream out of her mouth. Anthony caught the skull but dropped the light, retrieving it within a second's time. Rosalyn was a step from the trees, back to shrieking. Michael gave the bestial yell of his primordial ancestors. His muscles swelled with veins that carried to his forehead, fueled by the fiery eyes that pleaded with him for rescue.

As he pulled, his hands intertwined in a seat belt grip around her back, exerting a might powerful enough to rip the bones from his body. His feet went down into the Earth, feeling the black appendages fight with a strength unexperienced. His tendons became chords of compressed steel. He would rip his arms off before he let her go.

In the struggle, Michael had been caught himself, unable to avoid the seizing appendages pouring out of the trees. Anthony steadied his legs, having stepped out of the two lines his feet had dug in the ground. He brought the skull and flashlight closer to the fight. The light stream directed on Rosalyn's captors. It weakened the spirit's restraints enough that Rosalyn gained the ability to squirm. She uttered continual loud groans of struggle.

Michael yelled an atavistic cry of adrenaline, feeling the give. Rosalyn's mid-section moved toward him. Anthony touched the light to the black wraps, recoiling each individually. Rosalyn raised a hand for her mother. Anthony placed Lavinia in her palm. She recoiled her daughter's restraints at an exponential rate.

Michael was caught around his legs, feeling the spirits trying to pull them from underneath him. "Tony, get my legs!" Anthony lashed down, finding his light glimmering in a puddle of yellow water. He double-gripped the flashlight handles, shining the two lights on Michael's legs. The spirit's whispers amplified to an electronic hiss. Michael whipped around and Rosalyn went chest to chest with him. He avoided tripping, pulling himself out of an ankle lock.

Michael broke free, running through the bushes with Rosalyn cemented in his arms. He checked for Anthony, who was at his side on the trail, running free and keeping pace. They ran full steam ahead together. The spirit's rumblings petered off behind their rain beaten tracks.

"We're safe!" Rosalyn said. Michael threw a glance over his shoulder, then spun around carrying her in his arms, walking backwards. There was just enough light to see the divided tree line and its deceiving placidity. He stopped and looked at Rosalyn who hovered over him to block out the rain.

"My turn to ask…are you hurt?" Michael asked, catching his breath.

"No," she labored back. The two shared a long-eyed embrace. There was forgiveness in her eyes, repentance in his.

"I thought I might have hurt your back."

"I'll live. Besides, it beats…the alternative. But…since you mention it, could you let me down? It is tough to breathe."

"Yeah." Michael sniffed, setting her down. Their hands stayed on each other.

Lavinia was in Rosalyn's ear; she approved of him. "What are they?" Michael asked, peering back at the deceivingly calm trees.

"Prisoners of Blackie's," Rosalyn responded.

"We're down a light." Anthony offered a flashlight between them.

"Mike, you take it. We'll share."

Anthony was glad to see the two worked out their petty squabble because what lay before them was an ordeal that would require teamwork. Rosalyn gave Anthony a hug for saving her life.

"We'll take the fence out," Anthony said.

"Yes." Rosalyn agreed.

The three surveyed the open area of weeds, following Anthony's lead. Everything beyond the field was rained out of existence, except where they knew their eyes must finally take them, Blackie's skulking Victorian mansion.

CHAPTER 16
Night Walk

Sunday, 5:45pm

1

Vince returned from Plarek for dinner, his stomach grumbling. He turned off his Metallica tape. Oddly enough, the house's abnormal quiet subsisted, inaudible under the rain's incisive current. Vince went to check on his parents, leaving his bedroom light on and his door extended open. The rest of the house was twilight. He hurried and flipped on the kitchen counter track light, rubbing his goosepimpled arms, casting his eyes at his parents' closed door. *Still resting?* Their bedroom door gnawed at him. Vince went over to it, contemplating whether to knock and use the excuse of dinner to ask how his mom was doing. His knuckles lifted to the pressed plywood. *I wouldn't, why be a bother?* Vince's hand retracted.

2

Vince sat on the floor in the bright living room, taking the finishing bite of his hot dog by the space heater. He watched the evening's rain out the backyard window, thinking about a night walk. At night his safety zones would have their lights on, an indicator of who was home and, conversely, who was not. He would use a flashlight to keep the Dwellers at bay in the event that yard and streets lights left any precarious sections unlit. If he could pull it off, it would be a significant step towards improvement. Vince fetched his flashlight and umbrella from his room, leaving on precautionary lights for his return as well as the front door unlocked. He left through the back door to avoid his parents asking where he was going.

It was cold for California. The night was moonless with not a star in the sky. The umbrella resisted the hard sheets of rain under which Vince's light roamed the orange, yellow and white reflective street. There wasn't a dark house on the block beside Melissa's. He continued to wonder where she was in stepping off his driveway's curb, a fleeting dissipation.

The night made for a pleasant walk, despite the conditions. There wasn't much wind, only rain and bearable cold. Being alone in the dark didn't bother him as he thought it might after his encounter with the bum lady at Jarrod's house. Not once did he spin around to see what might follow him. Not one *what-if* thought, nor did his perception disorientate his motion. The plan was panning out precisely, that is, until he neared the second Oak Street.

He was on Erdmore when the strange coincidence became apparent. Although the majority of lights in the neighborhood were on, he hadn't seen a single individual in any of the houses. No visible TVs were on, no comforting sounds like music or talking. Not even a routine dog bark. *The rain's too loud.*

Could be…? The realization might have swayed his confidence if not for the mystery lady's white car from yesterday's incident being in her driveway. *She's home.* Yesterday's attack refreshed in his mind and Vince's foot speed increased. *What-if the lady's not home?* The lights were on in what could have been an empty house. The bum lady from Jarrod's flashed in his mind. Vince concentrated on his beam surfing the rain-pounded asphalt. He ignored the distance remaining. *Get to Fred's, he'll be home. Old people are always home on cold and rainy nights. Stiff joints.* Brief glances upward assured him the safety zone was closing in.

Vince's heartbeat increased. The buzzing street lamps passed overhead, illuminating a profusion of fire drops in their globes of orange heat. The latent properties swung by his narrow depth of field. His sight was focused straight ahead. The dreaded tremble he feared would come, came. He ran. Fred's unlit house came into view. His heart rose and fell at the sight. An unexplainable premonition spun his torso around to look back down the street in mid-flight. He saw under the shine of a streetlamp a shadowed stranger running after him a couple lamps back. His heart launched into his throat. *It's the bum lady!*

The rain flew at Vince's face. His umbrella inverted from the pressure of dragging it through the air. A twin pounding of water raced him uphill. He did not look back once. He cut into his neighbor Bill's yard, jumping a hedge into his water-laden grass. With his chest thudding, Vince entered his house, careful not to disturb his parents. He had determined that he was no longer in danger indoors. He locked the door, kicked off his soaked shoes, yanked off his hoodie and tossed it down next to the inside-out umbrella. He hurried through the entry hall and entered the front formal living room, fashioning himself a hiding spot behind the front window's drapes. His flashlight remained tight in his trembling hand, shaking a bouncing yellow circle on the carpet.

From Vince's perspective, the long rectangle of glass showed a small extent of the street from the camphor tree to Bill's dividing line hedge, the same privet hedge Vince leapt over to enter his yard. He was positive that he outfooted the pursuer. *It can't be a Dweller, it can't. The lights? It's the bum lady. Impossible.* His eyes squinted from the inadequate porch light which did not extend but a hair's breadth off the curb. He wished Dick's property lights were on so he could see better. He waited for what would emerge. During which, he envisaged what lay deep and dormant in his subconscious.

The lurid Dwellers from his mind's eye strolled out of the black halls of his memories. They were back from the power outage years past; the precise reason Vince kept a flashlight on hand. Never would he be vulnerable again like he was that night. He vowed to remain two steps ahead of the Dwellers of the Dark from there on out. He reflected on how the enormous black widow spider shape was leaning into his mouth when he awoke and how its choking legs stretched his lips out of order. The panic he went through trying to pull the bone-tough daggers out of his throat while it's lookout, a sasquatch shape, kept watch and observed the assault. This reprised how he found his scream when the spider handles he fought just vanished inside his mouth. A scream loud enough to wake the block. When his parents arrived, candle in hand, he had not the nerve to tell them the truth. He blamed the incident on a black widow spider he said he saw crawling on his TV set. A spider they would never locate. He recalled his father's face twisted with disbelief and shame.

Vince distracted himself to the corner of the block, feeling a loss of breath come on and a twitch of panic press his nerves. The unnerving undertone of the house was around him like a heavy blanket tucked up to his ears. He began his breathing exercise. His eyes concentrated on the street next to the hedge. His pulse was beginning to throb. *Breathe.* The stranger appeared, hushing his breath. *It's her!*

Vince watched as the rudiment stepped before his property. He could feel his hair raise. The figure drew close enough for identification. He identified the man not in the porch light but in a powerful flash of lightening that jolted his eyes to the clouded heavens and back down. The unveiling amounted in a shock that went beyond the lighting. *Fred!*

The elderly man was drenched in his gardening overalls. His dark, shadowed aspect looked straight at the house from where he stopped at the curb. Vince ducked out of potential sight. *What-if he saw you running and thought you were having an attack?* Vince snuck another furtive look. Fred was walking away, back the way he came.

Shit, you think?

Yes, stupid. He'll catch pneumonia.

He'll be alright, he's right down the street. I'll apologize tomorrow, explain…I'll think of something to tell him. Vince focused on his breathing until the shakes subsided. He then found himself consumed with jealousy over Fred not needing a flashlight in the dark. *Why can't they see them?* Vince ground his tooth.

CHAPTER 17
The Layout

Sunday, 6:10pm

1

The streams of light glided over the chain-link fence to wander the facade of Blackie's Victorian ghost. Nothing better typified reclusive secrets, menacing darkness and groaning despair than this ramshackle heap. It was bloated, cracked and drowning from the rain water falling off its quantity of gabled ledges. Led up to by overused steps, it reached two divisions of leaning baluster railings. Its foundation was anchored on worn, chipped and aged brown brick and supported on softening wood pallets. The pallets were demanded to reinforce the high-peak gable porch, above which supported what was left of the turned portico balustrade balcony.

The second floor grossly fought to bear another limp, high-peak gable on its pathetic shoulders, which attached the third-floor tower to the rich-black sky. The plentiful windows were boarded like the spray-painted doors on the first and second floor which read "I can see you" on the first and "Can you see me?" on the second. The shattered glass teeth gleamed back at the lights from the trim. It was a horrifying sight in the daylight, much less being in it's awful presence at night. It reaffirmed for them why it had become a significant part of Yucaipa's formidable lore.

"Anything?" Anthony asked Rosalyn. She stared at the sagging wreck's intangible boarder, attempting a break through.

She let out a long-held breath. "I can't read anything." Frustration was in her voice.

Anthony's light drifted down to the gate's entrance and split the darkness over the combination padlock. He lifted the lock in his sodden glove. It read "666" underneath. He turned the numbers to 000, pulling down on the lock. It opened. "Dummy lock." He showed the others. "We'll come back. Keep your eyes peeled." Anthony took the lead, anxious to get moving.

They shoved off, wading the trail along the fence littered with "No Trespassing" signs. Darkness was in full effect. A kind of night that eyes could not grow accustomed to, where the lightless spaces created phantasmagoria. Michael stayed close to Rosalyn, his wet underlayers unsticking and re-sticking cold against his skin with every shift of weight. On the outskirts of his panning light, he thought he saw something move. Shadows oscillated in the swinging lights, turning reactionary heads like scared birds. A constant apprehension of an unwelcomed assailant appearing in the light was unshakable. The rustling of their hoods intensified this awful anticipation.

Rosalyn and Lavinia mulled over the unknown interference that kept her psychic skills undependable. The conversation brought on a look of uneasiness when her mother's connection was severed. The group was closing in on the blind side of the mansion when Rosalyn was surprised by the ability to feel a friendly presence out amongst the weeds. The sorrowful voice was that of a young girl, mourning. Her childish tone was a banshee's moan, a moan that belonged to the wind.

"Mike, can I see the light?" Rosalyn asked with some urgency. Michael handed it over. Rosalyn honed in on the density of bushes to her left, making laps with the light stream. Michael, curious, watched with cursory glances at his backside. "Tony!" Rosalyn yelled, stopping in place. Anthony swung backward. Rosalyn's light elicited the barest trace of an outline a stone's throw away. Anthony walked up next to her, his light tacking hers.

"What do you see?" Anthony asked. He and Michael waited for an answer. Rosalyn took several steps forward to the edge of the trail. Anthony and Michael followed suit.

Rosalyn narrowed the light in on a metallic silver sheen. *This is no child.* She drew upward on the spirit's skin wrappings, bound in a bulk of clunky, elongated humanistic projections. Anthony and Michael's gaze lifted the sizable height of perceived vacant air. The menace was the height of an entrance tree, posing like a prowler ready to spring on its victims. The produced childlike mourning hushed from the black crater of a mouth and two giant balls of stark white poked out of a top-heavy oval head in a stare Anthony and Michael were blessed to be spared.

Rosalyn surrendered her nerves at the pureness of the white eyes and the upward corded arms threating to rend flesh. She could not see the terror's nub of a nose twitch her scent beneath the layers of metallic sheen before the spirit leapt at her. Eager projected talons became the light in a disturbing cry that catapulted Rosalyn back on staggering legs where she was caught in Michael's arms. "What is it?" Michael asked.

"Rosalyn, what do you see?" Anthony shouted over him. She wrenched at Anthony, speechless, frozen in Michael's grip. Her face had become a bundle of fear. She wanted to say '*Run!*' yet her mouth did not move. The panic-stricken look she gave Anthony was fleeting but felt like an eternity. She and his light turned back out at the attacker. There was a moment of sheer dread watching the field. Rosalyn pulled away from Michael in a shock, staggering a couple of brave steps forward. Her eyes searched behind the running water of her hood. The spirit was gone, the false feeling of a friendly presence as well.

Michael and Anthony gathered around Rosalyn. "What did you see?" Anthony asked. She swung around, shaken. Her breath puffed a cloud of condensation at the two.

"A magic is at play over me. I can no longer hear my mother. I cannot trust myself. Let's be quick, I want to leave!" With that, Anthony led on. Rosalyn placed her mom back in her handbag under her slicker. She offered Michael the light back.

"You keep it." Michael put an arm around her and pulled her close, walking side by side. He could feel her trembling as she looked back.

Twirling lights, smoking breath and sloshing gaits put Rosalyn's episode behind them. The blind side of the mansion gained sight where a scarred exterior and broken boarded windows extended on their right. The profusion of wild Earth emerged from everywhere else the lights roamed. Their paranoia was heightened from all manner of things shifting in the stirring rain. They headed east, the blacked-out mountains ahead.

"Come here!" Anthony conducted the group together at the fence's farthest back edge. He cast his light across the mansion's back yard at the faint melted words. Rosalyn merged their lights to discern the vague writing. "Charnel House" was spray-painted in runny letters above what appeared to be a descending staircase. The three shared a faceless look and continued on the beaten path.

The mansion drifted away and the end of the tree wall soon succeeded. The area became vast, yet despite its openness, a suffocating quality could not be escaped. The group somehow maintained their nerve, even with this interminable vulnerability building underneath the skin. Michael sneezed hard and he shivered from his under layers that were soaked from the fall. Rosalyn clutched him for warmth. Anthony's face was flushed in a hot sweat, his eyes seamed by wrinkles from straining into the great unknown. His light drew out slats of splintered wood under a waterfall of sliding rain. "Barn!" Anthony puffed. The group approached the site with caution for safe examination.

The shabby walls and protruding, triangular roof gave shelter to a doorless square opening at the front of the barn. The group gathered themselves parallel to the ominous entryway. It neighbored the trail perhaps ten feet, treacherous in every sense of the word. Will and reason impelled the group to move on.

"Are we going in?" Michael asked. The two lights were being eaten alive by the interior's black quintessence.

"I have to," Anthony said.

Michael had no second thought. "So are we."

"No, I am," Anthony said with a swing of his head.

"Tony, we're coming with you," Rosalyn demanded.

There was no time to argue. "Eyes peeled then."

The three traversed the weeds with striding steps off the trail. The path leading up to the access point was overgrown to the size of kids. Tumbleweed snagged and perforated their camouflage pants. It was a workout keeping light on the entrance and their backs while navigating their steps. Anthony lifted his light on a whitish discoloration of the wood atop the entrance, thinking it might possibly be the old hanging place of Iosk. A closing sweep of their outside surroundings found their lights on a sanguine carpet inside. The two-story barn crowned their heads at the entrance.

They swatted their hoods off. The heft of rain was respite under the barn's projecting roof, an interlude they were grateful for. They could now see, hear and think more clearly, basking in the freshness rolling around their heads and neck. Anthony spread his arm across the front of Michael and Rosalyn, barring them from entering. A serious inspection was needed first. They stood before the square of darkness, surveying the interior. "Smell that?"

"Yes," Rosalyn said, covering her nose.

Michael did a stuffed sniff. "I can't smell anything, my nose is plugged."

"Decomposition," Anthony said.

Their lights organized a search of the high roof's expanse, but like the roof, the walls were of a black abysmal color and likewise impenetrable. Ornate floor chandeliers gleamed back with reflective crystals. The rows of dark mahogany pews below them were positioned in a Greek lower case Lambda fashion. These rows extended from the blood-red carpet to a walking space between the chandeliers. Their lights could not espy the furthest extent of the barn's boundaries.

"We're in a place of concentrated evil. Be ready for anything," Anthony said.

"Like what?" Michael asked.

"Anything."

Rosalyn, crestfallen, said a private imprecation as she fought in vein to get a reading. With that, they pressed inward. The carpet had a cushiony surface that bowed underneath their footsteps. The three stayed close in a single file, aligned down the center of the barn. They spread out their lights in a constant back and forth. The rotten odor intensified. Michael felt Rosalyn pressed up against his back. He in turn pressed against Anthony's.

The outer wood creaked as rain pellets knocked to get in. Their coats swished as they walked, creating more noise than was welcome for surveillance. Rosalyn thought about how easy it would be for them to be boxed in with no visible exit besides the one they'd come in from. The black-colored structure absorbed their light rays into an oblivion. This did not escape Michael's notice, he had wanted to ask why the walls did what they did but was apprehensive about speaking out loud.

The carpet directed them down the individually inspected pews where the odor bred and dust covered the seats from non-use. The chandelier's crystals reflected starlit cataract eyes from the back of the extended seats, giving loose nerves over to fidgets. "Whoa, hey." Anthony shifted sideways to give a view that amounted in a momentary moratorium of the faculties. "The smell." He pointed his light.

The female corpse was nude, blue and bloated under a gloss coat finish of reddish-brown blood. She died in a curled position. Her right-side parts were folded over her. Her blood-encrusted fingers were knotted and toes constricted to her heels. The swollen arms hung awkward and rigid across her gassy chest like the crusty hair across her vacant glass eyes. The upper half of the face lay gaunt. The other end was flabby with collected fluid. The skin of the twenty-something-year-old swelled off her bones. It was an extensive slit that had disemboweled the once impregnated belly. The ghastly sight told a story of self-mutilation by way of the weapon at her arched heel, a sharpened butter knife imprinted in glittered crimson. There she lay next to a red robe; a Jane Doe puddle, enveloped by her own vital fluids upon the diffused carpet of similar essence.

Michael became sickened at the sight of the first dead body that he'd ever seen up close, especially in the manner she died. Rosalyn swung her light towards their backs. "What?" Michael asked. Anthony was reading the words written in the victim's blood on the podium when he jerked back.

The Layout

"I thought I heard something." Rosalyn's voice quavered. Besides the pews flaunting eye-chasing shadows on the carpet and the black walls bordered with cataracts, the interior was as it had appeared when they walked in. However, Rosalyn did notice the exit could not be distinguished from the walls and it leant an uncomfortable sensation of being confined.

Rosalyn's metallic spirit roamed her timorous thoughts but these fears were shelved when she began receiving a marginal signal from her mother. This signal is what she had heard. "It's Mom!" She hastened to retrieve Lavinia's skull from her handbag for a stronger signal. Michael explored the void surroundings where the light could not stick. He shivered a chill down his spine, which he blamed on his damp undergarments. Anthony watched his companion's backs and his own.

Rosalyn produced the skull, facing her mother in an intense concentration. The entrance flashed a square of brilliant-white flashes that exhaled in a thunderous crash. "Run!" Rosalyn yelled, dashing for the exit. Michael and Anthony were galvanized at her heels, looking for the undetected threat. "Run! Run!"

The barn's frame outside united in a series of amplified creaks. The chandelier crystals collided in a riotous jingle of tumultuous shakes. The carpet shifted and the three were flung in a fluctuating imbalance. Michael caught Rosalyn from falling, having no free hand with which she could brace herself. Michael took the flashlight, her arm and the lead with an enhanced speed. "Get us out, Mike! The barn is alive!" Rosalyn yelled. Michael's light was pointed at the exit, a square aperture that was shrinking. "Faster!" Rosalyn shouted. Michael fought the moving floor, balancing their combined weight.

The bones of their bodies seemed to separate with each jarring eruption of the foundation. The exit was rising and falling from the top and bottom like the maw of a beast sealing its meal. Anthony's ribs rammed a pew corner and he cried out. Michael whipped a glance around. Anthony was behind him, pushing him onward. The exit was a narrow letterbox opening.

"Get ready to jump!" Michael yelled. Their feet were on a roller coaster. "Jump!" They leapt through what was left of the void's compressing jaws, feeling its teeth sink and raise against their slickers. They emerged outside in a white burst of rolling grunts being force fed bushes.

Michael heard Anthony's urgency. Swift and agile, he was on his feet. He could see the nature of his friend's emergency in the flashes of lightning. Anthony was ensnared in the barn's inimical entryway from the knees down. The vice-like structure was attempting to crush his legs. Anthony reached out a hand for Michael to grab, attempting to free himself with the other by pressing against the steel jaws. Michael dropped his flashlight for a double-handed clasp. Anthony hollered out with a wince, his shout choked off. Rosalyn joined the tug of war and, inch by inch, they gained movement but it wasn't fast enough. The thunder cracked like a bone breaking and it was hard to distinguish if it wasn't Anthony being broken apart at the seams. Then, with a throwing release, the three hit the dirt.

Michael rushed to retrieve his light, throwing back on his hood to shield off the onslaught of rain. He barely had it in hand when Anthony and Rosalyn drew him upright and away from the barn. Anthony showed a minor limp in keeping pace but made on. A chain of puffing breath led them back to the trail where the three looked back in steadfast awe. The sky cracked above as the rain continued to beat down on their heads. The barn's entrance was covered over by the interior void. Their eyes strained against the elements at the inexplicable sight that culminated in illuminating flashes of continuous lightning.

Something was trying to break down the barn's outer walls from inside, rocking the exterior. The wood stretched out of shape, it's slats tested to the extreme in a chaotic display of random bowing. Whatever it was, it could not get out. "What's happening?" Michael asked as the thunder broke.

"We awoke the wicked church with our lights!" Rosalyn answered. Bemusement overwhelmed Michael.

"Let's find the altar," Anthony said.

2

Lightning blinded overhead, crashing down to Earth. Farther into the unknown they advanced, amalgamated fireflies in a storm. The wooden creaks of

The Layout

the barn were rained out. The morphine of adrenaline was wearing off and replaced with a subtle, ever-increasing ache of overtaxed muscles and joints. Rosalyn and her mother were discussing the all-too-coincidental reconnection to one another. They had a feeling Blackie had a part in their escape, but for what purpose they could not ascertain.

"Did either of you catch the message the girl wrote in her blood on the podium?" Anthony asked.

"No," Michael said.

"Rosalyn?" Anthony called.

"What?" She came out of her private conversation.

"I said, did you catch the message that the girl wrote in her blood?"

"I didn't. What did it say?"

"She wrote, 'Kill the babies' which leads me to believe the sacrifices are being bred by the Watchers. This also means, by my count, they're down one. If the church was attended, she'd been found and removed." Michael and Rosalyn's hold on each other's waist tightened. "Iosk is perhaps required for service. There was a bleached area on the wood above the doorway. I assume that's where Iosk hung. It's about one hundred centimeters from what I could tell."

Lighting flickered around their world. The black and white flashes brought out their surroundings where a face appeared. A prominent screaming face, released from the mantle of night. The three stirred, their nerves unhinged at the abrupt grotesquery. The flashes stopped as fast as they started, leaving the weak streams of flashlights to uncover what the mind did not want to assimilate.

The obtrusion rested perhaps seven feet from its visitors where the trail ended and the mouth of the poignant rock formation leapt upward in a fixed agony. The loose-jawed trio explored the rock's rugged edges. It upraised from soil with deep-set orifices bound by facial contortions. Rain slid down its projections from graven eye pits onto a jutted, off-kilter pyramidal nose, draining into a mouth wherein darkness lied.

"That must be the altar. I imagine the face personifies the sacrificee's anguish," Anthony said. He stepped from the stalled line of his companions, digesting the unsettling information with a wearied, degenerative brain.

"Tony, what are you doing?" Rosalyn asked. He was getting too close to the mouth for her comfort. She had seen a brief vestige of teeth in the movement of their light streams.

"It's okay!" Michael kept an unobtrusive light on his friend. Anthony hunched under the mouth's reared lips and examined the rock up close. He gauged the elevation to be roughly fifteen feet to its peak and a diameter of nearly twenty feet. The anthropologist rallied back with the others. "It's an anthropoid altar, preternaturally sculpted out of volcanic basalt. It's tiny for a crag, but it's not just a crag. The mouth is a descending pit covered in mineral formations, stalactites and stalagmi—"

A flash of lightning stole Anthony's breath and opened the rock's harrowing recesses. The crash amplified a gaining reluctance to stay. "Rosalyn, can you tell us if the offerings have been made yet?" She thought about it, her morale low. There was only one way to find out. Lavinia argued to the contrary in her ear.

"I can try." Rosalyn detached from Michael, placing her protesting mom back in her handbag. "Brace my arms." She lifted her arms for support. Anthony took one armpit and Michael the other, looping her arms around their necks and their arms around her poised back.

"Why are we bracing you?" Michael's worry was evident.

"I will project out of body and take a look inside."

"Is that safe?" Michael asked what Anthony was uncertain of also.

"The body will be disconnected. Without it, I cannot be damned." The content of the conversation was out of Michael's league.

"Rosalyn, are you positive? I just meant for you to get a reading," Anthony said.

"We haven't the benefit of choice. It's incontestable when it comes down to it, isn't it? Marissa needs me, so let me get it over with so we can go home. I've had enough for one evening."

Michael and Anthony held Rosalyn. "Wait!" Michael said.

"What?" Rosalyn shouted. Michael sneezed back to back and shivered to readjust. She felt bad for shouting at him but she was terrified.

"Sorry. I'm ready," Michael said, sniffing.

"Alright, here goes," Rosalyn said in a shallow breath. Michael had questions he couldn't ask, such as how long would it take and how she could see where she was going. The three confronted the mouth's sepulchral throat. Rosalyn's stark trembles shook her male pillars. The light beams peered inside at the shimmering teeth, building a reluctance to let her go through with it.

It was too late. Rosalyn's vessel uprooted from her body, causing her to sink in Michael and Anthony's arms. Her incorporeal self floated into the screaming recess. Flashes of lightning played over her second body. The cavern's icicle-shaped teeth tapered an upper and lower row of impalers from sources undetected. Rosalyn slipped between a gap in the teeth guided by her handler's light streams and, as she drifted down the pit, everything went black.

She dropped downward into its depths, feeling the craggy rock chute compress her. The deeper she delved, the tighter the pit squeezed. Her vessel was becoming too constricted so she decided to head back up. She lifted and found herself stuck. She challenged the fetters of rock and sank deeper from her struggles.

****

Michael and Anthony held onto the eerie limp manikin of Rosalyn's dead yet alive physical shell. Neither could look into the mouth of the rock face while Rosalyn remained inside. Their worries were too numerous and supernatural. Out of their porthole hoods, they surveyed the settings. Rolls of rain, flashes of lightning and crashes of thunder extended the expanse. The flashes created legions of demons out of paranoia. It was best not to think what could be out there, yet be ready for what may come.

Michael's thoughts deviated into an idle second wind. He thought of how he'd miss everyone he cared for. How his parents would react to his death.

What would be his final words? He thought of his dream of being a judo champion and how it seemed so important yesterday, but meant nothing today. How he'd been so wrong about his father. How he wished he had time to make things right with him.

A shift of Rosalyn's body weight pulled Michael out of his head. Anthony's arms waned. A lifetime of serious adventure had left its dents. "You got her?" Michael asked, sore himself.

"Yeah." Anthony readjusted his grip. Michael sneezed, causing his nose to run.

"I can hold her?" Michael offered.

"No!" Anthony's voice fought from the shallows.

"How much longer, you think?" Michael asked. Anthony regretted letting Rosalyn travel down the pit.

"Not long." Anthony was tired with regret. Tired from apprehension. Just plain tired.

****

Rosalyn was being crammed down the pit into a score of infernal chants. Her frantic writhings dug her deeper and deeper until she was wedged into a narrowing crevice. The edges pinned her astral self still. The plethora of voices began to heighten in tempo and overwhelm her.

"*We've got you.*" "*Yes, we have her.*" "*Sarah? Sarah?*" "*Mom, Dad, where are you?*" "*I can't see!*" "*You're mine.*" "*Ha,ha,ha,ha,ha,ah,ahh,ahhh,ahhh!*" "*Does anybody have a light?*" "*Let me out! Let me out! For the love of God, let me out!*" "*Ho, ho, we've caught a fish.*" "*Kick and scream, kick and scream.*" "*I can't get out!*" "*Can you get me out?*" "*There's no escape.*" "*No, you stay.*" "*Impressive dark, wouldn't you say, my dear?*" "*I can't take it anymore!*" "*Nobody's home.*" "*Call my parents, they'll be worried about me.*" "*Give me back my soul!*" "*God help us!*" "*There is no God, but you have me!*" "*I have to call my parents!*" The immaterial tongues were a tumult of madness. Rosalyn was entombed in their yammerings, buried alive amid rock and her own cries.

****

Rosalyn's physical body juddered out of control. "What's happening?" Michael looked at Anthony for answers he didn't have.

"Rosalyn? Rosalyn? Hold her tight!" Anthony said, shining a light in her hood.

"I have her, what's happening? What can I do?" In her thrashing, they could hear the rattling of bones, the bouncing of teeth and the swishing of saliva. The convulsions shook the hood off her head, spraying rain across her deathly pale face. Her sable hair had fallen in a clump. Her eyes rolled back in her head. Her mouth hung open, her blue tongue slipping back in her throat. "Tony, do something!"

"Rosalyn, can you hear me?" Anthony used his fingers to clear her windpipe. Saliva and rain drooled out. He drew down her drooping face to keep her from choking on her tongue. "Oww!" Anthony pulled his glove from her mouth, shaking his hand. She had convulsed and bit him. Anthony switched hands and straightened her head in a subtle lean forward, controlling the jaw so she wouldn't bite her tongue off. "It's a seizure, I think," Anthony said.

"Why?"

"I don't know. Hold her steady!"

"I am!"

Michael's heart pounded and his eyes were blurry as he watched, powerless. A gurgling sound emanated from Rosalyn's restrained vocal cords, sinking the men's hearts and bringing them closer to her colorless lips. Anthony's light saw no life in her eyes. "Rosalyn?" "Rosalyn?" "Rosalyn?" They called numerous times.

"Tell me what to do?" Michael pleaded, listening harder than he ever had before. The gurgling created nonsensical noises. A terrible sound formed, similar to discharging phlegm from the throat. Neither man spoke, afraid to miss any word that she might utter. There was a deep-set concentration between them. The sound that proceeded was like a record player stopped in mid-play, a sound of life winding down. Rosalyn wilted, her head falling forward in a pose of death.

3

"Rosalyn! Rosalyn!" Anthony smacked her face. Michael's heart jackhammered.

"What's happening?"

"Mike, stop, you are not helping!" Michael clenched his teeth. Anthony was no stranger to the sights and sounds of death. He had seen and heard it more times than he cared to remember. Anthony checked Rosalyn's vitals. "Let's get her to the Jeep."

"We can't! She's in the tunnel!"

"She's not breathing, Mike!"

Michael carried a blank stare of disbelief, waiting for her to come back, for her turquoise pupils to return and look upon him as lovely as ever. "What can we do?"

"We need to get her to the Jeep. Yucca will know what to do, I don't."

"What happens if she comes back and we're not here?"

"Mike, she's dead."

"No!" The atmosphere was heavy enough without the weight of the Earth crashing down. "She's not dead!"

"Mike!" Anthony was in no condition for the right words. "Either way, we have to get her to Yucca. Help me get her to the Jeep, I can't do it without you."

"She's not dead! She can't be! She's in there!" Michael's light signaled the crag's hideous mouth.

"You might be right but, like Rosalyn said, she can't be damned, which means our chances of retrieving her astral body are possible. We will get her to Yucca, he will know what to do for her. I don't! I knew I shouldn't have—Just help me get her to the Jeep." Anthony gathered her hair and fixed her hood over her lolling head.

"I got her." Michael sniffed, swinging her ultra-light shell up into his arms. "We'll get you back," Michael said to Rosalyn.

"You can have her back." Michael and Anthony's insides shuddered from the stranger's voice. They threw light on the dark-figured throng blocking the trail. A recognizable spirit stood at the forefront. *Hearth!* Anthony's mind reacted.

"Run!" He pushed Michael south while he ran north, his inner compass guiding him through the multitude of bushes. It was a miracle Anthony found track at the rate he was moving.

"Stop!" the stranger's voice commanded.

Ankle-deep in tacky mud and knee-deep in bush, Anthony split west. If his instincts served him right, he would find himself at the barbed-wire fence. It was in the swing of his light that a methuselah character descended from the wringing sky wearing a vermillion cowl and vestment. The robe was striped by a gold cross with a black circular centerpiece. The descender's wizened features were filtered heavy in shadow. Two ravened dots peered out from its hood. Anthony slowed at the unbelievable sight. The stranger was accompanied by a slew of grounded allies. Anthony darted south for the trail, his heart travelling faster than his feet. He was surrounded by numbers he couldn't conceive, reaching for him in the chasing expanse of perpetual darkness.

From the side, a hand of flesh caught Anthony by his slicker's arm and the woman's excited breath caught a reactive slug in return. The sock made quick work of the red-robed figure. "Stop him!" yelled a male's voice. Anthony found the trail and went west in a blast of rain. There was no time to grab his gun, only to run in a life or death sprint. Things of the dark dodged his light. He panted as a burn was building in his chest. Adrenaline coursed through his veins. He swatted at the touchy-feelies all over him, throwing his light at his back to ward off light-allergic spirits. The crude figures kept on coming in a dizzying array of ghastly hooded faces and darkling anatomy. Anthony connected with the crowd and from every blindsided angle he reacted to their grasps in jerks of near misses.

A glint of silver chain link came into view of Anthony's light. A kick to the back of his foot compromised him in a few clumsy steps which he turned into galloping strides. He showed impressive coordination under such fire. The trail swept under foot. The mansion might as well have not existed and, in Anthony's view, it didn't. Only the nasty noises behind and to his right.

He reached the trail at the front of the house, knocking the water off it and headed straight through the dense bushes, realizing full well that the tree line was a death trap. The road was straight ahead. He was wheezing from the burn within his overloaded chest. Survival instincts kept his mind on auto pilot. He would jump the fence when it came.

Anthony maneuvered the scores of bushes like a panther. The back of his raincoat ripped with a tearing sound, spurring him into a sudden conniption fit. He leapt over a bulky bush of thorns. There he was, stuck in an airborne commitment of uncertainty of whether he would make it. He landed at the edge, the thorns snagging his pants. Anthony yanked free with parts of the bush attached to him. He was awarded by the shrieking cries of some of his pursuers that were not so fortunate. It was a small victory which chased his ears. The horde quieted, leaving Anthony with his own sounds of panting exertion. He carried on, showing no ease in his lunging steps, led by a cunning knack to survive.

Images of the barbed wire cutting him off sprang into his mind. It became an immediate reality. The three lines of rusted barbed-wire fencing came up to his abdomen, crotch and knees. In that moment of delay, he could feel the pile of appendages come down on him with throaty moans of miasmic pleasure. Anthony huffed a breath that burned his chest. He performed a sideways jump, pressing down the top coil, fully aware of the descending drop on the other side. What he didn't see was that his boot hooked the bottom coil, lifting it up and over with him.

To Anthony's dread, he found himself caught upside down, hanging by one leg. The back of his head slapped the sinking hill. In a frenzy, he tried to fight the groping fiends dragging him up. Rusted points ripped throughout Anthony's clothing, the barbs connecting with his skin. In the tussle against the gathered contours, Anthony dropped his light down the hill. He was left fighting in the dark.

The barbed wire which had been his downfall was also his savior, making it difficult for the horde to drag him over to their side. Anthony let out a cry as a barb went deep into his back. The pack grew excited with bizarre moans. "Stop fighting and we'll free you!" someone shouted.

The rain beat down on Anthony's face with wet hands smothering his openings. It was impossible to execute an exit without vision. Anthony's heartbeat expanded his temples. He was going to pass out. A fresh stab of barb awoke him in a scream under the dog pile of clutches. His eyes exploded open and his torso jolted forward, just to be pushed down on the same barb twice. The blood oozed out of his wounds across his back and sides. The sting of metal twisting in spurting skin locked his teeth.

His hands would have gone for the area to move the wire if they weren't busy trying to pry the copious attachments off him. He would get one appendage off and another would follow. It was a defenseless position and he found himself wanting to give up. As more barbs stuck him, he would let out bloodcurdling shrieks that were answered by excited breaths that yelled, "Stop fighting!"

The rain did away with his tears as it hammered his burning eyes. In Anthony's blinking shuffle, the debilitating barb punctured him again and again in his recoil. He screamed as the nails dug through him. Upmost pain and dread accentuated to a suffocating zenith. In a last-ditch effort, Anthony shook with what he had left. His face was freed and he found himself dangling after a short freefall. His arms extended out in the air for a savior who wasn't there.

Anthony could see a hint of light from his flashlight below on what he could now detect was the ground. "Get him off the wire!" The horde gasped in a tenacious hold of his back, lifting him upward. His light began sinking. Anthony's pumping legs shook his body like a fly in a web, renewed by a chance escape.

"Stop squirming!"

Anthony's foot kicked somebody who cried out. He could hear his limbs being pulled apart, piece by piece. He fought with draining lungs when he lowered with a ripping sound that stretched out to a tear. It wasn't his limbs being pulled apart, he realized, it was the sound of his raincoat tearing. Anthony free-fell for a second before hitting mud and he was thrown into a downward roll. The darkness around him turned, slashed with the yellow of his flashlight. He landed flat with his face shoved in flooded dirt.

Anthony lifted on exhausted arms. His thermal was soaked and his back oozed with a fiery pain. Exasperated discontent from the hilltop mob robbed his hearing. He grabbed his submerged light, staggering to a stance and struck out in a confused, sideways gallop. The crowd quieted, ordered silent.

Anthony trusted his judgement on direction, despite his extreme head fog. He had forgotten the entrance flooding that blocked his way to the Jeep. In a huge dose of desperation, his light found some uprooted rocks that he was able to step on to reach the other side. His light shone upon his Jeep's green finish a short distance away. At that moment, it was the most beautiful thing he had ever seen. From what he could tell, the mob hadn't bothered to pursue him but, hobbling as he was, he took no chances.

Anthony plunked down in the Jeep, settling his dripping weight. He locked the doors with a trembling finger. The stab depressions excreted wet and sticky blood on his seat. The excruciating pains slowed his movement in getting a move on. Bracing himself from falling over the steering wheel, he coordinated the retrieval of his keys from his pant pocket. His wild eyes panned the windows, expecting an attack in the interim. It took multiple tries, but at last he got the key into the ignition. The Jeep started right up and he was off. The rutty dips in the road burdened his wounds. He weakened into a slouch from blood loss, watching for Michael and Rosalyn in the bright of his headlights.

The predicament they were in came back to him and he let out a cry of discouragement. Tears burst out of his raw, tired eyes. He honked the horn, banging on it out of frustration, hoping Michael and Rosalyn would appear out of the darkness. He drove with a controlled speed. The curve came and went, his palm on the horn. "Where are you?" Anthony said as he slipped off the wheel, semi-conscious. He grabbed it like a man sinking into the ocean and, with an intake of breath, pushed against the wheel to straighten himself. He had the feeling of being knocked over the head. A yellow light darted across his vision and he thought he was going out.

"Tony!" Anthony hit the brakes, hurling water at the flagging flashlight. Michael stood holding Rosalyn out in the road. Anthony managed an insane person's smile, his eyes chasing them in disbelief. Michael's desperate knock reminded Anthony the door was locked. He pitched forward, separating the holes on his back to unlock it. His head waved in a dizzy spell of eruptive discomfort. Anthony climbed backward with grunts of effort. The passenger side door swung open and the seat pulled forward.

"Hurry," Anthony struggled out.

"I am." Michael's voice was vigorous. Rosalyn's comatose body was strapped into the backseat. Michael kept a peripheral eye open. The horn went off. "Are they coming?" Michael yelled up front. He jumped into the front seat, eyes attentive at the windshield. He slid off his hood and looked over at Anthony in a stark pause. Anthony was face first in the wheel, dead.

4

"Nooo!" Stacked with panic, Michael pressed Anthony back into his mottled seat. The horn went silent, leaving only the resonance of pouring rain. Michael yanked off his glove and went for a two-fingered neck pulse. His pulse was weak, but it was there. Michael's breath released a held gust, his voice was poorly ventilated. "What did they do to you?"

"They? We're hardly responsible," said a pleasant voice from the backseat. Michael's gut wrenched inward. "Anthony tangled himself on the fence. We attempted to free him." Michael readied for who he would see behind him. He lifted his head, looking back at the lustrous black pools peering out of Rosalyn's hood. His head trembled of its own volition. "Michael, fear not. We are not enemies. I can return Rosalyn and Debbie to you—"

"Debbie!" Michael's stomach sunk. "You have Debbie?" he blurted out.

"Settle down Michael. We did what we had to do. I can explain everything." Michael struggled to maintain composure. "As I was saying, I can return Debbie and Rosalyn and provide safe passage for you, your family and friends from Argauthartera. I will explain how, and in the meantime, allow my subjects to treat Anthony before he bleeds to death." The driver side door handle lifted.

"No!" Michael leapt over Anthony to grab the handle, gaping up at the red robed mob outside the window. The mob stood staring in with deadpan faces, making no attempt to break into the locked door.

"Michael, we can save his life. He is losing far too much blood. Untreated, he will die. When you and I have finished our arbitration, I will give him back to you, fully healed. I have the capability." Michael continued to hold onto the handle. "Do not let your ignorance be his undoing. I assure you, no guile is involved. I come to you in peace." Michael's mind racked for what to do. His eyes wandered the lights of the Jeep surrounded by robed sentinels.

"Don't let him die," Michael begged out loud.

"You have my word, he will not. Let my subjects take him and I will see to it he lives." Michael's fingers lifted from the door handle and unlocked it. He drew back into to his own seat, optionless. Michael looked at Rosalyn's pale face that channeled the smooth male voice. From the neck down, her body remained limp and unanimated, still belted in the seat. The sight was unnervingly strange and reduced Michael to stiff breaths.

The driver's side door opened. "Bring him right back to you," said a friendly faced hooded man who hooked Anthony under the arms while another swooped in to take his legs.

"Easy does it," said the other man. Michael was confused by the amiable conduct. The door closed and the two were left to talk. The robed mob dispersed with Anthony being carried toward the farmhouse. Michael gained some nerve.

"You're Blackie?"

"To some. Let's call me that, for my precise designation is by a human, unpronounceable. My genuine appearance can be off-putting to your kind. Hence, I present myself through Rosalyn and speak to you in your own language. And I am here to tell you Michael, Rosalyn and Debbie can be recovered. I can see them back to you."

Michael thought to ask if Debbie was dead. "In return for what?" he asked instead.

"For your cooperation. The preconceived perspective you have of me is inaccurate. Our partnership will depend solely on perspective. What I ask is you at least grant me audience to an unbiased hearing. If at the end, we do not agree, so be it. I will return Anthony to you healed and you will be free to leave."

Michael sat stiff. "With Rosalyn?"

Blackie's eyes did not move. "In her current state, yes. Come to a reached agreement, different entirely. I will send her with you tonight, complete as she arrived. The choice will be yours in the end."

Michael swallowed, his tongue dry. "I'm listening."

"The Iosk skull is my property. It was stolen from me by three boys, two of which are dead." Michael's brows drew inward. "Be not so hasty in judgement over me, I didn't kill the boys. And assuming I were the killer, which I am not, perish the thought. Why would I kill them before I reclaim my property?"

"Then who did?" Blackie looked to the side, worried a misdirected hostility would show.

"A rogue betrayer of my inner circle. My subject wanted the power of Iosk for himself. He killed the boys during an interrogation. He would have destroyed Vince too, if I hadn't stopped him. Al was the fallen's name. He was the father of Jarrod. Jarrod and Ethan are the murdered boys. You know them as the Harbingers." Michael's ears perked. "Yes, I am aware of the Harbingers. Rosalyn's mind is open to me." Michael grimaced.

"Don't be upset at me, I have obstacles I must also overcome. What's necessary is necessary. I make myself vulnerable for a joint effort to solve our demarcations. I am aware of the obstacles you face. You are not aware of mine. You have a deal. I have a deal. Mine just so happens to have a hefty price tag. Thus, the deceased woman you found in my church." Blackie could see Michael's energy harden. "Before you jump to conclusions, my deal requires sacrifices, which you're aware. What you don't realize is, I have impregnated the women of Yucaipa with stillborn babies to mitigate the barbarity, for what is required. You must be broad-minded to avoid a lopsided opinion in a treaty to find common ground."

"I come to you because it is my conviction. You are capable of a mature dialogue. Let me share my side. We'll get back to what I can proffer you." Michael sighed. Blackie's eyes turned on him. "Tell you what, for additional good faith between you and I, I will dole out Rosalyn for you tonight." Michael shifted upward in surprise, looking around for the catch.

"You're serious?" Michael's eyes narrowed.

"No contrivance. She will leave with you as she came in."

"Okay...thanks. Tell me your side." Rosalyn's lips lifted.

"Gracious of you." Blackie's eyes softened a tint. "I was sent here as a scout around five millenniums ago. In my trips, I was to observe and report the status of a spreading parasite. Your presence was distinctly palpable on Earth, becoming more destructive as your kind was evolving. We have effaced similar, non-mutual relationships on other worlds, whose destructive influence had laid waste to their own settlements." Michael's features pinned to the thought. "After their removal, life restored to balance. Rarely is there a reoccurrence. It was decided from my reports that the pestilence of the human species was to be removed. Your kind is a plague on the balance of your planet. They must be quarantined. There is no other alternative." Michael stared after him. "Argauthartera's function is to quarantine disorderly parasites of such destructive types." Michael's tension grew.

"What makes you so dangerous is your rapid expansion. You procreate when overpopulated. Your species is at nearly six billion people with no signs of slowing. At that rate, what will the population be in one hundred years from now, on a human time scale?" Blackie waited for an answer. "I'm asking?" His voice remained pleasant. Michael considered the question.

"Eight billion?" He answered with an unsure flex of his shoulders.

"Try eleven." Michael was taken aback. "Eleven billion consuming parasites. Imagine that, Michael, if you can. In a fraction of time. Resources are already ill provided for your own. Soon, they will be rare and you will turn violent until no life is left on your planet. Your kind will take all life with you, not only your species. You're a self-serving parasite by no fault of your own. Your DNA is your god. You're at the mercy of sex and violence. You're a variety with the ability to cognitively discern your problematic developments, yet they remain unsolved. Why? I'll tell you why. Your primary function is to consume for yourselves. Your DNA demands it. You have avaricious billionaires yet starving populations. Can you explain that to me?"

"I can't."

"I realize you think I'm the evil one from what Yucca told you and the stories you've heard of me, but I would ask you to look at your own kind's behavior. You cycle in continuous warfare, in the name of freedom which you will not receive. You fish your seas barren. You pollute your skies and poison your water. You torture your food in ways my kind can't bear to watch." Michael's forehead ached from the mad scrabble of thoughts. His current state was not adequate for debate.

"You quarrel over the simple, judge without trial, hate over race. Your females are treated unequally. You erect dividing lines for your own petty ownerships. The best among you, the altruistic, cannot be expected to compete with six billion selfish strong. Even virtue by design can be corrupted into self-serving vanity which is often the case with so called, altruistic humans."

"If human beings knew what each other did behind closed doors, the acts you don't disclose. The thoughts you maintain private. Argauthartera wouldn't be coming, you would have killed yourselves off, long ago. I would not have been sent. I believe Rosalyn and you broached this subject already."

Michael waved back and forth, his eyes restless. "What about Argauthartera torturing people, aren't you being hypocritical?"

"Hmm, a perfect segue to what I can proffer. I will provide safe passage from Argauthartera for a list of up to say, one hundred individuals of your choosing. In exchange, you will provide to me Iosk before midnight tomorrow night at my home behind the trees. I will do the rest. Separate from our agreement, the genuinely righteous of your kind will additionally receive a pardon and safe passage." Michael considered the offer with a sideways glance out the window. The rain had lightened. He sniffed, rocking a finger under his nose to back off a sneeze.

"Sounds sketchy. What are your guidelines for determining a righteous person?" Michael asked, despite having no options.

"Fair enough. A person who strives to do what is morally and ethically right given their ability to do so. Obviously, this a general answer but how could I possibly do a check list of righteous behaviors, when they are different for different people. You seem to be grasping what it takes to be a virtuous person in your own life. I do not require perfection, for perfection doesn't exist. Don't forget in addition, I will release Debbie to you. She will be delivered to you upon Iosk's delivery to me."

"Is Debbie dead?" Michael closed his eyes.

"No more than Rosalyn is." Michael took in a deep breath, opening his eyes. "I will also release Vince from his bonds tonight, upon agreement in good faith, and call off Hearth. To rely on the Harbinger's agreement is tantamount to suicide. We'll all end up in Argauthartera by no fault but your own. Put the Harbingers on your list. I hold no ill will. That way you all win. You will have to put Rosalyn and Debbie on the list as well. Don't forget Darla, etcetera. You will only be able to take those you write on your list, so take heed. It must include yourself, everyone. You will be harmlessly transported to your next existence to live in a paradise where your kind's atrocities have no function. Think about it, a real Eden for you and your loved ones. A bargain, if I say so myself."

Michael's face bent uneasy, his mind unsettled. "Isn't there a way we can all get a deal?"

"Michael, you wouldn't want that. I sympathize with your virtuous stance but no…you are not grasping the big picture. The lowest of your kind have come to an end. The war mongers, murderers, rapists, serial killers, pedophiles, those who torture animals, those who mindlessly pollute the planet. They don't deserve a pleasant hereafter. You can't possibly find sympathy for these types of organisms. They are beyond forgiveness. They are the lost causes, the chaos of your planet. The reason I am here. I am referring to the parasites that don't care about anyone but themselves or are just plain sick and demented, which is a blurred line. I have seen the damage they have caused over my time here, my time elsewhere. While the strains of parasitical life forms are different from planet to planet, the results are not. I will not let it continue nor will I expose you to it because you will lose your mind from the concealed truth."

Michael avoided Blackie's black tears. "I can give you examples."

"No need."

"I beg to differ. A couple examples you have to hear, not see like me. I have seen…" Michael's stomach clenched. "your kind hack off the heads of children while their parents were forced to watch, all over access to clean drinking water when there was plenty to share. And after which, they gang raped the woman while the men were forced to watch. They raped the men while the women were forced to watch and then were individually tortured to death." Blackie shook Rosalyn's head. Michael's stomached squeezed, causing him to cough. "I have seen so-called children tear animals apart, just to hear the different types of screams they make, the sound bone makes when it breaks."

"Mercy, I get it." Michael held up a hand.

"No, Michael. No mercy. That's the problem, isn't it? I have seen a father rape his daughter until she was of age to bear his child. His child was born in a basement where they were locked up by their mother and forced to have family orgies."

"Okay, okay! Please, I get it!" Michael's eyes blinked on the verge of tears.

"Michael, I haven't begun to scratch the appalling surface and you ask me to stop. Do you question why I was sent? See things like I do every day and tell me how you would react, honestly? What punishment is suitable for these types? Argauthartera is just. Doesn't the sane part of you say something has to be done for the victims?"

"Yes!" Michael's answer was quick. "Are those the only types going to Argauthartera? No one innocent?" Michael searched for honesty in Blackie's glossy eyes.

"No one innocent."

"You swear?" Michael sleeved his nose, feeling it run down his lip.

"Yes."

"What happens to the rest of life? The animals, the insects? Some are violent."

"Agreed, but they are balanced by nature. They will remain. The human species is who has to be quarantined. None other."

"Then you have a deal," Michael said, with no reserve. Blackie tilted Rosalyn's lips upward.

"Deal. Judicious of you, young man. Think not of the suffering of the fallen but the suffering you're everting for the righteou—" Shots rang out from the farmhouse.

5

Michael swung back, scarcely breathing. The lights were on in the farmhouse but the activity could not be seen from where he sat. An additional few shots rang out.

"Anthony is shooting my subjects!"

Michael turned on Blackie. "Why?"

"I will find out. Michael, Rosalyn will revive soon. I will have Debbie for you tomorrow for the delivery of Iosk. Do not forget your list and don't tell anyone of our deal." Blackie's black pools reflected the importance. "And Michael, Vince will be at his appointment tomorrow. He was not cancelled on."

"He wasn't?"

"No, he will be there. See that you are as well."

"I will be." Rosalyn's eyelids closed and her head fell loose. Michael hopped into the driver's seat. He drove towards the farmhouse, his intense focus looking for Anthony. The windows were alive with robed commotion. Michael jumped when Anthony ripped open the passenger door and leapt inside. "Go! Go! Go!" Michael firm footed the gas pedal.

Anthony was in his underwear, his wounds healed. His pistol was perched on his thigh. The sight triggered Michael's unpleasant gun incident atop everything else in his overactive mind. The Jeep existed Cherry Croft Drive and turned onto Oak Glen Road, gathering speed. Rosalyn leapt forward with a vocal shudder. The world around her consisted of confusion.

"Where?..." she asked, testing her voice. Anthony twisted back. Michael stole a glance at lovely bright turquoise eyes.

"Rosalyn!" Anthony said.

"Where am I?"

"You're okay, you're in the Jeep," Michael said, looking in the rearview. Rosalyn gave Michael and Anthony a strange look.

"I can't tell what's real," Rosalyn said. Anthony's rucked aspect related a similar condition. Rosalyn looked about, recollecting the area. Anthony did the same. Michael coughed a sound of rumbled mucus.

"I'm taking you back to Yucca's," Michael said. Anthony touched his grimy flesh, the gun waving haphazardly. Rosalyn was stuck in stare out her window. The rain had stopped.

6

All but two of the cabin's occupants were asleep. The sound of the fireplace from the next room deepened in the minute of uncommunicative quiet. Michael was wrapped in a blanket, sitting at the kitchen table nursing a cup of warm tea that Yucca said would prevent a cold. Yucca cleared his throat. "Mike, did you make a deal with Blackie?" Michael propped himself up from the table, his blue eyes bleary but wide.

"No, I didn't."

Yucca let out a mocking laugh. "You did. You're a terrible liar."

"I'm not lying." Michael's mind was impaired. He didn't realize how obvious he was coming off. Umber, bold, tough-set eyes bore into his spirit.

"I'll protect your secret. Blackie's desperation is a positive sign. You ought to be proud of yourself for getting Rose and Tony back."

Michael's posture relaxed. "There's no secret."

"You can stop mining your own energy. I'm no fool."

"I never said you were." Michael gave a third-rate performance of being insulted.

"You want me to believe Rosalyn has no interest in you suddenly? Her gifts no longer available to her? That she escaped the altar and that there was no black magic involved? Can you explain why your stories don't match? Anthony swears he was injured beyond repair, yet there is not a mark on him."

"What do you want me to tell you?" Yucca looked behind him at the floor. Michael lifted to see what it was the elder looked at. He observed the blue and silver shattered pieces of the tea cup and saucer plate he'd broke earlier.

CHAPTER 18
Somnambulism

Sunday, 10:03pm

1

Vince heard the taps on the glass. Melissa was huddled behind a beam of light. Her green hooded face lit up at his and he at hers. He opened the window with a subtle squeal, letting the sound of pouring rain in. Vince leant his arms outward. "Easy, I'm sore," Melissa said, watching her steps on the ladder.

"Poor thing. You want some Ibuprofen?"

"I took some, thanks." Wet handfuls helped her in over the towels he laid down for her earlier. Vince closed out the rain as Melissa set down her backpack. They shared hands in a fleeting kiss on her frozen lips. Vince's warmth gave her goosebumps. "Brrr, I'm cold." Melissa shook.

"Yes, you are. Let's get you warm." Melissa slid off her hood in a burst of long blonde curls and rubbed her hands together while Vince fixed the blinds. "I stopped by your house today, you won't believe what happened to me."

"What?"

"I drove to Jarrod's house—" Melissa shot a glance at him.

"You did?"

"Yeah. The place is abandoned. That's why his phone number has been disconnected. I went inside and a naked bum lady was living in the house. Scared the shit out of me."

"You know there are bums around there. You should have waited and gone with me. You didn't get hurt, did you?"

"No. I wanted to face my anxiety in the rain, alone. Besides, I tried to bring you, I stopped by."

"Sorry, I was with friends. Hey, I want to go with you to your appointment tomorrow."

"Can't." Melissa's head jerked sideways.

"Why not?"

"Mom takes me from work. Besides, you wouldn't want to go. You'd have to wait out in the waiting room for, like, an hour."

"I don't mind. I want to support my man." Melissa's pink lips smiled curl to curl. Her emerald eyes refused to be denied.

"You know what?"

"Huh?" Melissa perked up.

"Let me think." Vince turned on the TV and muted it. Melissa removed her glasses, placing them on the nightstand beside their flashlights. *Don't mention Mom's baby, stupid.* "Nah, it wouldn't work, nevermind."

"Tell me what it was."

Vince ground his tooth. "Nothing, it was a stupid idea."

"What, what was it? Tell me."

"It won't work." Vince headed to the metal cabinet and retrieved the shabby blanket.

"I'm going to keep asking you until you tell me." She smiled, a guarantee she would.

"Give me a minute to think about it."

"Okay." Melissa tapped her heel.

The answer didn't take long. "I was thinking I could drive us, if I stayed home tomorrow, assuming my mom is not going to work. She still might be, and then I wouldn't have the car. Plus, you'd have to ditch school." Vince secured the blanket along the bottom seam of his door.

"We can use Dick's car."

"How would you pull that off?"

"Let me figure that out. You just find a way to stay home."

"That's easy. They'll be thrilled I want to stay home, as long as I can assure them they won't get bothered at work by an attack." The lights went out. In the lack of illumination, Melissa eased off her clothing in sets of blinking discomfort from her bruising. "What if my mom stays home?"

"Then she can take us. I'll stay in your room."

"All day?"

"Yeah, why not?"

"Don't get in trouble on my account, but if you're down, I'm down." Vince got into bed.

"I'm down." Melissa slipped into bed, sliding her delicate features against him. "Warm me," she said before he laid his lips on hers, rolling his hands through her soft curls.

2

Melissa's eyes snapped open, dried from tears. She had cried herself to sleep in Vince's arms, unbeknownst to him. She was roused by a low beat of nondescript language coming out of his mouth. Melissa's ears tuned in. Inhuman susurrations tripped over one another. She didn't know Vince to talk to himself in his sleep. He unyoked from their spooning and slid out of bed. Melissa faked asleep, her eyes watchful. The TV white noise bounced off the walls. Its glow brought Vince's static figure to the foot of the bed. He was moving in a helpless manner, his eyes closed, yet seeing. His strings were pulled to the TV to turn it off. He did and the room was steeped into momentary darkness while Melissa's eyes adjusted.

A dim light from the neighbor's house reclaimed a portion of the room's visibility. Vince stood stationary at the foot of the bed, facing his closet. Melissa eyed the flashlights within easy reach on the nightstand, giving her confidence she could react if it came to it. The extraordinary circumstance of what was occurring urged her to remain quiet.

Vince's head tilted back. His mouth opened broad in the light of the window. A batch of arched stakes sprouted out. The long, thick, flexible fasteners drew down on the skin of the host and, with an effort, bent the orifice out of shape. It gave birth to the likeness of an exaggerated black widow spider. The specter leapt off the host and into the blending dark. Vince let out a cavernous breath, accompanying the spirit's exit.

Melissa, aghast, couldn't move anything but her eyes. A tug at the bottom of the bed got her attention. Her eyes went sharp and aware. The bed blankets began pulling. Her paralyzed hands held the covers to her chest, not giving an inch. Her breath was especially silent. *It's crawling up on the bed!*

The mattress sank in and the tops of the legs grew arches in the weak light. A cold sweat ran down her skin. She could make out the bulbous abdomen undulating in her direction. Indents of pressure were felt dotting around her legs. *Do something!* The spider presence was over her midsection when it lifted its legs and cephalothorax. The muscles of Melissa's face bunched in an explosive movement.

"Vince!" She twisted to a tumble of weight off of her, snatching a flashlight from the bedside table and shining it in the direction of the spider. The malignant spirit was out of sight. The light shook like it was in an earthquake on Vince's closed face. "Vince, why are the lights out?" His eyes batted, bringing up a hand to fend off the fluttering beam. Melissa turned on the TV. The hiss filled the specter-free room.

"Turn it down," Vince said, confused by why he was standing. Melissa muted the TV, switching off her light. Her courage returned in the luminance.

"What am I doing?"

"Search me? I think you were sleepwalking. I woke up and the room was dark. I saw you standing there, all creepy like." Vince cast a look around.

"I don't sleepwalk."

"You did."

"It doesn't make sense…"

"Who cares, come back to bed."

"This is weird." Melissa patted the blankets, then lifted them for him. Vince climbed back into bed. "It doesn't make sense." She wrapped his arm around her slowing chest.

"Don't let it bother you." She snuggled, pretending to be tired.

"Seriously, that's wild. I can't believe I did that." Vince's head found his pillow. The beats of Melissa's heart lulled him quiet and eventually he did fall back to sleep. Melissa stayed awake, contemplating why Vince's bonded spirit left him and why it wanted to attach to her.

CHAPTER 19
The Appointment

Monday, 7:25am

1

Melissa stood rapt at Vince's sketch desk, observing the beauty of Plarek in the dawn of a blue and pink morning. The world was limned just how she imagined it, a variegated profusion of beauty beneath two green suns. The belated knock was unexpected, as they figured Vince's mom was staying home. Melissa snatched her flashlight off the bed and took to her pre-arranged spot in the closet. Vince bellowed the lyrics of Metallica to disguise the noise she made. Her joints eased her into a seated position, her flashlight shining as she closed the door from the inside to a cracked opening. Vince popped the door open with his trusted method.

The door opened to his mom dressed in her scrubs for work, her arms at her sides. "Why aren't you ready?" Paula spoke in a mechanical tone. His mom's complexion was olive and healthy, yet something was off. Vince regarded her in her pajamas, grinding his tooth. She had a blank stare with vacant eyes. An electric relay played in Vince's head.

Clean your room! "What are you talking about? I thought you weren't going to work after yesterday—" Vince caught his tongue.

"I am. Get dressed. Your dad's taking me to work and you're going with him."

"Mom, what's my name?" There was an awkward unmoved stare of silence on his mom's behalf. Her speech pattern became less mechanical.

"Vince, what's gotten into you?" She said it with a refreshed awakening in her aspect.

"Nothing." He shook his head.

"Get dressed or we're going to be late. Remember, you have your appointment with Bruce today at three-thirty." Her speech was back to normal.

Vince stopped grinding his tooth. "I haven't forgotten. About that…I was wondering if I could stay home and do my homework here today." His mother's eyes seemed to increase vacancy. Her mechanical tone resumed.

"Stay home…by yourself?"

"Yeah. I'll do my homework. I wanna push my anxiety. See how far I can take it." The answer was slow to process.

"You, alone?"

"Yeah. I won't bother you or Dad at work, I swear."

"You can't, your appointment."

"I know. Jacklyn offered to take me yesterday. I was going to go with Melissa after she gets out of school. She wants to go with me."

Paula remained still, in a blank stare. "Don't be late."

"I won't. I want to go, more than you want me to go. I wouldn't miss it for the world."

"Don't."

"I won't." Vince lowered his voice. "You're taking your pills right, Mom?" He noticed a moving shadow on the hallway cabinets.

"Yes, Vince." He flung his head out into the hall to see what was moving. His mom didn't move. He caught his dad standing at the end of the hall, dressed in his physical therapy uniform.

"Paula, we're going to be late. Vince, you have troubles, call me, not your mom. I don't want you to bother her."

"I won't." Vince looked at his mom. She stared at Greg. He wanted to tell her to stay home. *Something's not right.*

"Don't miss your appointment," Paula said, looking at Greg.

"I won't." She hauled off without asking for a kiss goodbye. Vince's eyebrows lowered.

"Bye, love you," he said, hanging his head out the door.

"Love you too," his dad answered. They walked out, without so much as a look back from either. *Something is definitely not right. The alignment! Oh shit!*

Once the door shut, Vince headed straight to the formal living room window to verify his parents leaving. On the way, he caught sight of his mom's car keys dangling from the mirror rack. He wasn't too keen on taking Dick's car. Vince watched from behind the curtain, dissecting the weirdness that had just transpired.

His dad ushered his mom to the Grand Prix; his demeanor was fidgety. *What's going on?*

Whatever you do, don't mention it to Melissa.

I wouldn't do that. The Grand Prix drove off. He half expected the car to U-turn, his dad to haul out of the vehicle, march up to the house and kick the door in, where he would be strangled for ruining the alignment, but the car didn't return. Vince was slow getting back to his room, his head tucked in serious contemplation.

2

The afternoon was a contradiction of yesterday, for even the shadows settled in a soft, honeycomb glaze. There was no rigor from the clear blue sky, no indicative signs of human life being on death row. The picturesque countryside eclipsed Yucca's cabin and the mountainside it backed. The evergreen pines filtered the sun's golden rays upon a luxuriant bedraggled floor. The sound of nature was wide awake. Birds sang from the boughs and squirrels squeaked from whence they foraged. Bees and flies buzzed in routine. The carpet of verdant Earth roved with a myriad of insects. Lizards scrambled underfoot while snakes slithered foliated coverings.

The Appointment

Michael walked out of an outhouse the size of a wooden telephone booth, incised with a crescent moon on the door. He didn't have to use the bathroom. He was avoiding Rosalyn so she wouldn't have to avoid him in their parting company's goodbyes. She confided in Anthony and Yucca in the early morning hours that she was repulsed by him. They had advised him in a sugar-coated translation not to try and change her mind, that this was all part of Blackie's attempt to ruin their deal. When he didn't take Anthony and Yucca's advice, Rosalyn was not so reserved in telling him that she couldn't stand the sight of him. The honesty hurt profoundly, though Michael knew it wasn't her fault.

As pleasant as the fall weather was, Michael was frigid in his thoughts. His nose was plugged but he wasn't sick, thanks to Yucca. His energy was up to the task but he would need more than energy to solve his precarious affairs. He would need absolute focus and, even then, who knew what was to be. He couldn't enjoy the unbelievable sights, sounds and smells surrounding him. Life was unaware. How he envied its imperception. It was a cruel joke in bad taste, all of it. He gazed at the damp ground, kicking the occasional stone. He thought about Blackie's deal and the list. How different things would be if he had life to do over. He wanted so badly for everything to be back to normal.

"Mike, we're off!" Anthony said from the Jeep, interrupting his thoughts. Michael waved at Yucca on the porch, whose large hand raised in return. At his side was Marissa, hand in hand.

"Bye, Marissa," Michael said, upbeat.

"Bye, Mike." Her small voice emitted an inner sadness, proving she knew more than she let on or maybe, just maybe, he was impressing his own feelings on her. Michael carried his leaden burden to the passenger side of the Jeep, bluffing a copacetic aura. He was about to board.

"Mike!" Yucca yelled from the porch. Michael regarded the elder when he drew close. "A danger foreseen is half avoided." Rosalyn came out, leading Marissa into the cabin and avoiding Michael. "Walk lightly, my friend, when meeting the reality of Blackie's magic, so when it meets you, you can conquer it. Take care of Anthony and your father, you are their strength."

"Yeah, I will."

"We trust in you, Mike." Yucca did not let the sentiment linger. "My tribe will be along soon. Be strong, life counts on you."

"See you soon," Michael said, getting in the passenger side of the Jeep. Anthony handed him the Chinese shaman mask. Michael looked back at his dad, glad to be out of Yucca's conversation.

"How you doing back there, Pop?" He reached back and patted his father's pant leg. Bruce's head was framed between antlers.

"Excellent, you?" His father's countenance was full of fearless vigor. Yucca's raven feather was held in his free hand, his cast anchoring the deer mask.

"Better now that it's not raining." Anthony laughed in agreement. The world outside the rear window turned. Michael faced front before the cabin came into sight. He strapped in, leaning against the headrest. Michael reached back and patted his dad's pant leg again. Father and son shared a smile in the side mirror. The Jeep was off.

3

Tension filled the front seat of the Jeep in a quiet that broke at the sight of Cherry Croft Drive. "Preparations," Anthony said. They'd seen the sight forming from afar; a strip of vehicles tailgating down the dirt road. The three huddled, looking out the muddy windshield. The vehicles extended the road as far as their eyes could make out. "It's the whole damn town." Anthony scanned the extent of stalled vehicles down Oak Glen Road.

They watched vehicle after vehicle passing on their right. The passengers were numb to the world, just vehicles filled with catatonic people staring straight ahead. The assembly line of motorists stretched down to Bryant Street where the traffic intensified at the intersection.

The street light at Bryant was disabled. Two sheriff units were parked in the middle of the road, directing the four way stop. The thoroughfare was jam-packed with vehicles waiting to head up Oak Glen Road. Besides the Jeep, all lanes leading away were empty. When it came their turn to go, a bitch-faced deputy did not wave them on. Instead, she approached the Jeep.

The Appointment

"Mike, give the mask to your dad. Bruce, hide the masks the best you can," Anthony said through thin lips. Michael handed back the Chinese mask.

"The deer antlers will show." Bruce adjusted in the back.

"Best you can." Anthony rolled down his window. The officer leaned in.

"Where we headed?"

"We have an appointment in Redlands. Blackie's aware of it." Her aviator glasses combed the passengers.

"Let me get your names."

"Anthony Pritchard."

"Michael McGrail."

"Bruce McGrail." The deputy's attention held on Bruce, the antlers in sight. Bruce could have cared less. Anthony felt persistent sweat beads on the back of his neck, ready to sprout.

"We're going to be late." The deputy turned on Anthony. "I don't think Blackie would appreciate you making us late. I would have to tell him you cost him Iosk." Anthony spoke with remarkable composure. The deputy pulled away from the window.

"They're clear!" she said to her male counterpart, who directed them across.

The city of impassive motorists stared ahead. The pregnant wives, girlfriends and daughters accompanied them. It was eerie for Anthony and Michael. The chain of fixed onlookers went on down Oak Glen Road, stopping just out of sight of Yucaipa Blvd where the gathering could be hidden from the main drag's fare. The busiest street in Yucaipa was a ghost town, except for one waiting sheriff's vehicle. The Jeep drove through another disabled light at the boulevard where that same sheriff tagged along behind them until they were seen entering the freeway.

4

Vince would appear lost whenever he was nervous, it's how Melissa could discern an attack was building. "We can take the boulevard," Melissa said.

"Why?" He could see the familiar concern in her face. "I'm not having anxiety." *Yeah, only because she's with you.*

Stop it. "I'm looking for a car."

"What do you mean?"

"Look around..." Melissa scanned the four-way stop of Live Oak Canyon and Fifth Street. "No cars." Vince glanced at the red light. He looked as far to the left and as far to the right down Fifth Street as he could. "There are no cars anywhere. Where is everybody?"

"I don't know." The light turned green.

"Is it a holiday?"

"I don't think so. Maybe an event on the boulevard. Street fair or something. I'm excited about your appointment." Melissa's emerald eyes flashed.

"Me too."

Vince rolled down his window and hung his arm out, attempting to enjoy the nice sunny weather. The smell of autumn was in the air. "Don't let me forget to stop by Fred's on the way back."

Melissa wasn't sure to what he referred. "Oh, for last night."

"Guy must think I'm a freak."

"No."

"You know what's weird?"

"What?"

"How come people like Fred don't see the Dark Ones, like us? Like my parents don't. Ever think about that?"

"How do you know they don't?"

"He didn't have a light with him, and he's an old man."

"Maybe it's only certain people who can see them? Why do some people see ghosts and some—"

"Shit! Sheriff. Don't look." Vince talked fast with a sharp stiffening. He cleaved his hands on the wheel at ten and two. Melissa's hand retracted from his thigh. She eyed the speedometer at 28 mph.

"Just stay in the speed limit."

"I am." Neither made eye contact with the mirrors. Red and blue lights whirled, accompanied by a high-pitched siren.

"Shit, we're being pulled over."

"I should have driven Dick's car."

"No you shouldn't have!" *Say you stole it. What-if they put you in a cell alone? Fuuucckk!*

The Monte Carlo pulled over. Vince dropped his shaking arms off the wheel. "I'm having an attack," he whispered, unable to even look at Melissa. He was ashamed he admitted it out loud, wishing he could take it back.

"Do your breathing exercise." She faced him, wanting to take his hand.

"I am." His voice quivered. He closed his eyes, locking out all distractions and concentrated on his hyper breath. He made a few shallow intakes, unable to form a decent flow of air. "I can't!" His eyes opened, his body convulsed. Melissa could see the medium-height officer step out of his unit. Scatterbrained, Vince wanted to run out of the vehicle and down the street. *AAAHHHHH, FUCK YOU! I'M TIRED OF BEING AFRAID! STOP IT! YOU HAVE TO STOP IT!*

"Fuck it, I'm a minor." Vince stroked his sweaty palms off on his jeans.

"What?" Melissa didn't get what he was talking about.

"You want to be afraid, you want real fear? I'll give it to you."

"What, what are you talking about, Vince?"

Vince's heart revved up. His convulsing arms leapt to the wheel, his hands white-knuckling the rubber. "Buckle up."

"I, I, am. Oh my God."

"Hold on tight." Vince grinned wide.

"Oh my God. What are you doing?" Vince gave the officer the finger and hit the gas.

"Ahhh!" Melissa cried out. The square-jawed officer went for the car's window, missing it by a long shot. "Vince!" Melissa was plastered to her seat and arm rest with digging fingers. The reckless move left her parted mouth open. The officer wavered in a run back to his vehicle.

You're not placing me in a cell alone, fuck you!

The street was flat and open before his charging fender. Vince ground his tooth. Melissa held on tight. Live Oak Canyon road weaved, taking a sloping left amid grassy knolls. The active freeway stretched into sight. Vince carved a skidding right at the three-way stop down the hill, running parallel with the freeway at an exorbitant speed. He slipped back into his lane. The two-way traffic was non-existent. He punched the gas for a straight chunk of asphalt that wouldn't extend for long. "Let me know when he makes the turn."

"Okay." Melissa hooked her belt between her thumb and forefinger to sit forward and swung a look back. The bend up ahead was fast approaching. "He's coming." Vince's foot eased the gas pedal as he wrapped the bend, blurring the knolls from both sides. Melissa's bones clung to what they could amid the seats. Vince drifted out of his lane, watching the road's edge get too close for comfort.

"Fuuucck!" He was off the gas now but the speed exceeded the turn. Vince pulled off a near-miss, kicking the roadside gravel in a wave of smoky pebbles. If there had been a vehicle in the opposing lane, they'd no doubt collided. He managed to straighten the car into his own lane.

"Sit down, Melissa."

"I'm trying to" Melissa straightened in her seat. They reached the intersection at Live Oak Canyon and Oak Glen. Vince ignored the light at the empty intersection.

"Vince!"

"I see it."

Two sheriff's vehicles were blocking his lanes to the freeway. Vince veered around the units onto the empty opposing lanes in a near-miss with the Monte Carlo's hindquarters. "Oh my God!" Melissa lifted off her seat. The deputies had not been in their vehicles. They were coming from the freeway entrance where they were placing cones. Vince nearly clipped a deputy whose hands were waving a signal to stop. He proceeded to run the cones over and enter the freeway.

Vince weaved through the traffic at a rate of speed he only recently thought possible with his parents' car. "You think he got my license?"

Melissa had to slow her heart rate to answer. "No." She pressed her glasses back, looking out the rear window. The freeway flew by.

"See him?"

Melissa searched the receding lanes. "No," she panted. Vince got off an exit early, just in case he was tailed.

He eased off the accelerator as the street wound underneath the freeway and caught the green light at Ford. He ignored the red on Highland in making a left to get off the main boulevard. Fellow drivers didn't seem to care about the infraction, not a single honk was heard. Vince huffed pent-up air. "Yah! Yaah! Yes!" He hit the car's roof with the backside of his fist. "That's what I'm talkin' about! We did it!" Vince grabbed Melissa's knee and squeezed it firm.

Her knee jerked. "Ahh! Don't, it tickles."

"Sorry, I didn't mean to do it so hard. Vince's panic attack had reduced to tame shakes. "Do me a favor. Don't mention any of this to Bruce."

Melissa's mouth was agape. Her head dizzied at the thought of what just happened. "I can't believe you did that." She fanned herself with a semi-smile of excitement at him. It turned her on.

"Believe it, baby." Vince smiled wide. Melissa brightened but the moment Vince looked away from her, she withdrew to the window. Her delicate fingers rolled inward, bringing her knuckles to her mouth. She bit down on them to keep from crying.

5

The Jeep sped into the complex, marking the pavement to park. The masks were left in the vehicle. In Bruce's mobile hand was the feather. Michael hooked his dad's casted side, Anthony his opposite, walking Bruce full-tilt to his office. The three entered the gated hallway. Bruce was kept in the middle to avoid adjoining colleagues and patients in the garden area that might inquire on his injury. They made it to his corner office. There was a note on the door. Michael unhooked his dad and snagged it, giving a brief look over at him.

"Sherri's mad at you." Michael gave the note to his dad who unhooked from Anthony to read it. Anthony read it over his shoulder. "I waited forty-five minutes for you! Did I not have an appointment at 10:00am today? That's what my card says. Call me when you get in. Sherri." Michael opened the door to the suite.

The door bells announced their arrival. Bruce threw the note in the waste basket. Michael switched on the lights to the waiting room, leaving the shades closed. Bruce's nose twitched. "They're here." Anthony could smell a slight putrid odor. Bruce followed the foul scent through the waiting room door to a hallway adjoining the receptionist desk. At its farthest end, the hall of bent shadows led to Bruce's office, where the odor sharpened. Bruce opened the door exhibiting his name.

The obnoxious stench was released as the door opened. It wasn't as offensive as Bruce recalled. Still vile, it was tolerable. "What are you doing?" Bruce demanded to know. Michael and Anthony jammed into the office.

"Pardon me, do you have an appointment?" The tall, costumed Harbinger said in a gravelly English accent, broken up with what sounded like dentures. The character played by Claude Rains, *The Invisible Man*, had his fancy black shoes on Bruce's desk. His partner lay on the patient's table, donning the identical costume in a shorter size.

"Take your shoes off my desk this instant and get out of my chair." Bruce slapped the wasted legs covered in black slacks off his table. The tall one leapt to his feet and skirted the bulk of Bruce, where the doctor reclaimed his chair with a flop of squeaky springs and a gusty breath. "You stunk up my chair, dang you." The shorter Harbinger sat up from the patient's table, making room for his cohort. In sitting next to him, they shared a perplexed look through side-lens spectacles. Bruce got comfortable while Anthony and Michael stared in length at the Harbingers. "Whose Jarrod, whose Ethan?" Bruce asked.

"I'm Jarrod," the tall one said.

"Ethan." The Harbingers eyed the feather in Bruce's hand.

"Here's how this scenario plays." Bruce spoke with authority. "You want me to retrieve the whereabouts of Iosk from Vince. Then, you do what you must from your end to work a deal with Abra so Argauthartera doesn't come.

My demands are not negotiable." The Harbingers faced one another at his audacity. This was not the same man from the hospital.

Jarrod spoke in an amiable, discordant cracked tone to both sides of the room. His bandages fluttered where his mouth would be. "We regret scaring you at the hospital, Bruce. We deemed it was necessary to drive home the seriousness of what was taking place. We thought about your heart later, it wasn't the right approach in hindsight. We were desperate. We thought we'd take a different approach today. You can see how that turned out. Our intention was not to make you angry. We wore these costumes for Vince; he's a fan of *The Invisible Man*. It was a way to break the ice and not scare him to death. And, I hate to tell you, the deal is out of our control."

6

The office bells jingled to an opening and closing of the front door. Vince sniffed twice. "Ew, it stinks in here. You smell it?"

Melissa sniffed. "Kinda, yeah." Vince looked around for the source of the scent while heading to the reception desk. He let go of Melissa's hand with a kiss on it. She gave a flat smile, dropped her head and left his side to take a seat. There was no clipboard on the table. Vince leaned over the desk for Susan.

"Hello?" Her dedicated section of front office was vacant.

The hallway door opened. The pungent smell wafted in Vince's twitching face. He expected to find Bruce but instead got Michael. "Hi. Are you Vince?" Michael closed the door in a rush that scraped his heel.

Don't be cancelled. "Yes."

"Hi, I'm Mike. Bruce's son." He smiled his high cheekbones at him and Melissa who was sitting in a facing chair.

"Hi."

"Dad wanted me to tell you, he has a phone call he has to finish and he will be right out."

The information roused relief in Vince. "No problem. I was afraid the appointment was cancelled." He rubbed his hands on his jeans.

"Oh, no. He wanted me to tell you too, he's apologizes for the smell, but we're having some plumbing issues."

"Uh-oh, somebody bombed your toilet?"

Michael burst out in an unexpected and much-appreciated laugh. "It remains to be seen. Can I get you two anything, while you wait?"

"No, I'm good." Michael checked with Melissa. She shook her head.

Vince started towards Melissa. Michael turned to leave but was detained by Vince's comment. "I love your dad. I can't begin to tell you how much I appreciate what he's done for me." Michael's hand rested on the hallway door knob.

"Right on, he'll be happy to hear it."

"Yeah, I couldn't leave my house alone a couple days ago." Vince snatched a magazine and took a seat next to Melissa. "One appointment and, poof, I drove to Redlands alone on Saturday." Michael's genial façade was crumbling. His high cheekbones dropped, his mind contrite.

"Right on. Well…I'll tell him." Michael headed back into the hallway.

"Did I say something wrong?" Vince said in a whisper.

"No." Melissa looped his arm in a snuggle. She buried her mound of hair against his shirt in her attempt to hide her struggles from him.

Michael stood in the hallway on the verge of losing it. Bruce came out of his office and Michael pulled himself out of what he perceived as weakness. He signaled his dad close for a meeting. "It's him and that girl, Melissa."

"We decided I'll treat Vince in the waiting room."

"What about the girl?"

"I'll send her to the garden."

"Gotcha." Michael hugged his dad, gentle yet hard. Bruce was caught off guard and not in a position to hug back. Regardless, he hugged his son the best he could manage. "You're the man, Pop. I love you."

"I love you, too."

7

Bruce walked into the waiting room, closing the hallway door. Melissa unlaced herself from Vince's arm. "Sorry to keep you waiting."

The Appointment

"Your arm, what happened?" Vince asked, placing down the tabloid fodder they were picture surfing.

"Ah, I fell."

Vince made a sizzling sound. "Ouch, bad weekend for falls. Melissa fell, I fell. We're all banged up." *Don't mention Goat's Head.*

I won't.

"I'm sorry to hear that." Vince went to stand. "Take a seat there, if you would for me."

"Can I help you carry something?"

"No, sit, I've got it." Bruce maneuvered to a chair facing him.

"What's with the feather, you have a tickle exercise for me or what?" Vince laughed and Melissa convincingly tried.

"It's part of today's session." Bruce placed a Newton's Cradle on the magazine table beside where the doctor sat. The five shiny, silver spheres swung in a connected line, slowing to a stop.

"Bruce, this is Melissa, my neighbor I told you about."

"Pleased to meet you, Melissa."

"Pleased to meet you." The doctor could see her suffering.

"So, did this weekend deliver results?"

"It did. I pulled myself out of several attacks. I walked around my block alone, even at night. I drove to Redlands, alone—"

"Vince, do you have a license to drive?"

He rubbed his hands on his jeans in a once-over, giving a guilty squint. "Not exactly."

"Well, congratulations on your achievements." He was surprised by Bruce's answer, expecting to be scolded. "What do you say we get started?"

"In here?"

"I would prefer it. The smell in my office is repellant. You wouldn't be able to concentrate, trust me."

"I do." Bruce gave Vince a gratified look. "What if someone walks in though?"

"You're it today, nobody else is due in."

"Susan's not here?"

"No, she's off."

"I don't mind. Wherever works for me."

"Would you mind, Melissa, waiting for him out in the garden area?"

"No, not at all."

"You can stay. I don't mind if she stays." Melissa waited for confirmation from Bruce.

"It's up to you."

"Yeah, I don't mind if she stays."

"Then let's get started," Bruce said, maintaining the raven feather in his functional hand. He leaned right toward the strung, silver spheres. "Vince, this is a Newton's Cradle. It's used to demonstrate momentum and energy. For our purpose, it will help you reach a deeper state of hypnosis. I want you to sit on back, relax and get comfortable."

"Okay." Vince did just that, sprawling out over his chair. Melissa sat back, providing him with extra space he didn't require.

"I want you to do your breathing exercise." Bruce demonstrated a breathing cycle along with him. "And, while breathing slow and easy, I want you to concentrate on the spheres." Bruce lifted the silver ball closest to him and dropped it to a clack. The energy transferred to the five balls, lifting one side and then the other. The room was given over to the sound of the clacking spheres. Within five minutes, Vince's eyelids bordered on collapse. At seven minutes, his eyes shut.

Vince's limp body appeared knocked out, his mouth parted. Melissa observed the procedure, her awareness torn between the present and the future. "Your body is loose…light…your mind clear. I want you to sleep, a deep sleep. Deeper than you've ever gone before." Vince's breath was but a whisper. "Deeper…deeper…deeper. Are you asleep?"

"Yes," Vince muttered.

"Travel deeper, to a rest so serene, you will not want to return." Vince's jaw slid further open. His body was draped over the seat like a coat. Bruce signaled to Melissa to get the others and be quiet about it. She headed back to his office. "Deeper...deeper and deeper." Everyone, including the Harbingers, entered the waiting room. The five stood around Bruce's back, their eyes riveted on Vince's sprawled anatomy. "Vince, can you hear me?"

"Yes." His voice was of the finest faintness. Bruce stopped the spheres from banging.

"Vince, I want you to dream. I want you to dream of the past. Dream back three years ago. It's Halloween night. You're at Goat's Head with your friends, Jarrod and Ethan... Are you there?" Vince's eyes rolled under his lids.

"Yes."

"What do you see?" Vince sat up, his stomach constricting.

"The trees!" Melissa cradled her arms around herself. Vince's breath was snatched. He lost color in his face.

"It's a dream, Vince, it cannot harm you. Your breath is full and deep, remember?"

His complexion eased back to normal. "Yes."

"What are you doing at the trees?"

"Going inside to get the skull. I don't want to go, but they'll make fun of me if I don't." Jarrod and Ethan traded a look.

"I want you to move past your attacks. What do you see?" Vince tensed, his breathing elevated.

"I'm panicking. The Ones Who Dwell in the Dark are chasing me."

"Past your attacks, Vince." Vince did not ease.

"I'm in a dark place. Where am I?" His hands went out, reaching for invisible walls.

"You're safe."

"No. I'm in the dark, alone! Bruce, get me out of here!" Vince climbed his seat.

"Vince, relax—"

"Get me out of the dark!"

"It's a dream. You are not alone, I am with you. I can get you out with a snap of my fingers.

"Get me out, Bruce! Get me out!" Vince's heart thudded through his white shirt. The onlookers were on pins and needles. Melissa tottered, about to have a panic attack of her own.

"Vince, find the light." Vince's rigid head swung sightless around the room. He found something that captured his interest. His muscles quavered as he slid back down into his seat where he captured a breath of relief. "Are you out of the dark place?"

"Yes, I fell." Vince was catching his breath.

"What do you see?"

His head craned around to the wall behind him. "I'm on the dirt road, trying to get up." He turned to the hallway door and raised his palms. His eyes rolled under his lids at them. "My hands are thrashed… My face feels full." He dabbed his forehead. "I think I'm bleeding?" A touch to his nose made him wince.

"Shit!" Vince tilted his head at the ceiling. "Ethan is yelling for me, I can hear him…" He explored for him. "He's stuck behind the barbed wire. I see him and Jarrod… they're glowing red… I can't tell what they're saying." The room was beyond silent. "Ethan has the skull." The Harbingers jostled each other from excitement. Melissa's eyes flared a shiny green. "Something's wrong." Vince's features hardened.

"What is it?" Bruce asked.

"Guys!" Vince's arms lifted, outstretched, taking on an invisible weight. "What am I doing? I'm running away from my friends! Go back, stupid!"

"Do you have the skull with you?"

"Yes. Why am I running away?" Vince slapped himself, causing Melissa to scream. She cupped her mouth. He searched for the scream, thinking it was part of his mind trip.

"Vince, don't hit yourself. Your friends told you to run for help, remember?" His face became straight confusion. "Where are you now?"

"Running to Jarrod's." He glanced at the wall behind him, the invisible weight of the skull carried in his hands. A look of horror gathered on his face which he flung at Bruce. "The Watchers are after me!" Vince hung off his seat.

"Let's move forward. Where did you take the skull?"

"They're coming after me, Bruce!"

"Vince, fast forward past this. Where did you take the skull?" The silence went on for too long. "Vince, where did you take the skull?"

"I...have to be quiet." The onlookers held their breath.

"Then whisper it to me. Where did you take the skull?" Bruce said in a low tone.

"Jarrod's." His eyes scanned his lids like a book.

"Where at Jarrod's?"

The anticipation was unbearable. "The tool shed." A low gasp came from behind Bruce.

"Vince, did you put the skull in the tool shed at Jarrod's house?" Vince bolted back in his chair, his hands on his thighs like he was squatting in a corner. "Did you?"

"No..." The answer was difficult to hear. "Under it, in the toolbox."

"You put the skull in the toolbox at Jarrod's house, underneath the shed?"

"Yes. Be quiet, they're right outside." Bruce could hear the movements of uncontrollable excitement on the carpet behind him.

"You're certain you put the Goat's Head skull in a toolbox, under the tool shed at Jarrod's house?"

Vince put a finger to his lips and then jabbed at where the Watchers were. He nodded a 'yes'.

"Vince, I want you to clear your mind." His body slumped down on the seat in a heap. "Get comfortable for me." Vince corrected his posture and draped over the chair in complete relaxation. Bruce waved the four out of the room. Michael looked at his father in amazement, while the controlled celebration continued into the hall. Melissa returned to her seat. She took a deep breath in sitting down, fanning her face.

"Vince, when I snap my fingers, you will awake feeling calm, safe and secure. You will be free from anxiety, free from *what-if* thoughts, free from stress. Your panic will be a distant memory. You will have no recollection of what has transpired during your dream and will awake feeling positive and refreshed."

Bruce snapped his fingers around the feather. Vince's eyes fluttered open. The physical world poured over him in sitting up. "How do you feel?"

Vince met the caring smiles on Bruce and Melissa. "Good. Did I fall asleep?" He circled palms in his blurry eyes.

"That you did," Bruce said. Melissa looped Vince's arm and rested her hair on his shoulder to hide in a snuggle.

"I have a gift for you." Vince looked at the raven feather Bruce held out. "Take it." Melissa lifted from him so he could reach. Vince eyed Bruce, questioning him. He took the feather in hand, studying it as he drew it close. The quill was a foot of solid black down to the stem where it greyed to a solid white of three inches.

"What is this for?" Vince asked. Bruce was getting up, his demeanor giving over to a gloomy resignation. "Something wrong?"

Bruce stroked his beard. "They will explain."

Vince looked confused at Melissa. Behind her glasses was an expression of sorrow and excitement. "You guys are acting weird."

The doctor walked toward the hallway. Melissa took Vince's hands in hers, careful to avoid the feather. "Hold on, we have a surprise for you." She slanted a smile at him.

"Have you been crying?"

"I'm okay."

Bruce closed the hallway door behind him, placing his functional hand on his hurting heart. He struggled for breath, wiping a layer of built sweat off his forehead. The distribution of shadows in the hall echoed his feelings of the unescapable coming event.

Without the feather, his mind now directed solely on his fear from the reality that was dropped on him from the Harbingers, a reality he couldn't treat. The sacrificial details Yucca and Anthony had spared him earlier. He clutched his chest, leaning against the wall. Shortness of breath walked him to his office door which seemed light years away. Ruddy and perspiring, his oily fingers wiped his forehead.

Bruce had a difficult time turning the knob with a slick hand. After a few tries, he got it with a determined grip and pushed it open. Four sets of eyes reared at him. "He's ready." The stink that wafted from the room pushed him back a step. His stomach was given over to swells of nausea. The four charged out of the office, electrified. Jarrod was leading them; Michael was the last out. He passed his dad, noticing he didn't follow.

"You coming, Pop?" Bruce struggled to conceal his lack of breath, using the wall for support.

"Yes, just have to use the restroom." Caught up in the traveling excitement, Michael carried on. Bruce lumbered towards his desk on rubber legs, where he fell on his patients' table. His chest ached. He steadied himself, sweating profusely. Taking a deep breath, he wiped his drenched head. His extremities were cold and clammy. His working arm crutched onto his chair where he flopped down on squeaking springs. He pulled open a top desk drawer with a wheeze, extracting a grey flask of hooch. He poured it down his throat until the voice of his father's discouraging remarks and the nightmare he was amid was insensibly drowned.

8

"*The Invisible Man*, alright. I love *The Invisible Man*," Vince said. He watched the four strangers take their selected places among the waiting room. Anthony and Michael stayed at length against the far wall, ear to ear in conversation. The classic-suited monsters sat across from Vince and Melissa. "You two stink," Vince said, uninhibited.

"Shut up, *Mee-yamee* face," the tall one responded. The slang broke the mysterious identities of the Harbingers in an instant.

"No way, Jarrod?" Vince looked at the shorter costumed twin. "Ethan?" He developed the biggest smile on his face. He couldn't believe it.

"In the flesh."

"Sort of," Ethan added. The Harbingers shared a laugh.

"Vince, old buddy, do we have an unbelievable story for you. It's a good thing you have that feather. We weren't expecting that. Minutes are not affordable, so any advantage is welcome," Jarrod said.

"Where have you guys been and what's up with your voices?"

"Dead. We died. Ethan and I were shot by my dad." Jarrod tossed a thumb and forefinger between them. Vince laughed at the presumed gag.

"We're not kidding," Jarrod said. Vince's jovial expression was replaced with a puzzled look.

"What happened to breaking it to him lightly?" Ethan asked.

"He's got the feather," Jarrod signaled.

"It gives courage, not an exemption from feelings."

"Guys, get serious," Vince said.

"We are. We realize this is difficult for you to process," Ethan replied. Vince fell back in his seat from shock.

Jarrod looked at Ethan. "See what you did, *Mee-yamee* face. I had a way of—"

"Jarrod, just tell him," Melissa said. Vince looked at Melissa.

"How do you two know each other?"

She looked him straight in the eyes. "We'll explain. It's all true."

"It is. Don't make me take off the bandages and prove it. And before you go feeling bad for us, don't, we lucked out. You have no idea. We came back to save our brother. If we hadn't died, we wouldn't have known any of what we are about to tell you. We'd be up a creek, us and everyone else."

Jarrod cleared his cruddy throat. "Here's the Cliff Note version. The night we got separated at Goat's Head, Ethan and I didn't realize you got lost." Ethan motioned in agreement. "We thought you were with us the entire time. Turns out, it was a spirit fooling us. Anyway, we spotted the red light of Iosk on the barn. Iosk is the Goat's Head skull. I knocked down the skull with a rock I found and in the light the skull provided when it fell, we realized the person we thought was you, wasn't a person. We both ran, but Ethan here had the guts to nab the skull first. So, we find our way back to the fence and see you. Ethan tossed you the skull so he could fit underneath the barbed wire while I held it.

The Appointment

Next thing I know, Ethan and I are being pulled away by Blackie's followers. We yelled for you to run and get my parents."

Did I?

"While we were being hauled off, I could see torches building from a crowd of angry voices heading in our direction. I heard my dad's voice from behind. It came from one of the followers that held us. He said my name. When I responded, I immediately heard shots. Turns out, my dad had a valid reason to shoot us. It wasn't as cold-blooded as it sounds. He didn't want us to be captured by Blackie. He then shot himself, because if he hadn't, he would have had to face Blackie's wrath for letting us escape." Michael reflected on the conflicting stories.

"When we took the Iosk skull, we sealed our fate. We broke a cardinal rule which cannot be broken. Blackie would have stuck us in the charnel house to be flayed alive and rot, that is until Argauthartera came to take us away for fallen punishment." Jarrod put out a palm in answer to Vince's nonverbal questions. "By my dad killing us and himself, our spirits moved on, thus releasing us from Argauthartera's punishment. My dad saved our spirits from perdition."

"The only reason you're alive is because you couldn't remember where you put the skull. Blackie bonded a spirit to you to find out what you did with it. Your memory loss saved you from some seriously nasty punishment. Blackie is a wicked sorcerer." Michael made a dubious expression. "He has summoned the God of Consumption, Argauthartera by way of Iosk, to come wipe out life on Earth. We, and by we, I mean everything on the face of the planet, are about to be harvested to the god's belly." Michael's expression deepened.

"At twelve o'clock tonight, life on Earth will end unless we stop the coming. The bottom line is, the belly is a permanent perdition for spirits where we will be stored and tortured for eternity in a pitch-black Hell. So, we came back to save our families and you, our brother, from the experience and, in doing so, put ourselves at risk."

"The Iosk skull, which is not a goat's skull, is a communicator to the darkest regions beyond and their ruinous gods and demons. Whosoever wields its powers is capable of unthinkable destruction. We need your help to stop Argauthartera and Blackie from expelling life on this planet and save our own asses at the same time."

"What can I do?" Vince asked. Melissa positioned herself sideways with one dangling foot from her chair. She squeezed around his hands, pulling his attention towards her, careful not to touch the feather.

"You know I love you, right?"

"Yeah, and I love you."

Melissa's chin dropped to her chest. "…That I would never hurt you?"

"Yeah…"

"You have a choice to make. We had to make a deal with a demon to stop Argauthartera. I…am part of that deal. I…offered myself to be sacrificed in order to avoid a deal my dad made for me." Vince's thick eyebrows frowned. "That's how I met Jarrod and Ethan. I would have told you earlier, but you were bonded to, like they said. Remember your sleep-walking?"

"Yeah…"

"That was the bonded spirit leaving your body. It tried to come into mine and it failed." Michael shifted. "Jarrod and Ethan came to me to help you and offered me an out from my dad's deal and safety for my mom in return. My dad…was not a good person, Vince. Please don't ask me how. I've never told you a lie and I won't. I don't like to think about what he did…and I didn't want you to think less of me for it." Melissa spoke with tears in her throat. Vince recoiled internally. Without fear, the disgust filled him wholly.

"I wouldn't."

Melissa spoke from under her mounds of hair. "In order for me to avoid my dad and be with my mom, I offered myself for the Harbingers' deal. They need a sacrifice, I needed out of my dad's deal. Abra, the demon we're involved with, is above Belum, the demon my dad made a deal with for me."

"You can't die…"

Her head tilted and her jeans caught her run-off tears. "Vince—"

"Not without me you don't. Where you go, I go." The room became still. Melissa didn't move for an extended moment. Her teary eyes lifted at him. The emotion behind the frames was unrestrained. Vince freed a hand from hers to stroke her hair. Her eyes closed to the touch, tears streaming out. He leant down and kissed her. Their lips parted. "I love you, I wouldn't want to live without you."

Her eyes opened, her lips quivered. "That's the feather talking."

Vince looked at the feather in their cupped hands. "It makes me lie?"

"No, it gives you courage. He's telling the truth," Ethan interjected.

Melissa's jaw trembled. Vince's eyes streamed tears from watching her cry. Her tone's pitch raised and lowered. "Abra has offered a deal for me, Iosk…and you." She did not mention their unborn child, a thought that cut through her.

"Do I get to be with you?" Vince asked. Debbie crossed Michael's mind.

"Not only do you get to be with her, you get to be with your friends, also. Don't forget about us," Jarrod said.

"Yeah, you freakin' *Mee-yamee*," Ethan said.

"I haven't." He looked at his friends. "I have been asking about you guys for years. I thought you ditched me."

"We're just giving you shit," Jarrod said, half-kidding.

Vince faced Melissa. "I'm in."

"That was easy." Jarrod exchanged a look with Ethan.

"Thank you, feather," Ethan said.

Melissa's pulsing emerald eyes searched him. "Are you sure?"

"I've never been more sure about anything in my life. You're the only reason I'm not dead now. I told you."

"I know…"

"You gave me the strength to pull the gun out of my mouth. I wanted to pull the trigger, I did. I just kept thinking about losing you and, to be honest, how much it would hurt my parents. That didn't help, but the primary reason was you. What about my parents, by the way? Will I be able to say goodbye?" Michael made an audible breath in the background. Anthony put a hand on Michael's shoulder.

"Fraid not. But, you will spare them an eternity of torture. You might be able to get a message to them later. That's how we found out you needed help," Jarrod said.

"How?"

"It's complicated. Let's just say, you can thank your friends on Plarek." Vince's eyes flew open in astonishment.

"You've been to Plarek? It's real?"

"No, we haven't been there personally, but your friends are responsible for our return. It is a real world. We had no recollection of our previous identities. Knowledge is always in a state of flux when you move on. Memories can remain from previous lives, but sometimes they don't. Your friends on Plarek restored our memories."

"Ethan and I were separated at death, sent to different zones, oblivious that we existed beforehand. The information of one another was wiped out in the loss of our brain. The people of Plarek figured out you were bonded to, restored our memories and reconnected us to help you. That's how we reunited and became aware of the danger you were in."

Vince sat back in awe. "That's exciting. Plarek is real." He laughed to himself. *Mom and dad will have the new baby to raise, they'll be happy without me. I was a burden anyway.*

"Like I said, it's complicated or I would go into detail. We haven't the time so, can we—"

"It's a no-brainer. My parents need me. I get my friends back. I get to be with the girl of my dreams." Melissa beamed. "What else can I want? Let's go kick some Blackie ass!"

"Oorah!" Ethan whooped to the combined enjoyment of Jarrod. A pleasant recall that lightened the mood, even if just for a moment.

9

Michael's eyebrows slanted inward, compressing the skin between. He didn't bother to wake his father from his drunken slumber to share his innermost feelings for him while he was out of sorts. Replete with disappointment,

The Appointment

Michael gave the flask on the carpet a conspicuous glance and left Bruce's office without a word or eye contact with anyone. "Mike," Anthony said, following him. Vince went to wake Bruce and Melissa stopped him.

"Let him be." Vince's temples pinched.

"Alright. Hopefully you can hear me, Bruce. I just want to say goodbye and thank you for all your help. I will help your son and your family from being taken away from you. You can count on me, I won't fail. Take care of yourself and thanks again for everything. I appreciate it more than you will ever know."

"Thank you, Bruce," Melissa said, ushering Vince out of the room to meet the Harbingers in the parking lot.

CHAPTER 20
Mean Road Ahead

Monday, 5:40pm

1

Anthony brought the Jeep around to a secluded part of the medical complex's parking area. He parked backward behind a brick trash enclosure beside a black-tinted Ford Bronco. Anthony watched Vince being suited in his bullet-proof vest. Vince's sour face and inflated cheeks went from side to side. "Man up, solider," Jarrod said, securing his Velcro.

"I'm sorry, you smell like curdled hot chocolate and B.O." The Harbingers laughed. Vince fed off their banter. "You make me plead for a fart."

"You're finished." Jarrod nudged him away.

"With pleasure, stanky." Vince checked to see if Melissa was laughing. She wasn't, she was elsewhere in her head looking at the asphalt. Jarrod was still laughing when Michael stepped in for his vest.

Michael would not partake in their loose behavior. His face made it frank and Jarrod read it, killing his laughter. Anthony stepped out from around the Jeep and Ethan retrieved his vest from the bed of the Bronco. The back of the Bronco was blocked from view by a black tarp. In the minimal leftover space was a storage container. The Harbingers retrieved black duffle bags from it and gave one of these forty-pound bags to each member of the party.

Jarrod took a commanding, wide-legged stance. "Alright, listen up! Although fighting is a last resort, Blackie will be waiting for us. So will all of Yucaipa, Hearth and his force, willing to obey his orders. You might see friends or relatives. You can think of these people as mindless slaves." Michael circled his neck.

"If Blackie orders it, they will try and kill you. If you hesitate to shoot, they will kill you. Leave your sentimental shit behind." Michael shared a disturbed glace with Anthony, who shared his concerns. "They have no emotion, no reason, no memories. Theirs minds are corrupted and will only follow Blackie. Got it?"

A united "yes" resounded from Vince and Melissa.

Jarrod unzipped his bag, pulling out a rifle. "In the event of an attack, you have been provided with an AR-15. She is good for thirty rounds at long range. The rifle has a weapon light for visibility in the dark and a laser pointer for novice accuracy. You have with you a supply of fifteen magazines for reload." Jarrod placed the rifle on the bed, retrieving a shotgun. "You will also find a riot shotgun, modified with bayonet for close-quarter fighting in your bag." Michael sighed.

"The shotgun will also have a fixed light for visibility but no laser, as it is not required. Shotguns are used for close-quarter combat for its spreading capabilities. Aim it and it will hit what's in front of you. You run out of ammunition, cut a path. If you should find yourself in close quarter combat with your AR-15, the butt can become a club." Jarrod demonstrated how to spring out the sharpened bayonet.

"The shotguns are chambered twelve gauge and have a hell of a kick. Melissa, yours is the exception. Yours is modified for recoil sensitivity. You and Anthony have also been provided with Walkie-talkies in case we get separated. Ethan and I will walk each of you through how to operate and manage your weapon properly. Unfortunately, there's no time to train you on how to shoot so conserve your ammo during a fire fight and use the lasers.

In a tight situation, the AR-15 can provide rapid fire by holding the trigger down. You'll want to remember the bullets empty quickly, so waste not, die not.

That's why we recommend the shotgun if you find yourself cornered. Any questions not pertaining to the weapons?"

Anthony spoke up. "Yes, I just want to reiterate for Vince and, as a reminder, my concerns I raised earlier. We should be sensitive in approaching Blackie in arms. He'll be put on guard."

Michael went on. "Yeah, I agree. He's going to think he's being double-crossed right off the bat."

"Yes, exactly. It will make our trade highly volatile," Anthony said.

"So, what's your suggestion that won't allow Blackie to just take Iosk by force, because that's what he's going to do if he thinks we are unarmed. Then we'll have a bloodbath on our hands," Jarrod said.

"We're on the same page. I'm just saying we should proceed with as little confrontation as possible. We have to give serious consideration for the welfare of the innocent bystanders involved. Let's be mindful to take extra precautionary measures not to brandish our weapons. That's all I'm saying."

"Agreed. Got that Vince, Melissa? No showboating your weapons. Weapons use is a last resort," Jarrod said. There was a united agreement from the two. "Failure is not an option, people."

2

The vehicles took aim at the hills to the northeast, riding on the appreciable blue hue of Mentone Boulevard. They were heading for Jarrod's old place. Anthony was driving the Jeep with Michael sitting in the passenger seat and Vince and Melissa sharing the backseat in an amorous embrace. In between their legs was the deer mask, splaying its horns over their laps. It was this love bird's position that kept the bullet from drilling a hole through Vince's occipital.

The sound of fireworks erupted. The rear and back-side window cracked with a whiz. There was a short-lived, dead ringing in Vince's left ear. Anthony swerved, his face contorted. "Get down!" he yelled, maintaining the wheels on the sinuous road. Three heads leant forward. Michael eyed the bullet hole in a swing-back look between the seats. A displeasing déjà vu it was.

"Vince, stay down," Michael said. Melissa was already pulling him down from trying to look out the back window where the action was.

"Is everyone okay?" Anthony asked.

Melissa checked Vince over. "Are you hurt?"

"No, I'm cool."

"Yes, we're okay!" Melissa answered.

"Mike, you?"

"Yeah!" His voice was rattled. Anthony eyed the ruckus in the rearview mirror.

Metal pitted metal in a screaming cadence of hell fire. The back side of the Bronco's roof had been removed at some point. In its place was an instrument of death, a M2 Browning aircraft machine gun, spitting .50 caliber shells down on a sheriff's cruiser driving the wrong way on a tree-loaded, two-way road. Ethan manned the jolting muzzle, which flared with sparkling fire. He was protected from the sheriff cruiser's pop guns by a shield mount.

The curve swerved out of the way, leaving the trees behind. The street straightened into rocky bushes of open terrain. The cruiser was sliced through like it was made of butter. The occupants rumbled in their seats, being turned into spurting swish cheese. Anthony watched the act of war in horror. He questioned if the Harbingers hadn't incited the fight.

In the blink of an eye, the moonlit sky lit up in a burst of flames. The unit hurled from the street like a Molotov cocktail on its head. The siren sang until the roof lights were smashed in on the rocks. "We're coming up on Bryant, it will be your next right," Vince said, as calm as can be.

"Keep your head down!" Anthony shouted back. Melissa was on it. The contours of her face advertised a deep concern. The orange street light of Bryant illuminated the turn-off ahead. Anthony couldn't stop thinking of the two deputy's bodies he saw waving in their seats.

A whizzing sound punctured a hole in the windshield glass over Michael's head. "Down, down, stay down!" Anthony yelled, not knowing where the bullet came from. The four ducked low as they could go. Vince sheltered Melissa, who pulled him down under her. He could feel her heart racing through her chest. Vince gestured her the feather and she rejected it.

The Bronco roared past the Jeep's windows. Ethan floated in the sky, encased in a cubicle of bulletproof steel. His spectacles were off and two caved in shadows peered out from the head wraps. "Light 'em up!" hollered Jarrod from the driver's seat window. Ethan's sturdy shoulders shook as gunfire erupted from the juggernaut.

"Stay down!" Anthony demanded.

"What's going on?" Michael asked.

"They have units blocking off Bryant...hang on!" The Jeep's passengers were tossed from a quick maneuver. Anthony got behind the Harbingers, his face hard-lined with plenteous wrinkles. The Jeep slowed to a crawl. Ethan hiked high over the windshield.

Vince moved aside the curtain of Melissa's hair that buried him so he could see. A queer Chinese mask on the floor under Michael gathered his curiosity. Pings were heard on the Jeep's right side. A maelstrom of sounds played, replete with chaos; the sounds of metal being riddled, tires being blown out, glass being shattered and skin being thumped and pulverized. However, the eeriest sound of all was the uncommunicative deaths. Not one scream was heard, not one yell of pain. Vince went to regain sight of the road but Melissa bore him down. "It's okay," Vince said to her.

"No it's not," she said in his ear. "Don't you dare." She combed a hand through his short black hair. It was a drawback of the feather, fearlessness but recklessness. The mayhem ebbed until it stopped in the last crackle of bullets. The passengers waited on orders from Anthony. Michael read the insecurity on his face. They felt the Jeep do a complete turn onto Bryant.

"You can sit up." Anthony permitted after a signal from Ethan that it was safe. "Keep your eyes peeled."

The three raised, Vince last after Melissa checked their safety for herself. It was hard to tell; the place was a doomsday wreck. Anthony was signaled to the right side of the halted Bronco. The passenger-side window was down. Anthony rolled his window down to speak with Jarrod. "Anyone hurt?" Jarrod looked at Vince in asking.

"No." He turned his bandaged head at the windshield and back in relief. "You know we gave you the rifles for this exact type of scenario."

"What happened back there?" Anthony wanted answers. It was evident he was not happy.

"Exactly what I said would happen. They're trying to take Iosk by force."

"We're going to have complications with Blackie because of this."

"What can we do about it? They shot at us first. They were trying to take Iosk. They don't know we haven't got it yet."

"Exactly, so why would they attack us?" Anthony asked with a doubtful expression. Michael seconded it at his side.

"You tell me?" Jarrod flipped his palms. Anthony adjusted in his seat, making the effort not to say anything he would regret. Michael turned to look out his window for the same reason. The mayhem around him seeded and Michael's mind was then made up. "Follow us," Jarrod said, moving out.

Ethan held a fist in the air for Vince. "Oorah!" Vince gave the reactionary fist back at the windshield. A gross, overwhelming sense of guilt at the looks he received from the front seats set in. Michael and Anthony's sick contours stared at him, the shootout still current in their ears. He was quick to put his hand away. It did feel in bad taste to salute the carnage now that he thought about it. *These people are victims too.*

They shot at Melissa, fuck 'em.

Anthony and Michael stewed as they drove on. Vince peered out the back windows at the deranged aftermath, left to spoil in the morning sun. No thought crossed his mind that there wouldn't be a tomorrow. The hatchet job covered the street in projected human hamburger. The cruisers were decorated with silver burnt peep holes; their cratered interiors with their passenger's insides. The slaughter stack smoked in copious flames from the awesome fire power. The mess of no survivors was to be commiserated, not celebrated.

Vince gave a deep breath. *I won't stop protecting Melissa. Don't ask me to.* His focus drew to her. She responded in a broken stare at his chest. Her expression, like the rest of the passengers, was pale with tremulous eyes. Vince sat back and pulled her to him. Her arms wrapped secure around his waist. He stroked her curls and kissed her on the head.

3

The Bronco and Jeep's travel down Bryant Street to Ivy Avenue was unobstructed. From the top of Jarrod's old street ascended a far-flung, mighty unifying light of yellow and orange that billowed into crimson. The two vehicles took up the street of astride ranches and farmhouses. Melissa lifted out of Vince's arms. She navigated her duffle bag past the horns of the deer mask and retrieved her AR-15. Vince and Michael followed her lead, slinging the strapped weapons around their necks. Each roll of the street brought closer the skin pulling uncertainty of the worst possible outcome. Anthony watched the sides of the Bronco, examining the blue outlined shadows for movement.

"Jarrod's house will be coming up on our left," Vince said. Ethan signaled a warning of danger ahead.

"On guard, people. We've got company," Anthony announced. Hands clamped down on their rifles.

Melissa tugged Vince's arm, beckoning him close. "I can't do this," she whispered, petrified.

"Yes, you can." Vince caressed her sweaty face. Her hand gripped his arm tight. "I won't let—" The words were drowned out by the gunfire, but she could read his lips. "…anything happen to you." The Bronco came to a halt. The Jeep was unable to see the fortified lineup firing.

"Get down, get down!" Anthony patted the air between the seats. Ethan's canon continued to go off in a barrage of .50 caliber slicing and dicing. Michael looked at Vince.

His exchange said, "We're fucked!" Vince did not listen to orders, Melissa was his only concern.

"I can't breathe," she mouthed. Her hands clang to him, desperate for a solution. She was about to be out of her head with mounting panic. The sight roused a fire in Vince's belly. He couldn't stand to see her like this, he had to put a stop to it. He ground his tooth, giving way to his shakes. A presence was being let out, something primal, thirsty for carnage worked his controls. A beast whose mercy was for none but one. This monster mutated his face into lines of absolute fear and matchless anger. His emotions had reached their apex, placing his body into maximum overdrive. He punched himself in the face hard enough to bloody his teeth, caught in an extemporaneous fit of rage. This thing inside him courted instability.

Anthony and Michael didn't know how to respond. "Vince?" Anthony said, gesturing him to relax. Vince managed to navigate his pack over his neck in the close confinement of the horns, crisscrossing his rifle's strap. "Sit down! What are you doing?"

"What are you doing?" Michael reiterated, sitting up. Melissa watched in fascination.

Vince looked into her vibrant-green pupils. "Stay here." His voice belonged to a savage. He burst from the back door of the Jeep to the perturbation of the front seats, slamming it closed behind him.

"Vince, get back here!" Anthony yelled, near to a scream. The sets of eyes followed him to the back of the Bronco where he began to fire off rounds, visible in the headlights.

"Is he crazy?" Michael asked.

"Melissa, what is he—?" Anthony's lost his voice for an instant. "She has the feather, Mike!"

"What?" Michael looked back to see the raven's plume in Melissa's hand. He palmed his temples in a whip back against his seat. "I'll get him!" Michael spun around and threw his duffle bag over his neck.

"Get out on my side!" Anthony climbed out of the Jeep, staying behind the driver's-side door. "Watch it, stay low!"

"I fucking hate guns," Michael murmured, taking control of his rifle in a hunched run.

Vince had moved to the left side of the Bronco. Bullets could be heard splitting the atmosphere, bouncing and whizzing. A continuous *ding, ding, ding,* could be heard. The Browning fire ceased to the strident sounds of metal clashing and the jingle of bullets. While Ethan was reloading, Vince fired on any sound or movement he could perceive in the orange-ish dark gloom behind Jarrod. Jarrod fired, moving backward out into the open, heading towards the back of his vehicle. Dust spurted out of him where bullets met unprotected decay. The sound of fireworks popped from invisible directions with the occasional spark and blowout of a shotgun.

"Vince!" Michael called, careful not to approach the armed lunatic unannounced. Michael stuck behind the coverage of the Bronco. "Vince!" The area sounded like the climax of a Fourth of July celebration. "Vince!" The closer Michael approached, the louder the .50 caliber was covering his voice. Vince went to reload how he was trained. Michael seized the opportunity and grabbed him. "Vince!" He turned at him, ready to throw the butt of his rifle in his face. "It's me! It's me!" Michael held up an arm in defense. The tension died in Vince's arms.

"Sorry! Take the right side!"

"No, we have to get you back to the Jeep! Come on!" Michael pulled.

"We can't, Jarrod needs us!" Michael hesitated from indecision. Jarrod found his way to the back of the Bronco where his bandages on the side of his head spurted dust from a kill shot. Michael went into a brief state of shock from the sight.

"Get some!" Jarrod yelled. The Harbinger shoved a full-loaded magazine in the chamber, returning fire in the direction of the bullet's owner until he emptied his stock. Vince joined in on the fray. Michael looked at the Jeep's headlights, conveying his dilemma. Jarrod punched his magazine out, fitting himself for another, directing the action. He made a gesture for Vince and Michael to follow him. The Harbinger had no eyes and, at separate times, Michael and Vince wondered how he could see.

"Where are we going?" Michael asked, close enough to waft the Harbinger's scent through his blocked nostrils.

"My backyard! Ethan has us covered! The bastards are cooked in all over the place for an ambush! It's suicide to attempt a forward entry! We're going in from the side and back up!" Jarrod stopped at the Jeep's driver side window.

Anthony rolled it down. "Kill those headlights!" The headlights went off. The mighty fire of Goat's Head grew over the land in a scant tint of pumpkin orange.

"We'll be back! We're going around to Jarrod's backyard!" Michael said into the window.

"Watch yourselves! Good luck!" *Please let it be there*, Anthony thought, looking at the sky. The three silhouetted men withdrew into the company of shadows, their fingers laced on their triggers.

4

Vince and Michael scrambled on Jarrod's heels through neighboring yards. Fence after fence, shadows were their setting, ceaseless gunfire their soundtrack. Horses, donkeys, goats, pigs and chickens spied from the safety of their enclosures, watching the three figures on the move. They came to the last fence with Jarrod's house just on the other side. Jarrod jumped over, then Vince. Michael was about to when he heard his name called.

"Michael." The voice belonged to Blackie and he swore it came from inside his head. He spun around where the imposing robed figure displaced from the dark of some bushes, with eyes gleaming black pools from inside a cowl. The figure's chest was ornamented in a circle of mottled speckles, like staring off into outer space. "Michael, I thought we had a deal?" Michael stayed put with a strong hold on his rifle.

"We did and your watchdogs shot at us."

"On the contrary. Your Harbingers did the shooting. Why would I jeopardize myself and my subjects? If we don't give Iosk to Argauthartera, we get taken. Did the Harbingers tell you that my people attacked you?"

"Ye— I saw it."

"What did you see?" Michael had no immediate response. "Your trust has no value. Tell me your honor does. Are they aware of our deal?"

"I had to tell them something in order to bring you Iosk."

"What did you tell them?"

5

Jarrod nor Vince noticed that Michael wasn't behind them. They reached the tool shed with only one thing on their mind. Jarrod's bony knees fell and printed on the ground that girded the base of the shed's door. Beneath the door was a raised wooden platform about a foot high. He swung his rifle and bag onto his back, digging at the sodden dirt underneath while Vince kept watch. "Where's Mike?" Vince asked in a twist of his head. Jarrod's gloves scratched upon a large metal object and in his excitement, missed Vince's question.

He pulled the brown toolbox free, dragging it from underneath the platform. Vince spotted a movement out of his left peripheral and swung on it. He hadn't time to warn Jarrod. The silhouette didn't match a body type he recognized, it was short and stout. With no choice, Vince flipped on his light and laser.

The stalker's eyes flinched from temporary blindness. It was a bald man with a machine gun pointed at him. Vince's fidgety hands aimed the red dot at the man's heart. Adrenaline surged through him. His finger squeezed the trigger and a shell shot out of the AR-15. In the fraction of an instant, there was a flash and bang and the target was hit. The man flounced, folding in a spasm. The stucco puffed from Jarrod's house where the bullet had wedged itself into the wall.

"Beautiful shot solider," Jarrod said, patting Vince's back. The world around him was a deep red. "We've got Iosk." Vince was half listening. The correlation of his swelling hunger for violence to control his anxiety claimed his thoughts. He ground his tooth, his heart hammering, but not from worry. He drove his eyes around the perimeter for others to stay his panic. Vince came face to face with Michael. His rifle flew under Michael's chin, giving a ghost storyteller quality to his face. Michael's reflex was instant. He had Vince's barrel in hand pointed at the sky where his face turned a deep red.

"It's me!"

"Where were you?"

"Listen…" Michael hushed him. "No gun fire." Vince looked in the direction of the street. "I'm going to let your weapon down." His attention drew back to Michael. "You got this?" Vince nodded his head, the hypersensitivity eased out of his glowing red face. Michael let his weapon loose, stepping past him.

Vince switched off his rifle's light. The deep red poured over the three. Michael and Vince roofed Jarrod's shoulders, stooping over Iosk in sublime fascination. The Harbinger looked at Vince and Michael with dug-out eyes in a wordless respite.

"I think the fighting stopped," Michael said. The group acknowledged the quiet. A terrible thought entered Vince's mind. *What-if Melissa is dead and that's why the fighting stopped?*

"Let's get back," he said, unable to bear mentioning what he thought.

"We go back the way we came in," Jarrod ordered. The Harbinger placed the glaring luminosity that was Iosk in his duffle bag and the orange tint reclaimed the night.

6

Compiled breaths released from Vince with the sight of Melissa stirring in the back of the Jeep. He had spotted her shadowed edging because she appeared to be searching for him. The three scoped the perimeter from behind a boxwood hedge. The Jeep's headlights were back on. Ethan was in their shine, talking to two red robed females off-guard, a familiar tall strawberry blonde and an average height brunette with curls. Their deadpan faces went on in conversation, awake yet asleep.

"My sisters," Jarrod said for Michael.

Terri and Becca? Vince thought. They had matured in his absence. Especially Rebecca, the youngest and still the shortest. "Don't shoot, unless they give you no alternative." Vince and Michael were stunned by the cold weight of Jarrod's statement.

The three made a surreptitious move for the Jeep, eyes roaming the unpredictable mass shadows of spacious yards. The Jeep's back door swung open, Melissa there waiting. Vince signaled for Melissa to be quiet. She nodded. "Men, it's time to see what we're made of. Let's save the day. Good luck to you, Michael," Jarrod said, shaking his hand. Michael was off-put by the feel of bony grooves penetrating the glove.

"And you."

"Vince, see you on the other side, my friend." Vince felt qualm. He took a deep breath, thinking of the feather as a safety zone to remain calm.

"I'll see you there." Jarrod gave possession of his duffle bag over to Vince, to which Michael gave a clandestine glance before he slipped in the back of the Jeep. Melissa tilted the deer horns out of his way.

"We got it," Michael whispered to Anthony in reclaiming the front passenger seat.

"Thank you," Anthony said low to the heavens. Vince looked for the feather in Melissa's hand while getting in. Jarrod closed the back door behind him.

"Iosk is in the bag?" Anthony asked.

"Yeah," Michael answered.

"This one." Vince distinguished Jarrod's identical duffle bag from his.

"Don't mix them up," Anthony said.

"I won't."

"What's going on?" Michael referred to Ethan's conversation with Jarrod's sisters.

"Peace talks."

"Sincere?"

"We'll see." Jarrod joined the conversation with his sisters.

Once Vince got settled, Melissa's hand guided his chin in her direction. "I love you." Her emerald eyes shined an intoxicating green.

"I love you." Her lips hung open, begging his lips without the responsibility of asking.

Jarrod broke from his sisters, heading to Michael's side of the Jeep. Michael lowered his window. The sound of glass brushing rubber separated Vince and Melissa. Vince found the feather in his hand. Melissa's loving demeanor was replaced by anxiousness. She made a clear gesture that she did not want the feather back when Vince offered.

Anthony shifted toward the passenger-side window to hear Jarrod. "My sisters will escort you to Blackie. We're to stay here." Anthony nodded. "Walkies out of sight," Jarrod whispered. His eye cavities wandered to Vince. "Later, Vince."

"Later, Jarrod. Later, Ethan!" Ethan waved at the windshield. Jarrod patted the window seal in a walk away.

Vince watched his best friends disappear again. Jarrod's bewitched sisters strode up Ivy Avenue. The Jeep's headlights framed their swaying figures pressed before two elongated shadows. The Jeep made its way onto Jefferson, avoiding twisted metal and shredded law enforcement.

"Vince, can I see Iosk a minute? I have to see it just once." The anthropologist in Anthony couldn't help himself. A brilliant, deep red glow filled the vehicle with an audible awe from the backseat that tingled Anthony's blood. His intrigue was provoked to the highest degree possible.

"I'll take it." Michael reached back. Vince handed it over and Anthony's divided attention drooled for a snapshot glimpse.

The red effulgent skull was stumped twice atop the head from what was inferred as a methodical removal of two horns. These circular mounds measured about four inches in diameter and were filled with what looked like keratin. They were similar in size and shape to the two protruding, sideways-facing eye sockets, smaller by a possible inch. The sloping nose plate hooded the gaping mouth from the precise middle with an attenuated V that stretched down at about seven inches where it was worn to a dull, arched nub. Mere inches beneath the nose's fringe were fractures, dislocations and splinters which comprised the upper mouth of jagged bone shards. Yet despite its frail appearance, it felt harder than rock and the shards piercing to the touch, as Anthony found out.

The lower jaw had a fallout with age, the shards representative of cutting teeth, being merely that of broken bone. The broken bottom went all the way back to what remained of a nicked, craggy skull cap. It had a rounded brain cavity about thirty inches in circumference that tapered out and down, to a sharp tail of twelve inches. The tail was snapped in a slanted break at the tip.

The most interesting aspect of the skull, besides its diabolic red glow, was its peculiar eyes. From their bowels on either side was a jumble of tiny, faint coruscating lights, suggestive of a pocket of remote space. With the slightest change of the skull's direction, the handler could summon a different map from locations beyond. Maps of worlds unknown and the communicator to those worlds was at their uncomprehending fingertips.

CHAPTER 21
Last Night on Earth

Monday, 9:34pm

1

"Now," Anthony said. Watchful, Vince and Melissa exited the backdoor of the Jeep. Michael held the duffle bag of Iosk in his lap, buried in his thoughts. He watched without looking at the open-ended stadium of vehicles parked row after invariable row in the field to his right. The metal and glass frames waved on fire from the reflection of abundant torches dawning the hillside across the road. The residents atop whose flames waved restless could not be seen, merely anticipated in number.

Anthony, aware of Michael's sensitive disposition, would have added words of encouragement but what can one say against uncertainty of ultimate victory or permanent torture. They would come off disingenuous lines. The Jeep rolled along with Terri and Becca, guiding the two men into the entrance of Goat's Head. The entryway had been smoothed over into a steady incline for their arrival which furthered Michael's suspicions of the Harbingers regarding who shot at who first.

Anthony entered the ablaze tree lines. Michael and his eyes were branded. Multitudes of torches floated in a red-robed association behind the left line, giving the illusion of towering tree arrows aimed at the burning heavens. The torchlights flashed brilliant-white dances through the plentiful interstice of branch space. They daubed the right line with an ocher semblance which enslaved the resident shadow people behind their keepers. Their eyes could not adjust to it all.

"Could be sixty thousand," Anthony said, his eyelids twitching from strain and sweat.

"Looks like it. Route six-six-six." The pervading heat was rising. The sweat redoubled under their vests. Anthony jerked his head at the air conditioning, turning it on full blast.

"Look, whatever hap—" Anthony began.

"It's okay, I know the score. You don't have to…" Both men shared a brief, meaningful look that said more than words could. Michael drew from Anthony to look out his window.

"The sisters are stalling us on purpose," Anthony said. The two looked out the windshield.

"No doubt, but does it matter?"

"No." Anthony wiped the sweat off his forehead. "No, it doesn't." He gave the expression of a sudden idea. He reached in the glove compartment, gathering Michael's attention, and retrieved a mix tape entitled "Best of Devo". "You like Devo?"

"Right on, yes. Play it." Michael's spirit lifted. Anthony pushed the tape in.

"If we're going down, let's go in style."

"I couldn't agree more. Crank it." The song "Beautiful World" blared. Anthony rolled down his window.

"Roll down your window, let's put them on notice." Michael smiled back high cheekbones, rolling down his window. The sisters gave a brief, mechanical glace of dilated pupils back at the noisy Jeep as they couldn't distinguish Devo from a loud verbal call. Anthony and Michael sang along. The boom box drove through the fire lines at the poor speed of its leaders; a rolling concert on wheels.

The missing tree's partition became visible. Anthony and Michael kept on singing aloud. The fears of the mind had collapsed with the first musical note.

The Jeep entered nature's doorway to a crowded field of red-robed locals placed shoulder to shoulder like the weeds they had pressed under foot. The slaves extended back to an orange shimmering horizon of blurring dots. The blaring Jeep was in stark contrast to the motionless, soundless, empty-faced observers sweating in the steady torchlight; each with his or her own rag stick aflame in the air above their hooded head.

Besides the sister guides, the trail was provided free of obstruction up to the point of the fence. Vince Marino's parents, under the same spell as those around, parted the fence open to Blackie's mansion. A single supreme beacon of flame dawned its ramshackle steps, ringing in a spherical blood orange. Beneath the flame, a figure ruled the porch dressed in a vermillion cowl and vestment striped with a gold cross centered with a black circle. The robed mob at the trail's border were sung Devo, like a celebratory parade coming through. The blank expressions and shadowed faces of the spellbound absorbed the singing with no reaction. Obscured beneath the folds of his cowl, was Blackie's adverse reaction to this spectacle.

The sisters stopped at the fence. Terri stepped aside the trail joining Paula, and Becca stepped aside joining Greg. The Jeep pulled into the fenced property and was pinned in by Terri and Becca. Anthony lowered the volume. "They're locking us in."

"Yes, they are." Michael glanced in the rearview between the deer's horns to see Terri secure the lock. Anthony and Michael shared an insiders' look, eyeing the time. "Here goes," Michael said.

"Be careful."

"On it." Michael stepped out of the Jeep and was met by the full brunt of the rallied torches. The heat threw another layer of sweat on him. In his left hand, the duffle bag of Iosk hung; in his right, his loaded rifle. He glanced back and at his sides. The locals grew on the fence, surrounding it. Their fingers crawled through the links in an abundance of blank stares and trailed Michael's every move.

Michael shouldered the sweat from his brow. He turned on Blackie, shut out his fear and maintained a sharp and focused eye contact. His mind was set for tournament fighting. The sorcerer's cloth swam in crimson fire. The black circle upon his chest projected an utter absence of color. It was a black so ultimate that Michael did not have the ocular means to define the coming of Argauthartera, as the god's anatomy of eternal darkness so filled the black hole.

Michael walked to the music. It had become his corner man, giving him a raised confidence in the face of death, equal to bleacher cheers. He reached the creaky steps when the music from the Jeep was lowered to a conservative level.

Blackie's orange skeletal hand and unhealthy nail beds beckoned him up the stairs, but Michael stopped halfway, a foot on two different steps. The sorcerers black-pooled eyes fixed on him from out of the shadows of his parchment-like face. Michael could see his wizened features in yellowish-brown sweeps of color too brief to reason a construct. The cowl and shadows seemed to have a mind of their own, making it impossible to obtain any distinguishable view. The patch of open door that framed the sorcerer's back raised caution flags from what may lay beyond it.

"Show me Deb." Michael's eyes searched the bare porch.

"You have Iosk in your bag, I presume?" Blackie drew in a glint of sliced, reptilian lips.

"For Deb I do."

"Marvelous. I will get her for you." Blackie twirled and swooshed to the side of the door in a wisp of flame and smoke. Michael considered its unlit depths. The sorcerer's torch could not touch the darkness within. "Deborah, come unto me, child." Blackie's voice echoed into the dark interior. An ancient hand unfurled at the door's passage. Michael felt a spasm of annoyance at how Blackie called her, indicated in a quick, distracted jump of his eyes.

Something in the unlit threshold moved with scant lambency and within moments, a curvaceous, orange, waving grace formed in its boundaries. Michael's emotions pitched, exploring her nude frame. Blackie's hand was accepted by model fingers. Debbie's naked body stepped out into the light, unabashed. Her nudity, enhanced by tan skin and shadow, etched her youth. She, too, was mesmerized like the others. Her light-blue eyes stared off at the nowhere place. Michael's heartbeat increased. Blackie carried her hand in hand onto the porch, presenting her centerfold to Michael.

"What have you done to her?" Michael found himself jealous of Blackie, Anthony and the crowd of people seeing her vulnerable.

"She will awaken when I receive Iosk."

"Why is she nude?" Michael said with some hostility.

"You are not plucked from death clothed. She has come to you naturally. Allow me to make the agreeable changes." Blackie's bony hand unraveled hers to be placed at her side. The sorcerer bent down to her feet, waving his dead hand up and over her to the mid of her neck and, like a magician, where the hand passed, a red robe formed. Blackie left her blonde wing-tipped hair unhooded. Michael sighed, his body caught in an eager tremble.

The sorcerer's back aligned, rattling the smoke from his torch. "Come, come, watch your step and take her hand. She is yours. A love reborn in paradise." Michael approached with caution. Blackie curled a smile, his hand unfurling with greed. "And now for your end of the bargain." Michael stood a trustable step over an arm's length from the dealer. In letting his rifle rest, he took the duffle bag in both hands.

"Deb." Michael called her over. A hesitation took place. She was pulled from the nowhere place to Blackie.

"You may," Blackie allowed. Michael's anger raised. Debbie went to his side, watching her master.

Michael's perspiring countenance looked at the sorcerer's veiled eyes. "I do have one last request." Blackie feigned a fist behind his fabric, weighing his response. The fist clasped the edge of his vestment's cosmic chart to find the whereabouts of Argauthartera. The blackest circle pulled to the sorcerer's hood opening, then was shooed away.

"I haven't long to prepare. Make your request brief," Blackie said with teeth as yellow as his flame's heart.

"You speak of honor and trust. Well, here's your opportunity to prove yourself honorable and trustworthy. It will depend on how I cooperate."

A slight hiss exhaled from the cowl. "I can't fathom your unreliable personality. Have you stabbed me in the back, after what I have done for you?" The words were laced with fear and venom. The sorcerer was infuriated with the human's insolence. If not for the position, he'd be regretful.

"No, but here's my problem. I have divergent stories being told to me and who to believe, I'm not sure. I had a chance to chat with the Harbingers and they claim you weren't sent here, but rather you were expelled from your own world. They told me your kind banished you for your terrible acts of cruelty and your punishment was to be left in cosmic solitude with alike parasitical organisms. Life no less destructive than yourself. They claim you want the world for your own and your subjects and that all other sentient life was to be removed by Argauthartera, not just the worst of us as you claim. I said 'prove it.' They told me you couldn't bring back Debbie because she was dead and you killed her."

Blackie grumbled. "And you believed them?"

"Let me finish…" Blackie raised like a pillar of strength that could crush him. "That you wouldn't have the power to resurrect life without Iosk. They said I got Rosalyn back because she was never fully gone. That you couldn't take her without the flesh. That's when a solution Yucca suggested represented itself and they were a little too game to participate for me to think they were lying."

Blackie's jangled voice cut in. "You have no trust, no honor. We had a deal or doesn't that mean anything to you?"

"We do and still might. That's entirely up to you. Regardless of the outcome, I want to thank you for making me a better person."

"Impossible. By default, you are sheep of pestilence. It's in your DNA. You think the Harbingers don't have their own agenda? Yucca his? You were manipulated. Why do you think I asked you to keep our deal a secret, you fool. Can't resurrect life? How did I save Anthony? Your friend died on our table. I resurrected him. Debbie stands beside you, resurrected. You have been lied to. Tell me I haven't been lied to back?"

Michael paused. "Like I said, we'll see what honor you have."

"Where's your list of names?" Blackie put forth a pronged hand for it. Michael hesitated.

"You haven't got it. I was the fool to trust a human. You can't be trusted. Your kind doesn't value trust. You live in fear because you are a wretched breed of—"

Michael pulled out a white piece of folded paper from his jeans that silenced Blackie. The dark-printed names bled through the paper from inside. Michael gave the list to the awaiting hand. Blackie drew it close to unravel its folds.

In the distraction, Michael pulled the Asian shaman mask out of the duffle bag, dropping the empty bag to the floor. Blackie took a step back, the wizened face corrugated where its temporary corners showed. Had Blackie's eyes been visible, Michael would have seen them sharpen. "Did you jeopardize yourself?" Michael asked.

"I would never." There was no disguise, Blackie's tone was scared.

"I think I've gotten my answer. Yucca said that if I placed this mask on Debbie that, if it was genuinely her and not one of your tricks, she would be authentically revealed and any black magic dispelled. Let's see how honorable you are?" Michael went to place the mask on Debbie. The mask slipped over her mindless face. Debbie moaned in confusion, her gasps played from behind the mask. Her head darted around, her arms signaling a trapped victim.

"...Deb?" Michael fought for her name.

"Mike?" She felt for him. Michael pulled the mask off her disoriented face. The spell was broken. "Michael!" Debbie clutched him in a firm embrace. "Don't let me go, Mike, don't let me go! Don't let me go back!"

"No, no, I got you. I—"

"Iosk, where is it?" Blackie demanded.

Michael blurted, "I'll get it."

Monday, 9:34pm

2

Armed with an AR-15 each, Vince and Melissa sought cover in the field's car lot where they followed the Jeep between the intervening spaces of close bumpers. The Jeep pulled into the tree line. Melissa and Vince ventured onward towards the unpopulated right side of the trees. They found a weak spot in the slanting hillside down the road where they could navigate the barbed-wire fence. They traversed the dense vegetation, guided by the dominion of torches over the sky. The avid shadow people spied from the trees at the armed trespassers, trailing them.

The Harbingers' instructions were simple. Sneak around the tree line to checkpoint 1, The Altar. Make your way past The Altar to checkpoint 2, Blackie's Mansion. Infiltrate Blackie's Mansion. Proceed to access checkpoint 3, The Charnel House, in the rear cellar while Anthony and Michael create a distraction. Once in The Charnel House, meet your contact Abra and give the spirit what was requested to complete your mission. Failure is not an option.

The sound of Devo stopped the doublet lovers in their tracks for a shared look of dissipation. The two studied the flame-outlined trees for explanation. Anthony and Michael joined the chorus. Melissa hastened Vince on with a wave. The two sped along in sight of the tree line. Melissa's tresses rippled to the rhythmic wind she created. Vince had to be warned by Melissa to keep a low profile more than once. He was plowing a path instead of gliding one, as she demonstrated. The area was open for latent spies. The various uncultivated expanse was unmanageable by perception.

The tree's lazy curve was spotted where the tree line ended. They rounded a safe distance from the lurking figures therein. In meandering the pass, they came to the bright side, leaving the shadow people behind. Vince was pulled down to the floor by Melissa. She signaled quiet and pointed at the black-robed guard concealed at the mouth of The Altar, checkpoint 1. The sentry was watching over numerous basketfuls of infants.

Vince was ready to take up the gauntlet but did not want to jeopardize Melissa. The problem was not the guard, it was the crowd of robed followers filling the entirety of bush and trail beyond the infants. Followers which drew far back into the eastern hills. Vince had that "we can take 'em" mentality. Melissa shook her head to the contrary.

Melissa perceived a low, imprecise movement. It interwove the infants laying in an assembly of dusky wicker baskets, their tiny appendages seen but not moving. She surveyed its motion, bringing Vince close and pointing it out to him. He followed her finger, spotting it. Steadily, the strip of what appeared be a moving piece of black sod moved closer to the guard. The guard was joined by a band of swinging shadows and then the robed figure fell, writhing. Vince pointed out another moving strip, then another and another until his eyes failed to keep up. Individual baskets raised up from what took a moment for the psyche to identify. They appeared to be dogs of some kind, bounding away with basket after basket, dangling from their maws. The sneaky abductions bounded southeast, away from the mob.

Sticks cracked on the ground from behind the two. Vince whipped around, rifle in hand, finger on the trigger. Melissa was not as graceful from nerves. Vince's weapon eased. Melissa didn't know what to think. She pressed back her glasses. The coyote's black and white maw dropped red robes from its jaws. The brown and white coat crept back into the shadows. The umber eyes were bold and tough-set against the flames. The marks of Kruktat were upon them. Vince and Melissa understood the robe's intended purpose. They looked at each other, unsure how the encounter came about but did not linger on it. They hurried to put the robes on.

Monday, 10:42pm

3

Michael's mind whirled. Yucca and the Harbingers had said that Blackie could not bring Debbie back from the dead, yet there she was. "Enough games! Where is Iosk? In the car?"

"I will be right back with it." Michael carried a clinging Debbie down the stairs, the Asian mask in his possession. He cast a quick shot at Anthony, who was leaning sideways through the windshield. There was a look of impending doom on him. The wrestled undoing of Debbie from Michael's side populated his face with that same look. Debbie gave an ear-splitting scream over Devo, being sucked back to Blackie through midair.

"My mistake was trusting a flawed animal!" Blackie shouted. Michael glimpsed the gathered mob, expecting them to push down the fence in turning to face Blackie. It was a turn he wouldn't make. Michael found himself hurling through the air from a necromantic pressure that interlocked on his bones with the strength of a hundred iron hands. The Asian mask went a separate direction. The untamed ground approached his fall, the scream of Debbie in his ears. He rolled out of what would have been a nasty collision, but to his benefit, the barrel stab he received from his rifle was absorbed into his vest.

Michael got his bearings back from the magic heave, coming out of his tumble in a defensive kneed position. He'd been freed from the hundred invisible hands. His head threw back at the porch. His eyes spread in terror, taking in a gasping lungful of air. Debbie dangled from the sorcerer's morphed hand. The hand had adjusted to a size which encircled her soft throat in a choke hold of two additional fingers. The torch the sorcerer carried was free-floating, bobbing itself at the fiend's bidding. Blackie was transfiguring before Michael's eyes. The sorcerer's hands became ice-like, translucent with a subtle azure color, flowing within like rushing water.

Blackie's spurious body, augmented with the cowl and vestment, lifting to the porch's cracked roof of twelve feet or more. The back of the cowl extended and moved like a bag full of loose snakes. Within the expanded hood, the face became latticed, the color identical to the ice-like translucence of the hands. Circuits of neon-white current flowed in the lattice intermittently, in no discernable harmony. The diamond-cut spaces between were of a purest black. The mass of abysmal diamonds conveyed a glaring threat from another world in some indescribable way. The creature was awesome, dizzying and terrifying all at once.

Debbie's brittle scream gagged from a strangle on her windpipe. "Wait, don't hurt her! I have Iosk, let me get it!" Michael said, standing, his arms in the air. He swatted sweat out of his eyes, racking his brain on what to do. Hearth appeared from behind Blackie. He could feel Debbie's loss already. "Let me get it!" Debbie's cries were choked out of existence and turned into a mess of tears.

"Let me get it!" He walked back toward the Jeep's passenger side, thinking of a plan. Blackie and Hearth didn't move. "Let her breathe, I'm getting it!" Debbie was turning blue. "Behooves neither one of us to kill her! I will cooperate, I just have to radio for it! Radio's in the Jeep! Give me a second, I'm getting it!" He improvised. Debbie made a choking noise from being shook in the sorcerer's powerful hand. "Easy!" Michael opened the Jeep door. He spotted the Asian mask some steps away on the ground.

"Looking for this?" It was Jarrod's voice. The crowds of numerous heads turned on the Harbinger. "Open the gate! I'll bring it to you!" Jarrod said, holding up a duffle bag. The Harbinger's red robe disguise was covered in an explosive device. A bomb big enough to blow the immediate surrounding into the stratosphere.

"Show me Iosk!" the chorus of slaves said in Blackie's tone.

"I believe I will when you put the girl down and let her over to Mike!" Indefinite seconds passed. What came next was Blackie's move. Jarrod held his gloved thumb over the detonator's trigger. A thud hit the warped wood of the porch, grabbing Michael's attention. Debbie scrambled to him in tears.

"You're okay. You're okay. I got you." Michael was stunned from Jarrod's welcomed intrusion.

"Bring me Iosk!" Blackie demanded from the mouths of the mob.

"You got it, big boy," Jarrod said. Michael took hold of Debbie with one arm, slipping his rifle out from between them, confused on what to do next.

Blackie's alien form flew off the porch with a snapping of wood bolsters. The creature screamed out something terrifyingly unheard of, an indefinable noise which curled the ears. Deer horns had impaled through the creature's robe in a squirting of green blood. Anthony pressed from behind in a full steam ahead charge that sent the protruding antlers into the soil.

Michael yanked Debbie over to the Asian mask, snatching it up. The mask placed itself on Michael's face. He couldn't explain it, but he could see through the solid mask. Hearth wavered from a run at him, changing course. The gorilla-like spirit was heading for the unzipping crowd. They were free from their spell, falling into and over one another in a riotous panic.

Michael searched the crowd for Jarrod. The Harbinger was nowhere to be found in the chaos. Wave after wave of Blackie's spiritual minions plunged out of the mansion's door. Blackie screeched, pinned between Earth, the deer spirit and Anthony. Hysterical, Debbie yanked on Michael to leave. "Not without Tony!"

Blackie agonized in a high-pitched, inhuman death call, similar to a buzzard being eaten alive. The antlers of the deer mask did not give an inch. The sorcerer's robed arms thrashed from the pain delivered, unable to reach back and pull out the prongs. Getting close, Michael and Debbie witnessed the green, oozing pus spilling out of the slits of the sorcerer's garb. The snake-like movements at the back of the cowl hemorrhaged, pooling a dark stain underneath. Blackie was in the final stages of passing the hard way.

Debbie looked away in disgust. The diamonds uprooted from the lattice design of the face as the head constricted and deflated in a convulsion of spurting green blood and white vapor. A green, bubbling overflow bled out the bottom of the sinking robe where the form of unseen feet kicked. Anthony sunk into Blackie's puddle of green slime. That's when Michael knew something was wrong with him.

"Tony!" Michael yelled from behind the mask. There was no response. Michael pried Anthony's limp head out of the deer mask. His neck was broken. Billows of smoke drifted by him; the land behind Michael was on fire. The unmerciful screams could be heard as the fat of flesh burned and sputtered. The stench of burning meat was on the rise. The land was crinkling in his ears like crunching tinfoil. Hearth and his minions wreaked havoc on the defenseless public, taking out their aggressions because of their inevitable fate with Argauthartera. The sound of burning alive and flesh and bone tearing was horrifying.

"Michael!" Debbie screamed, yanking at him to leave.

"Hold on!" Michael pulled his hand free, hoisting Anthony's inert body over his shoulder. There wasn't a second to grieve. "Get in the Jeep!" Debbie ran towards the passenger side, coughing and waving the smoke out of her face. Michael took in the insanity; the place was a tempest of fiery smoke. Flames bounded from the turbid clouds as if dragons ran free.

He made for the Jeep, the visibility dropping fast. He got Anthony in the back and slid off the Asian mask, placing it on his friend, hoping it would bring about a miracle. The toxic air snatched his breath, the smoke pouring into his lungs.

"Hurry, Michael!" He ran around and jumped into the front seat. The world around them was smoke. He had no time to think of how to escape without the possibility of running someone down. He drove on instinct.

"Hold on," Michael wheezed.

Debbie did just that. "Get us out of here!" His lungs were too crowded for a reply. He ran the property's fence down, hearing it bang over and jingle under his wheels. Things bumped his fender, things he didn't slow for. He had gone left, heading towards Jarrod's house. The ground jarred the Jeep, bumping the two holding on for dear life.

Red robes appeared and disappeared in the flickering clouds. The headlights did little to illuminate the situation. Peeling, ashy skin and melting faces lunged at the Jeep, shrieking. "Run, dammit, run!" Michael cried out at the top of his burning lungs. Debbie crawled out of her seat. The things under wheel kept bumping and Michael had to tell himself it was the ground's surface.

At a certain point, the Jeep tipped forward. Michael gritted his teeth, pressuring the acceleration, unsure if the Jeep would flip forward or not. "Buckle up!" Michael said over the screams of terror. Debbie scrambled to click her seatbelt. These sudden tips forward happened a total of four times. On the fourth, the surface went level onto pavement. Michael felt the wheels on the road, making a left. They had two chances; they were either heading the wrong way to certain death or away from the fire toward downtown Yucaipa.

The countless screams of choking agony heightened as the environment's crushing tinfoil decibels raged. The things bumping under the tires on a paved road were not as easily explained away from Michael's conscious. They were caught in Hell's inferno. Debbie was crying in Michael's arm and he didn't realize it. A Walkie-talkie sounded from the floor somewhere. "Anthony, do you copy?" The muffled message fell on deaf ears.

Shots were fired out somewhere among the myriad of those being cooked. In a flash of red flesh spilling forward in the headlights, Michael saw a person fall and go head to head with the Jeep's hood, then head over heels, rolling under the vehicle. A good portion of head skin peeled off the mangled person and was stuck, flapping on the hood.

Michael couldn't breathe, he was suffocating. He wanted to scream out but he couldn't stop. The images he'd witnessed within the smoke screens were indelibly brutal. How would he live with himself, if he lived? He was running people down and he didn't ease off the accelerator. He wasn't thinking: it was kill or be killed.

Without warning, the smoke thinned and scores of red robes on fire became visible, running wild in the widening street. Michael spotted a street sign. They were on Carter Street, crossing Fremont. He tried slowing down, but the mobs overrunning the streets tried to muscle their way into the Jeep when he did. "Get away!" Debbie yelled as they locked their doors.

"We don't have room! Run!" Michael tried to explain.

"Get away!" Debbie screamed at their hateful faces while they slapped at the windows trying to break in. The Jeep's speed shoved the building mob out of the way. They kicked and spit at the Jeep as it passed, yelling obscenities like beasts and throwing rocks. Michael blocked his face when a big one hit the windshield.

The people lowered in number the further down Carter they went. Most kept off the street. Some even dared a look back at the conflagration. Michael peered in his rearview at the narrow escape they made from the prodigious fumes burning down the landscape of Goat's Head in an apocalyptic tableau. He was on Bryant Street heading towards Mill Creek Road when he realized

Debbie was glued to his arm. He had tried to pull over but she had urged him on. "Keep going. Don't stop…ever."

"Anthony, Michael, do you copy?" The voice on the Walkie belonged to Jarrod. His background was familiar chaos.

"Find it." Debbie searched around under her seat.

"Does anybody copy?"

"I copy!" Ethan replied.

"It's under your seat!" Debbie said.

"Ethan, what's your status?" Michael pulled over in sight of the ranger station off Mill Creek, still on Bryant. The bloody aftermath from the sheriff firefight earlier was still smoking. Debbie moaned, looking through the windshield that framed a dark and lifeless miasmic road.

"I have your mom. We're on Pendleton, passing Date. You?" Michael's fingers groped about for the Walkie, grasping it.

"I have Vince's parents and my sisters. We'll meet you at the rendezvous."

"Affirmative. Over and out!"

Michael fumbled with the button on the Walkie. Debbie was terrified beyond measure, peering out each window. Michael pressed the long button on the side, coughing out the soot in his throat.

"Jarrod, can you hear me?"

"I hear you! What's your—!" The world descended into absolute pitch black in the split of a second. There had been no time to scream, no time for a warning. It was the epiphany. Midnight had turned on the digital clock. Argauthartera had come.

4

Galvanized by the scream from Debbie, Vince and Melissa left the infants and flitted through the spellbound crowd. They stayed close to not get separated. Vince looked over the hoods at the rising mansion. He could just make out the gables. Melissa pressed through the unmoving bodies while Vince guided and pushed them out of the way. None cared, they just swayed to rebalance themselves.

An eruptive outcry went out over the land and the crowd went berserk. "Vince!" A person ran into Melissa, knocking her down. She clamped onto Iosk, trying not to be trampled by the stampede. The two lost their rifles in the scuffle. For Vince, it was the feather or the rifle and he followed orders. He swept Melissa up in his arms, pounding his way through the panic-stricken free-for-all. The mansion poured an expanse of black smoke into the hovering firmament of reds and oranges.

The frenzy nearly faltered Vince in step. The screams wanted to blow out their ear drums. Vince fought against the pushing numbers, doing what he could to protect Melissa. The torches flew in their faces and he took the burn every time. Vince blinked to allay the rivulets of sweat collecting on his eyelids.

The air quality was plummeting. Melissa kept her eyes closed and her ears tight from the terrible noises strewn about. The atmosphere darkened and the mansion was becoming smoke screened. They coughed, heavy-chested. Vince was at the mercy of the sight of a single gable and it was not long before it, too, was smoked out. He kept on in that general direction, his lungs burning.

The sultry haze of marring combustion challenged their ability to breathe. Vince could feel Melissa's chest struggle for oxygen, an impetus which calculated his steps in a race against time. The smoke poured on. The crowd had dispersed outward. It was him against the smoke. The fallen fence jostled under his feet. "We're on the property," Vince said to encourage her. Melissa's eyes opened and closed. He slipped off her hood, running straight ahead.

The mansion's foundation showed an arm's length away. "See the house?" Vince said to Melissa, who was wheezing. Her eyes half opened under the dirty glass frames.

"Vince, hurry. I ca—"

"Be tough, we're there." Vince was dizzy. He ran along the building, coughing. When he reached the corner of the back of the house, he knew then, that he had gone the wrong way. Turning around, he ran with her weight gaining on his arms. Still, he had no worry that he wouldn't get her to safety.

"I love you," Melissa said in an inaudible whisper. Vince hit his pelvis against a bar. He took ahold of the rail with his feather hand and rounded it, feeling the ground fall away to steps. He braced his legs, feeling faint, and felt his way down. He went to say something reassuring to Melissa which amounted in a cough. Melissa's vocal chords made a soft, whistling moan that dwindled. Vince didn't worry. She wouldn't die, she couldn't. His mind would not except it as a possibility. They were led into complete darkness where the smoke was minimal and festooned cobwebs wrapped his sweaty face.

Melissa went limp in his arms. He was happy to feel her moving, regardless of why. Melissa coughed a great deal. Vince patted her back and, even though his arms burned, he ignored the pain.

The mansion whined and creaked above, swaying and straining on giving boards. Dust sprinkled down from the roof. He could feel Melissa catching her breath. The pandemonium had grown into the faint sound of a fire pit.

"You can let me down," Melissa coughed. Vince stopped wandering into the darkness, now on a level surface. He let her out of his giving arms, raking the web off his face. The two couldn't get their robes off fast enough. A great heat leapt off their bodies as they disposed of them.

The substructure's smell was musty. Melissa hooked her arm around Vince's waist and his arm around her back and, together, they moved forward in the dark, breathing stale but breathable air. It was the kind of dark that sees and listens.

Where is Abra? Melissa rubbed her throbbing temple. Then it dawned on her. "Hang on." Melissa unattached from Vince, who halted. She unzipped the duffle bag and out came the ghostly red glow of Iosk to light the way. Their sweaty, soot-covered faces reddened like two demons from Hell. Before them was an arched tunnel lined with limestone and a dirt-packed walkway with no perceived end. Looking back was the limestone's dead end that lead to the stairs.

The sounds of the outside world were snuffed out as they ventured down the passageway. Vince read Melissa's heightened fear. "Don't be afraid," he said, stroking her hair back in mid stride so he could see her beautiful face.

"We have to hurry. Where is Abra?" Melissa grabbed Vince's hand and pulled him forward and they began to run. They had covered a length of tunnel when they espied a wall. The closer it came though, they realized it was a dead end. Melissa let out an anxious cry. Her mouth held open with black-sooted digestion. *They lied to me*! She was having difficulty catching her breath when she spotted it; an ill-formed hole in the ground. She ran towards it for a look inside where she found another staircase.

5

Melissa descended the steep, narrow steps in Iosk's light. The red brilliance was not adequate for the depth of darkness. The steps spiraled downward in an ongoing plummet, suggestive of a bottomless extent. "Vince, watch your step." The smell of carrion filled the atmosphere. Vague skeletons and flayed carcasses floated in an innumerable amount, out in an inconceivable limbo. Their appendages were suspended and pulled apart from invisible sources. *The Charnel House*, Melissa thought.

Who are they? Where did they come from? Vince sought bygone answers.

"Abra!" Melissa yelled. The inefficient cadence of her voice drifted into the formless boundary.

"Are you quite prepared?" The demon's resonant tone rang out from far and wide, wobbling the stairs. Vince grabbed ahold of Melissa before she could fall off the edge. She sat down for balance. Vince pulled her back close to him by way of her vest.

"Stop moving the stairs!" Vince complained. Melissa spun and crawled on Vince, Iosk smothered between the two. He felt a wetness touch his hip. Melissa had urinated on herself. She held him, on the verge of a panic attack.

"I can't do it." She squeezed him, sobbing. "I can't do it. I can't do it." She was scared to death. "I'm having a panic attack."

"You can," Vince said, clasping her close. Melissa hid her face in Vince's vest, squeezing until her nails bent backwards in the lining. She was convulsing all over. "Stop moving the stairs!" Vince turned at a colossal Punch doll face forming from grey mist out of the great beyond. "Don't look and don't listen." The convulsions came in explosive spasms of hyperventilation.

"I can't do it," Melissa repeated in a whimper. Vince wanted to give her the feather but he was ordered not to separate from it again under any circumstances. Even if Melissa begged him for it. Under no circumstances was he to part from it or he would be their downfall. The demon's infernal smile spread into what would have been a heart-stopping sight.

"Look at me, Melissa," Abra dared. "Have you told your love of you and your father's precious carnalities. Has she?"

"Shut up, moon face, before I slap you in the mouth," Vince challenged. Abra chortled.

"The things they've—"

"Stop it!" Melissa screamed on the last bits of strength.

Why don't you share the feather? The simple wisdom struck Vince. So simple it was, he didn't think it would work. "Don't listen. Give me your hand."

"Yes, don't listen." The demon mocked him in a childlike voice. Vince undid her claw of a hand from his vest, pressing the feather between their connected hands. He interlocked his and her fingers in mutual contact. Her trembling eased. Melissa raised her head up to his. He wiped away her tears with his free hand. She cast a fearless look out at the demon whose baleful grin waned. The lovers hugged each other tight, staring at the outclassed demon in a bold, apathetic dismissal.

Melissa cleared her throat. "Let's finish this." Abra's smile was crushed.

"You heard her."

"Shut your shitty mouth, dog, or I will have you eat your own feces." The demon exuded the highest form of hatred from its enormous head. "You'll pay, underling! Mark my words, I'll see your life essence drained for eternity!" Abra boomed. The long aquiline nose jabbed at Vince's face as the words accosted him. The stairs threated to toss the two off into the oblivion below. Neither flinched and both were ready to die in a fall. With narrowing eyes, Abra backed away with a resurrected smirk.

The demon was avid for what was to come. The sound of water was heard rushing and rising from beneath. "We'll see, when your magic lapses, dog. You can live in my ossuary garden. Would you like that?" the discarnate demon asked in a low and sinister voice, gleaming with a repulsive joy.

With a brisk suddenness, the water stopped at a level Iosk's light could reach. It was a significant drop below. The fluid's consistency resembled blood. "Let's commence. Melissa, you have the floor. Jump into my bath and freedom is yours. You have to be quick about it, or your time will run out." Melissa fell into Vince with a brief, salty kiss goodbye.

"I love you," she said breaking away, staring in his eyes.

"I love you." He returned the equal passion that cut off all else. She gripped Iosk in her arm, not letting go of the feather, and especially Vince's hand, until the exact moment she leapt into a screaming freefall that took her down into a deep plunge.

The room filled with complete darkness without Iosk. A vast scream louder than that of Melissa's fall gathered around the steps, a panic-stricken scream of immense proportion. Abra had yanked the feather from Vince's hand. His fear awoke in the dark alone, his heart thudding to a pounding laughter. He hugged the steps, screaming madly in a total loss of his senses.

Fear was at an intensity he'd never experienced, one that would pop his heart. Abra relished in the presence of such extreme suffering. "You can't breathe, can you? Huh, huh, huh!" The discarnate voice of Abra mocked with mirth. "Huh, huh, huh!" Vince's screams were running out of air.

The stairs did not shake like before. "Huh, huh, huh! I can't catch my breath! I can't breathe!" The demon mocked and laughed a mighty wind at him. Vince went to run up the stairs in a stark raving panic and, on clumsy legs, he slipped, fell and hit his face. In that incident of distracted pain, a flick of reason appeared. *Melissa!*

The laughing of Abra stopped because Vince's screams did. Vince slapped himself harder than he ever had, breaking the twisted tooth free from his mouth. He rolled to the side until the ground fell out from underneath him. He flailed in the air to the high-pitched screech of a demon. His body smacked the sticky stuff below like he was thrown into a brick wall. Vince's world went black and on his submerged face was a dead look of satisfaction.

6

The light of the world was turned back on. Argauthartera had come and gone like instant death. Michael and Debbie looked at each other, stained and broken, and neither spoke. They faced the road ahead of them, conscious of its dark, uncertain and lonely aspect. As they drove away from those not too distant screams, they watched the damned inferno that burned like a flag from Hell.

CHAPTER 22
A New Beginning

We awoke super early, showered and changed out of our costumes. We had decided on a dawn heist of the brown toolbox. Our thinking was that the dirt bikers might be down from a Halloween sugar crash. We started up Ivy Avenue to Jefferson Street with our expectations dashed. Already we heard the revving dirt bikes down in the fields. Getting the magazines now would be dang near impossible. From our lofty vantage point, we regrouped, taking cover behind a purple flowered bush to formulate a risky plan. We would attempt to acquire the treasure under their very noses. Question was, could it be done? We would find out.

We went stealthy forth on Jefferson, down the newly paved road. The asphalt beneath our shoes felt like rubber. We searched Carter Street from a low profile for the bikers. The helmets would zoom in and out of the colorful field. Jarrod was the first to see her, or at least, to say something.

"Hey, check it out, you guys." He motioned with his chin. It was a new neighbor girl around our age. She dollied boxes down a moving truck's ramp and rolled them into the tree line.

"Let's help her?" I said, feeling confident in my clean, dark jeans and white t-shirt.

"You can. We have hooters to catch," Jarrod said.

"Yeah. We have hooters to catch," Ethan repeated.

"She'll be done by then. I'm gonna ask."

"Suit yourself, you freakin' *mee-yamee* face. We're going to get first peeks at breastages," Jarrod said. I started to walk away.

"He's ditching us for a girl. Can you believe this?" Ethan asked.

"For shame." They shook their heads at me, Jarrod tsking. I stopped, feeling like a chode.

"I am not."

"We have guaranteed hooters within our grasp. Do you get what I am saying to you? Hooters, Marino. Fun bags. Developed hooters, deeeveloped." Jarrod's eyes grew as wide as breasts.

"Are you willing to blow that over a girl?"

"Did you see where her house is located? Think of the advantage we would have from the side of her house for spying on the magazine's position from there," I said, hoping to sway them.

Jarrod and Ethan shared a contemplative look. "He's got a point. We get in there and we're golden," Jarrod said.

"How are we going to get past the girl and her parents?" Ethan asked.

"How are we going to get past the bikers? They may not take a break today. Have they ever? No. We could be waiting here all day again. What we should do is ask to help her. While we bring in boxes, Jarrod you sneak away or Ethan, whoever. Take a place in the field beside the house and watch for an opening and we take it. Beats getting manhandled senior-wedgy style." Ethan shifted. He knew.

"Alright, alright. But if she says no, it's back to the original plan, agreed?" Jarrod asked.

"Now you're talkin'. Let's get these hooters," I said.

The plan might have worked if fate hadn't interjected. When we passed Carter Street, the dirt bikers were speeding off. "They're leaving!" Jarrod exclaimed. "Here's our chance, Marino."

I can't explain why I didn't follow. I wanted to. Jarrod and Ethan hightailed it up the street, taking cover in the ditch. They looked for me like golfers out of a hole and dismissed me when they realized I wasn't coming. I felt like a tool. I took the walk of shame down the street, not positive why I hadn't followed. I soon forgot about it at the sight of the girl in her yellow sundress, catching sight of me.

"Hi," she said, shining a warm, pink dimpled smile. I smiled like an idiot, non-responsive. Her mother came out of the truck to see who it was.

"Well, hello." The two had identical winding honey-blonde curls.

"I thought I would come over and say hi and welcome you to the neighborhood. Also, see if I could help you with anything?" I found that I could speak to her mom normally, why couldn't I to her?

"Well, that's kind of you. We could use an extra hand, since you're offering." The youthful lady approached me. "I'm Jackie. This is my daughter, Melissa."

I glanced at Melissa, mouthing a voiceless 'Hi.' *What's wrong with you?* "I'm Vince, pleased to meet you."

"Where do you live, Vince?"

"I live here in town. I'm visiting my friend Jarrod. He lives up the street, on Ivy."

"That your friend?" Jackie looked behind me. I turned, giving the sight a double-take. Jarrod and Ethan were running down the street, the brown toolbox in Jarrod's arms.

They did it! Thinking on my feet, I said, "Yes, it's a game we play…called hide the toolbox." She seemed to believe it.

"What's in the toolbox?"

Porn "Comics. Where are you guys from?"

"Arizona."

"Cool, what brought you here?"

"My daughter and I are going to be opening a nursery in town."

"Oh, that's cool." I glanced at Melissa.

"What can I grab for you?"

"Well, let's take a look."

I could see Melissa staring at me out of the corner of my eye. I met her gaze and for an unrecorded period we were caught staring at one another. An incredible familiarity rushed over me I couldn't explain. She shied away, having realized she was staring. I, too, for the same reason. "Vince, if you could load the dolly for Melissa, I will take boxes individually. I was hoping we could fit the truck in between the trees."

"You tried?"

"Yes, almost didn't get it out."

I let Melissa go up the ramp first. She smiled, fingering a pair of black glasses up against stunning green emerald eyes, eyes as lustrous as our two suns. I couldn't get past how familiar she was, like I knew her from some place. She pressed her jungle of hair behind her little ears.

"Vince, start with any marked 'kitchen'. They'll say heavy or light on the box."

"You got it."

"For your help, we'll order pizza for lunch."

"Sweet. No problem." Jackie took what she could carry and I started loading the dolly that Melissa braced. For a stint, it was silent. Melissa took what chances she could to look at me and me at her. I couldn't believe how nervous I was being around a girl. When we'd catch each other's glance, her cute mousey face would light up, manifesting in nervous excitable laughs.

Then she said it. "I feel like we've met before."

My heart raced to speak. "Wild, you too? I was thinking the same thing. It's freakin' weirding me out."

"That is weird," Melissa said, looking down. I loaded the last box on.

"Here, let me take it down the ramp for you."

"Oh." She stepped away without argument. I skirted past her nervous body language and descended the ramp, wanting to pry further but show her mom we weren't dilly-dallying. Melissa came down the ramp and supported the boxes to stay in place.

"How long you been in town for?"

"Only today. My mom found the house for us." Melissa's petite frame aided the boxes up the slope of the natural driveway.

"Just you and your mom?"

"Yeah, my dad died before I was born."

"Sorry to hear that."

"It's okay." We started the long walk down to the house, accompanied with the fresh smell of sappy pine. The length would have been discouraging if not for the company. I was happy for the distance.

"Are you an actress?" She blushed.

"No, I'm not pretty enough to be an actress." She brushed loose locks from her glasses behind her ears.

"Yes you are," I said without thinking, to a delay of awkward silence.

"No." Her blush deepened, looking at the boxes.

"Unless you've been in town, I can't place where it is I would have seen you."

"You haven't been to Arizona by chance?"

"Not in years. So…where you startin' school?"

"I start at Parkview middle school on Monday."

"You're in sixth or seventh grade?"

"Sixth," she said with some hesitancy.

"Right on, I'm in seventh."

"Awesome."

"I could introduce you around, if you want?" She brightened, looking at me.

"Would you? That be great." Nervous of her reception from my invitation, I looked at the rows of trees.

"Beautiful property you have." I gazed at the towering evergreens, the emerald-green suns filtering through their glorious outstretched branches. I couldn't think of what else to say.

"Maybe you could show me around town? My mom wants to start the nursery on the boulevard."

"Yeah, I can show you around. Not much to do locally, but we can have my parents take us to the Redlands mall. You like comics?"

"Somewhat. I prefer books. I love used bookstores."

"We have two used bookstores. One in Yucaipa and one in Redlands."

"Do you like to read?"

No, but I was about to start. "Yeah, horror, science fiction, that sort of thing." She smiled and didn't press me for what authors.

"I'll let you borrow my C.L. Moore book. I think you might like *Northwest Smith*."

"Cool. You like movies?"

"Yeah, I like movies."

"You should come over and watch *The Invisible Man* at my house. I have it on VHS. It's my favorite film of all time."

"I'd like that." She smiled.

We turned into a break in the tree line. I glanced at the mailbox, reading a familiar-sounding name. "Plarek is your last name?"

"Yeah. What's yours?"

"Marino."

"Italian?"

"You got it." I turned to see what shadowed my back. There I saw the Victorian mansion that was to be their new home. The place was stunning and fit for a princess. It was a perfect fit for her.

"You know, I was worried about moving here. Starting a new school. Having to meet new friends. But the more I see of Yucaipa, the more it feels like…I'm home."

There was something in the way she said it that sent my eyes to hers. When our eyes met, she was looking straight into mine and I remembered where I'd seen her.

ABOUT THE AUTHOR

Brian Lupo

Brian Lupo is a writer, photographer, published anthropologist and independent filmmaker with four credits to his name: M.O.N., The Sickness of Lucius Frost, 13 Days of the Beast, and The Harvest, along with several short films. He is best known for weird, psychological horror stories. He lives in southern California with his wife and three dogs.

Made in United States
North Haven, CT
17 January 2024